AVALOVARA

BOOKS BY OSMAN LINS
IN ENGLISH TRANSLATION:

Avalovara

Nine, Novena

The Queen of the Prisons of Greece

AVALVARA
OSMAN LINS

INTRODUCTION AND TRANSLATION
BY GREGORY RABASSA

DALKEY ARCHIVE PRESS

Originally published in Brazil as *Avalovara* by Edições Melhoramentos, São Paulo, Brazil

First published in the U.S. by Alfred A. Knopf, Inc., 1979
Translation copyright © 1979 by Gregory Rabassa
Published by arrangement with Alfred A. Knopf, a division of Random House, Inc.

Introduction copyright © 2002 by Gregory Rabassa
First Dalkey Archive edition, 2002

Library of Congress Cataloging-in-Publication Data:

Lins, Osman, 1924-1978
    [Avalovara. English]
    Avalovara / Osman Lins.— 1st Dalkey ed.
        p. cm.
    Originally pub.: New York : Knopf, 1979.
    ISBN 1-56478-320-0 (alk. paper)
       I. Title.

PQ9697.L555 A913 2002
869.3'42—dc21

                                2002019294

Partially funded by grants from the National Endowment for the Arts, a federal agency, and the Illinois Arts Council, a state agency.

Dalkey Archive Press books are published by the Center for Book Culture, a nonprofit organization with offices in Chicago and Normal, Illinois.

www.centerforbookculture.org

Printed on permanent/durable acid-free paper and bound in the United States of America.

To Julieta,
who contributed so much
to the making of this book.

INTRODUCTION

A great deal of the fiction written in the second half of the twentieth century falls into or is near to a type of writing I call "the inventive novel." These are narratives where the author produces the raw materials and hands them over for the reader to give them shape or structure and sometimes meaning. It is a case of something much like the old Erector Set I used to enjoy so much, where the choice was yours whether to make a Roman chariot or a wheelbarrow. It is a less subtle way of telling us how to read a book properly than the feeling we get whenever we read something a second time and find that it is not quite what we had read before. Julio Cortázar gives us the essence of this method (if it is such) in Chapter 62 of *Hopscotch,* where the old writer Morelli lays out his scheme for how a novel should be written:

> Everything would be a kind of disquiet, a continuous uprooting, a terri- tory where psychological causality would yield disconcertedly, and those puppets would destroy each other or love each other or recognize each other without suspecting too much that life is trying to change its key in and through and by them, that a barely conceivable attempt is born in man as one other day there were being born the reason-key, the feeling- key, the pragmatism-key. That with each successive defeat there is an approach towards the final mutation, and that man only is in that he searches to be, plans to be, thumbing through words and modes of behavior and joy sprinkled with blood and other rhetorical pieces like this one.

This went on to be the basis for the title and shape of Cortázar's subsequent novel, *62: A Model Kit.* It might well have been the starting point of *Avalovara,* by Osman Lins.

Lins's novel has what could be construed as an architectural structure, albeit more in the mode of De Chirico than Vitruvius. At the start he presents the nigh-perfect palindrome in Latin: SATOR AREPO TENET OPERA ROTAS, which can be read with equal ease back and forth or up and down. He then shows us how the phrase just might be an allegory for the order of the universe. This palindrome is then centered on a spiral that emerges from the letter N and subsequently crosses over the various letters of the statement as it expands. As a spiral, unlike a circle, can be infinite in both directions, it could be that it comes out of the letter we use to denote infinity, the nth power.

Avalovara is a somewhat truncated version of Avalokitesvara, the avatar of the beneficial Buddha. In the novel it is described as a mysterious Great Speckled Bird of Folk Music.

> The Avalovara climbs even higher amidst the lightning flashes, and suddenly I perceive that a bird just like it—or the same one?—almost legible and also made up of small birds, is flying in our united bodies, light, among the branches, the butterflies, the crocodile, the rabbit, and the animals with noisy throats. It flies in us and sings. Strange: it sings in duet, with a human voice, and one impregnated with compassion.

This coming together and blending of bodies is part of the mystery. Lins introduces the idea of the Yolyp, a person who has two physical beings in one. The older one has the aspect of reality but the younger one is maturing inside and can be sensed by the bearer or even glimpsed in mystical moments. The Yolyp could be described as an inner doppelgänger and it might even be a start for describing the Trinity better than Saint Patrick's shamrock.

All three women in the novel have some sort of multiplicity about them. Roos in Europe, whom Abel pursues from city to city and finds that she is inhabited by cities herself, eerily reminds us of the characters in Cortázar's same 62 who, when they are together and only then, are mysteriously called "the city." Cecília in Recife is more than just bisexual. She is thought to be both male and female in one. We find as we read through the novel a trove of ambivalent and ambiguous yet nonetheless real creatures. There is much of Heisenberg's uncertainty principle in this novel. Every time we locate someone on the spiral that person turns out to be a variant of the one we thought we had defined or described. Roos can be one city after another or she can carry them all together and even be one that had not been thought of. In Recife, along with the ambiguous Cecília, we have the two old women Hermelinda and Hermenilda, who are so alike both in name and in presence that they often change places in a strange sort of way. Finally, in São Paulo, the last city, we come upon the woman who has no name but is represented by a kind of runic symbol, Ʊ, which is open to all manner of interpretation. It is from her that we learn about Yolyps. These creatures appear to have been born inside people as part of them, or a version, or perhaps a second thought of some kind. I think of those miniature peppers we often find inside a mature one when we cut it open.

This use of a symbol for the woman who is ultimately the most important one in the book as she leads Abel to his apocalypse is Lins's way of showing that she is both real and unimaginable. Much like the secret and true name of God in Jewish folklore cannot be named, her name is unpronounceable. Perhaps there is a sound that goes with the symbol, as with Chinese ideograms; maybe there are multiple sounds also with Chinese ideograms as they are rendered orally in divers dialects. It could also be that the reader must supply a sound as he attunes the character to his own interpretation. We have heard over and over that things do not exist until they bear a name, therefore it is the reader who must truly create this arcane character. This, of course, will also lead to some kind of variation in the many Yolyps brought into existence by this necessary nomenclature. I say necessary because when I first read the novel I discovered that we do indeed move our lips when we read. When I came upon this character I gagged mentally and couldn't go on; there had to be a sound behind it. I finally settled on the rather banal solution of simply saying "O" (the film *The Story of O* was around at the time). This would suggest that every reader will have to come up with his own version, thus making the character so depicted all the more multiple and furtive. At one point she speaks of her real name,

> not the one in the registry or on the baptismal certificate—mere appearances—but mine, the true one, the one I don't know myself and that would grant her the right to penetrate me truly, to open me up, a name that would be like the secret of a coffer.

Lins does not go as far as Cortázar, who furnishes an alternate version of *Hopscotch* using the same material but in a different order and reaching a different, opposite conclusion. As the novel is set up, however, a reader can organize the contents in what to him might seem to make for a more standard narration, or she might opt to render the story even more difficult to grasp and yet, by this same token, make it seem more authentic. This bears out the image of the spiral. Lins says that

> We are the ones who impose a limit on the spiral at both extremities. Ideally it begins at Always and Never is its end. By which we come to a conclusion even less trivial than the preceding ones; to wit, even though

we see it drawn on paper in opposite directions, its extremities (if they really exist) will meet at some mysterious point that is inaccessible to our stony comprehension, just like a circle, a much less equivocal and disturbing representation.

It could be that we sense reality to be the circle, the finite, and keep looking for it as we go along in the unperceived or only hinted at true reality of the spiral, which begins and ends at nowhere, whose coincidence of beginning and end gives us the impression that it is a circle. Osman Lins has his people aware of their hidden dimensions, their otherness, but they are completely unaware of how these will affect them in another moment, another place. They are really being led along by the reader, their inventor, who is never sure whether he will come up with a wheelbarrow or a chariot, the choice of which he wrongly thinks belongs to the author. The dilemma of Ö in a moment of drowsiness could well be that of the reader as he begins to understand this novel:

I am, at that moment, from that moment on, the terrible gorge of things, the point or being where converge, with their multiple facets, what man knows, what he suspects, what he imagines, and what he does not even think exists.

At the end, the murdered lovers lose shape and blend into the rug that is a woven depiction of Paradise, thus losing body as they become two-dimensional and go back to the Creation. We must remember, however, that this is a spiral, not a circle, so that T. S. Eliot's "In my end is my beginning" and vice versa does not obtain. This ecstatic last chapter where love and death are necessary ingredients of this epiphany, so Joycean in style, leaves the reader in abeyance as he must put it together and reinvent the novel to suit his own purposes of understanding. This is where creative reading, invention, takes hold, a far cry from certain sterile stylistic studies that remind one of ornithologists who study ornithology and not birds. The Avalovara bird deserves headier stuff.

Symbolic of the novel and its view of life is an actual part of its text: the story of Julius Heckethorn's clock. This is a complex mechanism put together not really to tell ordinary time but the creative time of music, invented ultimately to play the introduction to the Sonata in F minor (K462) by Scarlatti. The vicissitudes of the clock parallel those of the human characters in the novel and it is doubtful that the full phrase will ever get played as the novel ends. If it ever does, one is constrained to think that it will bring on an intuitive moment as does Vinteuil's phrase in Proust's novel. As we read this novel we keep Proust in mind and wonder if perhaps, unlike Bergotte, Osman Lins has succeeded in writing something like that piece of yellow wall.

GREGORY RABASSA
2002

... *the romance is mingled with the* CHANSON DE GESTE, *history, and a certain hagiography; it paints marvellous adventures, almost always linked by the process of the "quest" and woven together by amorous intrigues; ... the coherence of the work is assured by methods of numerical and thematic composition, rather than by dramatic necessity.*

—PAUL ZUMTHOR, *Literary History of Medieval France*

A creation implies a superabundance of reality, or in other words, an invasion of the sacred into the world. It follows from this that EVERY CONSTRUCTION OR FABRICATION HAS AS AN EXEMPLARY MODEL THE COSMOGONY.

—MIRCEA ELIADE, *The Sacred and the Profane*

Reaching the world is TAKING THE WORD, *transfiguring experience into a universe of discourse.*
—GEORGES GUSDORF, *The Word*

A primordial axis, the LINGA *shows, on joining with the* YONI, *that the Absolute is developed in plurality, but blends into unity. The* LINGA-YONI *combination needs the antagonism of the male and female principles—and it destroys it in a triumphant non-duality.*

—MAX-POL FOUCHET, *The Amorous Art of India*

Triads and decades are interwoven in the unity. The numeral, here, is no longer a simple external framework, but the symbol of the cosmic order.

—E. R. CURTIUS, on the *Divine Comedy*
(*Medieval Literature and the Latin Middle Ages*)

Avalovara

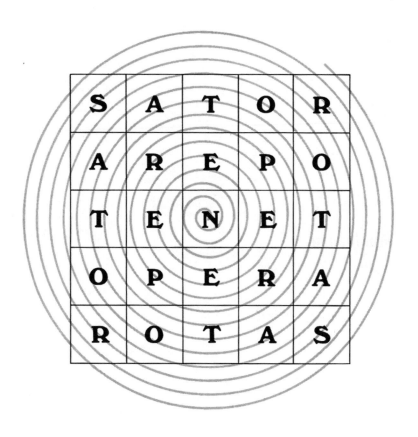

R

O and Abel: Meetings, Routes, and Revelations

In the still dark space of the room, in this kind of limbo or night hour created by the thick curtains, I can only see the halo of the face that the glowing sockets of the eyes seem to light up—or perhaps it is my eyes: I love her—and the reflections of the strong, thick hair, gold and steel. A clock in the room and the sound of vehicles. Does the vague, dusty, wavering odor come from Time or from the furniture? She beside the door, silent. Meteorites, dark during their pilgrimage, light up as they pass through the air of Earth. In just that way, after a short while, we lose opacity, she and I. Her brow emerges from the shadows—bright, narrow, and somber.

S

The Spiral and the Square 1

Where do they really rise up from—having come, as everybody and everything, from the beginning of curves—these two characters, still larval and yet already bearing? One cannot tell, whether in their voices or in their silences or on their hazy faces, the sign of what they are and what they are charged with. The door beside which they look at or appraise each other, face to face, surrounded by sounds and dust and darkness—what is it the threshold to?

Both go into the room and at the same time, perhaps, into the broader though equally limited space of the text that reveals and creates them.

R

Ⴒ and Abel: Meetings, Routes, and Revelations　　　　2

The curtains hide two broad windows with wooden Venetian blinds and glass panes. One window is shut and by it are the faded damask easy chairs, the coffee table in between, and the gold velvet couch. The other one, which is open, sheds light on the long table that has been set: on small oval mats—red, blue, and green—between the plates and the silverware, are two candlesticks, a bottle of wine, and the vase with yellow dahlias. Word and body, her face—fire and silk—next to mine: Ⴒ. I caress her hair, thick, strong, two heads of hair mingled. What links this hour to the vision of the City that comes down the valley like a bird? A distant explosion makes the pendants (some are missing) on the crystal chandeliers tinkle. I can also hear the slow movement of the grandfather clock. From the body in my arms, from the hair held tightly, the color of honey and steel, from the gay dress, a pungent perfume rises. The geometric motifs, the animals, and the foliage of the two huge rugs blend into a half-soiled pink. If the pendulum were removed, a child and his dog could hide in the wooden case of the clock.

S

The Spiral and the Square　　　　2

To believe that the two characters and the parlor with its declining luxury where they meet are clearer for the narrator than the text—slowly put together, where every word is revealed little by little, step by step, along with the world reflected in them—would be illusory. There would be no dream cities if real cities had not been built. They lend consistency in man's imagination to the ones that exist only in name and in design. Cities seen on fabricated maps, however, placed in an unreal space with fictitious limits and an imaginary topography, lack walls and air. They do not have the consistency of the drawing board, the protractor, or the India ink with which the cartographer works: they are born with the design and take on reality on the blank sheet of paper. How far would the unwitting traveler who is unaware of this principle get? Putting together a map of imaginary cities or continents, with all their relief and configurations, is very similar, therefore, to undertaking a journey through the void. Little is known about the invention or the inventor until he is revealed with his work. This is how it is with the construction begun here. Only one element, for the time being, is clear and definitive: it is governed by a spiral, its starting point, its matrix, its nucleus.

R

Ớ and Abel: Meetings, Routes, and Revelations   3

The amusement park, with its lights lost in the surrounding darkness, she and I on the carousel that groans around its axle, the floorboards groan when one of the other rare guests passes; I attempt, without success, to cut an ox's rolling eye with a sharpened knife; the suitcase falls to the floor, the sea groans in the mouths and bellies of fish, I hear or think I hear, face against face, a crackle of flames, the oaken planks groan under our feet, I don't know whether Ớ is pronouncing names she has invented or is giving shape to voices that seem to subsist in her flesh, the sound of the sea along the still half-savage coast spreads out in broad waves, embracing each other we whirl around on the carousel, the empty bed groans and the other one where we are; how can one comprehend that such hard instruments as the eyes retreat, burn each other, double over like a piece of silk?; the wind sporadically scatters the strident music from the park among the few houses of Praia Grande and makes the large window groan, the one with the hanging latches, maybe the heat of her face comes from her torrid eyes, I don't know the meaning of the names she scans with an artificial Latin eloquence (but does she scan them?), the chests and the bureau groan, the restless or circulating lights from the festival we spin around in are reflected on the cracked walls and on her face, no one knows this look which burns and does not go out, only I and some man whom she—in a different segment of Time—desires and loves, her voice is a breeze and it burns me, the bones inside me groan, a sound from the trunk on the floor in the sunset silence, birds of night pass by the window and groan, darkly, groan in the air.

S

The Spiral and the Square 3

Draw a spiral, with the help of a compass if it is your nature to be careful, or freehand if you tend toward easier solutions. Take a close look at the ends of the line, the inner and the outer. You will see at once that a spiral does not transmit a static impression to us; rather, it seems to come from far away, from forever, heading toward its centers, its point of arrival, its now; or, to enlarge upon it, to unwind in the direction of ever-vaster spaces until our minds can no longer grasp it. In truth, if we divide it into sections at its extremities, we do so arbitrarily; by doing so we save ourselves from madness. Eternity would not even be sufficient for us to reach the end of the spiral—or its beginning. The spiral has neither beginning nor end.

To a more candid look, which, we might say, deserves attention, the spiral would be without end outwardly; inwardly, however, there are the centers where it ends—or begins. Such a thought demands rectification. We are the ones who impose a limit on the spiral at both extremities. Ideally it begins at Always and Never is its end. By which we come to a conclusion even less trivial than the preceding ones; to wit, even though we see it drawn on paper in opposite directions, its extremities (if they really exist) will meet at some mysterious point that is inaccessible to our stony comprehension, just like a circle, a much less equivocal and disturbing representation. How, then, can one make the structure of a narrative, a limited object that tends toward the concrete, rest upon an unlimited entity, one that our senses, hostile to the abstract, repudiate?

R

O and Abel: Meetings, Routes, and Revelations   4

Kneeling on the rug, I take off O's shoes, I take them off and I kiss her small, curved feet, feet with hollow soles. Her painted toenails glimmer under the sheer stockings. I take her feet in my hands, both of them (she, on the couch, half curved over, stroking my head), and I rest my face on them. Invisible violets sprout and bloom in her feet, inside her feet, among the thin bones: I can sense them. The City floats silently through the air, alights in the valley. Face to face, the City and I, mute. To whom do they really belong, these feet under my face and inside of which I can hear voices? She repeats my name softly: "Abel! Abel!"

The smell of dust is dissipated by her presence or by the luke-warm afternoon air coming in through the window. Our tongues repeat the game of advance and retreat. Our incisors touch at times and then our muscles retract. I suck successively her tongue and her neatly carved lips. She does the same. Our tongues swell and shrink, advance, expand, try to fill the other's mouth entirely. O presses my tongue between her strong teeth, delicately. A bird of imprecise shape or a black pennant fluttering on the horizon and drawing near, filling out and waving in the pure sky—birds?—and suddenly I see the outline of towers, walls, the river, or an arm of the sea. The smell of the air I breathe, tepid, from O's nostrils, reaches an almost unbearable intensity. Even greater is the pleasure of sucking it in. Am I inhaling over a glass of wine? Crushed grapes, freshly pruned vines, dry leaves of the arbor burning in the rain, linen sheets in the sun, among tall trellises and vine shoots—there, among so many others, are some of the images brought forth by the breath that no one else possesses and that she herself, certainly, exhales only on rare moments with such intensity. The hot and agitated tongue, made to taste the flavors of the Earth, inverts that function and becomes food. It tastes like a liqueur. What kind? I drink in the ever-replenished juice of that living fruit. I steep myself in the noisy being I embrace—and on my chest I can feel her breasts growing as if they were part of me. Not only must they have the roundness but also the color of rose windows (two large rose windows over lesser ones), and in them is the glitter, I am sure, of most uncommon words.

S

The Spiral and the Square 4

As the spiral is infinite and human creations are limited, the novel inspired by this open geometric figure must have recourse to another one, which is closed—and evocative, if possible, of windows, rooms, and sheets of paper, spaces with precise limits through which the outside world passes or through which we observe it. The choice falls upon the square: it will be the enclosure, the precinct of the novel, of which the spiral is the motive force.

Conceive, therefore, a spiral that comes from impossible distances, converging on a determined place (or a determined moment). Upon it, delimiting it in part, place a square. Its existence beyond that area will not be taken into consideration: there, only there, is where it will govern with its mad whirl the succession of the constant themes of the novel. For the square will be divided into a certain number of other squares, ideally equal among themselves. And the passage of the spiral, successively, over each one, will determine the cyclical return of the themes spread out among them, in the same way that the entrance of the Earth into the signs of the Zodiac can generate, according to some, changes in the influence of the stars upon creatures. Let us adduce that the center of the square and the centers of the spiral will coincide, or, in other words, that is the imaginary point where—supposing that it is drawn from outside in—we arbitrarily interrupt it. Such are the foundations of the present work.

Other details will be added in due time. For now, we must suspend this explanation, imprisoned by the rigidity of the plan established more than two thousand years ago. Since our spiral comes from without, its spins become smaller and smaller. Inversely, because of a need for symmetry and balance in the conception, the one who constructs the work will always enlarge, in arithmetic progression, the space conceded each time to the various themes of the book, which are controlled in regard to the rhythm of their reappearances and the extension of the texts referring to them. The capricious broadening of these themes constitutes a kind of upside-down answer to that spiral, which is closing. In their own way, they will be spirals that open or cones that lengthen. The one who constructs it will exercise thereby a constant vigilance over his novel, putting it together with a rigor only granted, as a general rule, to a few poetic forms.

O

The Story of Ọ, Twice-Born   1

This man embraces me (he has been coming to me for so long that it is impossible to remember the length of time), a mechanical saw cuts pine boards, the pendulum in the clock is shaped like a sistrum, a warm breeze moves the dahlias on the table, a mixed sound of vehicles comes up from the avenue. Articulated in absence and described by me myself, in a chaotic, incomplete, and, to a certain point, enigmatic way, on feverish days of an imprecise date when my mouth seems to know more than I, our meeting now reaches its fulfillment and its end. Abel!

R

Ọ and Abel: Meetings, Routes, and Revelations   5

We go along streets we do not know, Ọ and I, questioning the clear sky, examining the light of the Sun on the ground, and attentive to all the changes in the air. Summer dress, loose hair, sandals with false purple jewels. I don't know how, our hands meet, we hold hands, she squeezes my fingers and shows me in the sky the trail of the first Nike Tomahawk rocket. It is exactly ten o'clock in the morning. A quick meeting under the trees, at nightfall, by the statue of Dante Alighieri. Ọ gives me her arm. We go slowly around the base of the Municipal Library, protected by the branches that dilute and fragment the light from the street lamps. Our feet become heavy, sluggish—and we embrace. Her mouth, always a bit open, opens more and she bites my tongue. Motors and horns, mingled voices, steps, the shrill whistling of traffic policemen. In her throat there is born and repeated an inarticulate appeal, born and repeated (the word, perhaps, that I must find?), repeated, it echoes between the clavicles, a suffocated shout (no, it still isn't the word, the phrase, the enunciation), in the formless and lacerating sounds I recognize my name. The funeral procession crosses the city of São Paulo under the midday sun, passing laboriously through points of congestion. The black and worn-out body of Natividade is going to the grave. We do not move and even motionless the bed groans, the men in the amusement park are asleep in the tents, in the ticket office, on the benches of the carousel, the waves die on the night sand and the noise that does harm can be heard through the closed window. Ỗ speeds up the car still damp from the night mist, goes around the Praça Roosevelt frightening the pigeons, the bells of Consolação Church vibrate solemnly in the morning haze and she laughs. The washed pavement smells of fish, of orange rinds. The ultraviolet camera mounted by Edwin E. Aldrin, Jr. on the outside of the space capsule and aimed at the fields of the stars Sirius and Velorum is seeking information on the age of the Universe. Numbers and names flourish in those regions. We go slowly through the long, deserted streets of Ubatuba. The grimy walls of the houses, with terraces and plaster decorations, gardens with half-broken trellises, weeds growing out of the tile roofs and eaves. Events are enigmatic and almost never show themselves as whole. A text that a hundred mouths pronounce, each mouth utters three words, four, one, each mouth ignores the words that the other mouths emit, does not know where the other mouths are speaking from, how many they are, or even whether they exist. A mouth can speak and not know what it's speaking about. We, under the sheet in the darkness of the room, lying down, holding hands, rigid and mute, naked. Blindness breaking up and a plant growing in the center of my body, tart root, red stem, harsh wrinkled leaves, a plant of flames, nettle.

O

The Story of Ⓞ, Twice-Born 2

My husband, an emptiness in him or around him, approaches me, I see him as a woman does and also as a child, he takes off my bridal wreath, he tears my two hymens, he deflowers me and at the same time he rapes me, a cry of pleasure, of horror.

We should not make the judgment that human existence, while unfinished, is an incomplete polyhedron whose last side is death, no, the polyhedron moves and its faces and edges proliferate, grow with us, a bit shiny, that's how it is with everybody and even more so with me, having a double life, born twice, with two childhoods, two ages, two bodies, so that the faces of the polyhedron trespass upon each other, some are reflected in others: I am inlaid, encrusted in myself.

All my life is here, then, in this instant—instant?—there is no instant, no instants, what you call by that name is your own life, a polyhedron of innumerable transparent faces, these, the faces, are what seem to be instants to us, contemplate one of these, one of the faces, and you will see that it is impossible to ignore the others. I see the world through a double glass and I speak with a double mouth.

A

Roos and the Cities 1

Through the night, Anneliese Roos and I, silent, on the streets of Amsterdam. All the houses with closed windows. Bicycles on the sidewalks, still damp from the quick May rain. We listen to our slow steps and look at the reflection of the streetlights on the pavement. Roos's arm weighs softly and with an undefinable aloofness on mine. I am a sanctuary into which a fugitive bird has penetrated and which it will immediately leave. Under the wet stones—or in some far-off block—the voices of men singing, laughter, a beating of drums, an uproar.

S

The Spiral and the Square 5

Around the year 200 B.C., in Pompeii, then at the height of its splendor, there lives the merchant Publius Ubonius. Extremely curious, he has a tendency to speculate upon the incomprehensible, he travels whenever he is able (he even sells Hindu goods), and he puts traders up in his own house with the sole purpose of listening to them. He receives across time and distances, diluted, adulterated, and anointed with magic, perhaps, the residue of Egyptian mathematics, Babylonian astronomy, and the teachings of Pythagoras.

A slave, Loreius, always haunted by enigmatic dreams, some true, others perhaps invented to cater to his master's easy curiosity, is considered by Publius Ubonius to be his ideal partner in conversation. It is not rare for the merchant to forget about wife, children, and business to hold discussions with Loreius.

As a consequence of so many and such increasingly elevating conversations, he ends by promising the slave his freedom if he can discover a phrase that has meaning and can be read either from left to right or backward. Not only that: by placing its constituent words on top of one another, it can also be read vertically, beginning at the upper left-hand corner or the lower right-hand one. From any direction, in short, where the reading of the phrase is undertaken, it will always be the same. Publius Ubonius, incapable of concentrating on the problem in spite of his attempts, wants to represent the mobility of the world and the immutability of the divine. The immutability of the divine would find its correspondence in the immutability of the phrase, with its beginning reflected in its end; while the mobility of the world would have its answer in the different directions taken for the reading of the same expression and also in the possibility of creating other words with the constant letters of that imagined phrase, which Ubonius does not know but which must exist.

Loreius's dreams grow more frequent; his periods of wakefulness are desperate. First, he decides that the length of the sentence must be no more than five words. Going beyond that limit seems ostentatious to him; he has a weakness for contenting himself with less. Furthermore, the number holds cabalistic meanings, important to him, having, among others, the illation between five and the starry pentagon, the universal emblem of life. Since the phrase is composed of five terms, each one of these must of needs have five letters, making possible— some grouped on top of others (if read horizontally) or side by side (if vertically)—the interchange demanded by Ubonius's insistence. As will be seen, the two men are preparing, without their knowing it, the scheme of this novel, in which they shall appear again and in which they are collaborators. The narrator gazes at them with gratitude over the two thousand years that join them to him.

A

Roos and the Cities   2

It is with such ill-founded hopes that I face this trip which I and Roos, Anneliese Roos, must take together! The other passengers in the compartment are reading newspapers. Ngo Dinh Diem at the White House, Dutch zoo to acquire a thousand crocodiles, a photo of Churchill. I look at the hay piles scattered over the green flatlands, lighted by the still tepid sun of May. Under the sign of Roos—whose symbol seems to be the circle, return, illusory progress—instead of continuing on to Lausanne, I can be returning to the cold open platform of the Gare de Lyon. If Roos and you, Abel, holding hands, could only whirl about among the piles of hay! Perhaps your heart would quiet down and perhaps you could catch a glimpse of what you seek in vain.

I swallow her absence like a drink gone bad, the certainty that she is traveling on the same train, taking, apart from me, I don't know in which car, this trip with no apparent meaning. I'll get up, I'll go to meet her in the end. She will say, with an air of censure and without much force: "You promised not to look for me." I'll ask: "What happened? Why shouldn't I have come?"

O

The Story of Ọ, Twice-Born   **3**

My husband, leaning over, looks deep into my eyes; with a steady, brutal deliberation he turns my face toward the lamp. He exclaims with a tremulous voice: "You've got four eyes, one pair inside the other. What eyes are those? How is it that I never saw this?" I close my lids, the childhood lids: I look at him only with the adult eyes. He puts out the lamp that hangs on the rough stucco wall and lies down. The sea breaks on the rocks. I won't tell him—now, ever—about my two births, my two bodies. In the glow of the night light, still visible—and distant—are the walls, the three oval mirrors on the dressing table, the wreath on the high hook.

Come, Abel. Penetrate me and make me grow. I am obsessed with sponges, creatures with a narrow life, always changing sex, now laying eggs, now fertilizing them, I am obsessed with sponges, they have existed for five hundred million years already, they have hesitated between one sex and the other, it's all they ever did and do, so they continue, a motionless formation that terrifies me.

I won't even live a thousand years, my life is quick, a scratch on time, just as one day a fish leaps up over the vastness of the sea and sees the Sun and an archipelago where goats are moving among the crags, that's how I leap out of eternity, as everyone does, here I am in the air, I see the world of men, soon I shall return to the depths of the sea. This brief leap, this aspiration to an act of flying is all that has been conceded me to go from graphite to graffito, to consume what spongeans, in half-a-billion years, cannot even have a hint of, limiting themselves to passing continuously from one sex to the other, from one sex to the other. Are you coming?

R

Ʊ and Abel: Meetings, Routes, and Revelations 6

Ubatuba on that November Thursday reminds me of a dead city or one whose inhabitants have fled. Ʊ's face, in profile in the cold clearness of the afternoon against the wet car windows, takes on a transparency that makes her untouchable and distant. Her dress rises as she shifts gear: her shiny knees. Some old and noble-looking houses, these, poorly cared for too, are the mark of an ascendant and restricted period. *Castelo Branco postpones indefinitely the implementation of new cancellations of political rights.* A cyclist, carrying fishing poles, passes in the fine rain.

"I have betrayed and I have offended. If you know despair, you may agree with me, Abel: despair, in its most acute forms, isn't abstract."

Leaving Rio Grande and following a straight line that extends from the thirty-second parallel between Lagoa Mirim and Lagoa dos Patos, you reach the city of Bagé; all of us—some coming from distant countries—are awaiting the eclipse announced for this windless, cloudless November morning. Our very existence is not always comprehensible; because it is, of necessity, not yet a completed event. Narratives simulate the joining together of scattered fragments and we rejoice in this. Eclipses evoke them. Black Natividade, lying on her bed in the Home, judges it to be almost night—incapable of seeing the light of afternoon through the window, and herself among old people in the garden, leaning on a cane. The hearse with her body crosses the streets of São Paulo (mechanical diggers, saws, pile drivers), slowly. The room smells of camphor, fatback, ensilage, wood fire, washboard, waxed floor, disinfectant, starch, oregano, vinegar. She brings her half-seen hands close to her eyes.

"All of a sudden, people find a strange body in their flesh and want to pull it out. Nothing abstract, despair. A root, a hot pebble, inlays at some point in the torso. A rotting cat."

Ʊ in the midst of traffic on the Rua São Luís, her head turned toward me, her dress and her skin crossed by the endless headlights. Is she hesitating? All the lights of night, the globes of the streetlights, the paint and chrome of cars, white sparks from the bus's trolley on the electric netting, signs, traffic lights, the polished marble and the glass windows of the Zarvos Building, the fleeting letters of the illuminated newspaper, "LE MONDE CONSIDERS GOVERNMENT VICTORY IN BRAZIL DUBIOUS," ruby taillights and the headlights of moving vehicles, everything is turned on and explodes, fireworks, a spinning circle and she the center of the circle, of the fire.

"I have betrayed and I have offended." (These words sound disfigured in her voice, tempered like an instrument archaic and subtle at the same time, rich in variations and at times breaking into ripping sounds, each syllable made iridescent, a scarab's back. Slicing blades, of steel? No, the mold of the blades.)

The sea resounds in the silent void of night. She and I, naked, holding hands, on the bed. The bed groans, and the boards of the room, with the violent throbbing of my blood and hers. A thin needle wounds my tongue. I spit the needle out onto the floor.

"Isn't there some way out, Abel? Some way?"

"To tell the truth, I can't see any. A way out? Oppression gets into the bones and invades everything."

O

The Story of ʘ, Twice-Born   4

In the brief leap, that lightning space in which the fish flies and sees the goats biting the rocks of the islands, in that brief leap we are confused by the light of questions, which are many. We emerge from the sea to query, Abel.

Who made my body? I observe my parents carefully, I compare them to each other, I compare them to me, and I see: it wasn't they. My body comes from so far away that they've forgotten what it means. They transmit it like a text ten thousand years old, rewritten innumerable times, rewritten, extinguished, lost, evoked, written again and rewritten, a clear sentence, once familiar, having become enigmatic as it passes, in silence, from one womb to another, while the original language disappears. And, as for speaking, who was my teacher? I hear my parents speak, they speak to each other with a dull, loving, clear violence, and I know that they were not the ones who taught me to speak. At the age of nine I still can't speak. I don't feel the voice in me. I'm like a human dog or a possessed child, a child carrying in herself the demon of understanding and muteness. I hear everything—the wind blowing, doors slamming, laughter, water from the faucets, orders, the beating of my heart, vehicles on the street, birds singing—I hear everything, but I don't dare repeat those sounds and everything remains undeciphered for me. Words rise up from amidst the sounds, but only like threads of some other substance in a skein that cannot be unwound. I can distinguish them, but not always with great clarity. There are two children older than I and like me. They stick pins in me, they throw salt in my eyes, they wet my nightclothes, they hit me on the head. I know that there must be a code, a signal to call me. I try to discover it in the confused coming and going of the things around me. Can it be a sound, can it be a smell, can it be a color, a light? Sometimes a hammer pounds, or I encounter the front of a building, or I see designs on a wall, or I dig my nails into my skin. I keep wondering if one of these things is my name: the ringing of the hammer, the glow of the wall, the scratching on the cement, the pain I feel. This is how I live, in this communion which multiplies me and tortures me, this is how I live, until I rush downhill on my tricycle, I and the world, I and the three wheels that spin around me, and everything grows dark, and in that darkness I am formulated again, I am given birth again, yes, I am born another time.

A

Roos and the Cities 3

I leave Roos on the corner trying to get a cab and I run to the hotel; I fly up the stairs; I grab my bags. When I get back, she's inside the taxi by the long red awning of the Dupontparnasse and she beckons me.

"Gare du Nord. Hurry."

Men and women under the lights of restaurants and bars (La Consigne, Bretagne, Paris-Rennes), places where I can see myself on other nights over a glass of wine or a cup of coffee slowly sipped. Roos wipes my forehead with an embroidered gauze kerchief, the smell of violets that enfolded her at the beginning of the afternoon comes back to life in the taxi, the night wind dissipates it. In short, a happy meeting, such happy and harmonious hours that I almost forget the planned trip. What if the train has left by the time we reach the station? London is only a city and there are so many of them in Anneliese Roos! The dreamed-of and implausible sequence: Roos, on her return, climbing the stairs of the Hôtel Sainte-Marie with me under the resigned look of the clerk, helping me put clothes and books back in place, transforming with her presence the small room where the morning sun reflected off windshields comes through the curtains.

The tepid hand—a new condescension—doesn't flee from my touch. The almost fugitive fingers now squeeze mine and I discover intonations unperceived till now in her voice, something fragile, a kind of disorder.

I open the cab door under the broad marquee of the Gare du Nord. We—in the midst of the crowd, rushing—still holding hands. Fluttering on her shoulders is the kerchief, a gift from me: a griffin surrounded by butterflies.

S

The Spiral and the Square   6

Loreius is of course aware that the central word in the phrase to be discovered—which will serve as a base for the other four—in order to fulfill its function must also read the same in both directions. So in the baths, in his dreams, alone, in company, at the theater, or during his customary walks up to the gentle slopes of the volcano, he reviews all the palindromic words he can remember, finally choosing from among them the one that seems the most dazzling. He selects the word "TENET," not just because it is an indicative verb of possession, domination, a factor of great importance for him, a slave, but as having understood beneath it (tenet: conduct, sustain; but who conducts, who sustains?) the existence of a third party, an agent, someone who acts, without his identity even being known or exactly what he does. Also weighing in his choice is the circumstance that by writing the word twice in the shape of a cross, so that the "N" acts as a point of inter-section, and by eliminating immediately thereafter the syllable perched—or planted or nailed—on the horizontally written word, it brings forth the disposition of the remaining letters, the design of the "T," with the beginning and end of the word having been broadened. This curious bit would not have had the slightest importance for Loreius if the cross, the cross in "T," had not been the instrument by which runaway slaves were tortured. In the dialect of his parents, na-tives of Lampsacus, in Phrygia, "net," the particle which remains of the word "tenet" once the initial syllable is eliminated, means "no more," by which Ubonius's imaginative slave glimpses in this play with TENET a kind of logogriph accessible only to his understanding as a slave. His interpretation of the charade is translated like this: "Loreius, if he dis-covers what his master wants, will lead a free existence and will be crucified no more if he tries to run away."

With the preliminaries of the problem established, four words must still be found, with five letters each, and the middle letter of each word must inevitably be an "E" or a "T." This limitation, however re-strictive it might seem, actually facilitates the proposed task: Loreius now has a path. With this central cross, formed by the verb "TENET" and so clearly recalling the cardinal points of the compass, he is no longer lost on the stormy, limitless sea of words.

In this way he arrives, from experiment to experiment, at his phrase on an angle, seen between invisible mirrors that cut it and complete it at the same time—and that, cut in stone, reproduced on parchments, will spread throughout the world, fascinating those who face it and who uselessly think they can take it apart, alter it, take away even one letter, because the phrase stares at us like an eye, inviolate, circular in its squareness, so perfect that to touch it is to stick a dagger into the pupil of an eye.

"SATOR AREPO TENET OPERA ROTAS." The exact meaning of the ex-pression, so concise, will be lost with time, becoming ambiguous. For Loreius's contemporaries, however, the sentence is extremely clear, and its only mystery rests on a double meaning. It says: "The farmer carefully maintains his plow in the furrows." And it can also mean: "The Plowman carefully sustains the world in its orbit." This latter meaning, consequently, also answers Ubonius's mystical yearnings. Over an unstable field, the world, there reigns an immutable will.

A
Roos and the Cities   4

The rhythm of the life and the bells of Eltville (there Anneliese Roos is born and there her people live) reverberate in everything she does: in her walk, her gestures, her speech. The language of Racine, which she uses in a literary way, dignified and even elaborate, with a pronunciation in which preciseness might be the only fault, acquires, interposed between different tongues—the languages that each of us brings from our country of origin and that the other does not speak—a magical and benevolent meaning: we, without it, are two mutes. The ways it opens for us, however, are limiting, and more for me than for Roos: rarely, perhaps never, can I express exactly what I am struggling to tell her.

Thus, in spite of my fervor, our conversations, fluctuating in an orbit that is neuter to a degree, equally alien to the atmosphere of the small German city where Anneliese Roos is born and that part of Brazil's Northeast which—always without success—I attempt to describe to her, illustrate, to my despair, the limitations of language and, beyond that, those of the writer, frequently the product of lands that are not too familiar.

When, withdrawn from this dubious adventure according to the ordinary vision of time, I undertake to speak of Roos, I shall be repeating, to a certain degree, our inadequate dialogues. Without effort I shall give the characteristics that belong to Roos as they emerge in other women: the easy smile and the tendency to assume a pensive look without transition. (Some sad and undesirable memory afflicts her.) Will I be able, however, to describe the cities that float in her body as if reflected in a thousand small transparent eyes? How can I say that I penetrate those eyes—eyes or dimensions—and verify that the cities there are at the same time reflections of real cities and are also real cities themselves? Innumerable, integral, there are the cities of Roos, built on her shoulders, her knees, her face. As an invader, I know their streets, their deserted buildings, their empty vehicles, their trees, birds, insects, flowers, and animals (no human beings), and the rivers under fragile or magnificent bridges. The Hague, Rome, Strasbourg, Reims, Granada, Hamburg. Yes, talking about all this is probably remaking my limited dialogues with Roos in a different direction, with the exact same lack of success.

O

The Story of O, Twice-Born   5

He stops kissing my breasts, slides off the couch, kneels, and, with hands made for repairing watches, picking violets, planning incisions, stringing beads, he takes off my shoes and through the sheer stockings contemplates the top of my feet, the tiny toes, the shiny nails that may still smell of polish. Can he be telling the truth? That he's never seen such delicate feet and soft heels? He tells me this and other things in his Northeastern way of speaking, the inflections of Inácio Gabriel, the very same, although less accentuated and, besides that, his loving voice seems to be hiding a certain degree of mockery. (Like Inácio Gabriel, who predicts you, you know, we know, Abel, that gifts carry demands and that it's not enough to open your hands, your arms, your legs, eyes, mouth, ears, it's not enough to exist in order to receive well, we know that receiving is taking in, keeping, multiplying, and also giving back, yes, we know.)

Sounds come from the street and the clock goes forward. I hear them diversely, from my thirty-two and from my twenty-three years. Doubly, on my feet, I feel the breath from his mouth: I, one woman and two, two bodies in one that only I truly know and that, from two different points, from two ages, act, contemplate, and find pleasure. Every time, Abel, that you kiss my knees, you do it twice. Can you see the letters, the words that I still see at certain times tracking under my skin and that are surely never silent? I hear them, inside my body, I hear them, distant shouting, a crowd gathered on a square, not as if I were on the square, but as if I were the square, the murmuring of the words echoes in my thighs, in my breasts, in my womb, flowing back and forth, continuous, I don't know if it's happy, I don't know if it's fierce, it flows as if the confines of my body were the limits of the square, and my shoulders and armpits were vaulted arches where the last echoes of the voices reach, and my arms—which I extend—were extensions of the square, avenues that are also filled with voices. He sits down again and starts to unbutton my blouse, with delicate hands always. Maybe muslin isn't right for me, maybe my body calls for a thicker cloth. However, if the temperature goes up just a little, it's enough for me to take my thin dresses out of the closet. I like this fluttering of wide skirts, of ruffled collars, of puffed sleeves. He holds the weight of my breast, finds the nipple with the tips of his fingers, I contract my legs. My right hand, moving autonomously, by itself, grasps his knee and goes up his thigh. How long have we been walking toward this moment? No one knows at what point in the world the winds are born, who brings them into the light or the darkness, who the mother of the winds is and by whom she was created. The beginnings lie in the shadows.

R

Ʊ and Abel: Meetings, Routes, and Revelations   7

Natividade examines her half-paralyzed hands. Two old women, one standing and the other seated at the head of her bed, her hand on Natividade's shoulder, accompany with terror and courage her peaceful death agony, heedless of the two policemen, the sailor, the burglar, and the maidservant who, with closed mouths, are present at their mother's death. In Ʊ 's temples, in the thickness of her bones, suddenly, a name glows, untranslatable. Beside the boats at rest I hear the waves and the light rain on the metal of the car, on the windows. Her face lights up facing the vague horizon and the hulls of the lighters: a transparent illuminated book in a language beyond my reach. The sharp and monotonous sound of a bell comes from the city, a sound made smooth by the mist.

Did I see? I see: time and time, the two faces. Times. I see and I am afflicted: I don't have the means of expression. Still, even knowing that it's useless, I must try—a signal—because seeing and not saying is as if I didn't see. A signal.

The crowd at Casino Beach, where the platforms for the launching of the Nike Tomahawk, Nike Apache, Nike Hadac, and Nike Javelin rockets are built, has emptied the streets and squares of Rio Grande. ☿'s face, happy and perhaps a bit defiant, passes through the shade of the trees.

"Abel! Is this the manuscript of the book you wanted to publish? 'The Journey and the River,' an essay."

Drawn by the eclipse, I coming from the Northeast and she from the Central West, our trajectories on Earth came together in a way not entirely foreign to the celestial phenomenon. How old can she be? A perplexing question. Her face, animated by a fleeting inner light and a kind of thirst (with excitement she observes the blinds, the walls, the sounds, the interiors of houses), hides another being, veiled and sensed. Another being: obstinate, multiplying, resting, torn, noisy, enigmatic, and one who contemplates me from another key in time, instigating my inclination for everything that hangs, like texts, between duality and the ambiguous. Presiding over this meeting are the sign of darkness—a simile for nescience and chaos—and the sign of confluence: the germ of the cosmos and the evoker of mental order. Earth, space, Moon, movement, Sun, and time prepare the conjunction of symmetry and darkness. *Marshal Costa e Silva supports indirect vote.*

"Yolyps never have brothers or sisters younger than they. They render the womb where they are generated sterile forever."

I stroke ☿'s hand. A swarm—of what?—glows, agitated, on her torso. A clamor wavers between us, as if the wind were bringing the half-muffled voices of a crowd gathered a long way off.

A sign. Yes, a sign, yes. Like the tracker who says: "A stray cow passed by here." Does he know the color of the cow? No. Does he know the brand of the cow, put on with a hot iron? No, the track does not reveal this. But he knows, the tracker does: "Here a stray cow passed."

The flesh without memory of the black woman advances over her fingernails, thin and shiny in youth, in spite of the rough work; it retracts, uncovering the implantation of the eight remaining teeth, and it unfolds on the whites of her eyes, joining the shadows that darken the world in her eyes. On the empty bureau—her clothes and a pair of shoes fit into the bottom drawer of the piece—in a hatbox, her memories are kept. Photographs of her employers, of the child she helps rear and sees grow, dead leaves, shells, pebbles, a prism, colored pencils half used and without points, medicine bottles, thread, a brass ring, the shards of a pitcher, pictures of saints, a silver doubloon. The darkness that invades the world and Natividade's heart shatters these memories. She does not recognize the tall black woman dressed in white who bends over on the sand by the shining sea and picks up some shells, which she hides in the pocket of her dress, so as not to forget, so as never to forget, the joy and beauty of that morning.

O

The Story of Ͽ, Twice-Born 6

He kisses me. His eyes swim and dive into mine. Oyster divers. They dive deep into the eyes of my youth, those of my maturity, they go from one to the other—and with two mouths I kiss him, with two tongues I suck his tongue, twice I desire him, I and I.

I put to one side the tricycle that I have decorated with colored ribbons: they hang from the handlebars and are wrapped around the spokes of the three wheels. I am on the roof of the building, lying beside the water tank. No one sees me open the apartment door, take the elevator, get off on the top floor, push the tricycle up the stairs, lie down on the rough concrete, in the sun. A sky with luminous white clouds covers me. A bird is circling way up high. It flies so far away that it becomes invisible at times, lost among the clouds and the gleaming blue. Abel softly brushes my face with his lips, the fuzz on my face, he traces the line of my temples, slips down my face, looks for the curve of my chin, his breathing bends my bones, I move my head quickly, I bite his mouth. The solitary bird grows larger and I lose sight of it less frequently. I have difficulty seeing that its turns are precise. It flies with discipline, tracing a descending spiral, which narrows toward a vertex. At this vertex is the point where I am lying, I can see this quite clearly, as if the notion of a cone were familiar to me, the vertex of the cone, the bottom of the spiral blends with me and for the first time I can feel the distance between myself and things. At the same time, I suppress a shudder: maybe that flight is my name. The bird is still far away, I can see that it is black, that its head is red, but I cannot hear the beating of its wings and it is still far away when I feel the point in the center of my body. In the cut on the stomach. It isn't a pain. It's a point, yes, a point, the beginning of a sound, as if a small calyx were quivering there. I close my eyes, I cross my hands over my breast, I hear the sound of wings, huge wings, I feel the air displaced around my body, my short skirt and my hair flying, a silence follows, I open my eyes, no bird is looking at me or flying, no trace of wind, no trace. Two small black butterflies perching on the handlebar of the tricycle are opening and closing their wings. I begin to laugh and the butterflies go off. I roll on the concrete laughing, two claws grab me by the shoulders, lift me onto my feet, and a cry of terror, then of joy. My mother, weeping, carries me back.

Abel unclasps the garters from my stockings and patiently undresses my right leg. I rest my left foot on his knee, I slowly pull off the other stocking, laughing, I toss it in his face. The clock chimes, an incomplete portion of the musical phrase that—they say—is only heard from time to time. I put a record on the phonograph: *Catulli Carmina.* The shadows in the room seem to light up with the immediate entrance of the chorus. *"Eis aiona! Eis aiona! tui sum."* On my bare feet I can feel the threads of the rugs, the threads, I could say that I feel their designs, colors, flowers, geometric motifs. *"Eis aiona! tui sum."* ("Always, eternally, always, I belong to you.") I walk toward him. Without waiting for me to get close, he stands up, comes toward me, embraces me. His knees bend, embracing me, he slowly drops down, embracing me, he kneels, kisses my dress at sex level, my legs give way too, heavy, we remain on our knees facing each other, holding hands, we embrace again, again, we fall onto the rug.

A

Roos and the Cities 5

We are, Roos and I, temporary residents at the Alliance Française. I see her frequently in the dining hall, where a glass partition separates the crowd of occasional customers from those who—like us—live in the big house on the Boulevard Raspail. In the wing set aside for the boarders, always more peaceful, we sometimes share a table and attempt, not without ceremony, discontinuous conversations. Beside her room key she places a small purse and, occasionally, Mauger's French grammar. My eyes are peopled with the groups of African, white, and

Asian women who fill the dining hall twice a day; some time passes until all those faces dissolve, with only two or three remaining afloat, Roos's among them. The most worthy qualities of a book are like secrets and they are revealed little by little, always parsimoniously. Slowly I come to know (a text conceived and executed with discipline?) Anneliese Roos's beauty, the elaborate charm of her face, and, later still, her secret gifts, accessible only to my vigilant and corrosive gaze.

Success and deception (just like surprises and expected events) are the texture of our lives—and they make up narratives. I still don't know that Anneliese Roos is also going on that Easter excursion to the Loire Valley on a different bus. I let myself go, with no friends, alone, like a dog, passing through the region adorned with princely residences—just like those which illustrate books read in childhood, lying down in some room of the villa—and preserved as rare examples of secular architecture of the period between the Middle Ages and the great maritime discoveries, country landscapes or small cities the names of which I do not even know (Étampes, Chevilly) and which make me wonder, scrutinizing their outline and form: Can it be here?

I see Anneliese Roos when we stop in front of the profusion of towers, chimneys, and dormers of Chambord and the passengers from the two buses, led by a single guide, mingle. We wave to each other from a distance in front of the great steps and then we're lost from sight, mixed up among the other visitors. We continue our trip, favored by the clear April Sunday. Day is breaking in Recife and the red sky is reflected on the sands of the beaches. A doubt begins to trouble me: did I really pass through a village of small, very old houses with pointed roofs, with red and yellow clogs sitting on dark walls—or did I just imagine it, guess it, glimpse it *in a face?* Children pass by in First Communion clothes. A couple are eating lunch in the middle of a wheat field that is still green, the woman sitting and the man reclining. A bridal couple appears in the field, arm in arm, those accompanying them are dancing, someone is playing a rebec, the sound of which doesn't reach the bus. The couple eating lunch wave to the bride and groom.

S

The Spiral and the Square   7

During the months in which Loreius, sunk in speculation, seeks to solve the problem devised by Publius Ubonius, the conversations between the two revolve interminably about the question. As, however, the slave senses that he is getting closer to a solution, he becomes evasive. Ubonius interprets his reticent air as incompetence and begins to withdraw the attention he has favored him with. He begins even to neglect him.

On the morning when Loreius, on awakening, sees himself quit of the problem, solved while he slept (in the same way that a boil, treated with poultices while we are awake, bursts during the night), his first impulse is to run to Publius Ubonius, give him the solution, and thus gain his freedom. But on the way he decides not to go. Now that attaining his freedom depends upon a simple act, a few words, a pleasure that might be even greater than freedom would be to postpone it. Furthermore, in his deepest self he no longer considers himself a slave, nor does he feel like one.

Ubonius, weary of the slave's haughtiness, reaches the point of admonishing him. At first, Loreius is amused by these reprimands, which pass over him. But one day, when his master goes too far, he rebels and demands: "Treat me as a free man. I'm really no longer a slave. I have discovered the words."

"Say them, then."

"No. I shall reveal them only when I feel it is time."

The master (is he still the master?) turns his back on him and begins to reflect. Is it true what the (perhaps no longer) slave says? If it is, and if he has mistreated him, the enigmatic Phrygian may be quite capable, out of vengeance, of preferring to remain in bondage rather than reveal the secret. It is also possible that he hasn't discovered anything, and that his affirmative pose is nothing but a trick. Ubonius's propensity for reflecting indefinitely on a question, whatever it may be, causes him to get enmeshed in prognostications, hypotheses, calculations, suspicions, precautions, conjectures, subconjectures, and corollaries of all these intellectual acts, multiplying them in such a way and with such persistence that he becomes, in spirit, the slave of his slave. It is as if Ubonius were playing a blind game of chess with him and hoped to exhaust, mentally, all of his opponent's possible moves as well as their consequences.

He ignores a detail that renders his cogitations vain: Loreius's behavior will not depend on any external injunction; he is determined that only at the hour of his death will he reveal his discovery, having decided that the five words should be inscribed on his tomb. The consequence of Ubonius's mental games, as he vilifies him today and favors him tomorrow, is that Loreius oscillates between plenty and poverty.

Vanity brings on his ruin. There are many taverns in Pompeii. Wine is served over a marble counter to those who come by. Behind that room there are others for the use of gamblers, with inscriptions on the walls and paintings that are replicas of the surrounding scenes: gamblers about a table, quiet or fighting; sausages, cheeses, and bunches of onions hang over them. On the upper floor, not always with an entrance that is easily visible, there are bedrooms for intimate encounters. In one of these houses, seeking to make himself bigger in the eyes of a courtesan—Tyche, whose name tradition will preserve—Loreius reveals his strange stratagem and the magic phrase. Tyche perceives the advantage she could gain from the secret and passes it on to the man she loves, a vintner. The vintner aptly sells the slave's five words to Ubonius. Loreius, seeing himself defrauded and recognizing that he has lost his only chance to be free, goes shouting through the streets of Pompeii, proclaiming himself the discoverer of the phrase that children will later scratch on walls and drinkers will write in wine on tavern counters, goes to Tyche's room without the vintner's being able to stop him, roars out the words of his perdition once more, and, drawing a dagger, kills himself in front of the woman.

A
Roos and the Cities   6

We're in Amboise and the members of the excursion are scatter-
ing. If, instead of wandering about the castle grounds, stimulated by
the chill of this bright midday, I head for the restaurant, I will never
really see Anneliese Roos. Turning, as I do, to the left and not to the
right, I head for one of the possible crossroads of my fate and entangle
myself in a way that has no name in the texture of her beauty—or her
magic. Would I have chosen a different direction, perhaps, even if the
meeting with Roos were to lead me to my death?

Over her shoulders she has a navy-blue jacket, which brings out
the whiteness of her neck and the canary yellow of her sweater. Her
gray skirt mitigates that contrast of colors. Still favored by the green
waves of the hills and the faint blue of the sky at the horizon line, Roos
is holding a bouquet near her chin as if she were breathing in its perfume, even though only the rose, fresh and red, holds any for me: can
poppies and geraniums also have a smell? The flowers reflect their
purples on Roos's face, which looks uncommonly vivid to me in her
meditation.

I am afraid of disturbing the happy combination of colors, lines,
and volumes by my approach. Standing out in the center of the sunlit
landscape is the solitary figure of Anneliese Roos, just as certain valuable works in museums are placed far apart from the others so they
can be contemplated in their integrity, without sharing the observer's
wonder with any other. I know, however, that she will shortly be
broached, she will leave her place or move her arm.

Lowering her head, she looks at me, looks away, and moves off a
few steps. I follow her and with schoolboy syntax I say that I don't
know which deserves a more prolonged or attentive contemplation:
she, or the rose she has in her hands. The fastidious vocabulary makes
the phrase impersonal. Barely letting it be seen that she hears me, and
imitating the cadence of the poetry in her slow walk, Anneliese Roos
begins to declaim with the tone of a psalm:

> *"La Rose est le charme des yeux.*
> *C'est la Reine des fleurs dans les printemps écloses."*

I see in a glimpse, without their catching my attention, ash-red roofs, and I note that a bell has begun to toll. To think that so many times at the table in the dining hall we spoke about the Suez crisis and how much it rains in Paris, while she is capable of reciting the poetry of Anacreon without mistakes! Moved by the interest that takes control of me, I, too, bring forth another fragment by the poet, perhaps proclaiming the summula of this brief instant when Anneliese Roos, distant, unapproachable—imprisoned in a youth immune from the woodworms of time—gives forth her halo, suggested in a text:

> *"Sa vieillesse même est aimable,*
> *Puis qu'elle y conserve toujours*
> *La même odeur qu'aux premiers jours."*

Thus the shade of a Greek lyric poet, put into a language that is neither Goethe's nor Camões's by a translator of the eighteenth century, read by me in an edition from seventeen-something that smells of smoke and old clothes, aloud, beside the villa cistern while the laughter of the Fat Woman and the voices of my various brothers and sisters ring out, speaks through our mouths over a distance of two-and-a-half millennia and establishes a provisional, yet not fragile, bond between us.

O

The Story of , Twice-Born 7

Eis aiona, eisaiona. Just as porous cloth absorbs dampness, so my body in its permeability drinks in the designs on the rug. They project themselves into my flesh and bones, white angles, bars, tawny fringes, branches, reddish stags, a rabbit, flowers, birds, leaves of an imprecise color. An abstract forest where things rise up, grow, but do not live: the stags do not bleat, the flowers do not smell.

At the turn of the century, the naturalist Wilhelm Bolsche publishes a book about animals. In it one reads that starfish can split in two; and all of the organs divide at the same time. The terrible wound doesn't take long to heal over. In time each half of the Asteroid grows and once more takes on the shape of a star. Then, Bolsche and his contemporaries ask, to what point does the starfish think as a unit and from what moment on does it acquire the rudimentary notion of its double existence? A bothersome and idle question, of interest only to a few, and one that cannot be answered, even if one lives an identical experience.

The small calyx, the sound in my navel, the quivering calyx continues sounding for many days. When the vibrations finally grow weak, there is a presence in me, a presence. Something like a beetle, no, like a slow-moving spider. Then it is no longer a spider, but a bird with short wings, no beak, its feet cut off, a gray bird, later a fish with four feet, afflicted and restless, swimming with effort in my green uterus. I open the window and the fish's eyes light up, I weep and the fish becomes sad, I am sleepy and it dozes, I run and its legs move, I am frightened and it curls up, I am happy and its scales shine. Without my knowing it, there is a split in me, I am being born from myself, I am invading myself. It is no longer a fish, but a dog, a dog ornate with feathers and large fins that occupies me. It has hands and feet. Sometimes it stretches its leg and with its foot it jabs my womb, my spleen, I twist with pain. It raises its fist and wounds my heart, pierces it: purple splotches appear on my body. It licks my throat and I vomit. I connect all of this to the bird that descends onto my stomach and, many, many times, I plumb the clouds. But the bird doesn't return—never again, never—it doesn't reappear.

Looking at the rug, you can't see the crocodile among the flowers and the birds. Camouflaged in the profusion of motifs, he can be discovered more easily on the other side, the side of the weave that is always hidden, where the threads are cut and knots show. Freed of the artful tricks that hide him, making himself present and invisible at the same time, the crocodile (absorbed like the obvious motifs on the rug) walks along Abel's extended trunk. The reddish stag, standing between our embraced bodies, looks at the face of the clock as if looking at the Sun, tail and hind legs on Abel's flank, head and chest on my flank. The crocodile, darkening Abel's torso, has his mouth at the level of his sex and presses against my thigh. The rabbit bites the tip of my breast, he bites lightly, as if he were nibbling a tender blade of grass.

I know what other men are like, I go to bed with them out of anger, I open my thighs out of rage, they give me pleasure and draw nothing from me, they give me pleasure, the pleasure one has when a mad dog is shot to death, a mute and lacerating pleasure, but I want to give myself to you, Abel, in a new and unique way, give myself with joy, I must open up my identities to your entry, my sexes, my bodies, I must receive you in my innermost parts and love you in two ways, with double desire, double anxiety, double consent, and you won't be an intruder, an enemy—you shall be the guest, the one summoned, the accepted one, I will receive you with all the doors of my body open, I, a cloven and reunited Asteroid, I, I, dual, I, one. *Morde me. Basia me.*

R

Ơ and Abel: Meetings, Routes, and Revelations   8

Flotsam, bounced by the small waves, hits the sides of the small T-shaped dock, little used now by fishermen's canoes. At the ends of the thick wall that corresponds to the leg of the letter, two lanterns hang from thin posts curved at the top (sunflowers on withered stalks) and at night light up the two flat dark stones used to moor the boats. One of the lanterns (one of the sunflowers?), the one on the right, was knocked off by the wind, which sometimes blows hard in Ubatuba. This accident points up the perfect symmetry of the dock, shiny in the light rain. It is isolated from the world somewhat by the thin mist that extends over the town, the beach, and the gray sea.

"The father of a yolyp, of course, can have children with other women. In general, this never happens. The yolyp is always the newest or only child. The mother of the yolyp never conceives again."

Natividade raises her hands and says to the other two old women: "Do something. Can't you see all these people in the room? Go get some glasses and some water. They want to drink. Very thirsty." Four men carry her coffin. When the Sun, at noon, grows dark, Ơ and I embrace, invaders of a firmament where we are strangers. Gigantic wings cross the darkness, the Nike Apache rises into the air, the great winged being makes the roofs buzz, shakes the trees, raises the dust on the square, and slips along above us with its hoarse song: heavy stones rolling in a long metal tube.

"No wisdom at all, Abel, put aside the conviction that the foreign body is in us forever. Our whole life finds its negation there. We turn against the intolerable presence."

"The exasperated and ostensible way in which oppression venerates Order makes me suppose that it hides an affiliation with Chaos."

To the right of the T, sitting on the stone under the post without a lantern, the mannikin protected by a sheet of inflated yellow plastic waits for some fish to come and bite his hook. Other shapes are fishing on the dock, all silent. Narratives are effigies of an order that we sense and that we are nostalgic about.

"Order, for the oppressor, is a degenerated reflex of the laws that rule the Cosmos: rigidly conceived, it tends toward petrifaction."

The ruddy setting Sun is reflected on the waters of the Praia Grande—a vertical sword of flames that, broken by the waves, comes together again. ☼, with a hat in imitation of daisies, laughs, putting her translucent and agile arms out to the side as the sea breaks at the level of her breasts: her red bathing suit becomes pale under the red sun. We hold hands and, with the waters making our bodies weightless, we run side by side, we run idly, slowly, lightly, imitating those sequences in movies where the slow-motion camera, drawing the characters out of the normal rhythm of their lives, points up singular instants. The sheet of fire is broken up on the agitated surface of the water and, from the foam, flowers more delicate than ☼'s are born. We run holding hands, slowly, in a field of ephemeral poppies and daisies.

Does the Father exist? In him and around him: a sound without silences, a noisy beehive, the sound of Eternity: around him and in him. Motionless bees buzz making sound: around him and in him. Buzzing bees in suspension—they don't move—in the whole extension of Time and the World. Having lived much with the waters and reading their surface, the fisherman says: "There are fish here." Where? How many? He doesn't know and fish are swift: they don't stop for hooks or question marks.

Natividade, alive and dead, seeing only what we see or judge that we see, we, those full of darkness, and now, with her sensitive and light vision breaking the limits of limitations, she raises her crippled hands to the level of her eyes and speaks: "I'm already dead. Why hasn't my flesh dried up yet? I don't understand. I smell like live people."

Ʊ's hands, well shaped and with long palms, emphasize what she says with quick movements. She raises them at times between one phrase and another, pushes her hair back from her temples. Thus, just as the thin shadow of the bones on the featherless wing of a bird can be seen, so I believe I have discovered in her hands, lifted and soaked in the transparency of the morning, another pair of hands, a secret pair.

O

The Story of Ʊ, Twice-Born   8

The fish leaps out of the vastness of the sea, the fish leaps and this leap does not always happen at the best moment, nor does it always take place near land, near islands, reefs, nor is there always light at that time, the fish might find a black and windless sky, or a night storm without lightning or a storm with thunder and lightning, so the leap, the instant of the leap, that quick instant might coincide with darkness and silence, might coincide with a sun-filled, moon-filled world, the fish in its leap might see nothing, might see much, might be seen in its flash of scales and fins, might not be seen, might be blind, and also might, in its leap, its leap, its leap, meet in its leap, precisely in its leap, a cloud of voracious birds, have its eyes torn out at the moment of seeing, be torn to pieces, turned into nothing, devoured, and the frightful thing is that those famished birds represent the only and re-mote possibility, the only one conceded the fish, of prolonging the leap, of not going back to the black gills of the sea. But aren't those birds, their swordlike beaks, another kind of sea without the name of sea?

Orff's music continues: a chorus of young men, of young women, a chorus of old people. The old ones proclaim the transitoriness of passions, *immensa stultitia*, but the young ones answer fervent with hope. Unhurried, Abel grips me, bites my naked breasts, takes them in his hands, rests his face on them, the navy-blue jacket thrown over a chair, his left hand (wing?) comes down my side, one of the shoes upside down by the crystal cabinet, his hand reaches my knee, another shoe with the beak against the gray baseboard (it looks like a turtle exploring the wall), the hand overcomes a kind of trembling, climbs up between the thighs, a tepid and cautious palm, cautious. "I can hear your heart beating. It beats as if I could hear the throbbing and the echo of the throbbing at the same time. I knew two birds like that. Two canaries. One would repeat the song of the other."

He turns to me, leaning on one arm, the other hand fondling my armpit, he turns, perhaps in my body I will shortly hear the voices that I only hear at dawn and that, since Inácio Gabriel, have been my company in this world, my only company, I take off his tie, I throw it to one side, I start unbuttoning his shirt, cars parade along the avenue, slowly. Will I hear those voices, the swarm of words that I can never make out and that still comfort me? It's hot on these November afternoons. My black bra, which he has thrown far off, hangs from an unpolished silver teapot, one of my stockings lying across my shoes, I don't know where the other one ended up, I put my hand into the opening of the white shirt, I feel his skin, no, not his skin, rather a force that exists under the skin, a magnet, my hands slide onto the magnet and can't get loose, the rabbit and the crocodile slowly leave my body, install themselves in his, he begins to talk again and his voice comes through the bonds, the flowers and the animals, in which we are both entangled: "I can measure your beats. When I move away from you, they slow down. I put my hands on your skin; the beating becomes faster and you breathe more rapidly." While I listen to him, while his voice enfolds me, while I raise myself up a little, loosen my hair, move my head, move it, my hair unfolds, languidly, covers my back.

"Beautiful, those colors. Honey and steel?"

He takes the loosened braids in his hands, delicately strokes them and doesn't see that two heads of hair are mingled on my skull, two. "Silver and honey." Where are the hooks of virility on his face? On the broad forehead, the clear eyes, the somewhat protruding teeth? The vaguely Mongol face and the faded amber tone of his skin. "How beautiful your breasts are at this moment. Do you know what I see in them? A maritime chart. An archipelago of names." "The names of islands?" He doesn't answer: he remains serious, in a way that frightens me. And he touches me on the chest, on the scar.

"What's that?"

"A bullet wound."

"How old is it?"

"Almost ten years."

"Who shot you?"

"I did."

We fall silent and both remain lying down, side by side, holding hands, looking at the chandelier, flowers bloom on my tongue, flowers with a prickly stem, and there is a flock of sheared sheep in my throat.

A

Roos and the Cities   7

We go through the garden side by side, Roos giving me the impression that she considers my company natural and even inevitable—and then another presence, more worthy than the rich estates we're visiting, than Anacreon's poetry and the countryside of the Loire (without the birds, the trees, the sultriness, and the violent light of the Northeast of Brazil), turns the atmosphere emblematic, in a manner of speaking, and in a foreign land overloaded with elements not completely absorbed by my vision, which is barbarian, after all, this mad love is revealed, I know it well—as furtive as its object. I once read that Leonardo da Vinci, and Girolamo della Robbia too, had walked about these parts and died here. Anneliese Roos asks me if I've visited his tomb yet. Here we are, face to face, silent (what could we say?), I contemplate her and she has a thoughtful face, her arms hang down, her hands clasped, the flowers at the level of her sex: she is looking at Leonardo's gravestone. The bell has stopped; the sound of voices coming from the garden grows soft as it enters the chapel. Then, suddenly and for a brief moment, as in a fall or a vertigo, in Roos's head I glimpse a city with winding streets, inhospitable, cold and windy in spite of the sun that inundates it, but with great white churches covered with marble. I exclaim to myself: "Dante's homeland!"

We are still standing before the dust or the memory of the dust of Leonardo's testicles and eyes—and reaching us, muffled, are the voices of those passing by in the garden. I catch the smell of the animal that, ever since childhood whenever I interrogate simple and unspeaking things like the surface of a mirror and smooth walls, appears behind me exhaling its rank smell, which means: "You don't make it, Abel." I draw back, trying to defend myself and banish the animal that is never seen, with his smell of excrement and rotting teeth, the sudden vision of Florence in Roos's pensive head, certain in the meantime that I will not escape and that, much as I avoid it (isn't that what happens to the villa with its porches and rooms sketched out in a hundred inept texts?), I will spend years and years searching for that point where the ungraspable and the word are reconciled: trying to make Roos and the cities she encloses visible. So, walking by her side once more under the flameless sun of this April Sunday, I almost believe that I am the same man I am before seeing her, silent, her hands and flowers at sex level in the chapel where sleeps the Tuscan bastard, painter, poet, musician, inventor of war machines and aquatic constructions, he also pursued by an ambition to knock down closed doors, with the advantage that he always opens or almost always opens them—like the Florentine whose mule-kicks open up Paradise. Seeing is a tortuous responsibility.

A chestnut-colored bird, with russet spots and two white lines crossing its upper wings, alights on the lawn. What's it called? Roos slowly bends her knees. In her left hand the poppies, the rose, and the geraniums; the right stretched out in the direction of the bird. Something feline and fragile breaks away from the crouching figure, from the concentrated face (where some city is shining through), from the almost black eyes, now squinting and metallic. The bottom of her jacket touches the grass. The bird, exploring the soil, approaches the ringless, empty hand. It acts as if Roos's hand were a branch, a drinking place. But the drinking place or branch, with almost imperceptible slowness, is also shortening the distance.

Can my companion be holding back some secret power? What is the affinity between her and the bird? Does a peculiar peace that is just right for the standoffish nature of birds flow from her body? I see myself losing control, submissive to her presence and following her like a cloak, a shadow, I go in her direction like that russet bird, and perhaps Roos, without my being positive of it, has stretched out another hand to me, one that I cannot see but that exists.

S

The Spiral and the Square

The square to which we have referred already and which constitutes, in a manner of speaking, the precinct of this work—which, without it, dragged off by the tireless gallop of the spiral, would be lost for want of boundaries—is subdivided into twenty-five: the twenty-five squares with the twenty-five letters of the sentence that cost Loreius his life. Each square, just as the divisions of the year cover the name of a month, as the rays of the invisible compass rose cover the designation of a cardinal or intermediate point—each square, we say, covers a letter. These, even though they are five times five in all, do not come close to including the whole alphabet. They do not go beyond eight, since the "S" and the "P" appear twice, and the rest—with the exception of the "N," which is not repeated—each come up four times.

There you have, then, the simple—albeit uncommon—structure of the book. Each of the eight different letters has a corresponding theme, which returns periodically, as the ever-narrowing spin of the spiral returns to it after having provoked the appearance or reappearance of another, of others. The spiral flies over several themes; and these do not return by chance, or from the arbitrary or intuitive power of the author, but are governed by an inflexible rhythm, a rigid pulsation, immemorial, indifferent to any kind of manipulation.

So that it will be easier to perceive the nexus of conception, which tries to be as clear as possible, we shall stress the relationship between the spiral and Loreius's sentence. At first both seem to be immensely far apart from each other or joined only by a common strangeness. Examining more deeply, we discover the mutual similarities, real as those which exist between a printed "Z" and a handwritten "Z" and obvious to anyone to whom the mysteries of writing are familiar, although inaccessible to those who still have not learned to read.

We have seen it clearly: the spiral, seeming to advance in a determined direction, is really an image of return, since its extremes, being inconceivable, tend to come together. Its beginning is its end; furthermore, whether as a figure that advances imaginarily toward the centers, or as a figure that goes away from them, it is always a spiral. Loreius's sentence has the same character of immutability: it can be read in any direction; on the other hand, in its apparent openness it closes in upon itself. It so happens at times that two brothers are dissimilar. We judge this way at least until we meet a third brother (or sister) whom both resemble. We still better perceive the obscure kinship between the spiral and Loreius's magic sentence if we keep in mind the relationship between both and certain mythical figures with whom, also at first blush, they seem to have nothing in common, like the two-headed dragon (one head being in place of the tail), the amphisbaena, and, principally, the god Janus, the ambiguous possessor of two faces, one turned to the front, the other to the rear, so that he has no back—or, rather, his back is also his chest. Does not Loreius's sentence, like that god (whose insignia, it should be noted, were the rod and the key, one to drive away intruders, the other to open doors), look in opposite directions? Does not the spiral represent, like Janus, a simultaneous coming and going; does it not pass simultaneously from Tomorrow to Yesterday and from Yesterday to Tomorrow? In its design, are not the Always and the Never reconciled? One must never forget, too, that one of the alchemists' favorite symbols was the marriage between the Sun and the Moon, represented as a hermaphrodite, a double body, rotting in a coffin. The thought that dominated this representation—where two heads, like those of Janus, were seen on one body—was that of death followed by resurrection.

The spiral, as well as the sentence we have before our eyes, seems to be taut with these fusions of contraries. There exists a point, a center, an "N" toward which everything converges. The "S" of "SATOR" is the same as that of "ROTAS." In the square and in the spiral, the Tiller has two faces and goes two different ways, comes from the edges of the field, plowing in opposite directions under simultaneous seasons. Lastly: all of these conceptions of human restlessness—god, amphisbaena, spiral, alchemists' couple, two-headed dragon, and palindromic sentence—are they not without beginning and without end, or, if an end exists, does it not coincide with its own beginning?

A

Roos and the Cities   **8**

How can I escape this irrational residue that induces me to read into things, where so many times I think I am deciphering (and am I not now reading into Roos?) representations of my life, texts taken down in a forgotten writing, in which, however, I identify my name? It occurs to me, facing Roos and the charmed bird, that my fate or a part of it—as twisted in spite of the Fat Woman's illusions as that of all my brothers and sisters, with their useless musical instruments—hangs on the scene I am observing attentively: if the bird climbs onto the hand of this foreign girl, I will be tangled up in a thread forever. Without trying to control myself, I clap my hands and the bird flies off, flees, the tension on Roos's magical face disappears; she gets up and turns her back on me.

As the afternoon goes on, I retain very little of the other castles visited. With my gesture, I had disappeared—like the bird—from Roos's eyes. Leonardo da Vinci writes that the testicles "increase the audacity and ferocity of animals" and he is horrified that man covers and hides his penis, "when, in truth, just as he does with a deserving aide, he should adorn it and display it solemnly." This is what the merry governesses do every morning with Gargantua, enhancing his "coral branch" with flowers, ribbons, and other trappings. Why, then, should I not decorate my coral branch with foliage? Why do I not, once and for all and with all solemnity, exhibit this deserving aide for Roos? I hide it at every stop on the excursion, without her speaking to me or turning toward me a single time; what I do is contemplate her and silently probe her spaces, wasps sticking their stings into my back, so that the salons, porticoes, stairways—everything I see as if floating in her image and mingled with the pain, with the angry wasps. Bits of phrases are exchanged in many strange tongues, a kind of pressure grows in me (I put the axis of the Japanese windup top into a tin cylinder, I put it in with childish hands, and the spring hidden in the cylinder, the spring whose curved tip sticks out, hooks into an oval opening in the top, I spin the cylinder and I feel the spring contract, ready to fire, but instead of pressing the axis of the top and making it spin, I squeeze it a little—just a little—to feel the contained force of the spring, and now it's as if there were other tops rising up in me, thirty, sixty, a hundred, held in their shining cylinders, their springs tight, ready to break out by themselves) until night closes in, back in Chambord, after that feverish day rich in images, and I hear a snort approaching, a roar, and I see myself surrounded by the headlights of dozens of motorcycles, driven by boys in leather jackets, girls on the baggage racks with their arms around them, the cycles zigzag back and forth, crossing paths, the cyclists, all in black, shout to each other, gunning their motors, the lights cross by each other in the night, new vehicles arrive, no one turns off his motor, the thunder coming out of the air and the earth surrounds me, I raise my arms in the midst of the turmoil of tires, gloves, faces, exhaust pipes, handlebars, and black jets—and I shout, hands over my ears, the name of Roos, a long cry, the longest I can give, in the belly of the roar provoked by the seventy exploding motors and with such violence that I lose my voice. As if they had been awaiting this appeal, almost at the same time, the motors fall silent and the lights start going out, almost at the same time, and I see myself free of the wasps, their stings, but split in two, out of breath, alone, surrounded by strangers.

I know that our interrupted meeting will go on (or is it going on?); the only thing I don't know about the sequence is its manner and rhythm. Like an individual condemned to death and waiting at every instant—from a cliff, from a corner, from a pepper tree lost in the backlands—for the bullets that, even if not fired, are already whizzing in his direction, I await every approaching minute—on the curves of the already, at the now—the beginning again. Through the window, closed against the still-cutting wind, the voices of the girls filter through as, having returned from Easter vacation, they expose their thighs to the April sun in the courtyard. I try to read: such is the lack of surprises and pleasure that I find in the reading that the book seems to have been copied by me. With a magnifying glass, I examine the tourist folders that are accumulating in the cupboard, divided by countries and tied with a string. The impulse to begin the search for the City comes to me again, demanding. I lie down and remain looking at the ceiling. Black cockroaches come out from the baseboards, climb onto the bed, walk on my face, my neck, my hands. The voices decrease. The cockroaches leave, with their frizzled wings.

T
Cecilia Among the Lions   1

Hermelinda and Hermenilda, that's what they call us. In this still-peaceful part of Recife, with a thick, hard name but with a precarious existence, where old age works without mercy on the poor thing that we are, few people are capable of telling which of us is Hermenilda and which Hermelinda. When the light is dim, we become confused ourselves. Twins? No. When we think about it, we can't even be sure that we were given birth, were born. Childhood, youth, mature fruits are unknown to us and we are both widows—but without dead husbands. Are lives a thread guided by a needle? Is your life a needle that sews without thread?

The Casa Forte district, the Estrada das Ubaias. We, two old women, live off the pensions we receive each month from the Fiscal Commission and from some help here and there, surrounded by cats and canaries, playing the mandolin (one of us, at least) with half-deaf fingers, all as if determined. The needle, falling point down, sinks into the water: the vice of sewing. Falling on its side, it floats and proves that water is a solid body. The function of leaders does not disappear with us. Can a needle, a perforating artifact, wound? It also helps in sewing. Hermelinda, Hermenilda. Needles, in this fable threaded by Death.

O
The Story of ⱺ, Twice-Born   9

A transition in the dog with fins, the dog dressed in feathers. It has human ears, the snout dissolves and the face of a child is revealed—with closed eyes, however. The fins are gathered into its body as if they were flapping ribs, as if they were tongues of the ribs. The front paws become rounded, the nails grow out into claws, into fingers, they rise up in the direction of the shoulders, the posture looks like that of a person crucified.

I go pedaling along on my tricycle and a sudden doubt holds me back. Timidly, I move the pedals in the opposite direction, I go backward. Verticals and horizontals are confused for me, height doesn't exist, what had been the floor of a room tilts, bends, wrinkles, the distance between the windows and the street seems passable. I would follow that route, on foot or on my tricycle, if all the windows of our apartment had not been reinforced with steel mesh that is slowly rusting. But the time for jumping has not come. The fall is being prepared, it awaits me, the mesh is no good, eroded more and more by the December and January rains, by the air that is always damp, by old age, perhaps by the shouts, by the constant noises that come from the neighborhood, by the trembling of the city. There is no lack anywhere of abysses, pits, there is no lack, and when there is, when there is a lack, we find within ourselves a void into which we can fall. For our own perdition?

They take precautions: I must be protected. I know nothing and therefore they must defend me, defend my life. Outside, however, a few steps from the door that is always closed, a few steps from the parlors and the bedrooms, mornings and afternoons, going round and round like a dog with an attack of colic, the windows fortified with thin steel mesh, I go round and round on my tricycle, many times each day the grille of the elevator opens. That is the place for the fall. There is where I must fling myself, and not—as they are sure—to die, but rather to be born. I have been spawned for the fall, that's why I grow, it is for that leap that I grow mature as the days rise up, pass, rise up and pass, the days. Who is bearing me another time? Whose daughter am I the second time that I am born? A word's? Someone gives the command: "Be born!," and then I obey, am I nothing? Shall I be, in my second birth, a being like others born of woman? Do I swim out of myself? Do I swim in the air, out of the air?

The dog with fins and rounded hands is in me, yes, it's in me, yet it's a stranger. The light inundates the eyes, they bathe in the light, but before a very strong radiance they retract, an intense and close flame wounds them. That body within mine is intolerable, too much light for me, an intolerable glow in my body, in the eye of my body. Invaded by it, my body closes up, closes up but the spark catches within, the flame, and it yearns for solitude, that darkness where it will find peace once more. A useless yearning. The incessant, painful, and increasingly clear splendor, I can only forget in sleep.

Suddenly, from some point, a subterranean voice, the fall begins to act upon me. It works its attraction on me, it calls me as the outside world calls a creature being born and I am not alien to that invocation. My restlessness becomes more intense; I let myself fall twenty times a day, from the tricycle, from my bed, from my parents' old and creaky bed, from the large round table, I climb up on the chairs (their backrests are decorated with a small cushioned medallion of light blue damask), I make them rock, they fall with me, I crawl along the floor, I run by the windows and beat against the steel mesh with my fists, my head, looking down. From the body within my body comes the smell of ripe oranges mixed with burnt lavender and flowers of sulfur. Only this odor, yes, it alone protects me, seems to defend me from everything, I can feel it weaving and making a cocoon thicker around me, hour after hour, so that I myself will be segregated. A cocoon.

I am in my father's room when the fan opens inside of me. It doesn't open gradually, with the slowness proper to the vegetable kingdom. It opens all at once, they're wings, the arms of the creature in me are still open, the hands almost touching my shoulders, but now, wearing two wings, these two wings clothe it, cover its nakedness, a kind of cloak, humeri, tectrices, and winglets are all of a brilliant purple, the pinions gold, principally on the tips, while the feathers between the gold and purple parts alternate, some the color of blood, others blue. Indistinctly, on the small features as well as on the pinions, a hundred marks like eyes (or can they be eyes?) contemplate themselves. I can see nothing more, I perceive nothing more except the wings I hide. These ornamental wings that will never fly last only a few seconds. They last only a few seconds or, if they last longer, they attract me so strongly that the days pass by far off. The hundred eyes on the wings close, they detach themselves, they fall apart as if they were dust and were carried off by a wind, they fall apart and the being that they had enveloped before appears naked, I run to the window and beat on the steel mesh, the sky is dark and the buildings give off a dull phosphorescence, there's a flash of lightning, the thunder and the brightness knock me down. Then the storm breaks. The Sun, wrapped in clouds, opens the door of Cancer.

R
♂ and Abel: Meetings, Routes, and Revelations 9

She lets herself float in the waters that are undulating and full of reflections. I dive, eyes open, under her body, I slip under the body that floats and I think I see, half hazy among the reflections, another body: I see, as if the reflections on the water were penetrating her, luminous points, purple, green, white, not just reflections but signs. (Letters?)

"Bent on the deciphering and also the ciphering of things (although almost always without success), I refuse to hold in what is seen and captured without effort. I investigate those planes or layers of the real that show themselves only in rare instances."

♂ and I look attentively at the rays of the Sun under the trees. In the shadow of the leaves, rising up and diminishing according to the wind, small clear circles reproduce the solar disk on the sidewalks and the streets. The light invades it, and that can be seen in the rays, where a small shadow, almost imperceptible, creeps into the circles. It's a little after eleven and the breeze seems softer, as if that November day were already dying.

The sailor, the soldier, the maidservant, the handyman, the burglar, and now, too, standing back a little, heavily made up, the cheap whore, Natividade's possible and only child, come close to the bed. A clatter of clothes, rugs, doors, chinaware, bobbins, workshops, and the voice of Natividade singing can be heard, a happy, strong voice, coming and going. The children she won't have—unwinding, exchanging her own solitary destiny for theirs, dull and difficult—kneel between the two frightened old women. They pray and look at the dying woman, all except the whore: her back to the group, she looks at the shape that is slowly crossing the sunny garden, a black child in a white dress, a straw hat, a strainer in her hand. The child climbs up the steps of the porch, she sees herself on the deathbed and looks at the adults, cautiously, as if asking everyone's pity. The whore takes a step in the direction of the child, uncovers her head, and strokes it. She looks her over, even so, with vengeful eyes. Natividade, for the last time, tries to raise her hands.

The damp façades and closed windows, motionless and faded streamers at the deserted Esso station, sea gulls fly over the gray cove. Two fishing boats anchored at a distance and rocking lightly break the uniform surface of the sea. The rain makes the boats seem farther off, separates the hills in gradations of gray, and accentuates the lethargy in which Ubatuba lives for most of the year. Outlined against the seascape and as if transgressed by the fine rain, by the gulls, by the harmonious hulls of the canoes turned upside down on the sand, is the face of ℧, half covered by her hair. The line of the nose, implanted firmly and perhaps on the extreme edge of balance, on the point of breaking the harmony of her features, when seen in profile reflects the straight line of the forehead in extension and rigor. The space between her nostrils and her somewhat prominent lips, of a precise cut, which she always tends to keep slightly open as if she needs air, is restricted. As clear cut as the lips, her chin shows more softness, especially when she laughs. She doesn't speak without putting her lips forward, and then I can observe between them and the wrinkle (a brief ascending curve) that prolongs the edges of her mouth a discreet, varied, and festive play. I vacillate between contemplating that moving of the mouth like a deaf man and listening as if nothing came to her rich-toned voice, now calm, cool, almost that of a child, with quick, sharp accents. In her whole face, in spite of the strength it suggests, there is a childlike look. (In what collection of antique toys was I startled to notice the steel-and-copper hair falling softly over the neck of a doll's head similar to hers?) Small wrinkles are concentrated on her eyelids and a shadow seems to adulterate her youth: she smiles. In her clear eyes, of indefinite color, inside them or even coinciding with them, other eyes—with a different age and certainly eyes of a different face—stare at me, if she is turned toward me or not, stare at me avidly. Under her transparent skin, to which waves of blood flow with the least stimulation, I sense—as one trying to remember—the hidden face and, even without seeing it, I contemplate it.

"Texts in a certain way exist before they are written. We live immersed in virtual texts. My whole life is concentrated around an act: searching, knowing or not knowing what for. My relations with the world are similar to those of one who has lost his memory. I hunt, today, for a text and I am convinced that the whole secret of my passage through the world is tied to that. The text I must find (which is in print, or perhaps I have to write it, I don't know) is like the name of a city: its reach goes beyond it—like a city name—meaning, in its concision, a real being and its evolution, and the paths that cross it, being still capable of remaining when such being and its roads are buried."

O

The Story of , Twice-Born   10

"I shot myself. I don't want you to despise me for that."

Abel, without answering, without turning toward me, clasps my fingers tighter—but gently. What's the age of the hand that did the shooting? Twenty-three? Fourteen? On the sofa, convalescent, I am resting, I touch the scar, the tender and still-sensitive skin, I stroke it, I struggle to get up. If I do so, I will stretch out again on the bed immediately or I will spend hours on end at the mirror, combing my hair, combing it. Which hand held the weapon? Could one have prevented the other from completing the motion, the pressure—so light—on the trigger? Useless questions.

I softly kiss his shoulders, lying face down on top of him, so that my breasts and hair smother him, cover him. His skin smells of silences and mornings. His torso is more fragile than his head suggests; fragile, lacking muscles, the torso of someone little given to exercise and shadowed by copper-colored hair. If it were not for the hair, it would be the trunk of an adolescent. I kiss his dark nipples, he turns little by little, I kiss his ribs, he remains face down and I kiss his waist, his vertebrae, his shoulder blades, the back of his neck. "In you, in you, in you," protests the chorus of young people, "resides all joy, all softness, all voluptuousness." I kiss his ear and nibble the skin of his shoulder (in you), I go closing my teeth like someone tightening a screw, in a little while (*Basia me!*) he becomes tense, I bite with more strength, the animals from the rug run between our bodies aroused (*Morde me!*), I stop biting, I pass my tongue over the red mark left by my teeth, I bite his neck and stick my tongue into his left ear, there, without saying them, I pour out some of the words that I yearn to say, he moves again and once more is lying in my direction. In you!

I get up off the floor, I look at the storm through the barred window. I remain waiting for the thunder and lightning to knock me down again. Space trembles and the walls light up, blue, under the flashes. Bolts cut the air; the thunderclaps explode as if they had been pulled out of the ground by their foundations. The wind blows faster, whirring on the quina trees, the roofs, the antennas, and the signs on top of the buildings. It's like an echo of the thunder or its prolongation. I sit on the tricycle and go around, I go round and round the table, the center table, in the living room (there is a metal vase without flowers on the table, dark brown), I slowly go around the chairs, and the nickel-plated vase, placed on an old crocheted doily, is the center of my turning, the center. Stronger and stronger, lashed by the wind, the rain falls. My mother appears, wearing slippers, in an old black silk dressing gown, a deep red hat with a very broad brim on her head and in her hand a white hat decorated with flowers. She goes through the room (doesn't she see me?), goes through, leaving behind the intense and caustic perfumes she drenches herself with all the time. The windowpane is wet and the wind blows through every crack, every one, in all directions, with drive, it howls and shakes itself, an invisible dog. Specters in cubic form, the buildings, dimmed by the water, have the same color and seem to take on the same consistency as the clouds. Rats are driven from their holes, they run stupefied on the ground, cockroaches come forth with their wings raised, they climb up on the chairs and fly off. All the people have disappeared; on the flooded streets only a few vehicles are moving. They go slowly. I hear a bell strike three, three strokes, mournful and as if lifeless, the bells of São Bento, and my turning continues around the vase. The downpour beats on windowpanes and sashes. The lightning flashes become more frequent, like blows on my eyes; they seem to burn the brown wallpaper of the room, singe its grimy flowers.

Suddenly, suddenly, everything comes together: in a direction opposite to the turning of my tricycle, the black bird with the red head is turning, turning over the city and the storm, it descends imperturbably, flies through the wind and the lightning flashes, its turning (lower and lower, smaller and smaller) is the opposite of mine but also answers my turning and completes it. It descends and becomes restricted. Prodded, I broaden my orbit, I move away from the vase, from the small table, I pass behind the chairs, the sofa, I broaden my orbit. At some spot in the house the woman starts to shout: rhythmic shouts in a terrifying succession. Pedaling more rapidly, I leave the

living room, the outside door is open, the entranceway is dark, behind
me I hear steps and roars, agitated wings, I see lightning flashes, I get a
quick glimpse of the grilled door of the elevator, also open, open for
the pit, for the void, the void of enigmas. From my throat, silent until
then, silent for years, a shout comes forth, I speed up the tricycle and
plunge, I am born, I am falling, we are falling, I, wheels, and shouts, I
no longer know whether mine or not, I don't know whether the
woman's, I don't know whether ours, or yet the bird's, I don't know,
we're falling.

The woman, sitting beside the bed, hands on her knees, her black
silk dressing gown wide open at the throat. I recognize her and also I
don't know her. All things are new and familiar at the same time; I and
the world, having changed, continue the same. She kneels, uncovers
her breast, brings it close to my face. She murmurs ceaselessly a monotonous sound. I take the breast in my hands, I suck on it, the milk
(or the breast?) goes down my throat, a thread inserts itself between
me and things, between one thing and another, I suck the breast, the
milk, the murmuring continues, and I go into a cycle I didn't suspect, I
have access to the cycle of identity, of delimitation—in the murmuring
of the woman beside the bed I recognize my name and I plunge into
the darkness once more.

T

Cecília Among the Lions   2

I'm sixteen years old: my eyes pierce shadows. Even so, I can
barely see my hands and arms, dimly reflecting, beside the cistern, the
few lights of Olinda. Not a star. The lighthouse rhythmically reveals
the surface of the water with its flash, the limit of things, the undulation of the fishing net cast clumsily by me. Some sixty paces separate
me from the villa. The lights on the porch and the ones that pour forth,
amber-colored, from the many windows, don't reach me; the zinc roof
that protects the cistern for almost its entire length cuts them off.
Mixed in with the breathing of the sea and the noise—less strong
now—of its attacks upon Milagres Beach flow the imprecise sounds of

a clarinet, a flute, a guitar, the raucousness with which the Treasurer imposes himself, the jovial voices of my brothers and sisters, twelve; in her rocking chair, the Fat Woman, instigated by the animal, redoubles her laughter. At intervals, I catch the smell of dampness in a more intense way. Sharpening my ear, I can make out in those seconds, amidst the vague sounds, the leap of some fish. It's hot: December is approaching. Inside the house winged ants are flying around the lamps, forecasting rain.

I throw the net again, I hear the lugubrious splash of the lead sinkers and the waxed cords. The weight of the sinkers is not well calibrated, the web closes slowly, and the fish—few in number—get away in time. That's the way, amidst the netting of my search, that what I'm seeking, the nature of which I still don't know, escapes. But careful, Abel. Pay attention to the net. Is it caught? There aren't any hooks or clasps underneath where it can catch. What holds it, then, in the dark water, multiplying its lead weights by a thousand or tens of thousands? Is some muddy spirit holding it? Dragging it malignantly to the cement bottom? You'll see whom you're dealing with. I grasp it with my left hand and with the other I start to open my shirt rapidly. Those cords at the bottom of the cistern caught on the horns of darkness are bothersome, like an annoying noise or the arrival of strangers, to my secret work, the blind search for an indication (the where, the name, the why) that would calm the punishment of searching in my veins. I glimpse more than I want to or can bear. Why, then, can't I see what I'm looking for?

A

Roos and the Cities 9

Residents pick up their mail in the large wooden square, with numbered subdivisions, between the first and second floors. I take out the two letters waiting for me and continue on into the dining hall. Roos is lunching alone at one of the tables beside the long glass pane, her pensive face turned toward the bright day, her navy-blue jacket over the back of an empty chair. April is coming to an end and even though the trees are green again, the weather is still cold. I sit down far away from Roos. I open the Fat Woman's letter: she sends news of Estêvão's engagement to a widow without means and the mother of children. "Just imagine, twenty-one years old, almost six years younger than you. Do you know how old this fiancée is? She carries thirty-nine years on her back and has varicose veins even in her touchhole. Those brothers of yours, my son!" While I'm here, I lose the certainty that even though she doesn't suspect, a word or a deed destined for me lies in everything that Roos thinks or does, even in the motion of lifting a glass of water to her mouth. "That person we know was here yesterday, much too merry"—I'm still reading—"with the news that you'd passed the exam, she asked how much the stipend was and kissed the Treasurer. She doesn't kiss me. She knows which side her bread's buttered on." Roos passes by me as if she doesn't see me.

In my room I open the other letter and find once more the small, twisted handwriting, the short, efficient sentences where the absence of lamentations or censure seems to instill the affirmation that I, Abel, always settle my accounts, all this mixed with allusions to facts that are foreign to us, like the heat, the first Mass to be sung in Brasília, or the state of public transportation. The pages smell of an evanescent and unrecognizable perfume.

I put the letter in the drawer and I answer the Fat Woman's. In the middle of the sentence I am attacked by the conviction that Roos and I will soon have a confrontation—and that everything will be set in motion. The letter finished, I write another one, a cold one, to the Treasurer, asking him to let me know when the term of the appointment expires and therefore how long I could postpone the acceptance. Telephones ring—and the calls are not always answered—in neighboring rooms.

I drop the letters in the mailbox near the Alliance, I turn the corner, I continue along the sidewalk by the Luxembourg. Women are selling flowers in front of the entrance to the gardens and the yellow tips of the grillwork glow against the greenish sky. I put off the idea of paying a visit to the Weigels before dinner. I examine, one more time, the objects displayed on a corner of the Rue de Vaugirard, all before 1930: dolls with faces like those that used to smile on postcards of the period, locomotives, tea cans, decks of cards, toys, children's books (*Bobine chez les fauves, Aristide et Bobine*), posters, labels, medicine bottles that belonged to dead people and still have a bit of the potion left. Shouts echo off the shopwindow. A woman, not far from me, is insulting a man; without answering, he slaps her, he cuts off the words with a slow, firm hand. The woman is wearing a dull-colored cape, without buttons; her companion a long and mournful topcoat. He leans over to pick up the beret that has fallen; the woman kicks him in the ribs with the tip of her shoe, runs, and opens her arms in front of a car, which veers and continues on. She is seven months pregnant. The man comes forward, drags her back, and hits her on the jaw—with such precision that she spins around twice before regaining her balance. Some people are watching from a distance. Without calculating the implications of my decision and indifferent to the circumstances of my being on foreign soil, I place myself in front of the man. I see him put his hand under the topcoat (my brother Eurílio, shot to death on a cloudy and suffocating afternoon in 1953, still not nineteen, in a brothel in Recife) and I wonder if maybe I'm not mistaken in placing in Roos the event I've been waiting for for ten days and of which I would be the target. Beside me I hear the sobbing of the woman. No, this isn't the moment, there's something else, somewhere else, lying in wait: my gateway or my trapdoor is in Roos. I take a step, the stranger moves too, we cross paths, we continue on slowly in opposite directions. The woman breaks out in curses.

With no uncertainty or conjectures, I cross the dining hall, which is lighted up and echoing with laughter, Roos, alone at the table, is reading a magazine, I hurry, nobody but me must keep her company, they call to me, I pretend not to hear, I sit down opposite her.

Before I can speak, she puts down the magazine and asks if I know Holland. She's been offered a job, a receptionist in Amsterdam at MACROPACK-57, she's going to leave in two days, she'll spend seven or eight there, maybe more.

Without any possible error, I recognize the instant, this is it. A flash of light. I wait for it with uncertainty and now it leaps out at me, unmistakable, I stand before a dividing line.

I clench my fists and: "Roos, I'd like to have your address in Amsterdam. I'm going to Holland to pay you a visit. May I?"

There is authority and pleading in my voice.

S

The Spiral and the Square 9

In its continuous turning toward an illusory center or centers, the spiral that governs this book has passed in turn over the "R," the "A," the "T," over still other letters, and thus certain themes of the work have arisen and are developed. During this time, the Sun advances through the stellar degrees of the Zodiac, it being opportune, indispensable to mention this phenomenon: our novel is ruled by a mechanism that means to be as rigid as the one that moves the stars.

The idea of rigor and universe are present in the sentence that proved so costly to the Phrygian slave of Pompeii: "SATOR AREPO TENET OPERA ROTAS." "The farmer carefully maintains his plow in the furrows." Or, as it can also be understood: "The Plowman carefully sustains the world in its orbit." It is difficult to find a more precise and clear allegory of Creator and Creation. Here is the plowman, the field, the plow, and the furrows; here is the Creator, His will, space, and the things created. The universe rises up for us, evoked by the irresistible force of the phrase, like an immense arable plain over which a shape, with sovereign care, guides the plow and makes his crops rise up, glowing, immediately to be burned, harvested, or crushed under the bloody hooves of horses, his crops: plants, heroes, animals, gods, cities, kingdoms, peoples, ages, celestial luminaries. Identical is the image of the writer, given over to the obligation of zealously provoking in the furrows of the lines the birth of a book, lasting or with a brief life, exposed, in any case—like meadow and kingdoms—to the same galloping horses. Despite this certainty, this menace, no lack of care can be tolerated. The Plow in its direction is sustained with zeal and constancy.

Are the ideas of universe and exactness less present in the spiral? We can conceive of it being drawn century after century by a firm and unknown hand. Its beginnings are lost in an aquatic abyss, infested with mermaids, singing fish, great winged hippocampi, and birds that do not alight, just as the then-known world and its imperfect maps ended for the ancients. The spiral's precision is its soul; without this, the spiral would curl up, never reach us. It is from this eventuality, that of the spiral's becoming a net, that the idea of the labyrinth probably emerged. If we examine labyrinths closely, are they not merely spirals that have lost their direction and have become fragmented in such a way that a man, caught in their web, knows nothing else in respect to his own steps? But the spiral can only become entangled through a malevolent human device. As rigorous as the twenty-five letters that refer to the plowman and his work, it never becomes as entangled; and it always bears us, each and every one, along its furrow.

We sense still other deductions between the fleeting natures of the spiral and the magic square, dissected here with instruments that are not very sharp. We cannot grasp them, however. Even if we could read with other eyes, and not those that darken the visible, the five Latin words on mollusk shells, in cyclones, as well as on the horns of goats, rams, and antelopes, many relationships would remain beyond our grasp, like music that, while we nod on the bank of a river, we hear deep in the night, sung by someone in a canoe that floats downstream. Our mind assures us that the melody continues, while our senses cannot confirm such a certainty.

We discover, indeed, a difference to keep in mind: the square arouses the idea of space; the spiral that of time. In that respect, it is always curious that watchmakers, in their attempts at perfecting instruments to measure hours, have thought up a delicate piece in the form of a spiral, the hairspring, the heart of watches. Closed in a spiral, too, is the spring that drives them.

It can be concluded that the basic idea of the book rests upon clear, neat elements that, even so, are no less elusive. In its principal points, it imitates an ancient morality poem. It seeks, however, only to describe the relationships between several women and one man, with the tracing out along this profane route of a trajectory of which the protagonist is ignorant and the meaning of which has still not been defined for the author. Since the spiral and the square are present, a point becomes evident that illuminates the creations of the novel with a powder that transfigures them. There they are, man and women, invented in order to help the author reveal an island of the world—and everything, characters and actions, comes from an unreachable beginning. In their gestures, trivial or obscene, they are seeking to decipher an enigma. They must do it. Inside of them a presence that cannot be denied or forgotten vibrates. "At the bottom of the cistern," says the poem by which the book is inspired, "I look through the waters and glimpse the All. Sun and fishes mingle."

With the function of making the plan of the work quite clear, at the top of the subdivisions of the text, along with the title, a letter and a number appear: the letter locates the theme in the square; the number indicates whether the theme is being introduced or is returning (for the fifth, tenth, twentieth time). As for the nature of the themes, eight in number, they correspond to the vowels "O," "E," "A" and the consonants "P," "R," "S," "T," "N"; any word would be excessive.

A

Roos and the Cities   **10**

Railroad workers' headgear, male hats, porters' numbered caps, women's loose hair, Anneliese Roos is at the Hotel Beethoven, incomprehensible phrases are exchanged, I check my baggage, I go out into the cold and still afternoon. Beethovenhotel, Beethovenstraat, 49. On the map of Amsterdam I study the urban transportation routes, I take a streetcar and follow its turns with my eyes on the map and on the street signs—those constellations that confirm the indications on the map—I go past gardens and city blocks, closer and closer to my destination, I advance, simultaneously, through a city and a tongue that I do not know, and suddenly, in green luminous lights, the name of the hotel.

She still hasn't returned from the MACROPACK. I leave a message, now I take a taxi, return to the station, pick up my bag, put up at the first hotel I find.

The voice of Roos, coming to me across the canals with elms along their banks, churches, banking establishments, diamond cutters' workshops: "Is it really you? I didn't think you were coming."

"Shall we have dinner together?"

"Tonight, yes, I'm free. I can't always get away, you know. We work quite late at the Exhibition."

At the door of the Chevalier d'Or a golden suit of armor with the helmet closed: an irresolute crusader lost among the customers who are coming in sprinkled with rain. The voices echo back and forth across the room, untranslatable. Was this how the voices of the invaders—Joost van Trappen or Caspar van der Ley—sounded, the Flemish soldiers and merchants who drop anchor in Pernambuco in the seventeenth century? Roos, in a gray woolen dress, her neck covered by a yellow kerchief, talks to the waiter and I can't tell which of the words she says corresponds to the fish, the vegetables, or the wine. Isolated with her on our common linguistic island, I listen to her and—zealously searching for the exact terms—I tell her about my trip, intent on the way her skin, a soft and in a certain way illusory texture, absorbs the light. The lamps, the reflections on the plates and on the silverware, the aromatic wine—as golden as the armor—everything seems to make us expansive. Roos speaks to me (of maps and treasures?) in her composed and neutral French, and in the same way that peacocks show off their tails, to hide them afterward, the cities that she shelters—all radiant on this night in which, in ecstasy, I forget the weight of the world—become visible, without her interrupting the sentence she has begun and without any gesture that allows me to conclude that the revelation is voluntary.

We put on our coats, we approach the empty gauntlet of the suit of armor, we go out, and then I understand that the sounds and the glitter of the dining room are talking for us. The lights on top of the lampposts are reflected on the wet streets, and we go along, side by side, exchanging banal phrases. Large wreaths of flowers set up along the promenades—the names of people executed on the ribbons, which are still damp from the rain—alternate with parked bicycles. "You can take my arm, Roos." The vivid impression that a procession is following us, invisible—but the tenuous and slow sound of our steps dissolves in the silence. "Do you write, Abel?" "Yes. But I've published so little so far. One or two stories. That's all. And I'm almost twenty-eight years old. I'm one of those people who have a hard time ripening, and maybe I'll never ripen. I feel and act as if I were twenty or twenty-one. I think it's about time I wrote something worthwhile." An unexpected gust of wind carries the sound of voices, men singing. Drunken sailors? The white window frames, the gray-brown façades making the molding stand out. All the lights out inside. The light, winged weight of her arm on mine. Some touch of intimacy in that confidence, but the pressure, being so light, worries me; it's as if her arm were held up by birds in flight. I feel escape building up and I pretend to ignore it: a gesture will bring on the end. "I don't know whether I'll be able to get away from MACROPACK tomorrow. In any case, if I can, it will only be at night. I'll call you." We're close to her Hotel now. The stroll ends and maybe only in Paris will I meet her again. Our words become less frequent, quieter, our steps slower.

"Roos, I love you."

We stop. Her face, clear, as if lighted by moonlight, turns to me. For the first time, with a lightness just like that of her arm on mine, I kiss her. I hear a drum roll, it's a large drum, the invisible procession that has been following us comes up out of the shining pavement, a bloody standard waving between metal lances over the conical felt hats with broad brims, a glow (coming from Roos?) puts the animated faces of the men in relief, ornate with wigs that reach down to their shoulders, the starched, smooth collars, the garments of the woman who slips among them, the casing of the drum, and, most of all, the embellished personage who comes at the head of the watch. Lances strike each other, the rhythmic beating of the drum grows stronger, the rat-a-tat on the hills of Olinda, closer and closer the troop of boots with batiste linings, voices, laughter, guffaws, the noise of chain necklaces, an explosion of tongues, the rustle of cloth, we are crossed over like the street itself by the men, by the woman who follows them, the drums vibrate on our flanks, the noise of the boots (the same that shakes the walls of Recife) echoes strongly in our feet, the throbbing of their blood pulsates in us, and over our uncovered heads we hear the flutter of the immense wine-colored standard.

T
Cecília Among the Lions   3

If I spend hours in the somber dampness of the cistern and if I throw the net until I am no longer able to, it's not to catch any of the few fish imprisoned there: out of this idle action, which I do poorly, I'm trying to make an axis around which my headless inquiries can spin, never coming to an end. Alone, under the covering—the zinc sheets explode on the hottest nights—I keep throwing the net, pulling it in, and asking. (Where? What? Why?) Not a sign of answers.

I'm shirtless, I throw my shoes onto the ground, and I take off my pants. I can hear, as from another point in time or memory, the voices and the laughter—that of the Treasurer, the Fat Woman, Leonor, Augusto, Mauro, Cenira, Cesarino, Isabel, Janira, Lucíola, Damião, Eurílio, Dagoberto, Estêvão, dispersion and discord already installed among us without anyone's perceiving its smell in the clothing, in breath, and behind the doors. The decision to leap, to dive into the gloomy water and unfasten the net, drives me on. A firm order that I dare not reflect about. Once more I tug on the net, which doesn't give way, and I stiffen my body for the leap. It's then that a who, a what, or a nobody grabs me by the kidneys and disarms the impulse that has started. Are you diving into Nothingness, Abel? Eh? In payment for what? The sea breaks on the rocks. Once more the luminous and light wing of the beacon. I kneel down, naked, next to the cistern. I see myself (as a person who picks up a revolver, spins the cylinder—Russian roulette: the cylinder contains a single bullet)—turns the muzzle toward himself, repents and aims into the distance, squeezes the trigger, hears the shot), I see myself in the black waters, among the fish, tangled in the net, trying to come to the surface but unable to. The one who added that weight to the lead of the net is Death. I think that, and the spell, if there is one, is broken—the net becomes uncaught and I gather it in. A fish struggles in its webbing. Feeling around, I grab it. The body raging with affliction in my hand. I toss it into the water and lie down on the concrete, exhausted, as if I really had dived, had fought with the No, escaped.

Voices and the sounds of musical instruments roll down the slope, Eurílio's flute, a precocious musician, Leonor with her mandolin, the childish fingers of Janira or Isabel on the half-hoarse piano. Fat and white, my mother in her rocking chair, the soles of her shoes a little thin now. The impression of hearing dead footsteps going away. The footsteps of the Light-Footed Woman! Can I be the who, perhaps, Abel? The where? The why? Isn't it I you're looking for? Still lying on the edge of the cistern, inventing those questions and hearing those steps, I'm not reached by expressions or ideas of terror, gratitude, relief. I turn face down and from my closed teeth there flows, is spat out: Cercília. Cercília? Ercília, maybe? Cecília? On this night Cecília and I are not yet in love. I still don't know her. I do know an Ercília, however. I'm nine or ten years old and someone pushes me in her direction. In mourning, sitting in the parlor, beside the piano and wrapped in a heavy halo of abandonment, she looks at me seriously. "This is Ercília, your Uncle Abel's widow. He drowned. Don't you remember?" I kiss Ercília's fingers, cold, with this same cistern smell, slimy and damp. Where can she be? She hasn't visited us again, her figure is forgotten, her name is forgotten. My Uncle Abel, dragged off by the undertow. We have the same name, he and I.

O

The Story of Ọ̀, Twice-Born   11

The woman's breast, a white full sphere, falls apart in a tepid taste. The thick perfume that envelops her penetrates me. I see her for the first time and at the same time I meet her again. She doesn't know that I see her. Pale, she seems even paler in her torn black silk dressing gown. Black or scarlet? In the shadows of the room everything is equally vague and clear, familiar and strange. I no longer contemplate in my body the creature in me; scales, feathers, or temporary wings no longer exist; feet, trunk, hands, and face, inserted in mine, belong to me; I have her eyes in my eyes, incorporated into mine. I see knowing and I see not knowing, I see having seen and I see without ever having seen; I begin this double look that never blends into a single one. I suck greedily on the woman's breast, she murmurs. In my hand I see slipping along (braids? little fluid salamanders?) delicate swarms of splotches still indecipherable for me.

I dive into the darkness again, into the soot. I cross slowly through the nights, nights without day, on horseback. The horse has a brilliant horn between his ears, and on the left rear hoof there is a wound, he walks on three legs, weeping at the leaps. In the interminable nights a white-hot star passes from time to time, and I see by the light of the shooting star that the animal is green. We go through dark cities, rivers of black mud, we climb mountains of shadows, and we go down slopes even more shadowy. One of the cities, situated on this road, which I don't know if straight or crooked, smells of fruit; all the people, shut up in their houses, are eating in silence, not seeing anything, harvests of oranges, pineapples, melons; inside the houses or in their yards there are peach trees, pear trees, apple trees, heavy with fruit. In one of the invisible valleys someone is hammering on a piece of metal, not continuously but with long pauses, and one blow is just like another.

A luminous sign lights up in the night (what night?), lost, suspended, under this mist of fifteen years, white and red, an immense shield with stars over large letters. It lights up and goes out. A pulsation. I go through another city—it has no profile, it has no name, no one is visible, no one has a name—all the doors slam, doors and windows, those far away and those nearby, they slam, I'm already far away and I can still hear them, they slam.

All I have on are the dress, the rings, the bracelets, the necklace, and the earrings. Abel, his feet bare, touches mine, his hands and his breath disarm me. What do I still control in my invaded body? Crocodile and rabbit run in my blood, run in his, pass from his shoulders to mine, from my knees they slip into his. Inside the geometric motifs, inside the black foliage, inside the fringes and the peaceful branches, she-goats with long curved horns are born, goats with white hair, in heat, bitches with a human head, lionesses, all lifeless, but they gallop and leap, the goats bleat, the lionesses roar, the bitches bark, I stick my tongue into Abel's mouth, I stick my tongue among the flowers that sprout from his mouth, two famished goats come up from my feet, come up to my tongue, devour his flowers, he says that he loves me.

I balance myself, hold myself up on my legs unsteadily—and I take a step. How strange is the weight of my body on the floor! It is many weights, they hang and oscillate—from my arms, my head, my legs—in search of a center. I go in front of the mirror, I see an infantile face. Mine? Under certain circumstances (the great majority of people are forbidden that opportunity), under certain circumstances, lying down, under appropriate lighting, neither too much nor too little, the eyelids half-closed, one can see the membrane over the pupil. Laid out in circular fashion and with the extremities turned toward the center of the iris are five or six shapes (impossible to count, owing to the rapidity with which they move) like leaves, ovate leaves, whose stalks remain hidden. Only the edges of these leaves without color and without veins, composed of a kind of metallic luminosity, can be seen; and they move swiftly, they don't stop moving, as if some force were attempting to undo them and the whole existence of these shapes consisted of a resistance meant to maintain intact the appearance of leaves and the circular layout. Seeing them fascinates, frightens, and terrifies: one has the impression that the eye is inhabited by serpents. When I see my face in the mirror, my reaction is the same. I can make out a threat trying to undo all of my features. My face goes back to what it is at each instant, several faces fighting, furious faces, endowed with spurs, claws, filed teeth, fighting among themselves like a hydra's several heads. My braids, grown longer, held in with blue velvet ribbons, touch my shoulders. Closer to the mirror, I examine the part along my head: between the hair, combed in braids, now a light down has been born, almost the hair of a newborn child, hair that is mine too, from another head, mine too, encrusted in mine. Two? One?

Still mute, I evoke my name day and night, sensed and sought for such a long time. I pronounce it in myself, I make it run through me, roll in me. A stone with lots of edges, it becomes round, a pebble. Then it dissolves, dissolves in me, aniline, a tint. I discover the word "mouth"; "I," the pronoun; the verb "to be"; a particle, "in." Two terms remain magnificently illuminated in my new world of limits, impossible as it is to elucidate whether they designate a fraction of the world or the whole world: "here"; "place." I take possession of the additive "and," with its dual power of joining and separating, and then I amuse myself by finding and placing face to face affinitive notions: "to flee" and "to fly," "vein" and "throb," "dog" and "bark," "depths" and "fear," "I" and "you," "I" and "I." My teeth fall out. Others are born, smaller and more fragile than the previous ones. Even though I still cannot speak, I go along putting together in me words that still do not exist. "Tenderne" is that light which reminds one of porcelain and which we see in the bedroom before dawn. "Lanstous": the air of a person who wants to attack us and doesn't out of fear. "Emarame": the act of going and coming at the same time; and also the dual, the indissoluble movement in front of the mirror of a body reflected in its glass, provided that both—body and reflection—are seen by someone.

R

Ʊ and Abel: Meetings, Routes, and Revelations　　10

From the reddish earlobes, close to the head and perhaps a bit long at their upper curve, hang the earrings of varied shape, which Ʊ takes off and puts back on. Her hair, almost always, hangs over her face. She throws it back with her translucent hands and with a raising of the head that emphasizes the protruding line of her breasts.

"Many times more painful than ordinary births, difficult as they might be, is the expulsion of the Yolyp. Nothing, however, makes the bearer suppose that she is carrying in herself such a rare variety of the human species. It is known that the number of yolyps in one generation never goes beyond six in the whole world."

An old woman of rough appearance has stationed herself almost at the foot of the T-shaped dock, sitting to the left; the brimless felt hat covers part of her face; having crossed her legs, she covers them with her faded skirt—purple or black—as grimly as her red blouse. With mechanical movements she changes the bait on her hook; she hasn't been able to catch a single fish. Still on that side, but on the wing of the T, a second fisherman stands out, equipped with gloves and warm woolen clothing. On the extreme right of the dock, under the post whose lantern the wind must have torn away, the poor man barely covered by a sheet of yellow plastic—with just as little luck as the old woman—holds his pole with resignation. Between him and the man with the gloves, closer to him than to the other, we see the fourth figure in the picture, his back to us, his feet hanging over the water: he takes his hat off and puts it back on at intervals, an unusual hat, blue and conical.

These fishermen and the other elements of the scene—the delicate silhouettes of the posts on both sides of the T, the mooring stones set beside the posts—are governed, all of this is governed, by a precise and clear rhythm, a symmetry that, we know, chance never offers and that the existing lack of balance makes even more tense.

Ơ and I, disturbed by the coherence that we see, wait for the event already in elaboration, a piece to be performed, announced by the capricious disposition of those elements, its introduction or opening. Here, through the always tangled threads and knots of things, here, dispersed fragments have become associated and among themselves establish a nexus that, in its way, makes one think of narratives. Narratives and eclipses. A motorboat passes in the distance with a figure standing in the bow; it makes a turn by the two anchored fishing boats and continues on, the muffled rhythm of the motor spreading out in the silence of the afternoon, seeming to separate with a stroke the scene on the dock, static, from those which are to come.

Natividade before her lacemaking cylinder, four bobbins in her hands. The clean sink smells of potash and the pans gleam on the tile wall. Natividade prefers to work on her lace at that time in the afternoon, when the quiet of the apartment follows the morning chores and the position of the Sun makes the pantry brighter, favoring her eyes, which are beginning to see less. She goes changing the pins along the outline and crosses the lines around them, the wooden bobbins click against each other, always four at a time, one pair in the left hand and one in the right, she puts them down, takes another two pairs from among the many on the square, fastens them. The dry, short sound of the bobbin heads, polished by use over the years, rings merrily in the silence. Natividade finds it similar to that of pinwheels in the wind and the sound of water trickling over pebbles. She begins to sing in a soft voice. The boy on whom she concentrates the whole weight of her love—and who at times startles her with his eyes, which are rapacious and neutral at the same time—half-opens the door, stiff and graceless, hard, the gray uniform with red on the cap: "Mama's sleeping on the sofa. Don't sing." She stops her song and the door closes noiselessly. The bobbins click less rapidly.

Two new characters approach the dock, one in dark clothes, wearing rubber boots, and fat; the other with blue shorts and a T-shirt, protected by an old umbrella. They come along slowly, chatting, fishing poles in their hands. They hesitate a little on the platform, looking around, as none of the others turns toward them. *Congress to decide if 1970 elections for governors and President of the Republic to be direct.* The stage they have come onto already has its laws: between objects and people there is a balance so precise and clear that the indecision of both is a refusal, I think, as they resist occupying the places on the dock toward which a subjugating rhythm drives them. Finally the one in boots picks up two crates, advances resolutely, and places them side by side, more or less in center stage, between the fellow with the gloves and the one with the conical hat. The symmetry, obviously, is not perfect here either. Between the bourgeois on the left and the first crate (where the man with the umbrella sits down), there is a space a bit larger than that observable between the crate on the right (the one in boots sits on it) and the obscure supernumerary, who, more than once, takes off and puts on the strange blue hat, without turning sideways. ♀ moves her head and looks at me, her nostrils flared: her strong hand squeezes my thigh. The somber double thud of the crates has just marked off, the same as the passage of the motorboat in the distance, one more unit of the composition, which, like a text, is being organized before us and of which we are a part (for would it not be incomplete and, in a certain sense, lost, useless, if there were no consciousness here, which, contemplating it, would learn the meaning it contains—or, at least, seems to contain—and in its way translate it?). The yellow splotch of plastic puffs up before the murky sea.

O

The Story of , Twice-Born   12

The wind blows uncertainly among the antennas and tall signs on top of the buildings. A golden sound of bees, similar to a rain, descends from the Sun onto the city in decomposition. Abel says that he loves me and exalts my body. The phrases that he murmurs: trivial, trite (oh, my love! how round and soft your knees are), words without inventiveness—flattering in spite of it—and they proliferate, bend me, bind me without his thinking or pronouncing them, they bind me. Garlands. You're beautiful and desirable. When you walk in the middle of the crowd, I can hear your face as if it were a hymn, a solemn and jubilant hymn rising up out of the brutishness. Even without seeing you, I know that you're approaching. Even absentminded people, even brokers can hear your beauty. I love you. Your body is a somber and sheltering chamber surrounded by slime. Flowing into this sanctuary, purified (or only evoked?), are the nauseating breath of Stock Market criers, the black oxygen given off by factories, the exhalations of dead people and automobiles, the tomb smell that floats between open coffers and cash registers, the dust of demolition, the sweat of the oppressed, the feces turned over in sewers by mechanical diggers; you yourself shelter some kinds of rottenness, but in you the world is transfigured. As in a text where the penuries of the world echo, but dense and rhythmical, and written tomorrow. You're beautiful. Being with you is a gift like that of sight, like the gift of hearing. It would be insane to be with you and not reap the benefit of what you are. Since I can hear, must I act like a deaf man? You must never forgive me if, knowing you, I do not undress you and join my body to your chosen body. I love you. Your tongue, warmed by desire, smells of musk.

That's the smell with which the death's-head moth, the Acherontia, calls its mate. Keep your tongue hidden in my mouth, then. Moths in search of a female shall not invade the room and attach themselves to your perfumed tongue, certain that they are making a new species, ruddy and agile. Your tongue shall not pass me by in favor of some moth evocative of death. How I love you! The celestial vastness is perfect in its nakedness. Not even then is it excessive or is its beauty marred by the presence of passing clouds. The piece of paper still not written on is perfect in its nakedness. The words that darken it do not restrict or diminish its perfection. So, too, the jewelry you wear around your neck, on your ears, your fingers, your wrists: clouds in the brightness, words on the whiteness. I've wanted you for so long! Your breasts, pale and plump lambs, idly stroll upon my skin. Their copper beaks tinkle when they move. I can hear them: delicate bells.

I take his risen sex in my hand, I can feel the pulsation of the satin glans and the veins. The blood throbs, throbs in his sex, in the heart of his sex—that bird. A shudder: it is as if it were trying to flee, to escape the pressure of my nails. A landmark, the center of the body. I fondle it, I softly fondle this obelisk, this erect and elastic harpoon with its little wolf's snout. I probe inside the flesh with the tips of my fingers for its beginning or its end and I can't find it, it continues on inside, inside his belly, no matter how much I dig with my fingers I can't lose it, it continues on (where does it begin? where?), the impression that it keeps on going all inside the body, it winds into tails, turns around, a plant, a stiff and vibrant bush encrusted in the body of this man, with flowers at its roots, flowers and fruit, flowers of heavy green, fruit of a redness similar to that of figs.

Does light decompose in prisms? His words are like that. He talks to me and his words, inside of me, open up into others that have not been articulated: Darling! Wrap me in your soft arms. Wrap me in your tender arms. Beside you my body no longer knows how to express its contentment and fills with restless wings. Take me in your perfumed arms, so that my winged joy doesn't pull me away from my joy. My love! Your stomach is hot. A stone in the Sun. Your stomach is cool. A stone under water. I want you. How my fingers slip into your sex! Hidden, under untouchable fuzz, between the round and undulating cheeks, your anus. Absent violet. The firmness of your haunches is silence. The honey of your delight dampens my palm and smells of roses. Your sex is calling me. It calls me from the depths of your womb, it's a clear call and as imperious as the one that comes to us sometimes in dreams. Your sex is calling me and proclaiming its gifts: "I am made of mouths, of clay in the shadows, of hands, of flowers, of avid fish, of summer afternoons, of glowworms. You will see how I shall suck in your virility with ten mouths, you will see how you slip between damp, oozy bricks, you will see how with uncountable and discreet fingers I shall crush your penis (as one crushes grapes, but your penis will be a cluster of grapes that is crushed and always renewed) and how I shall try with those same fingers to make your virile pouch, more valuable than a pouch full of pearls, more valuable than all bags of gold and diamonds, make your pouch, that zealously hidden treasure, flood me, flood my uterus with the warm broth of your blood, you will see how I shall turn myself into petals and what softness there will be around that invader, you will see how there will be nothing to crush it, how I shall gird it with red and yellow flowers, crowfeet, azaleas, fuchsias, and foxgloves will rain down upon the guest, how I shall bite your lure and how, so as not to come to the surface, I will anxiously drag bait, hook, line, pole, fisherman, and afternoon down to the bottom, deeper and deeper, you will see the soft warmth with which I shall gird it, the warmth of a sun-drenched ground, of sultriness, you will see how in spite of everything I shall enwrap your sex in my pleated silks and burn it, make it glow in my fire, in my fire without ever consuming it." Beloved, your sex calls me and speaks all the letters of my name with sweet vehemence. You're beautiful. I love your hair, your look, the little spirals on your pubis, your rich thighs, I love the beauty that you show. But more than anything I love your delicate feet: they brought you to me.

In the hollow of my hand, I softly heft his seeds and it occurs to me that I am holding his voice in my hand. The voice that speaks to me, that enwraps me, that exalts my skin, the splendor of my flesh, everything is born there, in those seeds, yes, not only desire, the force that puts words together and distills them, but also the timbre of that voice, its sonority, the voice, that voice of a bass viol. My beloved, love, my sex calls you, invokes yours, that god which pulsates and is surrounded by flames. You will see how your salamander will grow inside of me, will expand in me, take over my stomach, my haunches, invade my body, be my body, reign in me, in me reign, in me. *Morde me.*

T

Cecília Among the Lions   4

Prostrate on the damp concrete of the cistern, the mangled name that I pronounce is another—not that of Ercília, my uncle's widow—and I speak as if within a blindness. A blind man still. Only when I take the face of Cecília, mortally wounded, in my hands, only then do I see clearly: it's her name, hers and not Ercília's, that slides along in time and makes itself audible here between my closed teeth: it's her life, hers, not mine, that receives the sentence tonight; it is I who marks her hour—and also the place and the circumstances—not letting me collect, die, caught in my net. Shapes that I love stiffen, fall mute in her face, contemplating her I catch again this smell of cistern, I hear a fish leap, once more those distant voices resound and those instruments, then silence—and in the depths of my decomposed being I deplore not having dived, died of drowning, caught in my cords. I would have saved her, like this, for so many other mornings! The sea beats on the stones, advances, erodes the foundations on Milagres Beach. Cecília, the city of Olinda, the Treasurer, the Fat Woman, and my brothers and sisters—everything on the road to annihilation.

Hermelinda or Hermenilda moves among the aviaries and canary cages in the sun. From the hammock, I look at the other one, the sister, slowly taking the mandolin out of its case. Cats stroll on the porch. Sixteen years have intervened between this Sunday afternoon on the Estrada das Ubaias and the night when I am tempted to release the net at the bottom of the cistern. (In the big house in Olinda, they don't get together as much, they're incomplete, under the leadership of the former Treasurer—with his insolent hoarseness reduced to the soft cough of a humiliated person, and always with the scissors in his hand, clipping the daily *Official Bulletin*—the singers and musicians of my sixteenth year.) Beyond the main portal, gnawed by rust, with its small copper bell, I can see the sun beating on the old housefronts and grillwork on the other side of the street. A man accompanying a pair of children points to something in the distance, maybe a kite: we're two weeks into August, a month of winds and heavy tides. Hermelinda, sitting on a mahogany bench, her old face tilted, has her hand in the air, the right one, ready to strike her mandolin. The sister, in a wicker chair, her fingers locked between her knees, leans attentively toward her sister and looks at me out of the corner of her eye, half smiling. It's four-thirty in the afternoon, and the shadow of the villa has already reached the aviaries and the celosias and the faded dahlias planted between them. The birds in the aviaries and the canaries in the cages hanging from the walls or the thin columns of the porch wait, their ears hidden in their plumage, for Hermenilda's pick to awaken the tense strings. On the porch steps a cat is lying down; another lies beside the main doorway; a third is sleeping on the windowsill, its tail hanging down; from the door of the dining room, coming in our direction, yet another, one of its paws lifted. The predictable dialogue has already been pronounced: "You must remember that I used to play much better than I do today." And the sister, her hands between her knees: "That's right. She's over the hill. Today, at her age, the fingers aren't what they used to be. But I could be lying."

Hermenilda breaks her immobility and strikes the strings of the instrument with unsuspected energy. The cat by the door puts its paw on the ground, the man on the other side of the street lowers his arm and goes away with the children, the caged birds leap, lift up their bills, and release their song in many different ways, not only the birds that I see or that I know exist, but even others that I have no suspicion of and that are answering Hermenilda, so that the villa grows, expands, revealed by the voices of the singers hidden in it. Birds even sing on the tiled roof and in the yard, under the fruit trees. What is the kinship between old age, incongruity, and chaos? Can the loose threads in the world really be the reverse side of the rug to which some thinker makes reference? Who can guarantee that the face of the design exists, hidden from our eyes? What predominates, I can see clearly, is old age and the reverse side. Even so, a point or an act exists in which everything assumes order and begins. Isn't that so? The singing of the birds comes back to the mandolin, comes back to Hermelinda, she plucks the strings with more force and spirit, the sister claps her cork-encrusted hands, without making a noise, the cats, creatures with delicate hearing, continue lying down or move indifferently, the mandolin player's white hair becomes disarranged, her flesh swells, the wrinkles smooth out, she closes her eyes and with the teeth she has left goes on biting her tongue.

A
Roos and the Cities   **11**

How I would like to find the City whose image appears to me one afternoon, like a miniature, seen through seas and seasons, like the specter of a bird or an ancestor! Would it be possible, however, to recognize it? It cannot have come to me complete. Towers and roofs, in its migration, have gone partly to ruin and it's possible that vegetation, walls, and even bridges have been added to it, lost from who knows what other cities. I believe, for example, that the triple walls don't exist: they might have been captured by the City along the way, encircling it, a garland. A garland of stone with battlements and gates. Many examples exist of such gains and losses. How many times does the Treasurer recall the episode—never explained—of his relative who dies with both arms and years later is seen to be mutilated? On his head a hat that he never owned in life, covered with canary feathers and worn a little to the side, picked up in who knows what flea market of Time. One hat more and one arm less. I also have the newspaper clipping with the story of the Norwegian engraver Helge Nielsen. In London, Nielsen exhibits several etchings of the quadruped seen by him one August afternoon beside the wall of his house in Oslo, licking its left paw. The naturalist Edwin C. Porter identifies this species, which disappeared a million years ago, stating that *something* has changed in its formation, for in Nielsen's etching, the original tail— along with other small details, such as the sort of trunk it displays for moments beside the artist's wall—is entirely implausible. Designs found in the excavations at Enussia corroborate Porter's assertion.

Yes, the City, certainly, is not the same as the image that appears to me one day and then submerges. I believe, however, that I will recognize it—and so I seek it. Not that I know what end and why. Yes, I do know. Seeing it, *I will find*—and the verb, in this case, ends in itself; it is as if I said: I will sing. An aria is sung, a song; one cannot escape that. Is it necessary to add, so that the sense of the act of singing will be understood, *what* is being sung?

All in all, it's possible that I shall come to discover something in the City—and my attraction to Anneliese Roos, my interest in her, the continuity of which I have occupied myself with since the Sunday in Amboise, my mind and senses, leads me to ask, uncertainly, whether clarity might not be waiting for me in the sought-after City—or an object, a being in which clarity is the substance or even the opposite. For clarity is the mark of Roos. A clarity that doesn't help one see and may even obfuscate. Even so, Roos, she of this cities, impresses me by her opposition to shadows. Imagine: she goes through the world with the mission of not letting night prevail. The light with which Rembrandt signs his paintings, or the reflection of flames on a piece of metal, a bottle, a face, leads me to see, irresistibly, resonances of Roos. Something like this is what drives Melville's captain on. Would he have given himself over to such an obstinate search had the whale that impelled him to traverse the Ocean without surcease been of a bluish color like other cetaceans—and not white?

These are suppositions that seem to be confirmed as I wander among the canals, the streets, the museums, crossing over the day, this long and sun-drenched river, where on the opposite bank, on the nighttime bank, perhaps, I shall meet Roos again. I scat(in a thousand impressions)ter. I mingle with hurried businessmen and unworried visitors, listening to the surge of the waters and the motor of the boat, I see buildings whose names (Rembrandt, Cornelis Ketel, Salomon Mesdach) come drifting along, passing by me, the House of Sculptured Heads, of Grain Measurers, Old Arsenal, I am traveling with a group of schoolboys dressed in red, some blowing on piccolos, all with yellow flowers on their chests (Frans Hals, Pieter Pietersz, W. van Valckert), I watch the boats that are docking, slowly, with gulls about their rigging, while others leave with a sound of whistles (there are delicate curtains in the windows of the houses and the boats), I study the evolution of Van Gogh, I wander among the women selling flowers (geraniums are in bloom on many windowsills), I observe the flight of the pigeons, the resplendent eagles perched on the roofs (and the many flags that are flying evoke festive bells). As if these impressions were not numerous, they concentrate in two or three, becoming simplified: pigeons, gulls, metal flutes, reflections on automobiles, on bicycles, on waters, lace curtains, sun on the windowpanes, cottony clouds—all form one single thing, one single word, incomprehensible and luminous; Vincent's painting came out of the shadows, the grime, into blinding wheat fields and sunflowers; the light passes like a melody through hands and faces in the paintings of those Dutch masters, reigning with such eloquence over the darkness of clothes and interior that one has the impression of hearing, even in lesser artists, the same phrase: "Little by little we are advancing toward clairvoyance."

In Roos those slopes seem to converge. She shelters, among all the cities that at propitious times I can make out in her body (which I enter and become lost in, knowing that shortly I will be pulled out of there and that then I will have to return to the city where I am waiting for myself, I wait for myself, in front of her), the one I am seeking, all alone; at the same time, a splendor flows from her skin, as if many candles were lighting her up inside—perhaps the visible expression of what I dream of finding in the City, in a concrete way, thus uniting the expression and its object, just as if over the years I had read, in dissimilar words—"*vida,*" "*ave,*" "*uva,*" "*sonho,*" "*hoje,*" "*ver*" ("life," "bird," "grape," "dream," "today," "see")—the scattered letters still not united of the word "*vinho*" ("wine") before wine existed, and one day, suddenly, I discovered wine and I drank it and I got drunk and I knew that wine was its name and that in it there are also dreams, today, life, birds, grapes, seeing.

S

The Spiral and the Square 10

On the day that the desperate Loreius kills himself in front of Tyche, Publius Ubonius, amidst the tossing of a restless sleep, dreams of the Unicorn. The beings and objects of dreams, according to general belief, are unsubstantial. The terror of Ubonius on awakening is due to this incongruity: on his left breast is a slight scratch; lines that are quite visible and that then disappear run diagonally across the palm of his right hand. In the dream, upon seeing the Unicorn, he had run his nail across his chest to make sure that he was not dreaming; then he had gripped the horn of the beast with force in a show of rebellion against the orders he had received from it. The horn, not smooth or of a single color, but gold and white (two parallel threads, more or less waxed, twisting about it in a spiral, in the manner of Solomonic columns), had left its mark on Ubonius's rebellious and fearful hand.

Such strange signs make the merchant's dream known in every

corner of Pompeii, make it cross the Tyrrhenian Sea, the Mediterranean, arriving in Egypt, and transcribed on documents. The Unicorn gave orders to Ubonius. "The Magic Square is the Earth," it told him. "Move, then, from where you dream, turn around inside 'N,' inside Pompeii, invade the 'E,' the 'P,' the 'E,' the 'R,' again the 'E,' still the 'P,' the 'E' once more, do not hold back." The determinations of the Unicorn oblige Ubonius to walk without cease, not, for example, in the direction of North, but in a spiral over a map never seen, marked out by the five symmetrical words. In other words, he is condemned to move for the rest of his days, seeking the tail of Eternity, at whose end he will find, stuck on a pike, the head of the slave, the only being in the world with the power to forgive him for the evil of having stolen the secret.

Publius Ubonius had no illusions: the pilgrimage will be endless. Even so, he decides to undertake it, discussing it first with every person he meets. A merchant from Lampsacus, the land of Loreius, having debated with Ubonius for twenty hours on end about his dream, and concerned not exactly by the orders given by the Unicorn but rather by the fact that the Unicorn, the creation of a dream, had given orders, convinces Ubonius that all of this must be understood in a different way. A Unicorn, and much less an oneiric Unicorn, even though he can leave the mark of his horn on our hand, does not have supernatural powers. Make the distinction. Having engendered in his dreams a Unicorn that gives him orders means that man—be it in life, be it in art—must elaborate, along with other things, creations that regulate his acts and his own creations.

"What meaning, for example, do your preoccupations with divinity have if you cannot attain a moral? What is the importance of speculating, as you do, about the incomprehensible, to the point of promising freedom to a slave of yours if he can discover a phrase that placates your hunger for mystery, if you are capable—heedless of the immediate mystery of the relationship between man and his discoveries, and without any regard for the terror of a man facing his own creations—of stealing from him what naturally belongs to him, violating him in his intimacy to the point of bringing him to death? The dream, Publius Ubonius, means that you have still not created your Unicorn and that you need it. Without that, you are only a man who sleeps, even if you talk in your sleep."

The propitious circumstances admit these words of the Phrygian merchant. Publius Ubonius sees in an instant the extent of his deceptions. Abandoning the habit of finding out about everything and asking questions about everything, he concentrates his energies in transferring the Unicorn of the dream into his waking moments. One morning, upon awakening, he finds the Unicorn lying beside the bed, looking at him.

For the last time, the spiral drawn over the magic square crosses the letter "S." One of the themes of the book—which entrusts to the reader, with the permission of Janus, the available keys to the organization of the book itself—will not be taken up again. That organization, let it be made absolutely clear, was not invented by the novelist. It imitates, point by point, the long mystical poem probably written by a contemporary of Ubonius and dedicated to the Unicorn. The poem remained unfinished and the only existing copy, in a Greek version too, is found in Venice, in the Marciana Library, with three hundred thousand other manuscripts, all precious. In it one can see, as an Incipit, in beautiful Latin characters, grouped five by five, the letters of the magic square; over them, with the centers on the "N," dim in some places but visible enough, a spiral in vermilion. The anonymous author attributes a mystical meaning to each of the eight different letters: "A" is the City of Gold; "T," Paradise and Unity—there man comes to know death and is expelled; "R," the divine word, giver of names to things and order to chaos; "E," the human pilgrimage in search of wisdom; "O," the double nature (angelic and carnal) of man; "P," the inner equilibrium or the equilibrium of planets, a total eclipse being the perfect expression to represent the exact, albeit temporary, alignment of errant stars; "N," the communion of men and things. These themes, in the poem, are taken up or reconsidered in the order in which the vermilion spiral touches the respective letters. In the present book, only the organization of that ancient poem is preserved. The grandeur of the themes has disappeared. There remains, at best, a nostalgic halo of the ambition that inspired its model, millenary twice over. And perhaps the idea, insistently repeated in the old manuscript, that the Unicorn circulates among these pages.

A

Roos and the Cities

Lying on the bed, the lamp on, I wait, on the other bank of morning, for Roos to call me. The room is low, tiny, and the only window faces another. The telephone is in the hall, and time and again I get up, go down the stairs, steep, narrow, and so many of them that it's hard to find my way back, I examine it to see if it's working. I still haven't had dinner. Am I hungry?

When she finally calls, it's after eight o'clock. I follow the long explanation with difficulty and I have trouble answering. One thing is clear: we won't see each other tonight. She won't be leaving until very late and it seems that the stand where she works is going to be visited by some customers from Bonn. There will be dinner. Today? Tomorrow? She has to be there. She's not going to ask me, it's obvious, to stay in the city.

"How long are you going to be there?"

"Until ten, ten-thirty, maybe a little longer. We'll see each other in Paris."

The syntax, more rebellious now, hampers me as I try to show the incongruity: did I travel three hundred miles by rail from Paris to Amsterdam to hear that we'll meet in the place I came from?

"Listen, I'm on duty, I have to be brief. I'm very grateful for your visit, I didn't think you'd come. Try to see things from a different angle."

Lying down again, I go over the conversation. Knowing how far the allegations go doesn't interest me very much. What bothers me, in a manner of speaking, is a diagram. The main motif of our relationship, as in a musical composition, has just been presented to me. I identify it: we will go from one extreme to the other without alighting or without any real encounter. I'm convinced of this, as if the events in which we will both participate were to be born out of my own invention—and the leitmotiv sensed in this kind of opening, no matter what great afflictions it might bring upon me, takes hold of me. I try to resist that abstract entity and I yearn to observe its development.

I put on my coat. I buy some roses, I go to the MACROPACK. This

man with a perplexed look, facing cement mixers, bulldozers, typo-
graphic machines, winches, spotlights, information panels, graders,
tools for metal industries or destined for oil prospecting, not to mention the exhibits related to the science of navigation, is me. I almost
don't recognize Roos with her heavy receptionist's makeup. The sector
where she works: diamond drawplates for the wire-drawing of metals,
instruments destined to verify the polarization of light beams or to
separate them into determined substances, and also glass, natural, and
artificial gems, like the hydrothermal ruby and beryllium coated with
emerald, in addition to jewel boxes and gold casings for watches.

She lays the roses on top of a showcase of transparent stones,
diamonds, opals, and obsidian, protected by a crystal plate. She seems
less tired than she said on the telephone (or did I misunderstand what
she said?), and our conversation, not very extensive and always interrupted, revolves about her temporary job. I shall forget the data that
she furnishes, with the usual neuter correctness, about the making of
eyeglass lenses, and the temperature and other conditions to which the
lime, sand, iron, and potassium carbonate are exposed; I shall not pay
great attention to what she tells me about the difficulties encountered
by specialists in distinguishing between false and genuine black
pearls. What captivates me is her concise and ordered explanation
about birefringency or double refraction, discovered first in calcite,
especially in spar from Iceland, but verifiable in the majority of precious stones and in all crystallized ones in the triclinic, rhombic, and
other systems.

"That's why gems are separated into two series. Here [she points
to those lying under the roses with a gesture similar to the one she
made to attract the bird in Amboise] the monorefringents. In opal, for
example, when a ray of light strikes it, a single ray is refracted in the
interior."

I try to ask—and I desist, lacking the courage, calling on verbal
help I don't possess—if she noticed the double stairway in the center
of the castle at Chambord. Two people who use those two helicoid
stairs at the same time, Roos, see each other but don't meet. Perhaps
written there, or outlined—that is what I want to tell her and cannot
manage—is the fate of many people. Including us. We're not going to
go up the same stairway, Roos, no matter how much I—and even you,
perhaps—want the contrary. Both stairways lead to beautiful bedrooms with canopied beds. But a woman and a man could only occupy
the same bed if they went up the same stairs. How can I say this and

add that I'd like to sneak through the balustrade, be joined to her in every sense?

"Sometimes," she continues explaining, "one can only see the double image with special instruments. As an andalusite, where the capacity for birefringency is minimal."

Would her voice have gone on so firm and unconcerned if I had managed to interrupt her?

As I continue by train to Antwerp, I register her information with what details I can remember. Subsequently, besides Antwerp, I connect all the cities en route that I can include in my search. On two points at least I have an advantage over Melville's unfortunate hero: cities are larger than whales and don't swim as fast. In most cases they remain where the maps have put them.

It's after midnight, I'm in Bruges, beside the Ostend gate. No living thing on the streets, the canals, the bridges, or in the windows of the mansions, all closed and dark. The city, completely deserted, recalls those that I glimpse sometimes in Roos, all empty. Icy, incessant, the North wind cuts through. I hesitate taking a step. In my mind there are two hotels where I am staying, both identical, located in different parts of the city, both built on ninth-century foundations and at a place where there had been a stagecoach stop in other times. The only difference between them is that one is true and the other illusory. I can choose, indifferently, either of the two paths, which I hesitate to do, fearful of taking the false direction and thereby getting lost at once. A hotel and a route refracted in me?

"In all these stones [Anneliese Roos's hand points to the showcase], in topaz, amethyst, the ray of light as it lands is refracted into two distinct rays. In titanium, zircon, you can observe the phenomenon with the naked eye. The two rays imply the duplication of any image, whether light or an object."

T

Cecília Among the Lions   5

Hermelinda and Hermenilda pass through each other. I watch them at the beginning of every month at the counters of the Fiscal Commission. They wear false teeth, one set furnished with gold ca-

nines. They put either set in their mouths. Having always lived together, they have lost, distracted, the control that we have over our
bodies. They both let themselves be invaded and each invades the
other sister. If one arrives wearing earrings, with a shawl around her
neck on colder days, all they have to do is pass each other in the
entranceway—one through the other—and the ornaments change ears
and the wrap shoulders. Not just the earrings, not just the coat or the
cheap rings. The ears they wear in May appear in June on opposite
heads; they exchange tongues, voices; their four eyes are always
changing sockets: a transmigration is effected, a perpetual exchange
between those bodies, which are emaciated but still erect. I would go
so far as to suppose that the nightmares of one frighten the other.

Hermenilda? Hermelinda? . . . On making their acquaintance I establish that they interpolate each other, using those names loosely. I
end up not knowing which of the two I am talking to. In spite of the
fact that both habitually reveal little, and much as I desire to study
them intimately, I observe them from a distance. It is they ("Which
one? Both of them?") who approach me in a friendly way beside the
Cashier's cage, give me the address, and insist that I pay them a visit,
not as a consequence of any incident—my pleasure, niceties—that
flattered them, but so that they may have a function: that of getting me
away—me, the survivor of the cistern—from Cecília's distant paths,
placing me, by our joy, my mourning, and her perdition, here, where
her existence will be announced to me and where she herself will finally appear, will open the main door and come onto the porch with
her sandpiper walk.

Hermelinda's music continues and the birds respond. I get up
from the hammock. One by one I look at the wicker cages—made by
the old women, some of original design—with their singing birds (I cut
and cross the names of birds: Baltimore cardinals, chickhatches,
swalls, seagles, robs, red-winged sparrows, bullbirds, moonlings); I go
around the table in the dining room, I go into the workshop: unfinished cages, the primitive tools, the wild perfume of varnish and
planed wood; everywhere Hermelinda's evocative waltz, everywhere
the active throats of the birds; I venture into the room with the clothes
closet, the large double bed, the bureau; on top of the case for the reli-
gious image, medicine bottles, a money box; the red brick floor of the
house must have been washed very early in the morning; idly avoiding
stepping between one brick and another, I return to the dining room
and on the table I see in the center of a round lace doily, I see a photo-

graph album. Hadn't I noticed it? Decisively and rapidly, as if I had been hunting for the album on the porch and in the rooms, I pick it up. I go back to the hammock, I examine it.

Works from the times when photographers—instead of capturing the artifice that exists in the impossible naturalness of their models, trying to give an impression of life to their work—fix attitudes and gestures that are only acceptable far removed from the lens. The yellowing of the images and the damage from the bookworms are an answer to the painful appearance of action.

"Whom are these pictures of?"

"People. Most of them there already know the right hand of God, have been well judged."

"Is a good judgment always received?"

"It depends on their misdeeds and their contrition."

Two children kneeling on First Communion day. Men with ats and cane , side by side, one l g outstretched and a distant look, as if the camera had caught them in a short silence between profound dialogues; women sitting, lbow resting on a able with wisted egs, graciously closing a fa   between their ands; girls with lack s ockings and long white dresse , a large w ite bow in their hair, holding a book with a posy between the pages and with their y s in my direction; others in between rocks and royal alms reflected on the backdrop;   beside dogs; famil s in a group, each family looking in one direction; in the center of the group a pair of children with tra hats, dressed in ailo suits, holding a arp   . . . In the midst of this composed and faded gallery, where now even the identity of the models has dissolved, a rather clumsy photograph suddenly leaps out at me dated a month ago, taken at some circus performance: a young girl smiling at the camera, holding in her arms a lion that is still young and is muzzled. On the back, in squat and rather pretentious writing, this inscription: "*Cercília is not afraid of lions. June 15, 1962.*" The "*r*" of the name cut out, however.

I hear (on the street?) hasty sounds crossing, wheels and axles, a heavy structure falling apart. The album trembles in my hands. No movement at all on the street: the same peace. But Cecília, the one who isn't afraid of lions—the bars and the vertical shadow of the bars putting stripes on her yellow dress—opens the main door. Opening it, she begins a metallic phrase: the tinkling of the bracelet on her fragile forearm with small stars and little gold coins, the creaking of the door's unoiled hinges, the bronze clapper in the little copper bell hanging from a flexible steel arc. The bolt falls heavily into its slot. The same sound, exactly the same, as that of a cage being closed. Cecília, the Madonna of the lions?

O
The Story of O, Twice-Born   **13**

I still don't speak. Without speaking, I detach things, take them apart, separate some from others, reorganize them in me. I remove our apartment from the building; the building (its name is Martinelli) I remove from the block; I isolate the block from the city. I set up breaches and empty spaces. The world is a constellation of spinning swords, and every morning this question assaults me: "How can I survive?"

My father is tall, light-skinned, and speaks little through a trumpet of horn that he carries around his neck on a silver cord. He puts the trumpet into his mouth and his voice seems to come from far away, disfigured and without inflection. It's impossible to read what he's saying in his eyes: he stares at me sometimes for a long time, as if I weren't across from him, as if he were looking at a memory. Always with his beret on. The beret, worn to one side, helps keep a pink rubber artificial ear in place. The walls of his study, which also serves as a bedroom, are covered with photographs of singers from the twenties and the thirties, almost all with dedications. On a piano, which is never opened, one can also see his portrait, his wavy hair, the stubborn chin, his eyes fixed on a point a little to the right of the lens, full of ardor and confidence, clinging to illusory realities, the innocent and self-assured look of someone who doesn't perceive the spinning of the swords. His face from the time he gives piano lessons and my mother is still his pupil. There he is, at some point in time, correcting with excessive indulgence, perhaps, perhaps with excessive rigor, the position of the fingers of that flourishing and impetuous adolescent, her nostrils always quivering, who looks at him with unfathomable designs as she listens to him speak of Stefania Doratti, Del Nigro, the Cordays, Norma Bergantini (could those be the names?), brilliant, tragic, and willful characters, like those in operas, with whom he was intimate, whose perfumes he smells, and whose dedicated photographs he owns. He belongs to orchestras, he moves happily in the midst of a fictitious population of sopranos, basses, tenors, contraltos, baritones, maestros, impresarios, almost always foreigners, who go back and forth under the drapes of the Municipal Theater, smile at him, receive pay and applause with the same fatuous disdain, with a kind of unctuous arrogance they scribble their names on the photographs and leave. He doesn't see the swords.

One day, with lowered eyes, at the moment she feels the hand of the teacher on hers, my mother, without turning around, places her feverish face on the man's fingers. With that gesture she brings hours of unrest for the family and flings herself—capable of having chosen ten other paths, for she had no lack of opportunities—flings herself into a labyrinth of reflections where, always in hope of better days, she goes along living in places that get worse and worse, renouncing everything in that world of shadows and high-sounding fleeting names.

What, besides time, has destroyed my father physically? An accident? Some illness? Do ravenous animals gnaw at his voice in dreams, at his flesh? I don't know. The beginning of the destruction can be measured by the dates of the last dedications. Without his left ear and having to speak through a piece of horn with silver trim, he loses his students and is no longer acceptable in orchestras. He is reduced to tuning pianos (his only ear can hear for two), and he makes collections for a banking house.

My mother, in order to see the effect that her hats cause or to transport herself by magical action to the parties and solemn gatherings where they will be worn, always keeps on her head at home the ones she has just finished or those she is creating; and on them she experiments, with innumerable ribbons, paper flowers, beads, feathers, and stickpins with pearls or colored glass, before deciding. Coldness and pride more than suffering, also a little tedium, can be read in her eyes. The hats, among other things, serve as a pretext for her to get out of less interesting obligations. Our meals have been reduced to eggs and canned food. The dust accumulates on mirrors, windowpanes, and the shadowy eyes of the prima donnas.

The keys now remain in the doors and the screens rot in the window frames. From the window I can see a building being constructed. It's three or four o'clock in the afternoon and a truck is picking up wood that has already been used. An old man, his loose pants held up by a piece of rope, is giving a hand to the other workers. With effort, he picks up a sawed-off plank, a short lath, he comes along dragging his feet, throws the load into the back of the truck, and looks around. He takes off his cap, runs his cuff over his bald head. A sound at the window: sparrows peck the screening, the screen breaks. I put pressure on it with my fingernail, the strands give way, separate. I go away, frightened. I can move about at will in the building, there is no precaution anymore as regards me. In the elevator or on the stairs I explore by myself the long corridors where mottled globes hang from the ceiling, some without bulbs and others with very weak ones. Just as one goes about getting to know a neighborhood, I undertake the conquest of that small vertical world, almost always poorly lighted, with corridors, doors, rooms, stairs, numbers, that world without trees, without wind, without horizon, without firmament, an echoing, repetitive world, where each floor, with insignificant changes, is superimposed on its own reflection or image. But it is a world. I find lawyers in its corridors, justice officials, prostitutes, families, on the sixth floor there's a school of dance, a poolroom on the tenth, a labor union on the twelfth, on Sundays my father takes me walking along the Rua 15 de Novembro and everything we see is marble façades, bronze plaques, silent iron gateways, he goes to the Praça da Sé, people take streetcars for places that I can only imagine, hawking lottery tickets from his wheelchair I find a cripple who lives in the building and fondles my thigh when we take the same elevator, an old woman, on the mezzanine, bribes me with cookies to let her anoint my fingers with margarine so her cat can lick it, the harshness of its little tongue on my skin makes me laugh, at some point there's a clinic, the perpetual smell of ether, dentists' offices (carbolic acid), a vegetarian restaurant, the tenant in 128 who always argues with the voices on the radio, a teenage girl is found raped and dead in the shaft of an elevator and not even then am I stopped from opening the door when I want to and circulating aimlessly through the Martinelli Building. In short, and this intrigues me, no one knows that I've been someone else ever since the fall in that same shaft, or that the world from then on is a different one for me, no one, and even then no key is taken out of the lock, the screening originally meant to stop me from falling out the windows is coming apart, it can't even resist a sparrow's beak, and I wander all alone, freely, through the corridors where there is a rapist. Why don't they continue to protect me?

My father in an easy chair in the parlor, his legs stretched out, is pasting clippings into an album. Surrounded by artificial flowers, colored ribbons, and women's hats, my mother occupies another easy chair. I look at one and the other. It's Sunday, the afternoon is dark, it's threatening to rain, we certainly aren't going to the Praça da Sé. I get up, looking at them both uneasily, I open the door which leads to the corridors.

R

Ỡ and Abel: Meetings, Routes, and Revelations   11

We see, then (the pressure of her agitated fingers on my thigh), we see, against the misty sea and outlined in the direction of the reading, the post with the light not burning and the flat, unoccupied stone; standing, the gloved fisherman; more or less in the center, the one with the old umbrella and the one with the boots on the crates; the one in the blue hat, sitting on the dock; on the stone to the right, the one wrapped in yellow plastic; the post without a lamp, the final end of the sequence.

The color of Ỡ's arms is not identical to that of her face or even her neck. Lighter and touched with a soft down, only visible under proper illumination (proclaiming her emotions by standing on end), whether exposed to the solar brightness or not, it absorbs the regnant light. Throbbing at her pale wrists, the blue of her veins.

The old woman's irritation increases as she replaces the bait on the still fishless hook. At some distance from the posts, the mooring stones, and the other fishermen, her isolation is deceptive. A dissonant and solitary motif, in her earthy figure she concentrates the lines of force coming from the people and the things that otherwise would have remained unconnected. This convergence integrates her—the axis of a fan—in the symmetry of everything and renders her indispensable.

Imagine a river voyage. The boatman, from source to estuary, follows the flow of the waters. Does that passage begin? Does it end? The boatman thinks that's how it is and that's how it looks: and in truth there's an aspect of the passage where the beginning and the end do exist, where a reading or execution of the voyage exists. There is an aspect of the voyage where past and future are real; and another, no less real and more difficult to find, where the voyage, the boat, the boatman, the river, and the extension of the river mingle. The oars of the boat cut the whole length of the river at one time; and the voyager, forever and since always, begins, undertakes, and concludes the voyage in such a way that the departure at the headwaters of the river does not come before the arrival at the estuary.

What place on the dock have the cyclist and the girl riding on the frame of his bicycle, both dressed as the damp afternoon demands, been attracted to? In the disposition of the figures between the posts there is a distortion, an inclination, although not obvious, toward the side where the individual covered with a piece of yellow plastic is fishing: a line of poetry where the tonic accents, divided equally between the two hemistichs, are heavier on the last syllables. Getting off, the couple goes over to the gloved fisherman standing on the left. They are still not led, we can easily see, by the mysterious impulse to obey the laws of the rhythm that governs the scene: they know one another. But then a demanding force moves them. They do not remain as a group, since the idea of occupying the mooring stone still available on the extreme left of the dock, in imitation of the man in yellow plastic on the right, doesn't seem to occur to the cyclist or the girl. By doing that they would break the clear, tense harmony that we are silently contemplating.

From here on, much of the questioning and uneasiness that are part of my way of being are joined to the moving or still profiles on the dock. Am I reading what I see? The calm and implacable gestation of an ordered event? Am I reading the rhythm and the symmetries? Such realities speak to me directly—not like a piece of writing—and reach me in a zone that is not easily accessible. ♀ and I come through the world (our steps mixed up?) to this point of intersection, and here there is no disorder. We are in a sphere of miracles, where the fragments adjust to each other and the one is remade. Our shock is just and our intoxication legitimate. This fragile equilibrium: a pencil with its point on a flat base, the axis of gravity, thinner than a strand of hair, descending along the graphite and falling onto the tiny base. It is going to lean and fall, we know, and never more, we know, never more. A text is being coordinated geometrically within innumerable disconnected letters.

The veins, half hidden on the wrists, are completely invisible on the pale reverse of ♀'s hands and in her spindle-shaped fingers with oval nails. In the joints between the phalanges, the skin does not become dark and gives way to delicate hollows, almost without wrinkling. The couple, moving away a few steps from their common friend and remaining on the left wing of the T, take a position facing us on the wall of the dock—which is thick, about ten feet across—opposite the sea, compensating in that way for the slight overload in the final hemistich. Ờ puts on her earrings again, laughs exultantly, and shakes her hair, which gives the impression of a being with a life of its own. Does the fleeting and perhaps mysterious perfume that passes by come from her hair or her exultation?

The dock—up to now the scene of an abstract play of forces where the only indication of conflict is the impatience of the old woman sitting on her legs, while the other fishermen, equally unlucky, hold their poles with resignation—is vaguely agitated by an unexpected event. As soon as he throws his hook into the half-dirty and wavy waters that partly hide the muddy steps formed by the construction at that angle, the cyclist catches a fish. He shouts with joy, pulling off the hook the struggling prey, dark and unshining, almost the color of the steps in the dead light of the afternoon. The other fishermen, even those who don't turn around, show that they have heard the shout. All except the old woman: hat and arms motionless. New shouts from the cyclist successively announce his luck at fishing.

No adornment on Ờ's right hand. She moves it, however, a bit more than the other, where only the thumb is undecorated by expensive rings, two and three, of silver and gold.

The impatience of the old woman—seated a few yards away from the fortunate fisherman, with whom she forms in contrast an axis of tension—is becoming less visible and perhaps more concentrated. A dissonance has been set up in the strange equilibrium of which we are a part. Other strange and seemingly arbitrary forces (is it simply expertness that keeps filling up the basket beside him with fish, six or seven, caught one after the other, while the other hooks, there long before him, catch nothing?) are creeping in. *Decree by Marshal Castelo Branco unifies institutes of retirement and pensions under title of INPS.* The motorboat, the impassive figure in the bow, crosses the tin-colored waters in the opposite direction.

O

The Story of Ʊ, Twice-Born   **14**

My father, in silence, the horn trumpet on his chest, is pasting newspaper items into an album. With no access any longer to actresses and singers who appear at the Municipal Theater, yet unable to renounce that world completely, he will not get rid of the piano, an instrument he never gets to play in public (in the photograph, he is holding a guitar), and he keeps a scrapbook of celebrities with pictures cut from the newspapers. My mother, involved with her hat orders, occupies another easy chair. In the shadows of the parlor, darkened by the thick clouds that are forming, her shiny legs. Suspicious, I look at one and the other, I go to the door that opens onto the corridors, stairs, and irregular elevators. I turn the key, I go out. From the two in the parlor not a word. Not a gesture. Am I mistaken in supposing that I sensed a rapid look of expectancy between the two of them? I go over to the elevator, the same elevator into which I had flung myself with the tricycle, I call it; I don't take it; I go back, close the door, and retake my place on the sofa. Both have their eyes lowered. My father has his hands on the photograph he is cutting the instant I go out; my mother continues attaching the same orange cambric flowers to the hat. Are they my parents? Or are they my murderers?

I look at them, with my double sight. I feel myself protected and at the same time irate, but also run through with terror. I hide my right hand under my thigh. I move it as if twisting a cork. Under my thigh between my fingers I crumble the indications of the past weeks. This one more than the others: coming back from a stroll on the other floors of the building, I find the door locked; I ring the bell, I kick on the door, the door is a long time in opening, finally it opens, and my mother, when she opens, doesn't look at the level of my eyes, she looks three hands above my eyes, at the level of *her* face, the face of an adult. Why? Am I unjust in supposing that I have guessed it? She's waiting for them to bring the news of my death. The indications coincide; the negligence: keys in the doors, and screens that a sparrow can make holes in. I lift my hand to my mouth and bite this certainty, this terror, this bitterness, this hate, this wrath, I get up and decide I won't be silent, I'll put an end to silence, I'm going to speak, I open my mouth, but it's not easy to speak, my tongue and my larynx are full of cobwebs, I inhale the air and exhale it through my mouth with difficulty, they look at me, my father lifts the trumpet to his lips, my mother's fingers tighten on the hat, and I shout, I spit, I vomit in their faces: "Mell. Mell." That's not the word but I have to say it, the effort drains me, I fall onto my knees, the convulsive movements continue, and I try again like someone attempting a jump, a dive, an acrobatic leap, I try again, with more force now, with more hate, and I shout: "Hell!" It's the first word that I release, the first, I repeat it, four, five times, each time weaker, then I bend over, I touch the floor with my forehead and burst into sobs.

O me felicem!! The chariot of the Sun rolls with us in the fields of Capricorn. How happy I am, so happy I, wrapped up in my joy, oh! Happy me! here I am, happy, o me felicem, o me felicem, Abel. Happy me, ah! and I love you and I'm naked, my long hair unfurled, and rid of rings, necklaces, earrings, bracelets, everything, wearing only my nakedness, my adornments are the tips of my breasts, the cave of my navel, my pubic hair, my polished nails, I'm naked and Abel blows into my ear that there cannot be a more splendid mantle, laughing, I lay my head on my own wrists, happy to exhibit my nakedness, he kisses my shoulders and armpits, he rubs his face against my stomach, I feel the harshness of his stubbly chin.

Let my body give itself with all its animal load. For centuries sailors have brought birds stuffed with straw from Melanesia, stuffed birds of frightful beauty but without feet. They call them "birds of paradise" and it isn't hard to believe that they escape from Eden the instant the gate opens for the expulsion of the sinners. They seem to come from the privileged world where the hair of lions—not tawny—is silver, where fish fly whenever they wish to, and where the Moon rises each night accompanied by a dazzling cortege of peacocks who pair off in flight. In flight, the sailors affirm, the stuffed birds they bring from Oceania mate and incubate their eggs. Actually the savages who sell them cut off their legs. Let me not pull off my feet in this time of changing and lucid plumage: to dive into it with all my animal load. The Melanesians, refusing to accept that bird as a terrestrial being debased by the exhalations of the same dirty mud on which they live with their obscure unrealizable dreams and where almost everything rots, sever their feet. With that stratagem the dead birds are sent back to the heights, where, mutilated, they remain, thanks to man's cooperating imagination. Let me not pull off my feet at this time. We roll on the rug, we hit our sides against the table in the center of the room, the table falls and the unpolished silver teapot, once more I bring my hand down across Abel's stomach, heft in my palm the obelisk, the mark, the center of his body—I put my face against it, I rub it with my loose hair, I kiss it lightly and listen to it: butterflies are flying inside it, many of them, the innumerable wings hum, they try to get out, they nod foolishly on the walls. For how long has it been coming toward me with its energy and its butterflies? On seeing it erect, rigid, at its full height, I am proud of the fact that it lights its flame in me, that its enlargement is born in me. In my body, in the promises of my body.

My head still on the floor, I begin to babble. My father and mother think I am possessed by the devil. I speak in jerks, without thinking, without connection, my words are pus, my mouth an open abscess, I speak without stopping, sometimes muttering, then roaring, and so, as before, many words are formulated in me without my uttering them, I speak now of things that are beyond my understanding. I read one day in Virgil that the nations conquered by Rome, the triumphal celebrations, public games, ovations, sacrifices, choruses of matrons, warships, monstrous gods, and all the battles, placed in order, appear on the shield wrought for the son of Venus. When he girds on Vulcan's handiwork, he does not know that he is girding on the events and figures in which his line will participate. The words that I throw out in my endless and uncontrollable discourse also represent my own life, although as I pour them out I am completely ignorant of this; and my ignorance is even greater than that of the Trojan, because, unlike the battles chiseled onto his fearsome tool of war, all placed in order, the people and events to which I must be joined come to me fragmented in words, phrases, and names that I pronounce, names, phrases, and words of which many return, are repeated, from morning to night, on those days and nights when I speak and speak without stopping, how many days, how many nights?—many, maybe three, maybe five, it's hard to tell, days and nights in which I almost do not sleep and even when I sleep I still talk. Saddened visitors gaze at me from a distance, not daring to come through the door to my room, I eat little and poorly, swallowing words, I only drink enough to cool my painful throat, my voice is extinguished, exhausted, I close my eyes and even then my dry lips continue to move, I continue to speak inside of me of the walks with Inácio Gabriel, the messenger, the anticipator

of this man to whom I give myself and whom I love, of my adolescence
lived and relived, of the names of people who hang heavy in my destiny, of the disappointments, of the bullet fired and lodged in my
chest, of my death and, repeated, that of the yolyp, which I never
know and which I describe in detail, without understanding anything
and without knowing (how could I know?) that one day I will find it. It,
a yolyp. Yolyp?

T

Cecília Among the Lions   6

The light and rhythmical sound of Cecília's brass-heeled shoes
rings on the floor of the porch. Quick steps, those of someone who has
to walk a lot and lives with a certain urgency. The man on the other
side of the street lowers his arm and disappears with the children.
Hermelinda lowers her hand firmly onto the strings of the instrument.
The cat by the door puts his paw onto the floor, the birds release their
song. Hermelinda drives away the circle of lions that threaten Cecília
and kisses her on the cheek. The song of the birds also resounds,
clean, metallic. Cecília, with a smile, makes the lions climb up onto the
roofs, wagging their tails. I cannot hear what Hermenilda and Cecília
talk about. Cecília's tongue: a lascivious lion. Hermenilda makes a
gesture in my direction and points to her: "Her name is Cecília. She
works at the Pedro II Hospital. Social Services." She nods her head,
looks at me for an instant, and turns her eyes away. She looks at me
again rapidly (solitary bees, those eyes, scratching surfaces). "Abel is a
man of letters and books. A philosopher. He knows the other side of
the World." Black swift lions buzz in Cecília's eyes. Cecília sits down
on the mahogany bench beside Hermenilda and crosses her thin legs.
The bone structure of her knees is visible. Cecília's silence is crossed
by lions.

Thus, face to face, with our unhealthy help, behold Cecília and
Abel. The loop we have put together must tighten around them. We
would like to extend some distance between them both—so that they
wouldn't come together. We would like to? Vain desire. The die is

cast, and with it certain events over which we have no control. Abel considers Cecília's soft breezes and their opposites. He sees the discord between the soft curve of her shoulders and the lack of curves on her hips; between her prominent breasts (with tense nipples) and the chesty instep of her foot with its tendons, a bit long at toe level; he is startled that from Cecília there comes the echo of many branches, delicate, dry, carefully stepped on and that at the same time some sign in her face suggests determination; and, in addition, that that figure, winged and full of grace, should be sustained by an ungraspable framework of virility. This is still the beginning, of course. Without either's knowing it, or hearing it, two mouths are magically talking to each other. Then he will see her in a new way, varied and multiple, inhabited in her flesh by visions or bodies—and under reflections, as if lighted by a Sun broken up into a thousand oscillating blades. Trying to find direction in life is the same as seeking in a haystack the needle that might have been dropped somewhere else.

From the drawer in the boardinghouse I take the written pages of the story I am putting together. (The drawer gives off an inexplicable and never-dispelled smell of dust.) Beginning to be defined on paper are the profiles of the four sisters, all septuagenarians, each one burning to outlive the others. Why? They don't know. They live in the same house—this permits me to accentuate the hatred with which they spy on each other. But the stage where they move—the villa in Olinda, reproduced with all the exactness possible—continues to displease me. I try in vain to evoke the labyrinth of rooms and bedrooms, with clothing that sometimes smells of groins hanging behind the doors. I paint the wooden trim blue, on the stone stove I heat up the huge pots, and I pave the floor with mosaic tile. I introduce the unmatched furniture that increases along with my family and deteriorates as it is used by the old women. (Everything in the world sometimes smells of warts, scabs, and dry nails.) I fail to mention the musical instruments lying neglected in the drawers, the *East Coker* piano, the pompous pitchers, the enormous mirror between wall brackets in the main parlor and the oval wedding portrait. I maintain with some emphasis the German print from the times of Hölderlin showing three young spinners. I still have the sun enter through glass fanlights—colored in the real villa and white in the fictitious one. I represent, finally, with a heavy hand, the interior, where the lace curtains with hunting scenes flutter in the breeze that blows out to sea. The extensive description of the exterior is more inept. The peaked roof hanging over the side walls, the eaves shading the sides and the façade, the lambrequins of a faded blue accompanying the line of the eaves and rising up along the front with a lathe-turned pole on the highest vertex, the geometric flower, placed like a tympanum in the middle of the front wall, surrounded by a circle, and having a sphere of blue glass in the center, the white window frames, the porch to the left, also with lambrequins, every detail (and, more than any other, the paint on the walls, ocher, indigo, and white imitating transparent cubes, with a useless appearance of relief as a result) demands hundreds of words of me and always ends in a huge weightless construction whose roofs flutter like wings.

Beside the cistern, kneeling on the rough concrete, I try to see my face in the water. The water, which seems hard, petrified by the absence of fish and voices, looks at me dully—the look of a dead person. It reflects only imprecise lines, the interrogative splotch of a head against the cloudy sky. I spit in my face, in the vague reflection of my face, and I get up. The water of the cistern and the rancid smell of bedbugs. On Milagres Beach nearby the waves—strong, even at ebb-tide—abandon constructions of which only the markings are still left. Rust and sea air corrode the zinc roof. I cover the distance that slopes up between the cistern and the house, unhurried, throwing stones picked up from the ground at the trunks of the mango trees, all of them taking on the air of wild trees. Does the nocturnal cat with a monkey's head perhaps leap from among those trees when bored or superfluous? I stop at a certain distance from the villa, where for years the voices of the family have echoed and from which not a single sound comes now. I throw stones at the columns on the porch and the terrace. My mother appears, fat, holding a flatiron. She stretches her tiny thin-lipped mouth into its customary expression:

"Yes, sir! Thirty-two years old and still throwing stones at things. Is that the way you announce your arrival? Come in, man. Have you come for lunch? You didn't come by last Saturday."

I kiss her on the left shoulder, where she has the scar. She sprinkles rice water on the handkerchiefs she is ironing: "Of all the Treasurer's luxuries, this is what's left. Starched handkerchiefs." "He isn't Treasurer anymore." "Do you think he accepts that? He talks night and day about his reappointment. It had to end up like that. Ever since he was Treasurer of the stinking Bank he thought he was Treasurer of the world. What about you, son? The other week I was thinking: five years since you took on your job. The way time flies." "That's true."

The cat with a monkey's head, which she has carried on her body since birth, leaps onto the ironing board. It looks at me from there with its begging and affectionate eyes: two purple beads.

A
Roos and the Cities   13

I go along the Boulevard Raspail and I keep on walking, at random, only knowing where I am when I read the signs—Boulevard Saint-Jacques, Place d'Italie, Quai d'Austerlitz. It's a little after three, but the overcast sky makes it seem later; the wind wounds my eyes and not even the sight of the Seine under the bridges calms me. I return exhausted and aimless, a vacuum in my stomach. When I put the key in the lock, the telephone begins to ring and stops before I can answer it. I ring Roos's room: no answer. Having left an envelope with her name on it containing two glass eyes, bought I don't remember whether in Antwerp or Ghent, trying to convey the meaning that there was nothing of interest for me to see in her absence, I go down to see if they've been picked up: they're still in the big square wooden rack between the first and second floors. I go back up, unpack my bag, put the room in order after the changes from a week's trip, and I even count the coins I have left. How many weeks can I still stay and how many cities will I see? I check the calendar: May 10th. Tenth? What happened on that date? I can't remember. I distractedly thumb through some books, I find a text by Palladio on Chambord. In the center of the castle, the architect states, there is a set of stairs in *four* parts, with *four* entrances, serving *four* apartments, with the ramps going up one on top of the other, never meeting. All the facts are correct, yes, except for the number of parts. Palladio, an exact and objective spirit, raises the double stairs of Chambord to four, turning them into a more complex invention! I mark the passage in the book and I remember: on the day I turn nineteen, May 10, 1954, my brother Augusto comes into the world and never again makes news. Could he be spurred by an agitation like mine? Why didn't he ever talk to me? Aren't all of us, sons of the Fat Woman, given to searches, mistakes, disasters? I go out again, I head in the direction of the Rue Guynemer. I pay a visit to the Weigels.

The head of the family has been in bed for almost seven years. I imagine him as short in stature, even though I always see him lying down. Since he doesn't hear well, he makes me sit next to the bed. He calls me—no one knows why, perhaps because of my rust-colored beard—Lev Nikolayevich Myshkin, staring at me with his slightly cross-eyed look. When he's feeling better, as on this late afternoon, his subject is the great Russian prose writers. Then he becomes excited and runs his hands over his bald head insistently. He imitates, as I believe, the speech of Dostoevskian heroes: "How are you? Eh? Are you feeling well? You look pale. Do you think I've come to the end of my rope? Have something to drink. It's good with this cold. [In spite of the heating system, he always thinks it's cold. Maybe he imagines he's in St. Petersburg.] You see me today in a frightful mood. No, nothing I said is true. Everything passes and then I shall be judged by my crimes. You, Lev Nikolayevich Myshkin, don't know what old age is. Let's try to understand each other. What does all this mean?"

His wife comes to sit down beside us: skinny, with her knees apart and her feet crossed under the chair. Her hands resting on the empty space between her knees, she leans her head slightly backward, and as she looks at her husband she criticizes him, almost without unsealing her lips, so that he won't be aware of her censure: "So crazy, good heavens! When he's better, instead of resting, he keeps on talking nonsense. Be quiet, you poor lunatic." And turning to me: "I don't know how you put up with all this."

There's always a mandolin in the parlor, occupying an armchair. A fine instrument, it makes me remember the one that belongs to my sister Leonor (why didn't she take it to the convent?), which is falling apart in some closet in the villa, along with Mauro's guitar and the flute that belonged to Eurílio, riddled with bullets in a Recife brothel. Mme. Weigel's instrument isn't good for anything either: she played it when she was young and my interest comes from that circumstance. Sometimes I hold it in my lap—that mute survivor of happier days—as if I were protecting useless and dead things, while I chat with the couple's two daughters.

Julie is twenty-one. Fragile and calm, she speaks slowly and reasons slowly, although with precision. Her small, round face takes on an extreme purity when, separating her straight hair in half and combing it behind her ears, she fastens it at the back of her neck. I admire her hands, delicate and light, in spite of her nails, short and always a little darkened by the soot that is part of Paris. She makes a little money designing and sewing clothes for dolls. Only a temperament like hers could make dresses that in most instances are no bigger than the palm of one's hand with such detail and perfection.

Suzanne, four or five years younger, seems to have accumulated the energy and impatience that we find in Julie in moderation. Her features, not as pure as those of her sister, attract me by their vivacity and by something frank and generous that I can read in her slightly wide-set eyes. Her voice is serious, and when she speaks or laughs her upper lip sticks out a little. That habit and her favorite hairdo (she opens up her hair at the back of her neck, fastening it in two chestnut wisps at ear level) give her such a childlike air that it is moving. One thinks that she is destined for disillusionment and being crushed.

Sitting together on the ancient sofa re-covered with moss-colored damask, they are now enjoying a moment of relaxation on this third floor inhabited for seven years by the old man's illness. Suzanne puts her book aside, Julie stops her sewing. They talk to me in a low voice, as if their father, in spite of being half deaf, could hear from his bed. Why am I so pale? Ill? Grateful for the postcard I sent them from Brussels. How was the trip? Why don't I ever visit them anymore?

It grows dark. Suzanne turns on the lamp with the tall bronze base. Julie gets up, serves me a cognac. Sun in the cane fields. Lev Nikolayevich Myshkin, you're a useless man. The world explodes. Red birds at the windows, over the lamp, over Suzanne's hands and Julie's shoulders. St. Petersburg. Why is it so hard for me to ripen? Should one ripen? Sooty sea gulls. Poor lunatic! Cities drifting by on a phosphorescent sea or through the air. What are you looking for?

I wake up. The lamp is out, the house in silence. I get up without making any noise and leave. On passing by the mailbox, I note that the envelope for Roos has been picked up.

But what if she's avoiding me? I don't see her. I eat my meals slowly and linger over dessert. The rest of the time on that weekend I stay in my room. Why doesn't she call me? I listen to the oranges and apples rotting, the nails slowly leaving the planks, the springs in the mattress distending, the sheet wrinkling, the floor creaking, my beard growing, my nails and hair, the grease running down the door hinges, the knife losing its edge, my blood circulating, and the air shifting position in the room. I hear everything, except the telephone. A dark bird with a curved bill enters the room several times, alights on the table, and stares at me, predatory eyes, wings half opened. He disappears immediately.

R

Ὁ and Abel: Meetings, Routes, and Revelations 12

Less hazy and closer, the rain having stopped, the two fishing craft, boats. A few gulls float in the gray air: they dive, true arrows, at the light fish, and take flight again. Over the stretch that links the dock to the land come the gloved fisherman and the cyclist's companion in our direction. Their small heads with birdlike movements, a certain lassitude in their walk and a way of holding the left hand at the waist. Similarities. I hear the girl's voice, as if she were two steps away from us, telling the old woman: "When he leaves, you can have the fish. They're yours." An affable voice, without warmth, with something mechanical about it. The old woman, sitting, moves her head and lifts her hand. Again the cyclist's pole bends and the obvious happiness of his shout. A flapping in the air.

The balance of forces on the platform does not become undone—only the symmetry is altered—with the absence of the girl and the fisherman on the left. The cyclist, without his companion and with his back still to the sea, supplies the demand of weight—or presence—that floats audibly behind him between the umbrella and the stone.

Why is it I comprehend that this melodious unity organized before us has ended or is declining toward its end? Perhaps I'm right and the dissolution that I judge to be near has really begun in the contemplator: in me and not in what is happening on the dock. It could also be that a necessary proportion exists between the system—the rhythm—articulated in the space and its resonance. I ask, however, as if facing a loss and certain of a negative reply: "Is this all?"

A knoll to prevent the spread of an exuberant stream, the rounded projection of the ball of the thumb in Ὁ's broad palm, seems to repress the violent line where her fate might be written. (At what point in the interlocking lines, deep as scars, are my name and this day inscribed?) In her gestures, also modulated and vivacious, the harmony and ardor of her hands are echoed.

The sea gulls, motionless, less white, almost transparent against the dust-colored sky. Are they dissolving in the air? Rigid. They are integrated in the sudden and rapid schism that interrupts the flow of things: a hiatus where there is a collaborative cessation even of the sound of the water. All of the figures on the dock petrified, the woman in the red blouse, the torn umbrella, the yellow plastic, fossils on a slab. In the substance of that pause, in the fixedness and the perfect silence, a sound is born: a droning and with it the flow returns, other sounds and movement, the peaceful waves return, the lucky fisherman shouts, and—agile once more—the gulls descend avidly upon the fish. The droning, mingled with the pounding of horses' hooves and the sound of a rattling (I clench my fists), is defined: an automobile engine. Coming with it invisibly from the deserted streets of Ubatuba conveying other passengers—or perhaps the same—is there the ghost of some stagecoach?

Anachronistic and unreal, its large nickel-plated headlights a bit ostentatiously turned on, a green Packard from the early thirties looms up. The dark hood, the plaited wires on its wheels, and the white canvas of the spare tires between the running board and the black fenders, wet with rain, shine like new. When it turns in front of us, I see the thin metal charger on the radiator cap, heading—a leap—in the direction of the sea. The doors open, a couple gets out (the lights stay on), and three girls in gray coats fly off in the direction of the dock. There is something avid, implacable, and urgent in the children. Rapidly they go from one side to the other, silent. Are they executing a design? The oldest, suddenly, as if an order had been heard, goes toward the cyclist; the others, imitating her, station themselves beside him and remain motionless. The three of them in their gray coats, in the changing light crossed through by dull reverberations. Predatory birds lying in wait: a mute, motionless voracity quick to show itself. They scrutinize or become integrated, submissive, in the strange rhythmical conjunction that, emissaries of chance or destiny, or, perhaps, of a third entity disguised under that double face—did they come to lead out of the abstract into the living (a transposition announced in the tense axis extended between the woman in red and the lucky fisherman) and simultaneously to disturb, corrupt, break?

The tallest child, having come from who knows where, as in a ceremony slowly begins the few precise acts that would express little under different circumstances but here glow with intensity, illuminating our lives and our meeting in the world: bending over, she opens the basket with the fish. The fisherwoman, for the twentieth time, pulls in the hook without bait or fish. Sharp, cutting grunts punctuate the confused dialogue between the girls (or birds?) and the man: a word gleams several times, silvery, "fish." The youngest cunningly inserts her hand into the basket and back to the sea goes a fish. In the six childish hands, flashing like knives, the scaly bodies of the fish. The four come (the voices of the children, sharp and tense) in the direction of the old woman, obstinate and mute—a fish. The vivid balance of forces becomes disjointed and the whole weight of the picture now falls upon one wing of the dock, the right one; but it is around the fisherwoman, on the other side and closer to us, that the event articulated here according to the laws of narrative and with the precision of all improbables (a whole life can run out with this prodigious meeting, readable from a few fragments drifting in the explosion of the world, so rare—we know, with nostalgia and jubilation—that no one knows it twice, no matter how long he lives) is going to culminate, simulating coherence and even a certain prophetic character: aren't there people who read things in the viscera of birds and fish? The girls and the man are next to the fisherwoman, but ☿ and I know, as certain as in a still-unfinished line of poetry, the advent—inevitable—of the final tonic accent is awaited, that the girls in gray do not come forth in vain; invaders emerging from another world, they hurry from afar (from the clouds?) to snatch away those fish. The couple from the Packard (the lights still on and brighter in the rapidly darkening afternoon) approach the fisherman and ask for the fish. The girls jump into the car, which rocks on its springs: in the dark interior the glimmer of the fish. The cyclist leaves with his pole and empty basket. The fisherman with the yellow plastic goes to the center of the dock, irresolutely. The one in blue shorts closes the umbrella and everything falls apart. I hear once more, as the car goes off, the metal of a small bell and horseshoes on paving stones, the sounds of the invisible vehicle previously joined to the Packard as a spell, which in direction opposite off goes now.

A

Roos and the Cities   14

When day breaks on Monday, a heavy rain is falling. Stretched out on my bed, I spend the interval between breakfast and lunch examining tourist leaflets. Close to noon a clearing more intense than the others tears the sky and I find it natural that a sharp tinkle should be audible in the pith of the thunder, that it should rise up twice in the middle of a rolling so prolonged and so intense that the doors of the closet open. Only on the third roll do I distinguish the telephone. I get up slowly and answer: Roos is telling me she's back.

"Yesterday? At night? Didn't you find the eyes in an envelope, then?"

What eyes? What envelope? She maintains that she doesn't know what it's all about.

"I thought you'd got back three days ago. Where are you talking from? The company?"

Yes. Lots of things left over. She's going to have lunch with the boss, near the office.

"When will I see you, Roos?"

A silence. The rain and the wind. The sound of typewriters, of muffled explosions and diligent footsteps come before her voice: "I may have dinner over there. But I can't promise. In any case, I can't say what time I'll get back."

She comes along the Boulevard Raspail under the fine rain, in the light of the still premature afternoon, with papers and folders wrapped in plastic under her arm. A gray cape, a hat of the same shade, brown gloves, and white boots, halfway up her legs. She is preceded by golden standards on invisible staffs, tall with scarlet designs of suns, griffins, to the right and to the left of her shoulders, standing out against the heavy sky, the damp roofs, and the blackness of the walls. She looks at me with merry naturalness, a little distant, seeming to insinuate that she's not responding to our meeting in Amsterdam or, as one says, washing one's hands in the light of the mistakes of some distant relative. She has to finish the report, change her clothes, rest a little, we can meet at eight o'clock. Drops of rain glisten on her face.

We take the Métro and she holds my hand, even though in a fleeting way (a muffled sound of fanfare encircles her), as we go up in the elevator at the Cité stop. When we come out, the other passengers have already broken that contact and it's over her shoulder that against the starry sky I see the arrow-shaped tower of Sainte-Chapelle. Dozens of people follow us quickly through the flower stands; there's going to be a concert at Notre-Dame. The night, after the rain, reminds me of polished bricks and transparent bottles.

"I'm glad to see you back."

Quai de la Corse, an acid and obtrusive smell of urine. Quai aux

Fleurs, parked cars, the construction towers on the other side of the Seine. We approach the cathedral, illuminated in such a way that it looks light, on the point of rising up by itself and floating. Scattered drops of rain fall around us.

We sit down, facing each other, under the green awning of the café. All the lights are on in the square. Vehicles pass almost incessantly and I can't always hear Roos's voice, which orients the conversation in a direction that is at the same time neuter and personal. Many birds in Brazil? Have I read Goethe's *Werther?* What do I think of the final scene between the hero and his beloved? What am I looking for in the world? Stone walls in her face, unrecognizable, bathed in the sun; wind in the plane trees; two hyenas sitting in the middle of a bridge, their heads between the iron pillars, looking at the river. I grasp her hands. They slip between mine, which I flatten, tense, on the red tablecloth. The statue of Charlemagne, under the strong lights of the square, seems clad in an armor of steel and clarity.

"Do you know Lausanne?"

"No, Roos. Why?"

"No reason."

The noisy parade of vehicles ceases for an instant, out of Notre-Dame flows the beginning of some Triumphal March or other, the calluses of the organ-builders slide through the tubes. Do I recognize the woman across from me? That must have been how the re-encounter with my brother August was. Today, after three years of absence, three, he ponders the nineteen of our living together as if remembering the taste of a fruit whose name he can't remember.

Oh, those twisting streets, those walls of sacred or profane buildings, those canals, those walls, all that varied architecture included in Roos's body—and so luckily that I'm not surprised on seeing, in the pure and symmetrical face, lights that come from within, yes, from the sum of her flesh (not from the outside world) and which come, for example, from the reflection of the Sun on the waters of Venice! The hundred voices of the chorus descend from the arches over the Rue du Cloître de Notre-Dame, punctured by the uproar of the vehicles. They seem, even so, to envelop the yellow chairs of the café in a patina of dream, its conical lamps, the lights on the square, Charlemagne among the trees with his damp armor, and from the other side of the river the profile of the old buildings. One more time I try to talk about Chambord and also about Palladio's deception, just as the connections I see between all of that and the minerals she talks to me about in Amsterdam. What I'm trying to say is that in Iceland spar a phenomenon can glow that is real and illusory at the same time: the image opens, is duplicated, it's one and two. But there are also living beings on Earth who unite or multiply. Sometimes, and what is most admirable, not a single being, but two or three or more that a quirk of chance reunites, transforming into four the double stairs built between four vestibules of a castle in one of the valleys of the world. I want to ask if she doesn't find it fantastic to know that there are minds with a power that is selective, multiplying, unifying, and also conservative. She tries patiently to help me translate my thought, I get confused, however, and only manage to say—but without any connection to the rest—that phenomena so fleeting and silent that they can't be classified or even noted wander about in the universe.

"The world, Roos, is full of reflections and concentrations."

"At first sight you seem calm. But you're upset and upsetting."

The bell tolls twice and then a third time, sharply. Nine-thirty? Ten-thirty? How long have I been here facing Anneliese Roos?

Her eyes slip over me and suddenly stare at me, rapid: "I'm going to Lausanne on Thursday. To visit a relative. I'm taking the afternoon train. Why don't you come with me?"

Her hands in mine, restful, cool on the back, warm on the palms, with innumerable cities appearing, and reptiles, insects, birds, fishes, and quadrupeds inhabiting the houses, the rivers, and the walks.

"What can I expect?"

"Actually, nothing. Then we'll be so far away from one another!"

The cities: ten, twenty, silent lightning flashes, some with the living rooms lighted and others with the windows glimmering in the sun. Their designs cross, labyrinths imprisoned in other labyrinths. A confused sound rises up, I don't know where, the sound that comes from a large lighted stove when the top is opened. It mingles with the voices of the chorus and with the orchestra, once more conquering the less and less intense trembling of the vehicles. I know what they're singing now: the Psalm "In Convertendo Dominus," by Campra. Is there really harvesting in the midst of songs when we sow the seeds amidst weeping? Notre-Dame, a resonant vessel among the brutal noises of the night.

T

Cecília Among the Lions   7

The business area of the second floor of the branch of the Bank is smaller than that on the first floor: the central part of the floor opens up into a rectangle whose vertices rest on marble columns; a railing surrounds that opening. My desk, on the upper floor, touches the rectangle on the side opposite the main entrance. Through the openings in the white-painted railing, I can see a part of the street, the imposing door of forged steel, the movement of the people, and the lines by the tellers' windows. Callus Face, the ragged and impassive coffee man, appears with his tray and his rheumatic walk. A boy? An old man? He avers that he has taken a turn through mirrors, reflections, and repetitions, coming back together, old, in the same body and at the same age as in the instant he leaves: "I am the One and Only." The domestic sound of the coffee cups cuts through the shouts of the tellers and the customers, the tinkle of telephones, the pounding of typewriters, the call of buzzers, the thump of rubber stamps.

I go down the steps—marble and worn. Callus Face fills my cup. A broad head with tiny monkey eyes. I invite him: "Leave that tray there. Let's go up and catch pigeons." He resists, tempted and doubtful: "I have to wash the cups. If I was in the Ascendant today. But out of the house and in the Descendant? I could be fired. No. Not today. Orders from my Legislator." Suddenly, near the counter, I seem to see Cecília, present for eleven days—a deafness, a dormancy—in me. I go over. None of the faces gathered there reminds me of hers.

The Treasurer visits me at the boardinghouse. I give him the only chair in my room and I sit on the bed. It's hard to recognize in this man under the light bulb—large and frightened, always coughing—the same rough figure with an authoritative voice and sweeping gestures who decides to take my mother out of the red-light district, along with three fatherless children—(I among them), marries her, and registers them as his, never admitting any difference between the adopted ones and those of his own blood, engendered without respite in that womb which even the wind and the shadows made pregnant. He shows me clippings, taken from the *Official Bulletin*, relating to the complicated lawsuit in which he's involved. He falls into contradictions and his arguments aren't convincing. He interrupts the justifications to say that the paper lampshade smells burnt: it could start a fire and there were enough fires going in the cane fields. Tomorrow, Saturday, am I coming to Olinda? He chides me for not locking the door to my room. With the disorder the State is in, gangsters disguised as workers sacking sugar mills and invading cities with sickles in their hands! Thieves don't sleep, Abel, no precaution is too much. What will become of the country if João Goulart holds his plebiscite and restores the presidential system? Seeing the books on the shelves and the manuscript spread out on the table, he warns me. It would be prudent to hide from my bosses my interest in activities that clash with the banking life. Falling silent, he goes back to looking at the clippings. From the ground floor the voices of the other boarders playing cards rise up. He dozes in the chair, his chin on his chest. The long cut of the mouth and the square jaw, which in good times accentuate the energy of the face, aggravate his look of an old man.

The bus goes along slowly because of the storm. Through the damp and foggy window I can barely make out the houses and the trees. On my left, in the other row of seats, with a raincoat, a red umbrella dripping water, and a book sprinkled with rain, Cecília is riding. The book has the face of a black man on the cover, severe and stony, lighted from above by a green light, the author is Antônio Callado. The afternoon light, diluted in the clouds, in the rain, reflected on the puddles and the nickel-plated trim of the bus, makes Cecília's skin more tenuous in my eyes. Her profile, which the reflections always make changeable, is projected against the glass of the window and shines like an ancient medal in the shadows. Cecília. Otherwise, on the street—roofs and doorways, other buses, lights, walls, human forms—everything flows, the imprecise disconnected parts of an ephemeral and remembered world, over which, alien to the passage of time, her figure reigns, subtle and tempered by a kind of audacity. By the Archbishop's Palace she gets up, looks at me in her intense and rapid way, pulls the cord, the bus stops, the door opens. When, holding the metal pole, as she is about to get off, she turns again toward me, now seeming to have recognized me. Simultaneously, as if a thick liquid had covered my eyes, or maybe as if I had unknowingly made myself cross-eyed, I see two Cecílias, and one emerges slightly from the other. Cecília caught by a tremulous camera lens. Here, however, all comparison is incorrect: the other people and the inside of the bus remain clear; and the two faces of Cecília, identical, are not looking in exactly the same direction. The bus starts up. Through the window I make out her shape beside the steps of the State Museum, thin and one again, under the bright-colored umbrella. I get off at the next stop and come back looking for her. I don't find her.

Sunday afternoon at the house of Hermenilda and Hermelinda, both in white dresses. On the porch hammock I go through the photograph album and I listen distractedly to the stories they tell me. The simple fact that the faces, clothes, expressions of the turn of the century stay in the pages of the album now that the models are already old or dead and, in some way, nothing more exists, if it had existed, of those hours whose substance the universe of the camera tries to assimilate accentuates the boundaries—not always comprehensible, not always perceptible—between those two spaces: one, unlimited, continuous, fleeting; the other, restricted, unchangeable. The circumstance that I don't recognize any of the constant figures in the album (what connects Cecília to these models?) isolates the portraits even more from injunctions alien to their specific reality. An autonomous gallery of figures of whom the substance is not in the blood, in the gestures, in the palm trees, in the stones, in the looks, in none of the improper tricks with which they aspired to live on the paper—and yes in the light, in the shadow, in the chiaroscuro. The birds sing, without continuity. Cecília doesn't appear and none of us mentions her name. It is impossible to say from where I get this certainty that we're all waiting for her.

We walk along the Rua Direita and the Rua das Calçadas before dawn, Callus Face and I, throwing stones at dogs. "August has begun, Callus Face. The month of mad dogs!" We try to kill rats by kicking them as they run from one hole to another, frightened, along the curb. A woman half-drunk, coming from the edge of the market square, decides to accompany us, hooting when we fail in our attempts at rat-hunting. Somebody opens a second-story window and throws empty bottles at us. The woman and I run, she slips and falls, hurting herself on the stones. I help her up. We end up embracing, she weeping loudly and I consoling her. Callus Face accompanies us at a distance, his legs stumbling. He runs up: "I'm leaving." The light of the lamp-post falling on his graying hair. The woman: "Who's that?" I explain: "He's an old man. He's a boy. The One and Only."

Sleep suddenly conquers me. It ties up my ankles and makes my eyelids heavy. Thoughts slowly roll around. We climb up the dark stairs of a town house. Over the wide bed a large green crêpe-paper lampshade. I go sit in a wicker chair. I am bent over, my hands on the arms of the chair, when everything goes black. I feel a pain in my leg, my shoulder asleep, and inside the room I hear a noise of ironware rolling over paving stones. The pain, the sleepiness, the paving stones, the ironware—do they exist? In the darkness the lamp with the paper shade is still on. Its light, however, illuminates nothing.

O

The Story of ʘ, Twice-Born 15

Many days in bed, between asleep and awake, in silence. Without even the spirit to open my eyes, although with a new and passing feeling lying in wait at some point in my being (or is this feeling my total being that has become sharpened?), I perceive the slow and solemn movements of the world, the mounting of the machine. Could that immense apparatus which is shortly to be organized in space have another name? I remain attentive to the habitual sounds of the apartment, to those coming from other points in the building and those coming from the street. But my mother's soft steps, the squeaking of the unoiled elevator grating, the cement mixers and the mechanical saws of the building under construction, automobile horns, vendors' cries, a scissor-sharpener seem to be disguises to me, a curtain of small illusory events to hide the real one, the one that calls for my respect and is related to my fate—the formation of the machine. The great pieces are rising up (who knows where they come from?) and being adjusted, organized, the rusty plates of a ship with the keel turned toward me. The whole machine is being set up to function from the point where I am. Is it like a ship? Perhaps it evokes, in an even closer way, a large fleet, not anchored on the sea but in the air, the ships disposed in a conical formation and in such a way that I am the vertex of the cone. The advance of time is marked by the clear striking of the bells that irradiates from the Monastery of São Bento. Night and day, in an elaboration that seems endless, the gigantic machine or fleet is being shaped, it is taking on form, growing, and its parts creak if the wind lifts it. It seems to be finished, ready for its mission, I don't know what that is. When I least expect it, one unit or another is dislocated, the parts from which it separates go on to fill the empty space, while the dislocated units reappear beyond or return to their unknown origins.

It is three or four o'clock in the morning when it is finally completed. No sounds are heard in the building or in the city. Only, at more or less long intervals, the squealing of a streetcar on the tracks, perhaps rolling along empty. Even the women who early in the dawn wash the grimy pavement of the cafés located between the Praça da Sé and the Post Office have certainly all left for their homes on the outskirts. The eleven elevators of the building have stopped: two on the ground floor, one on the eighth floor, another on the seventeenth, still another on the top floor, and the rest who knows where. Some must be out of order, there are always some in need of repair. The clock of São Bento strikes the half hour, three unequal tolls, which are repeated. Half past what? I wait. Lying on my back, my arms extended alongside my body, the fingers clutching the sheet, my legs elongated, together—and I wait. The machine, ethereal but real, its intangible scaffolding invaded in part by the concrete structure of the Martinelli Building, the machine, crossed through by bats and so tall that the last pieces are engulfed by the black clouds, by the clouds of that starless night, the machine moves and alights delicately upon me. It spins and hums, it is like a top in motion, it spins, a slow spin, it hums and the sound it produces is almost inaudible. I have no difficulty in understanding that its slow formation is purely symbolic, that nothing would prevent it from forming more rapidly and that even the phenomenon of the formation of the machine might be dispensable, since, in truth, its existence precedes the consciousness that I have of its presence and its own fabrication. The machine spins softly on me, its tip resting on my stomach. Its spin takes in the *fasti* of the world, the resonance of the *fasti* of the world, it grinds things and events in its wheels, pours them onto me. In the darkness, in the silence, with no one to help me bear that moment in which, under the vertex of the machine, I support its weight, not a physical weight, let it be understood, but a weight that is born of its grandeur and its austerity, a change of periods is being processed in me, a consecration. I am, at that moment, from that moment on, the terrible gorge of things, the point or the being where converge, with their multiple facets, what man knows, what things he thinks he knows, what he suspects, what he imagines, and what he does not even think exists.

A few stay-outs—coming from where?—stop, conversing in loud voices by the Praça Antônio Prado, one plays a clarinet, plays a waltz, the performance has something of the dragging monologue of a drunkard about it. I can still hear the clarinet from far off when a group of confused voices rises up, innumerable shouts lost on some distant side street. Who is shouting at that hour of the night? It's the voices of children, a band of children in revolt is crossing the city, waking it up. I think about joining them, protesting against my parents, against this world of poorly lighted corridors and marble doorways. But the tip of the machine, this machine which is like a whole fleet, with lights out, hanging in the air and maneuvering slowly, in a circle, in the same direction, nails me to the spot where I am. The childish voices do not get closer or farther away. A few men's voices come to mingle with the clamor of the children. I can distinguish single words clearly and suddenly, as close as if they had been spoken in my room. Then I feel myself flooded, peopled with voices, voices in my blood, my ribs, my jaws, my hair, my eyes, my nails, many voices. Shouts and words swimming or flying in me, I am invaded by a multitude of voices, I am broken up into voices. As if I were a piece of sculpture of fine sand and each grain a voice, a word and its damnations.

Orff's music, through the voice of the old people, warns that nothing lasts indefinitely. As if time were important at this moment. The hippopotamuses of eternity breathe on me with their burning breath. Where are my breasts? Where is my neck? Arm. Back? Torso . . . These words—and others—slide, begin to slip out of the parts of my body named by them. I no longer think about my arm as being an arm, but as feet or mouth; the mouth is called navel or ankle; the sex is called eyes, then breast, then shoulder. Between my mind and my dismembered body a small arbitrary lexicon fluctuates. It surprises me that those designations haven't completely lost their ties to the parts of the body with which they are associated by norms: that the word "mouth," meaning "arm," surprises me, keeping an aura of what it ordinarily expresses, so that I don't know, on thinking of the arm as mouth, what changes there really were, what transmigrations, if it was only the name "mouth" that was dislocated for my arm with its sheaf of suggestions (voices, palate, gums) or if really the mouth, the mouth, not just its name, had violated all limitations and installed itself, avid, speaking, in the space occupied by my arms. Whether I am not embracing Abel's trunk with my mouth, or with my feet.

Oh, my love (will he hear me if, for example, it's my temples that speak?), bite my teeth, nails, pupils, bite my shoulder, thighs, put the real name onto every place. The names, however, continue to be dislocated. Do his hands slip over my eyelashes, the wings of my anus, my elbow, my spinal column? Does his mouth run over me, kissing the hollow of my knee, the roof of my mouth, my chin, my kneecaps, my anklebones, my hipbones? The hippopotamuses breathe on us. Rhythmically, Abel sucks the points on my waist, his hands stroke my waist, he sucks my finger bones, sucks my fists, his breathing burns me, I close my flanks, I open my eyebrows, his strong tongue penetrates the back of my neck, I give a muted cry, a shout: "Come." Everything darkens.

My parents are arguing. The offenses they offer each other are harsher and harsher. He lifts the trumpet to his mouth and with effort brings insulting expressions out of his esophagus. Without changing the tone of her voice, the look on her face, without growing pale, she hurls back the injuries received, while she tries to button a black dress that fits her body poorly. The seams split. A smell of camphor mixed with the perfume on which she seems to have squandered half of the money obtained in the manufacture of the hats. When she looks at the man, it is as if she didn't see him, or as if she saw him from a great distance, a cold and annihilating look. She dresses me in black too, and combs my hair, without interrupting her insulting litany.

O

The Story of Ø, Twice-Born   16

The brown fur stole, kept in a cylindrical box and protected by innumerable sheets of tissue paper, smells more of camphor than the black dress. Its fur reminds one of that of an old dusty dog. She puts it over her shoulders and places a new hat on her head, also black and with a veil. From the wall hangs the mirror, looking like another empty frame among the portraits of impresarios, prima donnas, musicians; it isn't large and it has a slight tilt, so that adults, in order to examine themselves from head to toe, have to advance and retreat in front of it. My father is in the bathroom, I hear him flush the toilet. The woman, coming and going, studies the hat, the makeup, and the light brown stole. I find her like the building, with its walls marked by pencils, its elevators stalled, and the smells wandering about the corridors like sick animals. I'm next to the piano, proud of my black dress and having my hair fixed up. She turns and commands me: "Come." My father comes into the room still buttoning his pants; he puts the trumpet into his mouth and gives a cackle. A spin by the woman, so quick that the wing of her stole hits my face:

"Don't do that again."

She seems to have leaped from within herself. He retreats before the aggressive and unexpected movement, hesitates a second, and points the horn trumpet at us:

"Why shouldn't I?"

"When you're asleep, I'll cut off your other ear. That's all."

The contrast between the rosy skin and the clumsy rubber artifact is greater. The man lets the horn fall to his chest. She takes me by the hand sternly, slams the door, and takes me to church. She leads me in a calculated way, she exhibits me, the way a beggar exhibits his rheumy eyes. With the aim of getting pity. This is her plan. But plans continue on beyond what is foreseen, they continue on beyond what is foreseen, everything foreseen, and they bite their tail. When, in the apartment, she stops me from falling so that I won't die, I fall in the shaft of the broken elevator and I am born; when by leaving the keys in the doors she sets traps so that I will explode once and for all, I catch that intention and kill her in me, I kill the father and mother in me, those two emissaries; now, when she tries to raise me up to the level of which she was deprived through marriage, thus incarnating my words or simply those emitted by me (and which do not evoke—rather, anticipate, if they do anticipate—her calculated steps), she begins to hurl me in the direction of the yolyp and the .38 caliber bullet that I lodge in my chest. That moment, however, is grave, much graver than she can suppose: part of my leap into this world will hang on it, as a pocket watch, caught in the current, hangs from a nail in the wall.

The church is full and this hinders the plan. Nevertheless, only the right side door, which is perhaps no more than three feet wide, is open; the main door is closed so that the wind will not blow out the hundreds of candles set up side by side on long tilting tables. Why not stay next to the narrow side door or on the steps of the stairway that leads to it? She will be seen by all coming in or going out. My mother, as soon as the mass is over, sneaks out and stations herself in that spot, waiting. She wants the desired encounter to look casual. But if the church has only one exit, those provided by the instant are innumerable. So I escape and go back into the church. Not to see the angels with trumpets over the main altar, the churches painted on the walls of the vestibule, or the round somber-colored stained-glass windows placed high up in the dormers, a little below the ceiling, with paintings standing out from the exterior light. I am attracted, rather, by the fire and the animals that are there inside. The fire of the candles, the oil, the incense. The dove that flies from one window to another, the baby mullet that moves and swims in the baptismal font, the ram that bleats between people's legs, the bull that lows somewhere and that I hope to find, the eagle whose impious head rises up in the pulpit for an instant, fixing me with his rude eye where the reflection of the flames gleams, the invisible lion who is lying under some pew and of whom I catch the strong smell, a smell similar to the one there is in the Martinelli Building. My intention is to see the flames close up, and to look for those creatures, and also the child ornate with wings, with a senile face, posted beside the candles. But I forget everything: a woman is in front of me. I see her during mass, weeping in silence, she's a woman of some years, but her legs are still well turned. My mother's legs. She's in mourning, beside a man in mourning, older than she. The man looks at the priest, limiting himself to passing a handkerchief over his face at long intervals. Sparse white hair. His hand is strong and inspires confidence. The woman settles on one foot, on the other, puts her missal on the pew and picks it up again, blows her nose, opens and closes her purse. She can't find the right position for her veil: she pulls it forward and then drops it over the back of her neck, uncovering herself. I see her from the rear. Now I have her in front of me, I see her from the front and I forget about the dove, the lowing of the bull, the flames, the smell of the lion: a tiny gold scorpion is floating in her left eye. I follow her in fascination. My mother, looking for me, comes into the church and we meet each other, the four of us meet, I, she, the woman with the little scorpion in her eye, and the man with white hair, we all meet beside the hundreds of candles. Starting to weep, but without conviction, my mother goes toward the woman, who makes a movement of drawing back and looks at her. Up and down, with her injected eyes. The look turns a bit in that rapid lowering and raising of eyelids, the look takes me in. Embracing, my mother with energy, she in a cold and complacent way. My mother embraces the old man. He returns it with indulgence and says a word to her, yes, he talks to her, looks in her face, only the face, and there is no disguised examination in that look where I read resignation, frankness, and a little foolishness, a little. He turns to me and extends his hand. Shall I kiss it? It's a roll of the dice (odds or evens?), everything depends on alternatives and yet the definition is predicted, I foresee, I describe the option and its consequences during the hours I speak and speak without stopping. Foresight? Or isn't there foresight? Who knows if foresight coexists with revealed facts, reflecting them, yes, reflecting them through conduits that are mysterious to us? Foresight, narratives contemplated in the mirror, narratives, on the contrary, told in the future. It might be that everything exists simultaneously and that we don't have a correct or true idea of time, and do have one that preserves our integrity. We have to believe that we are a point, not a straight or wavy line; we learn things, not the sum of their dislocations. Be that as it may, what I mutter, on the exhaustive days when I narrate my own story, apparently in way of anticipation, and in a way comprehensible at times—it isn't that I bite the hand held out to me, the hand of that stranger, and I do kiss it. The hand, in the light of the countless candles, seems transparent. Can I bite it? By biting it would my fate be different? I lean my head over. I kiss it. At another point, in another time, I am narrating this gesture of mine. At another point, in another time.

Besides the old couple there are four or five young people, also in mourning. My mother, still holding me by the hand, slips away between them and the couple, she slips away and receives condolences. She seems happy. Then only the couple and the young people remain, all with an indecisive look. A little to the side, she and I. The young people also take leave of the couple and go away. No one turns toward my mother, they all pretend not to see her. A car drives up. The woman, not weeping now, lightly touches the stole that reminds one of a dusty dog and that my mother keeps over her shoulders; she throws again in my direction that look which is almost imperceptible and not, however, any less analytical; she gets into the automobile with effort. The man also turns to my mother and is going to speak to her; from within the automobile, the authoritarian voice of his wife tells him to hurry up. I raise my hand, I smile and wave goodbye to him. The automobile departs.

The sun comes out. My mother takes off the stole; I am startled by the coldness that her eyes have just taken on, a short while before they were remorseful, supplicant, and loving. It's the first time that I see her in the crude light of day and what most surprises me is the skin of her face: white, transparent, and as if chilling, giving the impression of falling apart. It doesn't seem impossible to me that in order to powder herself, all she has to do is rub pumice or sandpaper across her face, powdering it with her own crumbled skin. Her skin then unmade into powder, under the attrition of the pumice, the sandpaper. It's the first time, too, that she sees me in the sunlight, and therefore perhaps she looks at me with displeasure and such deep rage, the expression we use when we look at a tool with which we try in vain to loosen a screw, pull out a nail, or knock down a door. But the screw, without her knowing it, is already loose, the nail pulled out, the door knocked down.

T

Cecília Among the Lions

8

My sister Lucíola, with her profile and her gypsy eyes, to Mauro, our brother: "Why didn't you bring your wife? She could have helped wash the dishes."

Cesarino shows his rotting teeth and raises his waxen face, with purple rings under his eyes that make his cadaverous look even more neuter: "Damião, I'm surprised. What's your boss, the owner of the taxi, going to say? You, such a hard worker, quitting work more than two hours early to have dinner with the mother who isn't even yours?"

My mother scolds Cesarino. The cat on her chest turns its monkey head toward him.

Dagoberto's clear eyes, the eyes of a man destined to die tubercular (can they be contemplating with terror the lack of sense in our lives?), also turn to Cesarino: "Deolinda Rusty-Iron complained about you. She gave you money for a bus ticket and you never showed up again. Is that any way to act?"

"She's a slut, that one," Cesarino answers.

Mauro, who had let Lucíola's spiteful comment pass, speaks to her: "I can't accept one thing. It's your first husband, the counterfeit counterfeiter, running off with that chippy, leaving his clothes on the riverbank to make it look like he drowned—and then coming down to a spiritualist session."

Lucíola, her eyes lowered, pretends she doesn't hear and ignores the laughter. She's the one who is least far off today among the faces grouped around the table—faces on which the years have done double duty, with a double power of erosion—closer to her own model during the phase of splendor and the absence of worries. Even the face of Isabel, even hers, bent over the piano and half hidden behind the golden hair, suggesting intelligence and mystery at the age of thirteen, now reflects in her way the thick and obtuse face of her husband—twenty-one years older than she, retired, amateur smuggler, ex-stoker on a merchant ship—who eats by pushing the food onto his fork with his fingers.

Here we are, obeying a persistent and useless habit, celebrating our mother's birthday. How does this dinner, still full of laughter but impregnated with melancholy, recall the noisy celebrations before 1950? All the lights in the villa are on and the Treasurer presides over the table. He coughs, however, now and again, and talks whenever he can about his new job: collecting for a business with a reputation more dubious than his own.

"I want to see what my enemies are going to say when they find out that I'm working with money and that the bosses have complete confidence in me. A blind confidence. I collect more than fifty loans a day. Honesty is worth a fortune, especially today when the government lives by encouraging robbery."

My mother, on his right, tries to change the subject, she talks about the death of Marilyn Monroe:

"What got into that girl? A woman who had everything."

"She was a slut," Cesarino throws out. "A slut just like all the others."

The Treasurer coughs and reinforces what he was saying, alien to it all: "They trust me like a son."

Which of the sons trust him? They barely look at him and of them all, carnal or not, only I—in spite of everything—listen to what he's saying. The rest—Mauro, Cesarino, Lucíola, Damião, Dagoberto, and Isabel with her husband—only raise their hands to serve themselves some omelet or beer and exchange not-very-friendly words.

"Would you pass the sauce?" (It's Isabel's husband, gathering the rice onto his fork avidly with his thumb.)

The platters don't hold, as in the time of the Treasurership, kids and suckling pigs from the spit, shining with grease and amply garnished; or great red lobsters swimming in coconut sauce; or slices of marinated mackerel; or dorados with delicious stuffing. The fine wines are lacking; the imported cheeses, round, red, so fragrant; the cherry liqueur made by the nuns of Santa Dorotéia; the five or six kinds of sweets. The English china is no longer matched and the white damask tablecloth is beginning to fray.

Cesarino, who drinks without stopping, asks Damião what his next great role in the theater is going to be—carrying on a letter, or a glass of water.

"It's better to bring a glass of water to a countess on stage than to run errands for those cheap whores on the Rua do Apolo like you."

Cesarino defends himself impudently: "They're my friends."

Eurílio and Estêvão dead; Leonor in a convent in Bahia, after three broken engagements; Cenira living on the outskirts of Rio de Janeiro, married before the age of eighteen to a dentist without patients, having a rough time of it (her violin becoming unglued, without strings, in some drawer in the villa); Augusto swallowed up by the world for eight years, with no news and no way of knowing whether or not he's still alive; Janira running from the police in some fifth-class cabaret after doing what she did. Mute, along with Cenira's violin, Leonor's mandolin, Damião's clarinet, Mauro's guitar, Eurílio's flute, the *East Coker* piano. On the porch or in other parts of the house, lighted up today, not a shadow of the friends—so many—of the Treasurer; of the boys and girls, our companions, who invaded the house in those days, not a one. We, no one else, taking part in this show of a party and exhibiting a joy that is only a malignant version of the other.

Mauro turns his thick and almost black glasses to me: "What about our man of letters? Still unpublished, *mon amour?* Do you ever get back to Europe to see French girls?" His spasmodic and mordant laugh slices up the words.

Cesarino accompanies him in the questions, showing his rotting incisors: "Why don't you write a soap opera about your wife for the radio, Abel? I hear they pay well."

Eurílio's flute makes itself heard, from the grave or from the whorehouse where he dies riddled with bullets.

"Just yesterday the boss talked to me. He said he never had a collector like me."

Coming from who knows where, upon the table falls the nasal

voice of our brother Augusto, disappeared eight years ago: "Can you give me any news about Janira?" Leonor, from the cloister, erect in a high-backed chair: "One month after marriage she ended up in the red-light district, Augusto. God protect her. Killing her own children! Two of them!" The voice of Janira, soft and monotonous, that of a virtuous family girl: "They died before they had a name. Is that dying? After all, they were mine. If I could, I'd kill Father and Mother. I didn't ask to be born."

"Does your wife know how to read yet?" (Isabel to Mauro.) "The rumor is that you write anonymous letters to yourself, saying that she's putting horns on you. To have an excuse to get rid of her."

Mauro laughs, nodding. Laughter echoes at the table.

"All they have to do is count the money when I turn in my collections. They send a boy to check."

"How much do you make?" Lucíola's husband asks.

My mother asks if he's still retired.

"Of course."

"I thought you'd got a job as customs inspector."

With his tenor voice, a withered gift, Dagoberto sings: "Late at night, laughing sky. / It's all a dream here by and by . . ." Those brothers and sisters. Also the others, the ones wandering through the world or who die disastrously, the sister who bears children and buries them in the yard—are they my brothers only through blood? Doesn't some common project link us in our failures? Perhaps they're marked by the same obscure impulse that moves me. With other shapes, however. Other names. "Only you sleep: you don't hear / your singer . . ."

"I'm going into the kitchen to get my dessert," Damião advises. "I've got to go to work. After all, my boss trusts me. I've got to return that trust."

"At what time did you suck his nuts?"

"At the same time, Cesarino, that you suck the asses of those sluts."

"Happy you, if when you get married your wife has an ass as clean as theirs."

The animal, on my mother's shoulder, stretches its cat's back and leaps onto the table, its tail erect.

She scolds us: "Fine brothers and sisters you are. I don't see anyone remembering the ones who are dead or not here."

"They can go to hell."

Isabel: "Why, Damião?"

"Just because, they can go to hell."
"It's a company that's still going to grow a lot."

A

Roos and the Cities   15

From the telephone booth I watch the people sitting in the cafés or standing in front of the stands—for chestnuts, sandwiches, newspapers, target practice—that clutter the sidewalks of the Boulevard Saint-Michel. Young couples laugh at the shopwindows or go along arms around each other under the trees. Khrushchev's proposal approved in the U.S.S.R., René Coty at the Vatican. British ships pass through Suez. Guy Mollet and Algeria, Eisenhower, Middle East. What do I care about all that? Everything is set for the trip to Switzerland with Anneliese Roos and if I'm calling her it's to put off my impatience. But it's hard for me to recognize the voice that answers and the first phrases seem twisted, broken, emitted backward, what it tells me is so unexpected. I hang up, I pick it up again and now the words are clear, toothy, they cut me, she prefers that I not go, yes, personal problems—could I hold off?—yes, that, she'll explain later, later, when she gets back, don't think badly of her, hurriedly, or with rancor.

I leave the booth, I fly down the dirty Métro stairs, I start wandering from one station to another with no object, looking at the brick domes, advertisements, subway workers, tramps on the waiting benches, beggars posted in the long corridors of the connecting stations. Sudden winds hit my face, oily winds. Coming from where? I finally get out at Nôtre-Dame des Champs, pick up my baggage, head for the Gare de Lyon. Roos, in the huge waiting room, heads slowly toward the platforms. Should I go up to her? The series of paintings over the ticket windows, almost all referring to cities in the South: Nîmes, Montpellier, Toulon, Monte Carlo, Nice, Menton. So? The time of the question is the time of losing her among the hundreds of strangers. Now, having bought a first-class ticket, I get into a second-class coach and stand watching the platform from the corridor until the doors close and, except for the windows, everything starts to move.

I watch the minutes pass by as if time were a landscape, those cultivated fields that remain behind with sunflowers, poppies, sheaves of hay. What trip is this? Where am I going for certain and with what end? The seconds grind me, roll in me like stones, for every moment shelters the possibility that Roos will come and talk to me. The spiral stairs. Roos with her hand held out toward the bird. I clap my hands so that he'll fly away, so that I won't get entwined in the snare. Snare? Now it's the inverse that forbids me from going to see her, looking for her. I'm fearful of holding her hands and so losing her.

The landscape turns pale: the lights in the coach go on. (The trains, when they leave Recife, go through the black swamps. Men and women, the stinking mud up to their knees, hunt crabs and shellfish.) I know, I always knew that Roos hasn't been offered to me, nor does she offer herself—and also that I proposed to myself to reach her, break the barriers, eliminate the distances. I see myself, however, facing myself, indecisive, hesitant, afraid of breaking the glasses, the mirrors, the windowpanes, the pencil points. (The mangrove swamps are covered with huts, and children with shiny bellies wave. The mud smells of carrion and is always full of vultures.) How much is there still left of the trip? A third, a quarter? So we wait in our youth for years for some event we don't know too well, which can come out of a meeting, a letter, which never comes and the impossibility of which we only recognize when we discover we have fled the time that's right for its coming, that now we fear because it would be despairing to come after its time, to come when it can no longer give us pleasure.

I open the compartment doors from car to car. Anneliese Roos is standing in the corridor, maybe so that I can find her more easily, her hands raised and resting on the window, looking vaguely out at the dark cultivated fields, invisible now. I put my hands on hers; the fact that she doesn't move tells me that she was waiting, yes, waiting. Since when and how many times can she have opened the door, coming into the corridor?

"You promised not to look for me."

Her voice mixes with the sound of the pistons and the wheels on the tracks, it seems to slide along those hard sounds, slide along like an oil, softening them.

"I couldn't help it, Roos."

Our faces are close and I see in the glass, spectrally, my reflection and hers, joined by the hands.

"You promised. You shouldn't have looked for me."

"What happened? Why shouldn't I have come?"

Her hands slide down the glass, she turns and stares at me. Cities of dusk, unknown and, as always, deserted. From one corner to the next, however, from one building to the next, from skylights to the ground, from basements to roofs, as if in every part there were threads standing erect, a tension resounds. A sound, a buzzing.

"I have problems."

"What kind of problems? Speak!"

"I'd rather not speak. Besides, I hate questions."

Can she really have uttered that second sentence? Can it be that I hear before the proper time, scanned by a woman I still don't know and who doesn't know me? It's equally possible that I distilled it myself in my shadows, in order to stop myself from repeating it beside Roos and to keep the enigma intact, rich in its virtualities, so that it doesn't matter what the revelation is. In any case, Roos's obstinate silence, detestable as it may be, certainly relates to what I am. I have the right to inquire (by the entrance to St. Eustace's, in Brussels, watching the last light of the afternoon in the nave of the church, which, instead of following the line of vision, veers to the left side as it approaches the main altar, almost hiding it, I enjoy the benefit until the intimate imbalance provoked by that architectural anomaly is blunted) whether Roos's rejection might not be a calculated, precise answer to the dispositions of my temperament, whether she's using it as a transparent veil.

"I'd be so grateful if you didn't insist." She takes my arm lightly. "Don't get off in Lausanne."

Do I manage to make her understand that, according to the reproductions, she looks like the model for "Madonna col Bambino," by Giovanni Bellini, which exists in Milan and is related, they say, to the altarpiece in Pesaro? I think, Roos, as if Bellini, as a kind of anticipation, had received the grace of seeing her. Does she understand that for years I have wanted to examine in the Brera Library the maps in the Geography given by Lorenzo de' Medici to his wife? That I'll do what she asks and will continue my trip if she promises to spend a day with me in Milan?

My voice drier and harsher, thick sand mixing in with the sound of the train.

"Why don't you continue on with me? Why don't you send caution to the devil? Roos, I counted on these five hours of travel to . . . It wasn't possible and I . . . have a minute or two to say what only in a little while . . . I don't see your body only, not in the ordinary meaning, I want to reach you, I love you, Roos, no, I don't know if it's that. Roos! Roos!"

Softly, she closes my mouth with her hands.

"Do you think I don't see? That I don't know? But all this is useless and has no future. And without a present. It's my husband who's in Lausanne."

"Sanatorium?"

The Pisan sun on the marble of the monuments and the old ocher or reddish façades on the banks of the Arno. In the center of the Baptistery, the echo of my shouts, three, four, echoing like a bronze bell. Her slow voice, the difficult word, the soft throat pierced with needles.

"Yes. Eight months ago."

"Do you have children?"

A city in a circle (Nordlingen?), another rectangular (Aigues-Mortes), others without a plan, all under the mist and the night. Wind.

"I'll continue my trip, Roos."

"And where can I find you, if . . . by chance . . . I go to Milan?"

"How many days are you staying in Lausanne?"

"Two. I'm returning the day after tomorrow at dusk."

"I'll be at the station. I'll wait for all the trains that come from Switzerland."

A

Roos and the Cities   16

We buy our tickets (I for Verona, she back to Paris) and we pause for a moment atop the immense stairs, absorbed as we watch the people on the steps coming and going. The sound of locomotives, the distant noise of a siren on the Piazza Duca d'Aosta, the sharp cries of birds in doorways, in the restaurant, in the underground passageways, in the information booth, in the lavatories, in the telephone booths. Petrels? We have only twenty-two minutes left, the air is cold and we're tired, we take refuge in the waiting room. Our Sunday excursion to the lakes: icy wind, rain, and rough waters. We go through the Borromeo Palace without any words, wet shoes, the temperature almost the same as it is outside. Ordinary paintings (the great Renaissance lords lent their prestige to the innovators of their time, not to imitators like these) and an absence of books, which don't merit the honor of horse-trappings, proudly exhibited (while the Ambrosian Library, active for three and a half centuries, was founded by a Borromeo, no less). The guide informs us that the family only lived in the palace two months out of the year. Roos, by the window, looks at the lawns and the flowers in the rain. A herd of peccaries runs slowly through my veins: they gnash their teeth. I close my eyes and listen to them parade by. They go away. From the glassed-in veranda that encircles the ocher-and-white building that is the hotel, forming a kind of winter garden ("Regina Palace, Orchestra, Spiaggia Privata, Equitazione, Sci Nautico"), I watch a sailboat struggling against the winds coming down from the mountains and curling the surface of Lake Maggiore. "I saw these lakes yesterday in Lorenzo de' Medici's Geography. It was there I got the idea of bringing you here if you came. It wasn't raining. It doesn't rain in Geographies." Her face, opposite the glass and the landscape, pale from the walk between the castle and the boat and from the crossing of those restless waves, recovers its usual color, absorbing the uncertain midday light: "I've seen some ancient maps too. They're so strange. They give the impression of those drawings of Asian or African fauna done by Europeans who've never been out of Europe and imagine an elephant along the lines of animals we know: dogs, horses, blackbirds." There's a pane of glass missing up above the waiting room, and some men with rather thin clothing are sitting on the benches along the walls, taking refuge, certainly, from the bad weather. Roos looks at her watch. "In general, I'd say I know quite well what I'm doing. But the truth is something else again. I know that I should be in Paris tomorrow. Do you know why I came to Milan? Why I'm here? No. And I don't know why I'm going away when I could stay. Nothing's stopping me." Waves beat against the windows of the launch. The frothy tips break against the companionways and wet the passengers. The moorings are cast off, the door is closed, the launch is taking us to Isola Bella. Three Australian girls, their governess, six Japanese, eight or nine matrons from Alabama (all in flowered hats), a German couple on their honeymoon, and three nuns from some convent in Campobasso. The wind whistles, the waves come, one after another, the vessel lurches, the timbers creak. One of the nuns, still quite young, coughs incessantly. Are we witnessing our own wake,

perhaps? Thirty corpses floating in the rain amidst the debris. Fog, life
rafts, searchlights, sirens, Roos breaking into fragments, a cosmos,
cities empty of human beings, coming from countless points on Earth
and plunging into the lake like the possessed Gadarene swine, but in
silence, and with a certain grandeur. The docking maneuvers go awry.
The vessel shakes from stem to stern, all wings and twisted flippers,
and the wooden hull keeps bumping the pier with a hollow sound.
Cautious and energetic movements moor it to the dock; the waves
continue to wash the windows. In the rain and wind, more intense
now, we cover the distance between the anchorage and the Borromeo
Palace, hugging the walls of the small shops. The icy wind hurts our
eyes. Snowy peaks of neat design in the dull afternoon light; country
houses huddled together on the verdant foothills of the nearest elevations, some climbing up the sides. Roos holds her cup at throat level.
While I talk, I can hear quite clearly the blood throbbing in her pulse!
"Designing an elephant based on what they know about blackbirds . . .
But maybe someone who only knew the elephant through those pictures could identify it when he came upon a real one. Which brings us
back to cartography. With those imperfect maps, navigators always
got to where they wanted to go. And when they got lost they knew
they were lost. That's something to think about. If a map is to be really
exact, it should have the dimensions of the country represented and
then it wouldn't be good for anything at all." The plants placed about
the tearoom slowly turn in Roos's direction, as if she were an open
window in that enclosure. The fragile voice of the nun can be heard:
"Io non vorrei morire senza aver visto il Varese." "Did you catch what she
said, Roos? That she didn't want to die . . ." "Yes." The panoramic
view of the lake: green, gray, blue, and violet, with its little boats that
look like beetles scratching on its banks. With that view before her,
the young nun will close her eyes. Even today, perhaps, or tomorrow.
Death can be seen in her face. But Lake Varese for her, never, neither
in dream nor in name. She located it on maps. I write on the napkin,
above the oval with a crown where one reads "HOTEL REGINA OLGA—
CERNOBBIO—COMO": "Je vous aime." Roos turns her face away, stubborn. Boats of different colors moored along the lakeshore, their bows
a bit high, some covered by tarpaulins. "There are so many ways of
loving and I could never be able to give you an idea of the way I love
you, a love that mingles the ungraspable and geometry." (Is the
strange instrument moving in my mouth?! Yes, lexicon and syntax
obey me docilely, and in association become a less scratchy and more

precise map.) "But, Roos, when I write that I love you I'm expressing the substance and the nature of what you kindle in me. Isn't that like a map? What I'm saying is something incomplete and faulty. But you reach port. You orient yourself with these words and reach the understanding of what I'm trying to say." "You could be lying." "In this case, it's a question of a tricky map. The map of an unreal continent, not an imperfect map." The flowers and the leaves lean more in the direction of her face and its strange symmetry. "A little while after you go on back to Paris, my train leaves for Verona. There's no better city in the world for me to tell you in the flesh what I could have told you with words. You've got a few minutes to decide. Why don't you come with me? Maybe once there you'll know why you went." She came to Milan and is by my side, the heat of her right thigh goes through the wool and softly warms my side. Even like this we're not close. Without that constant rain, yes, who knows, without that swift and tireless wind! Silence returns and I stare idly at the molding without glass at the top of the wall. Another boat, a larger one, docks at Isola Bella. Through the rain we can make out the formally dressed occupants and the tables set with flowers. We seek shelter under an awning shaken by the wind. Festive music bursts forth on the boat—xylophone, recorders, a cornet, tambourine, mandolins. A wedding feast certainly. Women in hats and stoles get off, gloved waiters protect them with green-and-white dotted umbrellas, the gentlemen leap along with their hands over their heads, a dog starts barking. Planks are laid in their path and, even so, the women's stockings get wet, their satin-covered shoes. The bride appears. There is an isolated shout, with no response: "Viva la sposata!" Damp palms clap. With her left hand she clutches the bouquet of camellias over her breast: with the other she holds the garland; the gauze veil, pleated and broad, flutters. Upon her appearance, the wind rises, blows more swiftly, breaks the veins of the blue umbrella with which they try to protect her, the veil, at the point of tearing, flutters, puffs up, blows to the right and the left of her shoulders, goes into her mouth, gets entangled in the remains of the umbrella, the pair of children dressed in red velvet who hold the long train make an effort to keep a grip on it, but the wind blows so hard into that lace-swollen sail that the girl hesitates, on the verge of flying. From the chapel where the procession is heading comes the sound of an organ. I turn around, Roos is two steps away from me, her face sprinkled with rain, and our glances cross with a strange force, I have the impression that she is seeing me for the first time, without fright, without passion, merely surprise. We are almost the only ones left under the awning, even the nuns have gone, she smiles, a desolate smile, looks at the restless waters again: "When I got married, it was raining too." What can I do, me, against that memory? I hold her close to me. She is shaken by two or three dry sighs, as if someone had hit her hard from behind. The wind and the growling waves of the lake mingle the sacred hymn with the profane music played on the boat.

T

Cecília Among the Lions 9

Damião and Cesarino have left, one behind the other. The rest remain, still around the table. On the porch, lucid, I take a deep breath of beach air. Of all the guests, I am perhaps the only one who doesn't leave the table a little drunk tonight. What presses on my stomach, making me worry about tossing up the dinner, isn't the drink, then, and it has no name. The lights of the beacon pass in the air. Oscillating in the night are the churches of Olinda, the Seminary, the convents, the Monastery of São Bento, they oscillate above the ground. Full moon. The tide is already rising, and at dawn the violent August riptide will knock some more houses down. That's why, in my mother, the simian cat is restless: I hear the back-and-forth of the rocker and the laughter. She is afflicted, I believe, by the silence the house lives in now, broken here and there by a dinner like the one today, by the former Treasurer's cough, and by the single notes drawn out of some poorly tuned instrument. At times her laugh gives me the impression that it hides madness and is obstinate in not seeing the fierce side of life. In spite of all, can I deny that I love her? It occurs to me to picture the people wounded by desire and solitude who enjoy the Fat Woman around 1929 when she is in the flower of her age, forgers, pimps, drunken sailors, thieves, vagrants, gigolos, smugglers, charlatans, murderers, police informers. I interrogate these impossible ghosts, created in my silence, searching in vain for precise antecedents. I see nothing in the shadows and no one answers me, only she—the Fat Woman.

She is my past. Is anything else necessary for me to love her? Yet: maybe her laughter doesn't exactly disguise madness and her decision to ignore what is destroying her. It might be an expression of rage and fear at the unintelligible essence of the world; and of joy at its appearances. It might be. In this, then, it is similar to my silence.

A woman (seen from a distance, her hair loose, the Moon hidden in the clouds, she looks young) is approaching the main door. Her haunches, not too heavy, fluctuate under her dress. I think she's indecisively looking for something in her purse—a key, perhaps, an address. Since the street is poorly lighted, I can't make out her movements. I go down the steps, I'll find out what she wants. I'm led, besides that, by vague projects: those haunches provoke me. Two steps separate us and not even then does she look at me.

"Where's the Treasurer?"

The question seems directed at someone walking along the sidewalk.

"He's inside. Some abortion problem?"

In her look there's a certain air of a cheated lover in search of reparations or help. That, however, doesn't justify my stupid question.

"If it was that simple, I wouldn't have come in person."

A collective, careless laugh rises up in the villa. A few piano notes sound. Everything like the sounds of other times. Something seems to be missing in the sounds, however, in the face of the strange woman, in her thin and vaguely perverse voice. I quickly step to the right. She's older than I suppose and the left side of her face doesn't exist. Ear, bones, eye, eyebrow: a hollow, a void. No manner of relationship between human diseases and the destruction of those tissues. What consumes the face in front of me is something more subtle and certainly more voracious, what is destroying it, turning it into an incurable sore, is nothingness.

Cecília in front of the Mother Church of Santo Antônio, her right hand outstretched (a casual and quick meeting), takes leave of me. A changing sky, between pale blue and faded purple. Remains of daytime clarity wrap the church in a golden light, the profane buildings, their windows, the asphalt of the Square, the signs, the sidewalks, the indistinct multitude, and our shapes. Headlights turned on prematurely are reflected on the paint of the vehicles. The urban tumult of this hour surrounds us. The iron doors of the shops roll down, the safes are slowly closed, the offices grow silent. The elevators reach the ground floor filled. The march of people on the street quickens and the vehicles slow down. We are surrounded, tense, by thousands of bodies, each one in its own direction. All, all of them, shut up in their unknown quantity. Impossible to know them. Impossible in the face of a reality so changeable, diverse, and vast is all relationship, except to be reduced to an abstract notion. Consequently: deforming and unifying. To know each one who goes along beside us? To feel each one? To love each one? I keep Cecília's hand in mine. How long? Three seconds, five, time enough to catch a glimpse of the gilt of the intaglios in the main chapel of the church, to go down one step, not much time. Her fingers tremble and I see her, see her duplicated. The way we see our own image in certain cheap mirrors: two faces superimposed, but with a minimal deviation between those identical reflections. In the tiny void of the deviation, I catch (a radiance) Cecília's hidden nature, her true identity. A radiance. Dazzled and at the same time having the unrestricted gift of sight, like someone who beneath a flash of lightning in complete darkness sees the unveiling of the thousand faces in a crowd and their story too, I see the thickness of Cecília's flesh, peopled by beings as real as we. In the substance of her mortal flesh, Cecília bears the integral and absolute being of every figure crossing the Square, not only of the men and women who now people the Square and its environs, but also those who peopled it yesterday, those who peopled it in May or in June, those who peopled it last year, those who are going to people it yet tomorrow, these and those who exist or have existed elsewhere, yes, no one is absent in any manner from Cecília's body. Cecília, in this way, is herself and others. By loving her, my love, with a kind of multiple and concrete individuality, takes in what in principle is ungraspable and abstract. Her thin hand slips between mine. Fragile in body and in name, Cecília turns her back on me and leaves me alone.

So it is, then. Sound and round. I and I and I, Hermenilda and Hermelinda, here we are, aides in the fable that is beginning to take shape, in which two lovers, brought together by us and in our way, are beginning to become involved, full of joy, of passion, and even more of fright. Tune the mandolin. Randy raids reels, Robert runs. Sun on the ground, breeze all around. Isn't it? Enormous. The things so runabout, so many noises. Ah, waves of time and dragging nets! What does the seamstress do with the rest of the thread? She silently sews the corpse's mouth and nose. This way and that. Zap. This ballad is unraveled. One thread holds it together: the needle. Run, Robert, read, rail, rant? Urn.

The Treasurer comes to see me at the bank. He lays his briefcase on the counter, leans over, and attempts to talk about the weather. His jacket is damp under the armpits. He heard tell that the view up there from the top of the building is worth seeing on an afternoon like this. I go up onto the roof with him. A cloudless white sky with the buildings baking in the Sun. The pigeons scratch and take flight. He talks without stopping. Eight years today since Vargas's suicide. Can it be that when we're dead we meet our ancestors? Not our relatives but those who people the land where we were born. He'd like to come across the old people of Olinda. The pioneers who came from over there and settled the whole coastal plain. Architects. Priests. Soldiers. But no. He's not going to find them. The building is tall for two stories.

"Would you get killed, Abel, if you jumped from here? You'd better get back down. You're still new on the job. You have to be visible."

"It doesn't matter. Besides, I want to ask you to talk to the old lady. I've been thinking about going away."

"Where to?"

"I don't know. I don't know yet."

The sentence, which I unknowingly pronounce or, in a certain sense, of which I am the executioner, may be conjured away. With my plan for leaving Recife, Cecília, condemned ever since the night I escaped death in the cistern, might receive a reprieve.

The Treasurer, blind to that sort of deduction, turns around: "Your mother's not going to like it. But that's the way it is. As for me, you ought to know that I won't interfere in any plans you have."

"Nobody can be sure of that."

"No, no. I'm sure of what I said. I've already played my part. Now I can leave the stage."

Is he sorry about what he wants to add?

He takes a few steps and stares at the distant line of the water: "How large the world is! And this is just a small part. I mean: facing eternal life. Isn't that so, Abel? But nowadays all they think about are strikes. Strikes and stealing. Everything's so uncertain!"

Stevedores, gleaming with sweat, carry large sacks on their heads, the cranes are working. The dock train passes slowly. Its nasal and powerful whistle, the lowing of a great iron ox.

"It's nice, all this. Well . . . I'm going home. Not now. When I finish my collections."

He goes ahead of me and I look at him face on. He smells of stale food. His collar frayed. I take him by the arm. His breath recalls the damp and sad odor of a hole in the ground.

"Be careful. A woman asked for you."

"When?"

"Last week, after the birthday dinner. The side of her face was missing."

He lowers his head and changes the subject, pensive: "Abel, forty-three years ago I discovered my great-grandfather and I'll never forget it. He died with two arms and appears to me with one, ever so long afterwards. He was wearing that hat he never owned, all covered with yellow feathers. My grandmother guaranteed: 'Never.' How do you explain that? Eh? He looked at my grandmother, startled, when he passed in the yard. I didn't know him in life. He was young now and she an old lady. Where had he been mutilated, and where, once dead, had he got the hat? Who in the world knows where that woman you saw left one side of her face! Back there. Dead or alive, we go on losing or getting things in the world. Isn't that it?"

O

The Story of , *Twice-Born*   17

From my two ages I contemplate him—with my four eyes open. The straight chestnut hair falls over his temple. When a child: not as dark and curly. Silvery threads among them, mainly at the temples, make the forehead broader. Strange, his head isn't large, no larger than that of any other man. Where does it get that look of mass, weight, and obstinacy? Delicate ears, almost transparent, small red and brown leaves slipping in among his volutes. Thick black eyebrows make the gold-striped blue of his eyes more ironic and deep. When he smiles, he closes his eyelids and the blue is hidden even more, intense, two sparks. Fireflies. The female doesn't have wings, the female firefly, the male flies over her, lights up, she stays on the ground, on her back, waits two and one-tenth seconds, and only then answers the male's light. A fraction more and they won't come together; a fraction less and they won't come together. Two and one-tenth seconds. My double love and my duplicate desire hinder me from seeing his mouth. The lines of his mouth, as if they didn't exist, fall apart in my eyes, fall apart as if they'd only been sketched, I can't see his lips and all I know, all, is that: hot and humid, they must surely hear my flesh, because they press me lightly, or with force, according to the tortuous whims of my body. His teeth are large, slightly spaced, and not very white, they're large but hidden between his lips. In a certain cunning way. The irony spread out over every point on his face reaches even to the long jaw cut by a cleft. The fragility of his trunk and the tone of his voice absolve that irony. The fragile trunk, with the foliage and the fleeting animals that move about in us, induces me to protect it, protect it, and the husky voice, veiled and agitated by sudden signs of drunkenness, is that of someone who will never have the pride or ambition of entering the world of dominators, the voice of a man who knows, having gathered them in and lived with them, fear, misfortune, loneliness, pity, ardor, and interrogation. Inácio Gabriel is his rough draft, his anticipator, Inácio Gabriel announces him.

Three times my grandmother takes me to her home; three times I return alone to the Martinelli Building on foot. The same ritual every time. A game, a repetition. She appears wearing a hat, too much makeup for her age, a long pearl necklace over the black dress; in her hands, always restless, the purse and a small silver-handled crop, as if she were going horseback-riding. There is a vague equestrian aura about all of her. The way she sits in the easy chair, erect, her raised breasts decorated with the pearl necklace, her legs together and turned to her right, so that they remain in profile, which brings out the still youthful line and glow of her ankles, so identical to those of my mother, everything brings to mind a person riding sidesaddle. From the first visit, I have abominated her restless hands gloved in gray holding the useless whip; and her habit of speaking as she turns the left side of her face toward me, even when I'm higher than her face, giving me a quick, dominating, and examining look, which always seems to come from up on a saddle. I search uselessly in her eyes for the tiny scorpion. She criticizes the building bitterly, complains about the elevator operators, and laments the loneliness in which she lives, now that her *only* daughter is rotting under the ground. My mother accepts the status of a dead woman, she knows that she has been dead for her parents ever since her marriage. From her grave she makes two or three soft and malevolent comments about her dead sister, assuming an air of extreme compassion and at intervals she releases a laugh, a nervous cackle, with which she thinks she is giving the impression of an unfortunate person trying to put on a show of euphoria. My grandmother cuts off the false conversation full of intentions and old undisguisable rages: "I don't want an innocent girl to expiate the sins of others." She points to me with the little crop: "Dress her. I'm taking her with me."

The way to my new residence, on the corner of Marquez de Ytu near the Charity Hospital, is slow and full of curves. My grandmother talks and waves her arms. A little ridiculous with her erect bearing, rocking on the seat of the car because she wouldn't think of leaning back, she always thinks the driver is going too fast; it gives her pleasure to see the street signs on the corners with the names of relatives of hers again, this also being the reason for ordering detours on the trip. She won't allow me to bring any of my belongings, considering them useless and replaceable, she doesn't know that turning slowly over my old bed is the large invisible mechanism, the mechanism that looks like a fleet in suspension, that captures events, and that I keep secret. On the first night, I lie down and close my eyes, my whole body at rest—and I wait for it. Will the huge ships come spinning to this house in my direction, slowly, through the night and the city? The feeling of absence and abandonment couldn't have been greater if I'd had a dog and it had been taken away from me. I wait, I wait for the machine, I can see the blue-and-white street signs on the corners, the gentlemen in the photograph album on the small table covered with crimson damask, hands in their pockets, posing in snowy stretches with leafless trees (and there are also smiling groups of dead people, on a beach, in long bathing suits), I see on the dining-room table a white fruit bowl with the figs I ate, my grandfather in a shadowy parlor beside the heavy Telefunken radio, the magic eye shines greenly in the darkness of the room (it's news of the war in Europe), I see the tall bookcases and the books with gold titles on their spines, I see the Erard piano, covered by a wide brocade cloth, the piano beside which my mother warps her fate, I see the lamp turned on in my room, inside a red shade, there's not only silence in the world, the silence is in me, in my empty body, it's terrifying, I get up, get dressed, climb over the garden gate, and flee.

The two other times, I run away during the day. Do the thick bedcovers at Marquez de Ytu hurt me? No, they keep me warm. Do the warm bath and the violet water hurt me? No, they make me light. Nothing hurts me in this spacious house, not the large windows through which the March sun enters, or the severe furniture all covered with crochetwork, or the chandeliers, which, when lighted, give off lace shadows on the ceiling and on the walls with cedar wainscoting, or on the highly polished parquet floor, or even the parlor where the radio with the green eye is, ventilated only by skylights, with false windows painted on the wall that open illusorily onto wintry countrysides. On the second floor, the paint on the walls is a little peeled, some rooms are neat and clean, while others seem to grow old, full of unmatched furniture, piles of foreign magazines from 1912, and perfume containers so ancient that they smell only of the past. Nor am I afflicted either by this presence of ruin and debris in a house where even the porcelain spittoons have something pompous about them. On the other hand, the Martinelli Building hurts me. With its dowdiness, its broken elevators, and its sooty windows that are opened to light up the stairways but that seem to be open in order to provide holes into a world where it never dawns. But there is a relationship, I know, between me and its grimy walls, between me and the old elevator operator with a hook on the tip of a stick to open the elevator's grillwork door, and the dark windows that look out into the darkness, and mainly between me and the mad multitude that works or lives on its many floors, silent, cursing, robbing, or being robbed—and that, without knowing it, sharpens my claws. That's why I come back, and as soon as I come back the corridors hear my steps again. On one of the floors now, a whole wing has been blocked off by an iron grille painted with tar, a gate with padlock and chain. I stand by the entrance shouting inside, into the deserted and isolated wing, no one comes and yet my shouts don't seem lost to me, shouts with no reply don't seem to be unanswered to me, in the Martinelli nothing seems useless to me, every shout I make, every step I take on the worn stairs leads me, that's what I think, to a culmination. In the house on Marquez de Ytu, in front of the photograph albums and the sideboards with marble tops, the world is reduced and wilted for me. In this building, with cypresses beside the entrance and many parlors, some thorn is being softened in me (in my ankle?, in my tongue?), as some point in the body is being dulled, I am being pruned of the violence that branches out in me. The fourth time, waiting for me at the entrance with the white uniform of a nursemaid, is a slight and fluttering someone whose job it is to seduce me. Her name is Inês and she doesn't have to make any effort to fulfill her duty. Seduction flows from every one of her gestures, every phrase, Inês loves earth and air, she loves loose lions, mangy dogs, the sharpness of razors, executioners, she would have an affable word and look for the headsman and the ax if condemned to death. She looks at me inside the eyes, affectionately, always giving me new names, Amália, Creusa, Sofia, Cristina, María Alice, with each new name I feel myself touched, each new name seems deeper, an invasion into the pith of my being. Inês goes on inventing other names as if she hoped to discover my real name, not the one in the registry or on the baptismal certificate—mere appearances—but mine, the true one, the one I don't know myself and that would grant her the right to penetrate me truly, to open me up, a name that would be like the secret of a coffer.

P

Julius Heckethorn's Clock   1

"Clocks," writes J.H., "have a strict relationship with the world and what they represent largely goes beyond their use. Since their beginning, they have put the transitory in opposition to the eternal and have attempted to be a mirror of the stars. Still more: they express in simple numbers—so simple that in our innocence we think we understand them—the rhythm imposed ever since the beginnings on the solemn and delicate movement of the stars. Consider sundials. Might one, after some reflection, continue to believe that Anaximander of Miletus, when he makes quadrants, simply wants to facilitate the division of the day into hours? What he aims at is to convert the solar light, its harmonious spin, into a geometric flower that withers with the dusk."

O

The Story of Ǒ, Twice-Born   18

For three days I vacillate between staying and running away. On
the third, I'm beside the piano, which is still covered with a brocade
shawl, I am standing beside the piano in the exact spot where my cred-
ulous father, without knowing it, involves his pupil in an adverse fate.
The clock on the table, braced by two lush caladiums in porcelain pot
racks, shows eleven-ten. All the windows are open, the fringed curtain
gathered, and the sun falls onto the carpet where a young girl in a thin
dress is enjoying herself between trees on a swing with flowered ropes.
Inês, all in white, sitting on a low chair and no less happy than the girl
on the carpet, is knitting. Reading a newspaper with great agitation,
my grandmother, erect and turned a bit toward the right, is on the
couch—wicker, with medallions on the back. Her gold-rimmed glasses
glitter. In the center of the couch and sitting sidesaddle, still with the
look of someone mounted high on a horse, queen of the sideboards
and the bric-a-brac with glazed shepherds playing rustic instruments
or whispering into the ears of shepherdesses, the colored porcelain
pitchers on silver trays, and, most of all, ruling over the twelve
chairs—some with armrests, others plain—all empty and all turned toward her. I see her reflected in one of the large mirrors with gilt frames
that hang on the wall. The repetition of her figure makes her even
more dominating.

It gratifies me during these ages to hear my own voice. It's still the
voice of a two-year-old child, hoarse, nasal, and strident, but I throw it
against the walls, many times not listening to what I'm saying, intent
only on its volume and inflections. In the same way that during my
long period of muteness I create unpronounced words and arrive at
thoughts I don't dare give out, in this second phase my mouth gives off
ideas, narratives, and names that no one recognizes, that not even I
recognize, that I can't recognize better by hearing them from my own
mouth, and that certainly startle even more those who listen to me, as
these are offered in an insecure, infantile voice, translating an experience that reaches beyond them and is not justified by my age or
experience.

The clock on the table shows eleven-fourteen. Inês's needles weave the woolen yarn. My grandmother, duplicated in the mirror, reads the obituaries. The sky becomes dark and menacing. Two swallows cross the space together, from right to left; in an opposite direction a solitary dove flaps its wings. A thunderclap is heard, dull and prolonged. The impulse to speak suddenly comes upon me. Then I speak. Inês, interrupting her knitting, looks at me with surprise. My grandmother, her paleness accentuated by the superfluous makeup, stands up and the newspaper drops from her hand; she leaves her glasses on and, in an uncertain voice, asks me something I don't understand. I keep on talking, exulting in the sound of my voice, a new thunderclap crashes, she repeats the question three or four times, and finally translates: "Where did you learn to speak German?" Further: "What monster is it that you're talking about that's in front of me? There's nobody here."

The last syllable of her words is still echoing in the room when the storm breaks: I hear the bell and the door opens. Through the windows I see in the garden, running bent over, a short, heavyset woman with a look of fifty years, running, and a still adolescent cadet who must be her son. With her eyes still fixed on mine, my grandmother speaks to Inês: "Go see who's coming." Inês, in a hurry, picks up the newspaper at her feet and runs to open the door. The woman and her son, with rain dripping off their clothing and hair, come in. He takes his hat off, Inês closes the windows. My grandmother, with a gesture, invites the visitor to sit down beside her on the couch. The boy, after an instant of hesitation, crosses the room, pulls a chair back a little, and sits down *in front of them*. I see him from behind, his back is a little heavy for his age. Over his shoulder my grandmother gives me a troubled look, no, a terrified and inquiring look. I go out from beside the piano and sit on the carpet by the young man's feet: "What's your name?" I ask, as if I were looking for someone whose features would match his or as if I were only trying to dissipate the last doubts about some evidence. He is startled by my acid tone and draws back a little in the chair before answering: "Olavo." "Olavo what?" "Olavo Haiano."

Two flat images, blended on the stereoscope, take on relief. I see Olavo Haiano with my double look, as no one can see him, I see him in relief, the military cap on his knees, a figure in a stereoscope. I grasp him in his carnal form and in the consternating emptiness hidden in the perceivable flesh. Olavo Haiano? No, that's not his name. That's what they call him, that's what's assigned him, but the name falls from his lips like a cloak that illusorily dresses a body, a cloak raised between the observer and the naked man, with a glass wall between the cloak and the man, it having been forbidden, however, for the man to get to put it on, and it is enough for the observer to move out of his place—a little to the right, a little to the left—to ascertain that the man is undressed, that the cloak doesn't dress him, nor can he dress in it. "That's not it." "Not what?" "It's not Olavo Haiano." The rain is teeming, noisy and heavy. Inês is beside me, her hand raised and pointing to the youth, urging him on certainly. I get up slowly, I get up and take a step backward. I look at him from my center, from the depths of myself, with impatience and rage, feeling that this rage, this impatience are hitting his eyes and coming back redoubled, I look at him as if there were a great river between us, a gully—and we would have to do a lot of walking, go a long way, before we really come face to face. But he still asks, hands clutching his cap: "What about you? Who are you? What's your name?" His coldness enfolds me, penetrates me. I leave him and I answer from the door without turning around: "I don't know."

At night, once more I lie waiting for the machine that spins for no one over my bed in another part of the city in the Martinelli Building. Olavo Haiano, posted in my mind, has the air of a supernatural intruder, joining together in himself the senses of enticement and warning. Behind him my fate is hidden in the same way that he is hidden under the opaqueness of his name. There is a yes and a no, a deep-seated option in the aura that surrounds him.

When I wake up, separated and lying side by side on the bed are the two that I am. I see myself still in the mirror. I see myself now outside of myself, and the faces that I look at surprise me. One of them is still a child's face, but the other is beginning to enter the shadows of adolescence. I look at myself doubly, the notion that I have of my individuality is single, I feel myself one, but at the same time I feel myself one in each one that I am and in the two simultaneously. So that by no hypothesis could someone say: "She is looking at me." Or: "I answer her." It's as if I were in the mirror, but without knowing which side my reflection is on. With the circumstance that these reflections are not identical; nor do they act like reflections; and no sheet separates them. The lamp is turned on beneath its red globe and there's no clock in my room. From here I can't always hear the parlor clock between the pot racks with the caladiums. I say: "I'm leaving. I need the machine." I'm sitting on the bed, wearing a woolen nightgown and standing beside the bed, naked. I'm covered and I feel cold. "That's it. I've got to leave. But maybe it's too late." "The devil with the time. I'm going in any case." The voices are different, both restrained, almost a whisper. "It's dangerous to walk the streets at night." A great disdain for me rises up in me. The answer is no longer offered in the same tone of voice, and is louder and as if aroused, yes, there is something of a wild boar on the attack in the voice: "And is it safe here? What does safe mean?" There's a noise, or a series of short, sharp noises, thirty pieces of chalk breaking inside of me at the same time. I raise my hand, I put it as far behind me as I can: the blow hurts me at the same time on the face and on the fist. Am I still talking? Answering? Insulting? I? I? The combat is long and violent. A duel to the death. I want to leave, leave again, as many times as necessary, I want to stay for a few days at least, the wills oppose each other and there is nothing childish about the struggle. Do two vulnerable eyes open? I try to stick my fingertips into them. Is the wall close by? I beat it with the head I hold between my hands. If I can reach the pillow, I'll use it to suffocate. If I can, I bite. If I can, I strangle, I elbow, I knee the chins, the ribs, the liver—and I collapse with every blow given or received. In the midst of the fight a problem cuts through me several times: if I destroy my opponent, will I continue on? Won't conquering her be the end of me? The question doesn't moderate the ferocity of the duel. Mounted soldiers pass on the street, the horseshoes striking hard on the paving stones—and I in a struggle. The lamp crackles, the flame grows brighter, goes out, and the room is in darkness: I in a struggle. Dogs bark and are silent, an ambulance passes, there are distant explosions. I struggle. Birds begin to trill on the roof, I struggle, the weak light of the morning slowly penetrates into the room, outlining the furniture and the walls, outlining the enemy—and I struggle, still struggle. Finally I roll on the floor, I remain on my back, lying there, arms open, breathing rapidly. I say: "I like Inês." With another voice: "I hate Inês." There's a pause and I propose: "No matter what, stay; no matter what, go." My voice, in reply, after a brief silence: "No separation. For whatever is given or seen, let it be a single life." "What about the Yolyp? It's coming. It's already come." "Let it come. We'll see who wins." I get up, I sit on the bed, I'm lying on the floor, naked. With difficulty I get to my feet and walk: with my back to myself. The singing of the birds is happier, and from somewhere, far off, the sound of bottles comes. Someone is starting to shout in the Charity Hospital. In my heart, discordant at first and then in unison, the newer heart is beating. Twelve years, six months, and two days I have been living in that house.

T

Cecília Among the Lions   10

When the office has been locked up, the clerks leave. Those in charge of the cleaning haven't arrived yet with their buckets, brooms, brushes, and voices. Out of the typewriter I take the paper on which I am trying to put in order vague ideas on chaos, I throw it into the basket, I distractedly open a newspaper. Alarming news items about the Peasant Leagues in which the Treasurer's voice seems to echo, frightened and vengeful. Perhaps I ought to envy his wild opinions, I who insist on the habit or deformation of always weighing all sides of a question, finding that only in that way can I reach a conclusion that isn't too distorted. Are the conditions of life of the canecutters inhuman? Then it occurs to me that landowners in the Northeast could never think or act any differently. I begin to doubt, however, that these worries of mine have anything to do with equity or that such a type of equity today serves justice most loyally and usefully.

The telephone rings on the Boss's desk. The sound of the strident bell shakes up the two silent levels: it flees through the tall windows reinforced by grime-covered grating. Putting down the newspaper, I get up, I lean over the railing and stand looking at the piles of useless papers thrown beside the wastebaskets down there under the lights that are on for no reason. Hesitant and with my ideas unwoven. Can this world really be a carpet that's all in one piece? Callus Face crosses the room gesticulating among the empty in-boxes placed without the slightest sense of order and covered with large green sheets of blotting paper. It could be the world, a carpet broken up into pieces and also a carpet that has never really been woven: its design would be coherent and complete only in the idea. Yes, it could be. Chaos is unhealthy and even repugnant. Isn't it?

The telephone rings again. I answer and several invisible jaw-bones around me slowly begin to grind glass or thick sand. "I know it's you, Abel. You've got to come back. The past . . . Have pity on me . . . The bonds between us . . . You can't ruin my life . . . I can't stand it anymore. You'll be sorry, I swear! Today—remember?—it'll be four years, Abel!" I look at the number 6 on the calendar and hang up without saying yes or no.

On the railing again. Through some kind of instinct, she knows all my weak points and there are many. When she throws herself to her knees in the hallway, blocking my way and begging me not to abandon her, she knows what she's driving at. She knows that for some individuals her gesture has no importance whatsoever, is even pitiful. In my case, she's sure that it won't change or even put off the decision taken. Of this I haven't the slightest doubt (I know how well she knows me), and even so I give in to the trick. Like that species of wasp which stings crickets exactly in their three motor centers—centers, of course, that are separated from one another—and immobilizes them? Their larvae feed on immobile but living crickets. I give in to the trick and make the play that, underneath it all, she has provoked, de-sired, awaits: I slap her face, I, a person repelled by acts like that, who never, before or after, has hit anyone.

Once more the telephone rings. The notions of symmetry, bal-ance, connection—all this favors us. It remains to be known, remains to be known whether, on taking a close look at the manifestations, ar-tificial or not, where the threatening contraries of those same notions prevail, we are not entering the real nature of the universe expressed precisely in what is disordered, illegible. I close my ears to the insistent telephone and I face the name that comes to my mouth, Cecília's. I say it several times, leaning over the parapet, looking down as if I were tossing small, shiny stones into a well, until the telephone falls silent. I can perceive in this way, with the weight of a jubilant solemnity, that Cecília and I, I don't know on what dark night—or clear day—I don't know, traveling or not, are already face to face. Callus Face reappears. He looks up, smiling, his child's face wrinkled and two teeth missing in his senile gums. He flees, leaping among the pieces of furniture.

My mother, sitting in the rocking chair, is eating a cluster of jambos and putting the remains in a plate on the table, laughing. Sometimes she laughs in her dreams: the cat with the monkey head doesn't go to sleep in her body. She laughs about the children who leave or end up complete failures like a donkey in the water, at the incapacity that most of us reveal for any permanent effort of continued obligation, at Eurílio, shot to death at the age of nineteen in a brothel ("Now, indeed, I have been fulfilled: I have given birth to a martyr to lewdness!"), at Estêvão, younger than Eurílio, giving up his soul before his time after hours and hours of dancing without cease, desperate, at the taxi-dance hall on the Praça Maciel Pinheiro, because of his broken engagement (the fiancée, with no dowry, a widow and mother of three children, is more than twice his age), at Dagoberto, ruining his voice in the Gambrinus Bar or in the whorehouse on Marquês de Olinda. "I have to laugh. Sowing all that seed and harvesting nothing from it? I wanted to sleep in the moonlight and I lay down in the nettles!" Through the door that opens onto the porch, on a clear afternoon, a touch of green from the trees is reflected in her eyes: they seem full of fright under the raised sketch of her eyebrows. Cecília's eyes (when will I see her again?), lively and biting, dance on things.

"Thinking it over, my brothers and sisters may not be any more mixed up than all those people who go around here as if they've got the keys to the world. But nobody I know has the key to anything—nobody—or knows where they're going: what direction to take or what to make of themselves. Is it a worn-out system of life, one that's no good anymore? Maybe. I, at least, look around and can't discover a strong, live current where I can plunge into, soul and everything else, once and for all and without hesitation. In the cane fields there's something new that interests me in a certain way: that occupation of land and even those fires. The object is to shake up and, who knows, to eliminate once and for all certain schemes that have lasted a long time now. But is this a current or a broken dam?"

She listens to me attentively now, eating her jambos. She doesn't grasp, of course, what I'm putting forth—and she gives a different meaning to this kind of monologue which leads nowhere. Is she capturing my thought? No, I know that quite well. She understands, in return, the perplexity and passive submission that lead me to it. There's already been so much of it! What about Cecília? Does she find meaning in what she does? Her thin legs are agile and the bones of her knees are clearly visible under the skin. Her presence sows lions.

"A domestic way of seeing things imagines that a man is sure of himself because he punches the time clock and because he goes on strike when everybody else does. That's not it."

The cat with the monkey head, sitting on the floor, looks longingly at the jambos. It jumps onto the Fat Woman's knees, from there to the table, and it touches the plate lightly with its forepaws, as if touching hot coals.

"The lack of sense that marks Brazil from one end to the other can be seen in the government's initiatives. When least expected, the man who by an act of chance holds the Presidency of the Republic takes a program out of his hat: march to the West, wipe out ants, pump oil, build Brasília. Those things have their importance, of course, I'm not the one to deny that. But they don't make up—how can I say it?—a meaningful aim. Above all, they're not coordinated with anything. They're not the consequence of anything and they don't lead to anything. The country, from North to South, is drifting along. In a picture like that, how could individuals be any different from what they are? Nobody here knows which side the Sun comes up on. Some people (I don't mean everybody, because the great majority don't even get that far) invent some kind of emergency project: *I'm going to be Governor. I'm going to be section head.* Unconnected and artificial ideals."

I'm silent and intent on the silence of the villa, filled in other days with boys and girls, voices, songs, and laughter resounding, even on Good Friday. Fireworks, music, improvised dances, the porch decorated with flags and Japanese lanterns—a disguise, a postponement. The Fat Woman in that chair—the monkey-cat inside her body.

"I'm no exception and I have my false project: I keep on writing. I'm not—and I doubt I ever will be—satisfied with this or sure of the choice. A choice that's not at all peaceful or merry, you have to remember. In spite of all, I have no intention of signing my treaty of peace with the world in which I live. My brothers and sisters don't know how to—or don't want to—invent an acceptable effigy. That's the difference. Between the declared disaster and the appearance of finality, they even prefer the disaster."

The animal, leaping away from the plate, draws back and stares at me, moving its tail, its ears standing up.

"The revolt on the plantations might be in Brazil today the only movement that doesn't constitute diversion and improvisation. But for certain intimate reasons that, to be frank, I mistrust, I'm not taking part in that struggle even in spirit. Besides, I'm not a man of action in the common acceptance of the word."

"That's all we need, Abel, you mixed up in setting fire to cane fields."

Her arched thin high eyebrows give her a look of surprise and she rocks in the chair. Her dark hair, half faded at the roots, reflects the colored glass of the windows. In my short story those panes are clear. The four old women spy on each other with hatred. Each one always tells her tale to the other old women and all the stories are similar. The nocturnal cat or monkey balances itself, mistrustfully, on the moving chairback: in a silent leap, it returns to Mama's body. It moves with agility and speed, as in a cage.

"Your wife paid me a visit. She wants you to think about the possibility of going back. You know I was never on her side. But you can start life over again here, if you want. There are plenty of rooms."

Yes, plenty: almost all empty. Mauro, Leonor, and I, children of who knows what fathers, bump into the younger brothers and sisters—Dagoberto, Janira, Lucíola. Isabel is still moving in the Fat Woman's fertile womb when the Treasurer takes up with a nurse and Damião is born of that adventure. "Well, the devil take the little innocent, I'll bring him up. But now, you old goat, you're going to find out who's going to suck out your strength. Get yourself ready!" The beds increase.

"That matter's closed. Besides . . . in a certain way . . . there's someone."

"Who? Married? Single? Free?"

"What do you care?" (Can the Treasurer have spoken about the trip?) "There's someone. Single, I think."

"How awful! A person with nothing to offer compromising a nice family girl. What will come of this?"

"Come? What do you mean? Maybe it won't come to anything and maybe I . . . We've seen each other two or three times. That's all."

I get up and snap my fingers at the catamonk. He turns his back and scratches my mother's armpit, furtively.

A

Roos and the Cities 17

"Almost time for your train, Roos." We go along side by side, suitcases in hand, toward the boarding platforms, sonorous names precede us, the names of our trip, I am afflicted by the height of the ceiling, the stairs, the dimensions of the station, its inhospitable spaces, that aridity, we pass by a magazine stand, I offer her some (*Burda, Stern*), we pass through the turnstile, I hear train whistles and peacock cries, Alpine countryside and splendid homes parade by in the train.

"Thanks for the lakes."

"If you can, send me a postcard at Ravenna. I'll be there for a week."

"I will."

"I'll never be able to thank you enough for coming to Milan."

She gets on the train, puts her suitcase up on the rack, looks at me through the glass. There's a minute left, she can still get off. Varese, Como, Intra, Baveno, Stresa, Chiasso, Verbania . . . I'm nudged by the hope that those lacustrine names and that rainy Sunday may come back to the woman who is leaving on some winter afternoon wrapped in the sun of other moments. She lowers the glass window, extends her hand to me, *Ciao*, the train starts moving and her gesture is the same one with which she tries, the same one, in Amboise to cast a spell on the bird that I scare off with a clap of my hands.

New hunting days. The last ones? The railroad complex (F.F.S.S.), miles of track, ties, innumerable poles, electric cables, locomotives, track and office personnel, regulations (VIETATO), timetables (PAR-TENZA), stations (SOTTOPASSAGIO), electronic controls, radios, telephone connections, an immense and well-oiled roulette wheel in which I migrate for thirteen days, always unsuccessfully, on limiteds, express trains, night trains, and narrow-gauge coaches that go slowly and stop at many stations, dozing over the rumble of the wheels, or looking for a way to obtain, with crosswise questions, indications of what I'm looking for. I go on and on, from Milan to Verona (96 miles), 24 between Verona and Padua, between Padua and Venice twice that, 120 from Venice to Ravenna (there's a holiday in the city, the post office is closed, I don't know if a letter from Roos is waiting for me), 42 or 48 separating Ravenna from Ferrara, 72 more Ferrara from Florence, 48 on the trip from Florence to Pisa, from Pisa to Rome 180 something, from Rome to Naples 140(?), not much less than 240—or maybe even more—from Naples to Assisi and from there to Arezzo, and 240 on the Arezzo-Milan stretch, not to mention the 444 that separate me from Roos (USCITA), to whom, at every stop, I send postcards on which I draw a map of possible australias, dream fauna, and a gulf where I write "*Je vous aime.*"

The 1,200 miles of that itinerary has something demented about it. Was there anything sensible in it? The very acceptance of the search goes against the ordinary norms of behavior; and, at times, the decision to go to a certain city rises up unexpectedly. Only in Naples—and not in Florence—does it occur to me, desperate now, as if I were gambling my last pennies on numbers I don't trust, to make the try of getting off in Assisi and Arezzo. On the other hand, I'm convinced, like that person so well versed in searches and journeys, that for some enterprises "a premeditated disorderliness is the true method." The premeditation, it is true, is done in this case with the help of maps; and my conjectures, at best, are based on the always-so-summary dice of tourist brochures. In the last analysis, I give myself over a little blindly to fate in this migration—now that I have become transformed into a gambler in this—and, in order to do it, I block off the intimate voices that warn me about the discordance between the proportions of the search and my possessions, which only allow me, in this game where the capital is also made up of the time of my existence and in more than one sense can ruin me, to take a chance on a number that is very reduced in possibilities. It doesn't matter, I'll bet what I can. It's the least I must do and this least is also the only logical access to the outcome.

I persuade myself that the City, as little as it may be identified—and it wasn't its appearance that imposed this conviction, reasonably developed, but the evocation of certain antecedents or the examination of similes—gives off a prestigious light. Ahab, to cite only one example: would he assume the duty that destroys him, would he accept the demands of his long hunt, if Moby Dick were not an immeasurable being where "all that stirs up the lees of things" is incarnated? This principle, up to a certain incontestable point, is put to use by me. It undoes the temptation to get off in every city I pass, limiting myself to those which because of precise reasons—history, works of art, dead—rise up over the general run. My look becomes more analytical, sharp, and cautious. In the cities covered, I, dog, scent an intangible prey, a hunt that I have seen, I, dog, in a mirror, but the smell of which I couldn't get to make out.

I couldn't assert, defrauded in my search, that these days were ruined. Silence over the codices and incunabula I see; and all these artistic realizations—contemplated at times in the places where they had been conceived—transmit to me instructions for the book I secretly aspire to write and the central theme of which would be the way things, having crossed a threshold, ascend by means of new relationships to the level of fiction. Doesn't Padua answer me? Doesn't Naples? I break myself apart in them, in different exercises. Eyes on the peripheral neighborhoods, nose in marketplaces, skin free in the air, feet wandering, mouth in cafés, brothels, sex listless, ears in stores and buses, I don't know where they're going, the suburban population, their houses, fish, vegetables, fruit, squid, the temperature and consistency of things, unknown streets, tired whores and timid pederasts follow me, wines and questions, sex listless, manipulated by women whom it will not penetrate, because that was how I had decided, so they could laugh at their possessor, judge him impotent, someone more pitiful than they, the voices, the shouts, the barking, the tolling of bells.

Yet it is mistaken to say that the undiscovered City is still unknown and hidden as before; that its identity hasn't suffered some unfinished process of revelation. Does Amsterdam reveal in its streets the existence of clarity or something of which clarity might be the sum? In Pisa I can read the declaration that an uncertainty, a maybe, a doubtfulness are probably present (in it, the City), without which my search would find no recompense.

Who can show me why? In every square of any city a white lamb rises up, gentle, with a bell and a red ribbon around its neck. It gently presses my thigh with its soft head and follows me in silence. Before the great cylindrical tower, unbalanced by the *male oscuro*, infiltrations, and subterranean erosions, two more lambs, also with bells and ribbons around their necks, come to join the one that always appears to me in the squares. Docile, they follow me. This end-of-May Sun, like an alchemist's potion, penetrates the marble, igneous oil that lights up the inside of stones, all the stones in bloom, in flames, in the core, in such a way that the light seems to come from without and at the same time is emitted by the Tower, the Baptistery, the other monuments. A sign? I contemplate these more or less leaning structures. I know that marine sediments in the subsoil mined by currents of the Arno are unbalancing the city, making plumb lines, the law of buildings, vacillate, that almost all the old structures give way or lean (Pisa, birefringent city built on zircon or Iceland spar), but not even then do I lose the notion of verticality. Beside these works, others stand out, resplendent in the same way with their marbles gleaming against the clouds, vertical, however, and this Tower, this Cathedral are illusory, because the real buildings lean with time, but it is in these, the leaning ones, that the shape of the unreal passes, precisely because installed in them is the tenuous thread between what persists and what passes.

As in Amsterdam, Roos, a doubtful and fugitive being—as well as making things unclear—unbalanced in her absolute symmetry, is not alien to that experience. In the same way that under other circumstances when she is present (limited flesh and constructed spaces) I am flung into her cities, I discover myself, before the Pisan doubtfulness and light, not before Roos, but introduced into the universe of her presence—a certainty not disturbed by the slightest shadow of a doubt. An archaeologist would with the same certainty recognize an epigraph or a frieze of civilizations with which he had lived if he discovered the relics hundreds of feet deep, and even though they were disfigured.

Thus, from out of the great spaces, a cosmic cat extends his claw to me. But careful! Don't suppose that he will belong to me because of that gesture. Then he will withdraw his claw and he himself will immediately retreat into another cat, of whom—who knows—he is the nail. Advancing through the web of enigmas can lead us to greater enigmas. In the end, I can state, back in Paris, that I have not altered the nature or the rhythm of the long phrase that, knowing it or not, Roos, a back-and-forth estuary, writes me: a correspondence of three or four days, even a letter from Lausanne and the message that, doing everything I can to lay siege to her, I send from Verona—a leaf from the vines that grow before the crypt with the presumptive tomb of the young Capulet maiden and the line "It is my lady; o it is my love"— awaits her return once more.

R

℧ and Abel: Meetings, Routes, and Revelations   13

The sky of Rio Grande, this morning, radiant, morning, filled with a light that I would call twisted, as if the Moon had acted in some way upon the rays of the Sun that the eclipse reduces, acquires a twilight tone and weight.

" 'The Journey and the River.' What's it about, Abel?"

"Mythical times and their relationship to narrative."

It can be perceived, even with the naked eye, that the luminosity of the Sun is dying, washed away by the celestial conjunction. ♉, avoiding the protection of the shadowed areas now, leaves the trees and goes where there is sunlight, compensating for the drop in temperature. The vultures glide lower and the little birds enlarge the intervals between one flight and another, throbbing for a longer time on branches or power lines. They give off little restless cries and at the same time seem to be desirous of fleeing, stupefied, as if under the eyes of serpents. ♉ is the first to see the white and climbing trace of the second rocket, a Nike Javelin, in the breadth of an ever-deepening blue, pointing at it with her left hand adorned with rings, while the shout from the multitude crowded into the square by the Casino acclaims the flight and echoes—a roar—over the roofs. Lions? I wonder if I am mistaken or if some stars—although not firmly, as if seen on the surface, only to sink shortly after—begin to perforate the noonday light. We busy ourselves, laughing, in discovering new fugitive lights, to the South, the Northeast, the Southwest, suddenly I hear the fall—into what waters?—of a fishnet, a damp nocturnal wind blows on my face and I look at ♉, who is motionless: she pretends to gather great sheaves of flames, as if the asphalt were a field of fire that glittered but did not envelop us, she pretends to grab those bundles and throw them up, where they stay. What does she tell me as the celestial space seems to absorb the imaginary bonfires? She speaks and I don't translate the words she offers: intent on the voice and the voice isn't the same, it isn't the same, a different voice surges up in hers and the hoarse voice, a voice known and touched by virile tones, is not the same, it doesn't belong to her. I take her by the wrists and scrutinize her, not only with my eyes, I scrutinize her with my whole being, as if she were—she or her face—an urn of memories or an enigmatic text, indispensable from then on.

"What do you see?" (Yes, this is her voice, a restricted instrument used with wisdom.)

"Nothing. Nothing yet."

The light of the Sun strikes the treetops, and the beams of light printed on the ground repeat what we observe through frosted glass: the sphere of fire over which the Moon advances, dead and black. The rays under the trees, corroded coins.

"You know, ♉? I open my eyes in the heart of the night, as if the night were the world. I open my hands before my eyes and I can't see my hands. I'm not even satisfied then: the room doesn't seem to be as dark as it should be. I press my eyelids, like this, my fingers on my head. Open. I create a cocoon of shadows and in the center of the darkness I ask the question."

"The question?"

The black hearse with Natividade's coffin stops at the intersection, lost among cars, buses, and cement mixers. The shack to store material—construction manuals ordain—should be built with ordinary planks already used and tiles laid on simply with mud. When the building is finished, tiles and wood, intact, can be used again on another job. The sun of this February morning crowns the wreaths of roses and the blue daisies thrown on the coffin. Only two cars accompany the hearse: an Army vehicle and a black Chrysler, somewhat used, chrome and windows gleaming. The driver, hands firm on the steering wheel, ignores the tumult, a style of action that he repudiates and considers threatening (don't increase any unusual start in the disorder). On his thick and impassive face, in the rigidity of his posture, a kind of fright can be sensed, one shielded by powers. As if the weapon that weighs on his belt, in the holster that smells of horses, brought him no security and he still expects, without deigning to look behind, a bullet in the neck. The heat accelerates Natividade's soft rotting in the pine box, under the lifeless flowers.

"It's exasperating, Abel, the presence of a strange body in one's flesh. It's as if your heart hurt, and in order to free yourself of the pain you prepare to tear it out. The strange body poisons us and poisons the air. Love or be loved, something of disputable value. Don't you think? The sources of love, the directions of love, they're what count."

The train slows down, and the walls and objects that pass in the still foggy morning, gleaming, lugubrious, with a kind of indefinable hardness as if the nearness of the rails and the locomotives infected them, give me the impression of shipwrecked or exploded things, without any order that in some way makes them coherent: I don't read what I'm looking at. Piles of wood thrown alongside the tracks, watchmen's iron posts, piles of sand, junk piles where wild black plants entwine, a bus down below, pointed roofs, and even the numbers and letters on the coaches—everything seen from the bed through the dim glass seems to me to be isolated forever in its own horror, holes in the world poorly plugged up, like the irregular pieces of canvas and cardboard that disguise the cracked windows of that old factory or warehouse. A damp wind blows on the platform, it's always there on mornings in São Paulo even when it's not winter, this cold wind that pierces my sweater and my denim suit. *Gemini 12 breaks record in space and completes successful mission.* I am comforted, in spite of the cold and the suffocation that large railroad stations provoke in me, to evoke, while I continue on among the other passengers, the existence in this strange city of a familiar island: secretly, someone is waiting for me.

"Even if it were possible for the mother of a Yolyp to conceive again, it's not to be expected that she would risk it: the placenta of the Yolyp is like a hedgehog. Its spines, of course, don't injure the pregnant woman during gestation. Retracted, more or less, they only really begin to grow and harden, one could say out of malice, during the last two or three weeks before birth. They are implanted on top of the placenta in various directions. One can imagine the lacerations they cause. It's as if the woman were giving birth to hooks or bottle shards. Never, no matter how long she lives, is she ever entirely cured of the wounds, and she suffers periodic hemorrhages until her death. Even those who happen to undergo a Caesarean section suffer from the spines. It's not necessary to add that the father and mother never stand in solidarity before that experience."

Sitting on the bed, she opens the kimono with blue chrysanthemums, and the mobile lights from the park, reflected on the white walls, reveal in part her stomach and voluminous breasts with their vibrant rosettes, we stroll along holding hands by the gift stalls and we head toward the carousel, the carousel creaks on its axis in the tepid nocturnal November wind, black nocturnal birds creak their wings (jointed with old hinges?), threaten to come in through the open window, and cross the agitated reflections that animate ℧'s loose hair.

A

Roos and the Cities   **18**

A week elapses, seven days go by, a week slips past. Uncertain weather, with sudden furies of water, dull thunderclaps, the rain lashing the windowpanes of my back room on Montparnasse, and then the clouds leave, this end-of-spring sky glows fleetingly and soft breezes touch the flowers on the other mournful windowsills. I wander through the museums (Guimet, Instrumental, Armenian), I listen to the radio (U.N., Leo Ferré, Sierra Maestra, Suez, Charles Trenet) while I write letters I never mail, or I sit in parks, idly. Have I been back a week? How many days of this waiting? Seven? Six? There aren't many visitors left on the benches and the portable chairs of the Luxembourg. Adolescents are playing tennis, and flashes of lightning pass by in the almost nocturnal sky. One of the players inexpertly hits the ball in my direction. I bend over to pick it up and I become motionless: I think I see Roos on a bench, her rosy legs crossed, pensive. Did she get back and not telephone?

She makes room on the bench without showing surprise, and I sit down. Pale, shadow of fatigue in her eyes, her gray woolen dress a little loose around the hips. She got back that morning. She was in Eltville, summoned by her father. "My mother isn't doing well." "What about your husband?" She avoids answering. We: the two banks of a river? The two edges of a knife blade? Evasive. The impression of being fearful or waiting for someone. She doesn't talk much, considering the time that has passed since our Sunday of rain and wind in Italy. Not many questions. Did I like Venice? Did I get her postcard in Arezzo? As for the ones I sent, they're in her purse. She can follow my itinerary by means of them.

Long whistles and words from the guards cross through the trees. They're going to shut the gates. We get up. Roos's feet on the gravel, the measured rhythm of her walk: the rhythm with which she follows the verses of Anacreon at noon in the Loire Valley. A gate slams in the distance.

"Is your hotel on the Rue d'Odessa any good?"

"Third-rate. I haven't got much money left."

From the lone window I count several others, ash-colored, all in the rear of other buildings. Few stars are visible when I lie down. I'm bothered by the idea that Roos will consent to see me, maybe get undressed in a place so far removed from her light and magnificence.

"In the hotel, at least, you can visit me. Roos . . ." I love her more and more. It's like flint in the stomach. Like a piece of glass in the eye.

She pretends not to hear, and asks me about my friends on the Rue Guynemer.

"I was there two or three times this week. There's a little more peace in the family now. The old man has been feeling better."

We go into a bistro next to the Théâtre de France. The glasses of port between us, her hands beside mine, our knees touching lightly.

Face to face. The name of the bistro in neon, Le Petit Suisse, is reflected in the mirrors, ruddy. Carnal and luminous, enflamed by the light of the sign, Anneliese Roos's skin glows. This is the woman I love. Night is approaching and the remnants of light flowing through the thin white curtains wrap around things as if weaving. I can barely see the people around us. Dazzled, intent only on Roos's face where unknown cities are now revealed and hidden once more in her skin, silent.

"I feel good at the Weigels'."

I neglect to say why, that I have observed that the enthusiasm of the head of the family when he talks about his own sins and the Russian novel has diminished; that his face has taken on a certain rigidity and the color of his skin has changed; that he's begun to die and only I can see it; and that, against my will, there's been unleashed in me the impulse to protect the sisters, to shelter them from the world and from the blow that's being prepared before my eyes, forgetting that I don't even have any defense against the violence, the refusals, the torments that are reserved for me. Even now the notion that some blow or other is on the point of wounding me is so clear that I look over my shoulder suspiciously. Behind us there's only a mirror on the wall and some thin jackets. Yet, among neutral phrases of the difficult conversation, like the profile of death leaping out from among the cards in a deck, out slips the phrase that I've feared hearing for a long time, knowing that it would be uttered one day: "This is the last time we can talk."

My look is like mold from the city where Roos silently flashes and sucks me in. I omniview the streets and the insides of the buildings, the barrels of drink in the storerooms under the street, the bridges by canals, and the dusty objects in the cellars, the topography (I identify it) of Utrecht, the light of an autumn afternoon, civilian and official interiors, everything and all that is inside everything, cupboards and chests, and what lies in the drawers of the furniture, and in those right there my voice resounds with the inflection of a condemned person.

"You just spoke those words, but I have the impression that they were shut up in your throat as in a jar, and that I've been hearing them for some time, held back inside the jar."

"I . . . don't love you."

Her hands flat on the tabletop. With the tips of my fingers I touch the fluid skin at pulse level, in the direction of the phalanxes (above the cigarette stand they turn on the lamp decorated with labels from

Dewar's) I touch the fluid flesh, lightly, softly, the gesture of one trying to stroke the surface of the water in a receptacle and not wrinkle it, but the water whirls, the flesh whirls, fountains follow one another—dry, slimy—pitted streets, bridges with broken parapets, desolate houses on the edge of a stretch of railroad tracks, posts with black wires wrapped around them, the fronts of ruined factories full of dusty pieces of broken glass, trash piled up in vacant lots, infested canals, abandoned gardens. She slowly moves her hands away from under my fingers. The gesture of taking her handkerchief out of her purse and discreetly passing it over her lowered eyes. Through what meanderings, through what play of mirrors placed in time, did Bellini see her?

"I'd like to know why I love you in such a cutting way."

"If you'd stop talking, everything would be easier." (Her voice perturbed, tense, a salt-filled vein on the point of breaking.) "I beg you not to try to see me. I also beg you not to leave here with me. I've got to be alone."

I can't make out whether she adds a farewell or whether the word "goodbye" is the gesture of getting up and leaving. With her passage the light white curtains in the bar flutter. I follow her, Rue de Vaugirard, along the Luxembourg, closed now. In the distance beside the black spiked grillwork, Roos seems smaller. Four altar boys—with scarlet cassocks and surplices, holding up a black canopy with poles and gold decorations—pass me, catch up with her. She goes along the narrow, treeless street under the canopy, and perhaps because of the night her suit also seems to have grown dark. The lightning flashes continue, more frequent and shorter, lighting up the yellow tips of the grillwork surrounding the Luxembourg. I hear a distant and rhythmic roar of cannon.

Restraining the desire to lick her the way dogs and cats do with their whelp, I stand still before the shop with items from the twenties, I look for an instant at the dolls, the ingenuous packages, the posters ("Rom Ste. Croix," "Koniak I," "Mate Θ AIOY"), then I turn left and go up to the Weigels'. Propped up on pillows, the sick man tries to breathe through his mouth. Bathed in sweat. In spite of everything, he says he feels cold. Suzanne is fanning him. I catch the mingled smell of hot sweat and sandalwood. Julie, with a threadbare towel, tries to dry him.

"Lev Nikolayevich Myshkin . . ." (He speaks in starts. His muted voice reminds me of a rust-filled current breaking into pieces under the earth.) "Life is definitely too great a burden for men. Living, Nikolayevich Myshkin, can it not be a crime? Nothing is more impotent and static, yes, static, than our love. Our love doesn't save others. Rather . . . rather . . . it can condemn them."

"You're seeing things darkly. Tomorrow . . ."

"No, no. Ever since yesterday I've felt clairvoyant, Lev Nikolayevich. Look at these two."

Suzanne advises him: "Don't talk. You get worse when you get excited."

I ask: "Where's your mother?"

"She went to lie down for a while. She's exhausted."

"Look at these two. What can my love do for them? Love has no instruments. It has the instruments of pleasure. Nothing else. It's an event in itself. Sometimes one can make the rivers of joy and fullness flow for the beings one loves. But it's by chance. One's love, underneath it all, isn't responsible for that."

Without looking at the sisters, but addressing them, and with difficulty, as if I, too, needed air, I let slip: "I love. And I'm desperate. That woman, I run in her direction. Do you understand? I'm launched, I fall into the web of the things that form her. We collide with so many shadows! You two, I'd also like to redirect the rivers toward you. But who can do that? Who can do it?"

The dying man has his eyes closed. I put my hand on his shoulder. Without opening his eyes, he grasps it strongly for an instant. The palm icy, sweaty. He lets go of it. I go into the living room and collapse onto the sofa, beside the lamp. My eyes burn. On the arm of the couch, a piece of silk, left there by Julie, full of sewing exercises: glove embroidery, backstitching, overlapping, double stitching, hemming.

Suzanne comes and sits down beside me. "Do you think my father is dying?" "I don't know; maybe." "Don't worry so, you're more unprotected than we are." I look at her hair, gathered, as always, at the level of her ears: "I believe you. But you can't know that." "I can. I know."

Confused, I run my hand over her hair in a protective gesture, an archaic gesture. The distant rumble of the city seems to form a part of the furniture, the floor, the walls. The old mandolin lies upside down on an easy chair.

T

Cecília Among the Lions

11

On my way to the Fiscal Commission, I cross the Avenida Rio Branco and see a crowd near the Buarque de Macedo Bridge. Cars and buses drag along, I hear comments about the man hit by a truck: he's lying on the sidewalk by the Apolo Docks. I go along the Rua da Guia toward the Marine Arsenal Square. I turn left, however, come out onto the dock, and go over to the crowd. Covered with newspapers in the two-o'clock sun, the dead man, with the patience of the dead, is also waiting for the Police to arrive. When did he die? Between eleven and noon. Why is he still there? There's a shortage of police vehicles. Do they know who he is? I go away and head toward the Commission. Hermelinda and Hermenilda already know about the accident. At four o'clock, on the way back, I retrace my steps past the Apolo Docks. The poor man is still on the street, a stray dog lying under a sun that burns less now, still waiting for a police van to come and take him away. Vehicles pass more rapidly and few passengers notice the crowd, which has grown smaller. The victim's shoes, worn on the soles. Faces appear at the top windows of a building across the way, indifferent hands point down. They disappear. A breeze starts up and the newspapers covering the unknown man's face flutter under chunks of brick. The Treasurer owns a pair of pants just like those which were torn in the fall. The Sun is reflected on the oily waters of the Capibaribe and, far off, from the other side of the Bridge, lights up the trees on the Praça da República, the statues that stand over the Forum, the gardens of Government House, behind the barracks of the Guard. At the Bank I call the Police. None of the public servants answering my calls has anything to do with corpses thrown onto the street: they all say call another number. Damião appears in the doorway of the building, distraught, he asks a clerk something and heads for the elevator. Before I talk to him, I already know who the accident victim in the street is. As we go down, I ask him how it can be that the Treasurer was lying on a public street without the company where he works knowing anything about it and doing something. Damião answers laconically: "He was fired. Three days ago." Cecília, for the time being, knows nothing.

We drive along the Rua do Pombal at two in the morning, Dagoberto and I in Damião's taxi, following the ambulance with the mutilated body of the man who has assumed the role of father and protector for those who had only a mother and no protection. Dagoberto, in the back seat of the taxi, is singing softly and Damião grinds his teeth. The ambulance, its siren on, goes down the Avenida Norte. My feet hurt and my head spins. Empty stomach, a hollow wounded animal. Impossible to eat after I don't know how many cups of coffee with a taste of formaldehyde, sugary, cold, drunk at the Institute of Forensic Medicine. Fever? Now the whore of 1930 is a widow and all alone. What will she and her hybrid cat do when the body arrives? She's nineteen years old, with almost five of them spent in the red-light district, a razor cut on her shoulder, plated jewelry, three dresses, a large yellow pitcher, two venereal chancres, a pair of silver shoes, and a live grenade hidden under the bed when the future Treasurer meets her, takes her out of the district, and marries her. What attracts him? The mad laugh with which she faces up to things. Razor cut, venereal disease, men's passions, bridal gown—she cauterizes everything, burns it with raillery.

"Do they think that with a white dress or a certified piece of paper they're going to stop me from being a whore? Let's tell the truth: I used to be anybody's whore and now I'm yours. You open your wallet and I open my legs. The game is just the same as it was before, except more restful. Why fancy things up? Do you think I'm going to play the fine lady and belch out puritan stuff? Give young girls advice? Oh, not a chance. There's nothing more sickening than to have a street bitch like me putting on the airs of a pet Pekinese or Saint Rocco's kindly dog."

Raul Nogueira de Albuquerque e Castro, the Treasurer, during the days of fireworks and a porch decorated with lanterns, takes pleasure in repeating, between coughs, slapping his thigh, those words delivered by the Fat Woman. His femur sawed off now, he travels through the night on the Avenida Norte. My eyes are heavy and we all go along in silence. How is the stranger onto whom they will graft the bone we have given up? The Treasurer is obsessed with the appearance of his great-grandfather, buried intact and coming back mutilated, wearing a hat of unknown origin. His great-grandfather's arm and his own femur are wandering through the world. We roll through the long straight stretch of Cruz Cabugá, cut through mangrove swamps, between black landfills, even blacker under the shrouded sky. Straw in my stomach, my tongue thick and salty, dry, an old in-sole. Damião breaks the silence: "What a fuckup. We'd be there now if it wasn't for that bone business." No one answers. I open the car window; the heavy wind blows in my face. They've turned off the siren on the ambulance. A few lighted windows in the Santo Amaro Hospital. Flat, infested with shacks, the banks of the Beberibe River. Out of the mud and its gardens of mangroves, shellfish, and crabs comes the smell of carrion. How sad it would be, Raul Nogueira de Albuquerque e Castro, if you—who in the years of plenty turn on all the lights in the villa while Cenira's violin, Mauro's guitar, Eurílio's flute, and everyone's voices challenge the stony sound of the riptide on Milagres Beach—could see, on this early morning, the route of your body, this journey in silence and darkness! In the misty shadows the few buildings are barely visible, the Naval Cadet School, the Tacaruna Factory. Damião passes the ambulance to show the way. An urge to vomit: I swallow dryly. We go into the sleeping city. The villa, as on its nights of glory, has its lights on and its windows open.

My mother comes to meet us, calm, a black shawl thrown over her shoulders, followed by Lucíola, Isabel, and some strangers. She only recommends: "Be careful with him. He's been bruised too much already."

I run to the bathroom. To void the hollow beast (no: mud-drinker, straw-eater) that occupies my stomach. A taste of gall fills my mouth, I feel bitterness in my throat and with violence into the hole of the toilet I throw all the curses I know. I throw them at the Treasurer, not knowing that the curses are not so much against him as against his death, baited into the deviation of Cecília's condemnation and premature end. Not being able, I, to vomit up myself and all my mud and all the mud of the Earth!

People on the porch and even under the mango trees, in the shade. Isabel goes over to the Fat Woman. In spite of the dull and undulating sound of voices (cut at intervals by sobs or a suppressed laugh), I can hear her say: "They've come." The animal leaps nimbly from Mama's body, steals under the coffin, and runs for the trees, its long tail doubled over its back. "Both of them?" "Mother and daughter." "Then I'm going inside. They may not want to see me." She turns to me: "You stay." There's a movement of people, a surge of voices that then dies out, a shuffling of chairs and shoes on the floor. The Treasurer's mother, led by Dulce, appears and halts on the threshold, not in a clear or conclusive way, her hesitation is necessary and, in a certain sense, calculated, a pause just like the pause with which, in reading, we separate certain words where there is no punctuation, accentuating, with that brief and subtle delay, the importance of the postponed expression. The old woman, with life's training, has an exact notion of the solemnity that marks this moment. Her hesitation doesn't escape me: it's an emphasis and she plays it exactly right.

She comes forward and contemplates the Treasurer. Here, however, her training and her years are of no use to her: this one here, lying in front of her, is her son. Giving in to the improvisation of her suffering, harsh, indisputable, and urgent (behold the dead man and his indifference), she takes him by the lapel of his jacket and raises him toward her. No, she tries to. As one who might have said, with vehemence: "Courage, man!" while the face, lacking in hope, asks: "Can it be true?" The gesture is lost, rejected by the rigidity of the corpse. She still insists. But then she lifts her hands and places them, useless, on the edge of the casket. The wrinkles on the dead man's lapels mark her frustrated impulse. Dulce goes around the casket and clutches her fingers around her broad suède purse. The creases of her mouth are deep and marked. Because of the loss? Because of the light of the candles? How many years has it been since she last wore that faded turban (it used to be lilac-colored), decorated with a false amethyst? She takes a seashell from her purse and lays it on her brother's stomach. The silence, as if from a distance, respectful—children holding hands, a circle—surrounds the two women and the dead man. This, all in all, the axial scene. How appearance can deceive us! The dead man and the silence in the parlor, the arrival and the actions of Dulce and their mother, the shell (in it, Dulce and her brother perhaps had heard in childhood the sound of the same waters, Time, the events of the world, including this moment), everything simply coincides— and only coincides—with a greater event, on the point of being fulfilled. A discreet event. Footsteps sound on the porch, light ones, someone with metal heels is approaching and not coming alone. Dulce takes the pearly shell from her purse, large, like two crossed hands, with its mysterious spiral—and places it tenderly on the dead man's navel. Then I raise my eyes. At the door, in the midst of the shapes lighted by the candles and the bright morning filtered by the merry glass of the transoms, bathed in a kind of unreality, I see, between the permutable shapes of Hermenilda and Hermelinda (but I see only what I can see, the innocent surface of the event), Cecília, a few steps away from me, caught after a thousand turns in the carefully laid snare, Cecília with her short hair, her luminous eyes, her narrow hips,

her thin legs, unlike anyone else, drawn by the dead man—that lure—
and thrown once and for all into the area of joys and evils of which I
am to be the bearer, the messenger, the provider, the instrument, the
hand. Ten thousand men are in her flesh: as in the center of an astonished eye. Ten thousand men are in her flesh: as on a path little trav-
eled for ten years. Ten thousand men, adorned with their own fables.
In her body there are bodies. Cecília, body and—at the same time—
world, looks at me from the doorway with the joy that is born in her
eyes and I don't know at what point in her face, maybe in all the lines
of her face, a new face, startled, avid, and happy, without the slightest
trace of evil, yes, without hate, yes, touched by audacity, decision,
strength, a face of one who isn't afraid of lions. In her stable and unstable flesh, real and magical, in her transparent and many times visible
flesh (in Cecília's flesh perception is repeated, grows in reflections, answers, and explosions), in her flesh, a simulacrum of memory, the
presence of beings I am to love by loving her. Hermenilda and Hermelinda lower their heads.

I perceive everything—the commendation of the body, the work
of the gravediggers, the dust on the gravestones, the discreet wailing of
the women—and, alien to everything, within a clarity that illuminates
me within and is like a globe made from the pieces of broken mirrors,
with thousands of beams crisscrossing, I contemplate Cecília in the
noonday sun. With her eyes (quick black lions buzzing in them), she
seems to tell me: "I have my life in my hands, Abel. Receive it. But listen: love, a difficult artifact to handle, is filled with secret buttons and
knives, which, with the slightest ineptitude or distraction, will leap
into flight and wound the flesh." Am I deceived, I, if I recognize my
substance in this companion? She emerges from me and my vigil, so
like a prolonged sleep—she and her beings, some naked, others
clothed, some weaponless, others armed. In her body simultaneously,
as it seems to me now, I contemplate my memory and hers. The
human presences in those memories. As if I were able to see, hear,
touch the visions, not always clear, but full of truth and never fixed at
one single age of her lives, the visions or specters that inhabit memory
and have, along with toys possessed before and the places where one
has lived, the dubious name of recollections. "Cecília, the balance is
not very sure and is illusory, I well know, when man is included in it.
Even in Eden, that state lasts much less than can be hoped for. How
many steps shall we take together?" This minute: a measureless,
spherical bramble patch, burning around me, as in a fire of diamonds.

O

The Story of Ø, Twice-Born   **19**

Twelve years, six months, and two days. Time, life, events—fenestrated parlors. On all the walls open windows, and the windows look into other rooms surrounded by windows through which the windows of new and strange parlors can be seen, and so numerous are the parlors that each one is the center of the rest. In this mobile, imprecise center, with ages that are not any definite age and two pairs of eyes that scrutinize as if they were one single pair or even one eye, in this center, probing the next windows through all the windows, I, inserted in a play of arbitrary mirrors where the repetitions, for being countless, tend toward the spherical, see myself, see the others, and also see myself in the act of seeing myself and seeing those around me. I see myself, I see the others, and the varied settings in which we move. All. All the settings. All of us. One pair of eyes sees from within another pair: it's as if they were of a different substance, they're more tender eyes, more innocent than the older eyes. In that way this world of windows opens on numberless segments of the flow of things that, by being numerous, evoke the spherical form, and is duplicated, refracted by my double look. Two dilatable spheres of salons surrounded by windows, some crossing through others, echoing, echoing from my steps, from lost voices, echoing, too, from my silences, and not circumscribed by those twelve years, six months, and two days: all my existence is there—and that mobile, fleeting center which moves from one parlor to another, as if it were the center of gravity of time, is one of the forms—a concrete form—of the present, of the ungraspable now. I, trying to read my name in the pounding of a hammer, and I, before Inês, perplexed, aware that her ways and words have something new about them, but not knowing what the new consists of and what its fruits are, I, squeezing the trigger; in the mouth a taste of blood—an afternoon in—the trigger of the revolver—August? Alameca Franca? I? A fearful schoolgirl holding up her hand. Faded marigolds in an old piece: of newspaper the early morning sky grows pale (I hear the sea beating on the jetty) and I with this man (   ) naked (   ) knees on the floor while he asks: repeating, the, words heard from another mouth at another time, gripping; my wrist with such force; that my hand goes to sleep what will become? of us? and I answer and sob as if sobbing really were the only. Passable answer. My grandmother sixty-eight years old seventy Olavo Haiano and I the funeral of the black woman at seventy-five the fire in the building under construction opposite the Martinelli. (I.) Visiting my parents the funeral of the black woman through the city Inácio Gabriel on the Praça da República one cold dusk toward the end, of June my grandmother, seventy-nine eighty, other ages the sun; at eleven o'clock I; with Inácio we I & he watching the geese glide along the lake not just. At those different ages. Turning to the husband the right hand turned toward me, no, against me, my grandfather at his writing desk piled high with writs under the light, of the lamp, he on his deathbed in some drawer or other his dentures, a metal lamp the girl behind him/occupies the leather chair and looks at the gilt/labels, of the books, on the shelves and—in Inês's—room taller now than Inês in her hand a pair of sewing scissors holding the scissors by the tip I offer them to Inês in an insti-gating gesture my face hard. A? Stone. The serpent biting me in the ribs. In this parlor: lying on the rug, the right leg bent and the thigh resting on Abel's flank: in another parlor, dark, still I, a dark being, looking into the rooms next door, some lighted, others not, I—old?, mature?—thinking shadows, acting. My act: a shadow.

With the trembling of my hands, I must have scratched the other side of the record, a rhythmic and disagreeable shock wounds the me-lodious voices of the singers. The wheels of the automobiles on the av-enue, slide along the brake, the wheels, ready at my feet; the sound of the saw in some construction work, sharp, crosses through my body; I can barely see my hands, my eyes hazy. I in the parlor, standing, bent over the moving record. A rhythmic shock. The dragging on the rug and the repeated kisses around my feet, shots that almost miss the mark. In the voices of the singers I make out the words *"aeternum,"* *"vita,"* and *"amicitiae."* Abel kisses my feet.

My grandfather refuses to have wrinkles like a magistrate; a point of honor, for him, to be up to date on the law and jurisprudence. At the same time, he is fearful of an alteration in the concept of justice that he had when he assumed his judgeship. This desire for coherence, converted into a dogma, transforms his activity in Justice into a jungle of sophistry. He shows me his extensive notes, accumulated over al-most three decades of service. For whom? His voice measured, as-sured, where it is possible to catch, by sharpening one's ear, a fright:

"No one can catch me in an inconsistency." (I sense that inconsistency dogs his heels, sleeps with him, gets into his pockets.) "I challenge anyone to find, in all my verdicts, any single one that contradicts another." He classifies cases by content. Organizing his notes takes up even more time than the time needed to put his verdicts together, but the files—Ark of Equity and Justice—do the job for which they exist: my grandfather, before giving an opinion, and even before forming a judgment about the cases that reach his hands, reviews his old verdicts attentively. "The skill consists in the management of jurisprudence. One of its functions is to give solidity to our suppositions. This is because a magistrate doesn't change. A magistrate has no right to hold two opinions, even if he were to live to be a thousand years old. Otherwise he doesn't deserve the position." It's inconceivable for him that time or events could in some way change, at the age of seventy-three, a judgment written down around the time of his forty-eighth birthday. A verdict by Grandfather, an exemplary old man, is something that has reached coagulation. *June '33:* indignant, he develops a cluster of arguments and asks for the maximum penalty for a carpenter who, having been cheated, murders his boss with his hammer. *September '58:* he suggests the same punishment for an identical crime, going back in time for his reasons and arriving at indignation from those reasons, so that all is finished and done and he can sleep in peace. A great man, I hear many times in the parlor that has been transformed into a funeral parlor while I move among the official-looking men and haughty women. A great man, the kind demanded by a world that was also dead.

Slowly I raise my left foot, Abel takes it in his hands and kisses the sole, kisses the heel and the ankle, thirty, forty times he kisses the muscles of my leg, slowly comes up, kisses the hollow of my knee, once more I touch the floor with the foot that is raised, he kisses my knee, I turn toward him and his face rises up between my closed thighs, I hear the abstract sound of his kisses, but he is no longer kissing my flesh, he is kissing the space between my thighs, on his knees, while in the back light hands accompany the contours of the legs, the roundness of the buttocks, he models my hips with light hands.

Perhaps born with me, and reborn, there was a serpent—Wrath. It poisons the image of my father, of my mother (are they really my father and mother? do we have fathers and mothers?), it struggles against the walls covered with brown paper, against the grimy flowers on the walls among which I spend one childhood and begin another, against, bites the world. I carry this serpent in me, coiled about my ribs, and I don't try to hide it: its scales sometimes peep out through my fingernails, sometimes its contractile body fills my mouth and I spit it out, it rolls about my neck and it serpent-peeps over my shoulders—right or left—at those who are docile and accept everything without complaint. Inês flies over things, she flies between me and things and distracts this reptile, puts it to sleep. Experimenting, through names always replaced and never repeated, to get into my being and know it, she weaves me into the things, the day-by-day of the house, into the temperature of the rooms and into everything that this pleasant island has and irradiates. A snake charmer. Even though after giving in I resist this full world, I learn to see it as irresistible. Wrath, sleek, prudent, coils up amidst my viscera. It dozes. Its long sleep exhales an odor of jasmines. Lost, adrift in space or time, are the pieces of the immense nocturnal machine. Are all of them the first acceptance? I accept the room, the house, the garden, the entranceway, I accept the street, I surrender, I forget the machine (proof: when I go to the Martinelli, its slow deterioration, like a suspended fleet that has scattered), I turn my back on the black and forsaken part of the world. Each time my going to my parents' place is less spontaneous, and each time the corridors adrift in the building seem longer and darker.

A honeycomb breaks, a sweet fig opens—and the honey runs between my thighs. He kisses my pubic hair. I wake up in the silence of the night; no voice at all, weak as it might be, can I hear in my body, wandering. Some kisses through the thick mass of my hair wound my flesh, wound my sex, the veins open, they seem too many and too thick for the blood that flees. The breakup of the machine. The words wander through its openings and hollows. From time to time I can still find the voices in me again. The kisses wound my flesh, I hold my breath, I take his head in my hands and I see that it has no weight. *Aeternum, vita, amicitiae.*

My father in an easy chair, his legs on pillows, still not recovered from the incrustations: metal plates on his shins. The horn trumpet hangs around his neck, answering the questions I put to him. Both ears rubber—the spinning of the swords. On the sofa, my mother and two children. She asks me envious questions; it's not for me to be accepted and she herself still excluded that she takes me to her sister's funeral mass. The children cut an old shirt of my father's into little pieces with shears. They look the way I do and their look is malignant. With aversion, with hate, and then with horror, I listen to them conversing and exchanging smiles filled with malice. The serpent darts its tongue in some secret part of my body. These are the ones, these, this boy and his sister, these are the ones who salt my eyes and stick me with pins on the days I go from one room to another wondering about my own name and wavering in an inconsistent world. Are these the ones? Then it's my turn to torture them.

P

Julius Heckethorn's Clock   2

In spite of the modernity of the lines and what it takes from current technology, J. H.'s clock, so far removed from those that pricked Plato's curiosity or the ones that marked the conquering march of the Persians in Egypt, is situated in the center of a web of relationships more complex and ambiguous than that which exists around a sundial or the one that gives astronomical clocks their justification. At first blush, nothing in that device arouses attention; unless, perhaps, a certain majesty that emanates from its bearing, the measured movement of its pendulum—one second to go, one second to return—and the neatness with which, in Roman numerals, the numbers on its face are painted. Otherwise it is a clock like all the rest and, among its kind, only a bit taller than average. It strikes the hour, however (an incongruous number of notes), and then we come to see it with new eyes: the sounds, different from what we usually hear, surprise us. Our amazement grows as we perceive that they are not repeated; rather, they are varied for the hours that follow without our being able to grasp the law—because there must be one—that governs such changes. When the principles that orient the workmanship of the clock are known, that law will also be explained along with a parcel of its implications. Our interest in such rare genius will grow, the narrative of certain human vicissitudes related to it.

O

The Story of Ꝋ, Twice-Born   **20**

That torment me? are these children? the two? If: I should ask my
mother. I will go down the smutty steps of the Martinelli Building,
continually more worn, I will go down those steps slowly and in the
middle of the stairs I will turn back. To ask her the question. I will remain before the door, hesitant, I will remain before the door, not daring to press the bell, I will hear the laughter in the living room
and—suddenly—the voice, the voice of one of them, an infantile and
depraved voice like that of someone on the top rung of vileness: "Is
she the Hernidom?" In the voice, shameful and offensive to perceive,
similarities to mine. I turn half around, I leave, I hold off reaching a
clarification. Days and days, intrigued, repeating that inexplicable
phrase: "Is she the Hernidom?" Wondering who or what the Hernidom can be. Hernidom, in the end, can it be the same as Wrath?

He kisses my sex and holds up my breasts, the crocodile strolls
beside the silver teapot that has fallen onto the rug, branches and flowers that grow out of the rug almost hide the walls and twine around the
chandeliers, twine around, hang out the window, the lionesses pass
through our bodies, the lionesses, the rabbit, nanny goats with white
hair and bitches with human heads pass through our bodies, walk in
the room, climb up onto the chairs. He strokes the nipples of my
breasts with his fingers, his posture is that of a man with a weapon
aimed at him, arms raised up, bright daisies bloom on my breasts, violets burst forth inside my stomach and the crocodile—purple, red, and
green—the crocodile slips along beside the silver teapot.

Inácio Gabriel, how old are you, Inácio? Too serious for sixteen;
too slim for twenty. An adolescent with a fragile frame, an ephemeral
foreteller, that's all. Praça Antônio Prado, cold dusk toward the end of
May. Ash-gray sky, damp streets and sidewalks. My childish steps
echo in the silence, I, holding my father's hand, over those same stones
on desolate Sunday afternoons. It's no longer raining; the tops of some
buildings lighted by the sun glitter against the leaden sky, and from
the ground one cannot see where the sun is coming from. Startling in
Inácio's eyes is the absence of ambition and gleam. Everything in him

makes one think of a pale watercolor, a landscape glimpsed through the mist: the thin eyebrows, the discreet smile, the veiled voice, and even his way of walking—the inaudible, cautious steps. He came from Recife less than a year ago and his well-pressed but cheap suit doesn't give him much protection against the cold. If he owned a sweater at least! The thick black book—he works at the 11th Registry—seems too heavy for his arms. Vehicles sprinkled with rain and people in a hurry pass, many of them with an anxious look.

"I hadn't seen an afternoon like this in São Paulo up till now. Everything so light! Notice the smell of the city. Different when the air's been washed."

"What's your name?"

"Inácio Gabriel."

I look him in the face, in the depth of his eyes, I look at him, in the face, in some part of his eyes I read the threats that surround him and I see him in his truth, innocent, unprotected, intent on the variations of smell, with his silent walk and his restless hands, I see him coming from so far off through so many byways, alleys, detours to find me in this small and brutal square, no silence and no trees, disoriented in the world, with death smiling inside his eyes in a cunning way, I see him destroyed and I understand that this casual encounter is the announcement of others, and something never sensed before unwinds in me and I look at the fugitive sun on the distant walls, certain that only we can see him—I take his hand and decide that I must give him something, that I will give him something with urgency, because he certainly isn't on the street to receive, he doesn't have the hands to grab, he goes in silence amidst the clamor and the shouts of ambition, he's a stranger and will be reduced to dust, I will save him from nothingness (who could save him?), but he will have company for a few steps.

The two, I and I, the two, contemplating things and the metamorphosis itself. Inês, although formed to go among people without being sensed, applies her fascination. She doesn't choose reasons to laugh with pleasure, even though with a touch of melancholy (the upper incisors always appear between her thin lips) and her measureless tenderness, she expresses herself with diminutive suffixes, applied to plants, furniture, nonexistent beings, parts of her body, belongings: "Where's my blousy?" "Have a sweetsy." "I put it in my pursy." "Did you hurt your footsy?" "My eyesies are so tired!" "What a warm bedsy." "How I miss my love, the Bird That Flew the Coop!" She blows me adulations and pet names: "Luisinha, you were made for silks. Look at your little fingers, how straight they are. Such skin, Lordsy. You're a lucky one, Vanju." She nourishes the idea, already strong in me, that it would be a disaster to lose my privileges, I, with these straight fingers, this tender skin, made for velvets, damasks. Behold me, then, servile before beadles and teachers, behold me carrying bouquets of faded marigolds, wrapped in a newspaper, my arm outstretched, the flowers taller than my head. "Did you notice your grandfather? He talks to you with such love! He works with the law. He's an important man, Naná. The heart of a dove." I agree, and then I'm proud of that bald, deliberate man, elastic bands on his shirt sleeves, visor on his forehead, zealously drawing up verdicts that are the altered reflections of others. Sitting in a leather chair, I read the titles on the bindings of the books on the shelves. I hear the scratch of pen on paper. My grandfather gets up to consult his files. Inês, half opening the door, opens her eyes wide, smiling, in his direction and retires in silence. Her gestures accentuate the distinction, mine, of being there, forming part of the shadow that surrounds Grandfather and his desk, while great questions take the direction he suggests with his coherence.

We get up from the floor. The stag, sitting next to the large grandfather clock whose pendulum goes back and forth slowly, looks at us. We roll in the air, among the foliage, the branches, the animals, we roll in the air, in a strong embrace, we alight on the rug. The noise of a crowd, some shouts, a laugh, a call. Can it be my voices that echo in me? Plants and animals return to our bodies.

My grandmother and her walled-in life, a web of intercommunicable cycles, restricted, so that her acts and words tend to be repeated with almost imperceptible variations, or an imperceptible piling up— acts and words—some upon the others, obsessively. Her face changes under the makeup, the line of her spinal column curves slightly as her chin, seeking compensation, is lifted, the words are spoken in the usual rhythm, but a few syllables, in growing numbers, are lost on her tongue, the quick and scrutinizing glance becomes less efficient and her hair blacker, for she increases the dye as the graying progresses. Almost unchanged, in spite of all, is the repertory of criticism, orders, meals, and strolls, that inopportune ritual which does not come together for any precise end. Words very often repeated: "How can you deceive yourself like that? A man who has lived so long and among the enemies of society! She's irretrievable. She's slipped out of our hands. What good were your thousands of verdicts and your law journals? In the end . . ." She doesn't elucidate a single time what that loose phrase hides, enigmatic, left suspended.

I move, at the age of thirteen legal years, among children of nine, learning in school the same things they do. We don't understand one another: I'm indifferent to their games and intent on the numerous things they don't yet perceive. Taller than all of them, older (and simultaneously younger), I also stand out because of my fatness and I go through the rooms and recess yard with a deep feeling of segregation. An anachronistic monster. Crossed in me are my two births and the daughters of those two births, two bodies in one, only one of them visible; the other, in wait, is only revealed by the voice that alternates with that of the visible body or by the extemporaneous teething, or by still less evident manifestations. At the mercy of those alternations, my periods oscillate, irregular and sometimes harrowing, with no one's knowing it. That is the rhythm of my apprenticeship. Months pass in which the double notion I have of things seems to be governed by the newer body, and I'm unable to progress. I'm suspended, expelled, one scolding follows another. The flowers I offer are thrown into the wastebasket along with the newspaper they're wrapped in.

How many times do we see each other, Inácio Gabriel? Ten? Twelve? Maybe less, maybe even less. And those few times seem to be one single time, one single meeting with interruptions. A hasty meeting, like that of two people at the station between trains. They blow the parting whistle, conductors shout, latecomers arrive on the run and throw their baggage onto the platform of the train. We know that something essential will not be said, that the most important, what must be confessed before anything else, will only occur to us when we will have left in our own different directions. Words stumble, gestures stumble, and there are silences, and the silences afflict us because we know that standing face to face is a fleeting privilege, but we go on without speaking. And suddenly we see: we're alone. Did we do everything? Did we say everything? Fleeting Sunday afternoons, almost all of them misty. A year of little sun, 1951. I quiver with joy, for the first time I know the pleasure of joy. But this joy gives birth to a bird still caged and restless. I look at Inácio Gabriel in the darkness of the movies; his attention on the screen, he doesn't know that I'm observing him; his placid face has something of a reflection, an old man is reflected in him. Suddenly he sees me, sees that I'm observing him, the old man flees and his youth comes to the surface. The Municipal Galleries, intermission during a concert; I come back from the ladies' room and I see him from a distance, his hand on his chin; he has nothing of the adolescent who a while before throws paper airplanes into the orchestra seats and, smiling, gives names to the women fluttering on the ceiling, even his color is different; I go over and the face that is lifted up to me is the one I love. We, in the Viennese Pastry Shop, buying sweets to eat in the Praça da República, looking at the ducks in the small pond. "What will become of us?" I am not to know that through his mouth another voice is speaking and I can't understand this sound of waves breaking on rocks, heard distinctly at the same instant he asks the question. "We who, Inácio?" "We who in one way or another don't want to oppress the rest." I take his hand: it's trembling, burning, he has a fever and must be cold. He takes me to the streetcar stop, he waits for me to get on and waves to me. Happily, in spite of the fever. I get off and go back, to observe him without his seeing me. He goes along the sidewalk among the pedestrians, slowly, his left hand in his pocket, looking at the trees. The line of his shoulder blades visible under the light-colored coat. How fragile you are, Gabriel, and how little my love takes care of you! Death, ready to throw her net over you, follows you subtly.

T

Cecília Among the Lions   12

Oh, human doings, oh, succession of things, halt ye if ye can. Time, go against thy course, violate thy rhythm, interrupt thy serene impassive flow, or tumble out over me without course, without sluice. Cecília is with me. Her face, seen against the stones of the beach and the sea—the sea red and green at this hour of the afternoon—seems simultaneously eternal and fluid, fleeing my possession and even contemplation. A face fluctuating between opposites. Her hands rest on the white towel beside the glasses of wine, somewhat restless. Men and women slip out of her body, walk among the rustic chairs and tables of this restaurant placed among coconut palms (some trunks penetrate the straw roof, and when the wind blows more strongly I can hear the brush of the palm leaves against the covering), they come out, sit on the stones, strangers, their footprints cross on the sand. One of

them touches me lightly on the wrist. A pale man, the forehead sloping, the nose aquiline, the chin delicate. His two eyes gleam, but one
has no sight, the right one: the other contemplates me, affectionately.
My father. Not the carnal father and not even an imaginary father. A
father of a different kind. I recognize him and catch the smell of his
body. A smell of constant but not arduous work. Cecília slowly talks
about what she does at her job. From early in the morning she moves
between the Pedro II Hospital and welfare institutions—dispensaries,
labor unions, social centers—dealing with negligent clerks and almost
always impassive doctors, seeking to solve tangled problems. A mea-
ger salary, sometimes paid late. The things she talks about, inserting
her into the vulgarity of life and revealing her way of living, active and
generous, impede me—I take her restless hands—at this first prolonged meeting, from seeing her in a cathartic way, with no dust on the
ankles. Intangible? "They expect nothing. The most difficult of all is to
avoid their stopping." Cecília, bearer of bodies, pomegranate of popu-
lations, is not—unlike me—a marginal being. Her working hours and
even, not rarely, her evening hours are tied in with the tribulations of
those who inhabit the mangrove swamps and outer districts—Água
Fria, Chacon, Vasco da Gama.

The shadow of the restaurant advances toward the sea, and the
golden luminosity of the sky adheres to the rare clouds. Cecília runs
her hand through her short hair. Green lions roar in the waves that
beat upon the rocks.

We go along the beach between the end of the day and the coming of night, between solid land and water, between. The sea seems to
be covered with half-rusted copper coins, red and green. Cecília takes
off her shoes. She's not wearing stockings and her feet, a bit long at the
instep, used to walking, are put down rhythmically on the wet sand.
My father and his rulers. With tailor's chalk he sketches a pattern on
sailcloth. The waves successively form and break up, noisily: and spots
of oil and coconut husks and pieces of tar thrown overboard by some
ship. The sky is a golden cupola with the effigies of turtles. Cecília: a
thin figure, bones of a bird, the magic of her flesh making her bones
even thinner. Plumage. I can't see wings on her. So light, however, are
the prints of her feet on the clear sand and such a charm exists in her
bones that I wonder: Is she floating?

We go along the beach, with no goal. We breathe September in
with great gulps. The instants are days. Growing, on this walk where
afternoons and evenings are concentrated, is my love for Cecília, the

necessity of incorporating her into my life (or of incorporating my life into hers), our intimacy and our knowing each other grow. Hermenilda or Hermelinda doesn't lie when she says that I'm a man of letters and books. I plan to write. What for? At a certain point in his so prolonged government, Vargas worries about sauba ants. He could have conceived of the multiplication of birds and anteaters as a program. Writing will come to acquire a more precise and elevated meaning for me someday. For the moment, it represents a way of not succumbing, of not living my life haphazardly. An artificial decision. Cecília. An honest woman in spite of all. I invent, along with the ants, imaginary birds and anteaters with tongues of fire. Throwing some words against others, exercising a kind of friction upon them, striking them until they give off sparks: until unexpected demons leap inside the words. In a society like ours, which, more or less like your clients at Pedro II Hospital, I mistrust, and which doesn't attract me, what remains to be done is to rub consciences together—until they, in the same way, burst into flame and light up the old carcass. Both, it can easily be seen, more or less gratuitous activities, and, in a certain sense, outside the law. I'm far from having the virtues required to inflame consciences, the way Francisco Julião does in the canebrakes. I lack the blind energy of reformers; and with my tendency, perhaps archaic, to rationalize with every given possibility of a problem, it would take a lot to make me decide what values should be burned or replaced. Nor, at least, do I know how to say with certainty if the profession that you exercise, fraternal and corrective, is even adequate to the reality in which we live. It can give a meaning to your life. But does it really make any sense today? I'm not capable of answering, Cecília. It remains for me, then—refusing in this way all official stupid forms of living with what I imagine remains of my competence—to attempt machinations with words. A desperate and ensnaring project.

A ram born of the sand and the foam of the waves accompanies us docilely. From inside Cecília, my father, intoning a ballad from his boyhood, looks at me and puts his hand on my shoulder. Felt hat, his black beard shaved, a scar on his neck, his shirt sleeves rolled up. Also docile, he goes along slowly beside the ram. His cheap wristwatch shows five o'clock, more or less.

Adolescents pierce the treacherous waves of the ebb tide. Sometimes a fish flops in the elevated wave. My father, apprehensive, looks behind and draws me aside in a protective gesture. At that moment I hear the sound of bells. A great silver-colored wheel, as tall as a town house, comes rolling along the beach. A metal wheel with eight spokes, wobbling a little, coming along alone, slowly. We open ranks. The wheel comes, giving off heat, it draws closer, full of bells and decorated with colored ribbons. The spokes and the rim, polished, reflect the golden sky, the setting sun, the coppery surface of the sea. The wheel looms larger, passes between us, slowly, the sweet sound of the bells making the afternoon lighter, it goes away, it leaves the rut of its passage on the sand, it curves in the direction of the adolescents who are swimming, the direction is corrected, a solemn wheel, new, shining, going along the sand with no one paying attention to its majestic and unusual passage. It turns to the left, cleaves a breaking wave without being shaken, slowly advances into the sea, disappears in the distance. Great swift clear birds rise up slowly at that point in the sea, fly menacingly, five or six of them, go high and immediately dive, rapidly, their wings folded, as if, famished, they were attacking a school of fish.

Before the birds dive, a new sound begins, this one in Cecília: tambourines. The sound is then answered on the right with a little more intensity by several other tambourines, played by girls between the ages of ten and thirteen. There we are, escorted by the two groups from the Northeastern folk play called the pastoril: seven figures on one side, with long red skirts; seven on the other, with long blue skirts, some faded. Between the two groups and in such a way that part of her body passes through Cecília's, Diana goes, dressed in red and blue, a sign that she belongs to both ranks. On her round tambourine, larger than those of the pastoras, which she shakes with lifted arms, red and blue ribbons also flutter. The long cord holding tight her curly hair is the same color. Diana's legs and Cecília's, the first one's dancing, the second's walking, intertwine. Not all the girls carry tambourines. Two bear a basket with jambos, oranges, and pink mangoes; two hold dahlias and white and colored lilies under their arms. Diana, ceasing her playing, raises her arms even higher, silence falls, and we all stop. Green lions roar in the waves, among the fish. The pastoras suddenly begin a carol, keeping time to the music with their feet and tambourines, the latter decorated with ribbons like those on the great wheel that has disappeared:

> "Come ye, come ye, young and old,
> come ye all here to behold,
> how good this is, how beautiful,
> how good this is and good too bold."

Night is coming on. Between the two ranks comes a man, aged now, with beard and top hat, in a wrinkled morning coat, waving his hands: "I am Modesto Francisco das Chagas Canabarro! I am known in these parts." The ram bleats, Cecília smiles, my father follows us silently.

I tell Cecília (the childish voices around us, the beat of feet on the sand, the festive sound of the tambourines, the breaking of the waves, the smell of Modesto Canabarro's salt and sweat) that I would like to inaugurate the world in her company, at peace with all creatures. Cecília, head down, reminds me that the harmony of the time when the leopard licks the fingers of man no longer exists and will never be found again. She squeezes my hand and with her other hand protects the skirt blown by the wind. Her body continues to people the beach. Following us along with the *pastoras*, accompanying the carol, is a small orchestra: clarinet, cornet, bombardon, bass drum, and a hoarse trombone. On the drum is written "LET SPEAK," the one carrying it, toothless, laughs with joy, dancing to the tempo of the piece. The musicians, of dark color and poorly dressed, wear no shoes. The ram's bell tinkles and the old bearded man continues: "I am Modesto Francisco das Chagas Canabarro!"

The sand, which creaks under my feet and always bore the name of sand, is not the same. Names and things (the word "afternoon" and the afternoon, loving and the word "loving"), things and their names, have been transformed. The world, as we go along the beach now, alive, real, holding hands, is different from the world that precedes this encounter. A dirty coin, buried for a long time, and its clearness after being cleaned. The profile of the King (which hadn't been visible) is seen, the date of minting is seen, the motto is seen, the value (which hadn't been visible) and the gleam of the metal are seen. Cecília's presence reveals the hidden world. Oh, if it were all really new, peaceful— jaguars licking my fingernails—and had a name for the first time.

At night, the house of Hermenilda and Hermelinda, without the warbling that the daytime light brings on in the throats of the birds, gives the impression of being smaller. One of them (are there bird nightmares?) gives off an afflicted peep and from time to time a dull agitation of wings or beaks can be heard. As if the group of birds formed a body—a body that contained all of them—and the body trembled or changed position slightly. Hermenilda passed through Hermelinda and was occupied by the sister. It can happen, I admit, that only their respective names have slipped from one to the other. There was, in any case, a radical exchange: they're not the same. Can it be for that reason that with so much indifference, somewhat somber, looking vaguely about, they hear my clumsy confession with regard to Cecília?

The vibration of the meeting persists in me and I refuse to fall asleep. How many places have I run through tonight? I go from one point in Recife to another and I look people in the face. Do they, those alien presences, evoke their own matrices, existing in Cecília's enchanted body? Might they not be, on the contrary, matrices of concrete beings who pass through the body and form it? How is one to know? I only know that the travelers in front of the ignoble ticket windows in the Bus Station and the filthy old man who watches over the useless rusty turnstile; the fishmongers on the Market Square; the prostitutes on the balconies of the Rua Bom Jesus, showing their tongues to the rhythm of the music that the phonographs are loudly playing in the parlors; the population of the shacks under the black ironwork of the Old Bridge and the blind man on the Santa Rita Dock, sadly shaking a few pennies in a cheese box with no one near, the jingle of the coins making the Dock even more deserted—all can exist in Cecília's flesh, and my love, taking them all in, ties them to me with bonds whose nature escapes me. Recife (lead-colored walls of the House of Detention, São Pedro dos Clérigos with its trim façade and the pavements smelling of rotting fruit, short-haul boats, their masts swaying by the Customhouse Dock), the Moon reflected on the river, Recife, a fraction of the world, many of its inhabitants distant no more, strange no more, integrated in my being through this love and Cecília, her substance and her treasure chest.

Offices and shops still closed. The wind on the sidewalk agitating fallen leaves in the early morning. The day a clear and virgin plain waiting for men. Cecília phones me. Her words, coming through half-dozing Recife, seem to inaugurate the morning for me: clinging to the sand of a beach on which passes, alone, the first swimmer.

A

Roos and the Cities **19**

I open the window: the moonlight brightens one of the walls and all the lights are out. The Venetian blinds open, I lie down again. Dogs with their hair on end stir under the bed or in the drawers; I hear them and I catch the smell of mange. I can wait until July 15th before taking the job in Recife; but it will be difficult, with the money I have left, to postpone my return until then, even in hotels like this one and eating poorly. My days here, therefore, will soon be over. Roos knows that I'll be going back, that I'm passing through, and she wouldn't think of abandoning the man dying in Lausanne; crossing the Ocean; entrusting her life to me, the poorly skilled child of a region that in her eyes is wild and uncivilized, even though fascinating: the fascination of an underground animal. Ambiguous, she is exposed, in spite of the enigmatic character of her body, to disfavor and suspicion. Involving herself with someone in transit and enduring the consequences? Her understanding closed to the always ephemeral character of human fruitions and encounters. She removes herself, therefore, as if definitively, before the series that has begun can take on order and come to an end, no matter whether for our despair or for our joy. In the meantime her aversion for me or not, her blindness or lucidity, everything is governed by the laws that rule our relationship: this coming and going, this sinuous diagram. Lying down with the window opened onto the pleasant June night while the remnants of the moonlight move along the courtyard wall, I lament last night's scene and Roos's frankness, aware that this still isn't the end (even though the end, inexorable, is already being outlined) and that not even the lament is arbitrary or fortuitous here. Roos, too, knows, in one way or another, that the goodbye at dusk is leading us to the new sequence in the series. These dogs under the bed and in the drawers, invisible in the light of the dawn that is starting to come in through the window, form part of the sequence.

Changing my quarters—I know—won't stop the dogs from following me. I move, however, to the Hôtel Sainte-Marie, with a window on the Rue du Montparnasse. I return before dawn after pounding boulevards and bridges that soon become deserted, my feet without feeling, an emptiness in my stomach, my back muscles heavy. The dogs have gone.

I go to the Rue de Rennes branch post office to pick up a registered letter and I run into Roos. Polite expressions, banal and vague, amidst the sound of rubber stamps and tinkling coins. I show the check that came with the letter from the Fat Woman. ("That certain person came by here again, giving to understand that you broke her cherry. Is that true, Abel?") Roos prolongs the trivial conversation and shows signs—discreet, however—that seeing me again hasn't upset her. Would she like a cordial? She looks at her watch: a little after one. She'd like some coffee.

She and I, sitting in the chairs that have a kind of lace-trimmed back, sheltered by an orange awning. Before us, among trees, the statue of Balzac under the blue sky. The dialogue goes on with pauses and, without anything important having been said or suggested, she goes off with her languid walk, so un-Parisian, the walk of a girl from the provinces used to hours that unwind slowly, marked by the tolling of an ancient bell, years and years under peaceful roofs. Eltville. Why not arrange a meeting where I could give her the scarf I brought from Venice? I follow Roos's tracks, rapidly. I don't catch up with her.

I cash the check, I go back to my room, and I lean over the travel folders. I study the map of London to such a degree that now I not only see its outline and the names—Kingsway, Oxford Street, Green Park, River Thames—but the city itself, real and imaginary, constructed in the room through the course of the afternoon, with stones, photographs, old engravings, pages from novels, headlines, newspaper stories. The vain hunt in Italy and the days that followed make me believe that the City, its three walls intact, seen one day (near me and as if situated at a distance, for it is not much larger than a dress, and, like a dress trimmed with gold and beads, sinks into the calm water and disappears), no longer exists in the world, and therefore my search is over. The City that rises up impelling me to find it and that I have engraved in my spirit must be inserted, encrusted in new streets and new blocks, tangled up in another one. I can cross through it and not recognize it. I also remember that many extant works of art have been dismembered, like the polyptych by Masaccio done in Pisa, where all I get to see is the figure of St. Paul, the only one left in the city, going on to find Calvary—isolated from the group—in Naples; saints and fragments of the lower frieze are in Berlin; in London, the Virgin and

Child, with angel musicians all around. The yearned-for City might be, like this, a dispersed polyptych, and if it is I'll never find it. At least I'll never find it whole.

Therefore, if I decide to take a quick trip to London, I don't expect to find the City's rivers in the Thames. On the one hand, I would like to pay my respects to the collection in the galleries of the British Museum that illustrates and documents the evolution of writing; on the other, I am driven by pendular laws, based on a kind of distortion of lines, that govern my commonplace adventure with Anneliese Roos, London and its graphic treasures in stone, plaster, metal being a reason and a pretext. The real motive for the trip finds its justification in an inflexible play of alternations.

The morning sun, reflected on the windowpanes opposite, comes through the window of the room filtered by the lace curtain. I go to the Gare du Nord and buy a ticket to London via Calais. Why on the Sunday night train? I don't know. Saturday afternoon the telephone rings and I imagine that I'll have the answer then. Roos asks me if I wouldn't like to go with her to Vincennes on Sunday and take advantage of the good weather. We could lunch first at the Alliance. Would I like to? "Why not go to Chartres, Roos? I'd like to see the stained-glass windows again and examine the clock next to the cathedral. We can lunch there and come back at sundown. I'll get back in time to catch the train." "What train?" "The night train to London." A brief silence. "I still don't know Chartres. We can go when you get back." "What about today, Roos?" Another silence and the answer. She's going to stay in her room, she has letters to write. Tomorrow, at twelve, we meet in the lobby of the restaurant.

A black silk blouse and a moss-colored linen skirt. Long sleeves, fastened with green buttons in imitation of shamrocks, just like her earrings. Light-colored shoes and a shoulder bag. A gray sweater in her hand. Silky hair. Her skin smooth, her nails polished, light makeup, and a light smell of lotion: violet fragrance. "So you really are going to London?" "Yes, tonight. Via Calais." When we go out into the sun, she puts on the straw hat, a hat with a flexible brim, decorated with a ribbon the same color as her skirt. Why the sweater, when it's warm and the sky is blue? We take the Métro at Saint-Placide, heading for the station of our destination, with its name and all it augurs: Porte Dorée.

We go through the park in silence. Her face speckled by the sun, she smiles for no reason under the hat. Golden Door. We, two terrestrial animals, male and female, side by side among trees and birds, under the sky that hangs down like a huge breast, a blue-and-white breast from which we drink our ration of joy. We, on this Sunday afternoon, a pause or cooling off amidst greed and tribulations, free of everything that weighs heavy on our chests, floating above the turf as if on the preceding days, not the six but the fifty-six, we had bred, in fatigue and anxiety, the instant we are living. The sun becomes a set of plates among the leaves. Reflected on the millions of leaves. The light, over the lake and its shores, spreads out, wavering, and I don't know where its limits are. Fish, we go along drinking it in with our mouths and eyes, with nostrils and skin, perhaps with our sexes. Men and women—lying on the grass in the sun or under the trees, rowing or letting themselves be carried along by the boats, walking or standing on the paths—keep us company. Are they soothed by the same certainties as I? We, near the lake, reclining. The sound of a small orchestra curls the surface of the water. Men stripped to the waist, some with hats or tattoos, half lying, facing the lake. The waters crackle with a sound of dry leaves being stepped on or moved incessantly by the breeze. I give Roos the scarf I brought from Venice: a griffin surrounded by butterflies and made up of strange creatures. Each leg is a fan of birds; the claws their beaks. The birds on the front feet are coming out of the anus of a simian; and those on the rear ones from the mouths of bodiless animals. Wolves, horses, lionesses, birds, little monsters, and the face of an old man like Aesop, intertwined, many with their heads in the mouths of others. The tail of a wolf is also that of the griffin. At the tip of the tail, encrusted in a plume, two identical people, woman and man. Are they conversing? All of this zoo seems not to fit into the body of the fabulous beast, and therefore the hind legs of two more animals can be seen in the air, their heads stuck in like arrows halfway up his spine: the one provided with a tail (somewhere between a dog and a gazelle) covers the other (a dog with the head of an iguana). The tail of the gazelle-dog (or dog-gazelle-arrow?), velvety, ends in a head with a viper's tongue. The griffin has horns in the shape of wings or flippers. His beak and eyes are aquiline, sharp beak and piercing eyes. The original, Armenian, goes back to the cycle of great discoveries and perhaps even before them. Roos, smiling, thanks me and with slow movements puts the scarf around her neck. The colors of the beast and the butterflies move between her skin and the black blouse.

She'll go to Venice one day. Is it as beautiful there as in the movies? Streets of water, aquatic avenues, all with palaces on their sides . . . I answer that the Marciana Library is also fascinating. One leaves the square filled with pigeons and goes into rooms inhabited by incunabula and codices.

"Some of those books are mysterious. I didn't just choose your scarf by chance. The central design recalls a poem. A rather strange poem. I asked for an Aldine *Odyssey* and an Egyptian manuscript, in Greek. I don't know Greek. I just wanted to look at it. Aldo Mannucci's book came. In the place of the other, they brought me the Greek version of a mystical poem by mistake. The introduction in Italian gives the characteristics of the text. Its basis is the spiral. One of the themes, the search for the Name. The author dedicates the work to the Unicorn."

Roos takes the scarf off her neck, looks at it with an indecipherable expression, and then spreads it over her shoulders. She takes off her nylon stockings, lifts her skirt, exposes her thighs to the sun. I can see the soft blue of her veins—rivers—under her skin. I begin to sing, in ecstasy, facing the fluvial cities that are scattered through her feet, knees, thighs, inlaid in the flesh, made flesh, as if irradiated from within, from the bones, which are intertwined by prisms.

R
Ö and Abel: Meetings, Routes, and Revelations   14

Ö's sparkling eyes and the inlaid leather of the chests tremble with the noisy flight of the nocturnal birds, holding hands we run, weightless and slow, in the sea, the oaken boards creak under my knees, I lean over and embrace her, her hands in my hair, roof timbers and tiles explode, stabbing and mixed with sea smells, her perfume penetrates me, the music from the park alternates, fragmentary and mobile like the lights, with the dull sound of the sea on the rocks, I rest my face on her breasts and I don't know if I warm them, if it is they that burn me, I don't know—she begins to talk to me. Talk to me? Is this talking? I can hear every syllable clearly and I could almost indicate without error the intervals between one word and the next, even though it is a new tongue, aimless and arbitrary. This discourse closed within itself goes grinding through the room, thrown out at times with violence and truth, an impenetrable sphere that I contemplate, disturbed, one step from knowing. Knowing? What?

"Oppression, if established as a norm and even more so when it appears with precise instruments—almost always garbed in a sacred aura—takes possession of the moral world in an absolute fashion: a replica of gravity in the physical world. It infiltrates our bones and invades everything. It infects the world. Infects the world, did I say? Yes, that's it. A sickness."

I fill my mouth with the nipple of her breast and suck it, as if I were drinking in ♀'s life, her passions and accidents. Rising up, interspersed in her discourse, are words that I know and am pleased to suppose belong to the same phrase, disjointed, intertwined with others, numerous: a dismembered body. Little by little, the language in which she speaks to me and with which, perhaps hunting the unhuntable, she broadens and enchants the world, returns to the limbo where it is made. Inversely, words of clear usage begin to occupy the field of her discourse, the verbal possession or demon is undone, and ♀ reveals to me—not with minutiae and clarity but in a cryptic and symbolic way, as if she were reading, ubiquitous, in the hands that she sees in hers—her own fate, reveals to me what she thinks she knows of her life and what she knows.

What is loved in the loved one? What, in the one we love, makes love show itself? The being (visible) or its story, which we hear? ♀ and I facing the eclipse: I read in the world and I am instructed, without words, about the eyes that spy on me from within her eyes.

"The worst of all, Abel, is when people accept the rotten carcass and decide to live with it in the flesh."

By the dock, in Ubatuba: she and I in silence. Here, the lamp in the room turned off and sometimes—I, she—staring at the floor or the walls that are barely visible in the course of this unreal night which the short diurnal night of the eclipse prefigured, the voices of events and things fall silent or become unintelligible—and her tongue moves convulsively between her teeth. "I have betrayed and I have offended." What is she trying to do, talking to me? *President of the Republic hands down nineteen additional decree-laws.*

"Even though the formation of the Yolyp is not well explained, the parents always find that the one responsible is *the other*, although they never reveal that conviction. The affable looks exchanged between husband and wife make one believe that each is trying to console the other for the misfortune. But what really exists in the depths of that look is hatred, an unexpressed hate, one that takes on innocent appearances: deciphering words exchanged, neglecting personal hygiene, or even coming out on top in life at all cost."

"I insist on the conquest of a poetic and legible attunement between the expression and faces of the real, which remain savagelike, protected—by their secret inclination—from language and thus from knowledge. They exist, but hidden, waiting to be named, this second birth, revealing and definitive. Sometimes I manage rapid passages— overtaking the pith of the sensible. The almost bodily combat I maintain with the word is joined to those perforations. An effort in which I get to master more or less benumbed aptitudes; and for which, still, the shadowy pauses converge, the intervals in which—without really seeing and, yes, only reseeing—I seek the occult. The clear and evident leaves me cold."

The park in silence, the tide rising and falling, the force of the waves changes, and the wind takes on a different direction. The throats of roosters. Is what I see what exalts me in ℧? This and what I presense without a name. Her long and painful discourse grows and peoples her spaces that were desertlike before with multiple images. "I never spoke like this, I want you to know. To no one." You meet a woman and she favors you with brief shore excursions. She opens up a photograph album for you when you least expect it. There she is, then, at different ages, leaning out windows that have disappeared, sitting in chairs thrown in cellars today, wearing lacework eaten by moths, under eternal trees that continue to bear the same fruit, behold the gallery of relatives and their death masks if they are dead, the Bride and the Groom, people, places, scattered objects, and erased voices. That existence, immediate and flat once before, projects itself now over a world in relief, which broadens it. In the space of the night, I don't know if the night is rapid or long, rising up and succeeding one another, among the dresser, the chests, and the dark wall, through ℧'s voice, are images of her or of which she is the center.

Selective and flattering, nostalgic notwithstanding, the old family albums. ℧, her kimono half open and the long sleeves waving with the lively movements of her arms, the chrysanthemums, vague, grayish, veiled glimmers of her pupils and the gems on her rings, breathing fire, rhythmless and smelling of nutmeg, resin, dry pine (how many fervid steps and embraces?), the creaking of beds and floors, the tenuous and ephemeral flash of hair in the darkness, an intense force, as if tangible, a lodestone, flowing from her bodies, the melodious and convulsive voice (in her mouth: pebbles), rejects the urbanity of the albums, and she doesn't know what nostalgia is, even when she passes by the evoked dead youth whom she loves.

"The race of Yolyps, besides not being numerous, is sterile. Do they mean by that a kind of terminal point for the race or an announcement of the end? Who knows? Sterility, of course, will only be revealed in the adult Yolyp. Apart from the spiny placenta, there is almost no outward sign to distinguish it from other children. When the memory of the birth has passed, the parents end up taking kindly to it and are not afraid of its fate. Why should they be afraid?"

Truth always has a false bottom where an essential word or event is hidden. That's where our integrity lies, the knot of bonds, the meeting place of forces, the center of the secret, our real Name. I won't get there, and not even she will admit it. She repeats herself and peoples herself, opens, as far as she can, and tolerates her secret, she carries me, goes on, introduces me without ostentation and without shame, into a jolly, convulsed, fragmentary, harsh world, subject to deciphering, and she doesn't conceal her detritus. Why does she do it? Does she love truth with so much fervor? Does she refuse to yield me a body without history—which would be yielding an object without ramifications, a neuter one? Does she believe in exorcism to the point of supposing that the painful experiences into which she plunges through decision and calculation can cease to exist as long as she keeps them hidden? The intertwining threads form the lacework. Tangled, they express nothing and tend to separate.

Speaking, Ʊ admits me into her intimacy, anticipating her yielding in the flesh, which, enlarged by this present unasked-for admission, unforeseen and certainly more difficult, takes on the weight of a confirmation.

"The gestation of the Yolyp is exactly the same as that of other children. The same signs and the same time. The parents await it without fear. Innocent and crafty, the monster."

A

Roos and the Cities   20

My head in Roos's blue rivers. I drink in the warmth of her thighs,
I see the Sun on high and its beautiful face through the foliage, I stare
at her, I smell her, I hear her, and with the usufruct of these favors I
move unfolded into numerous rivers—which ones? The Rhine? The
Rhône? The Arno? The Main? The Elbe? The Ebro? The Tagus? The
Tigris? The Guadalquivir? Alighting beside us and flying off in pairs
are birds whose name, foreign, escapes me. Roos glances at them: the
impenetrable and tense expression caught in Amboise. Is she related
to the beings of the air? She strokes my head. In her hand I perceive a
flutter of wings and a throb, the throb of a bird's heart.

Clerks, students, nursemaids having soft drinks at the small metal
tables or dancing. Balloons tied to the hair or the buttonholes of the
dresses of several dancers. Suspended by those colored globes, elongated light shadows flutter on the ground and among the shadows of
the trees—and I, by my side a lamb born of the wind, see myself in
Roos, I inhabit her timeless flesh. In the outskirts of this new city that I
discover, one of the so many that can be found in Roos and deserted
like the others, there resounds the music to which she and I dance,
embracing to the beat. To the heat, should I say? Rising up in the sun
are city blocks of neutral aspect, speckled with hunting standards.
With the white lamb trailing me, I cross a moat, which could have
been flooded but is flooded only with daisies, and, right after, the
walls, with turrets and battlements without occupants, laid out in a
regular manner. (The griffin and the flowers on the scarf around Roos's
neck roar and spin.) The path, long, made of oval stones, leads directly
to the Door, of cedar and iron; on both sides bas-reliefs in bronze representing battle scenes. It is the ceremonial entry to the city, which I
now reveal. Dominating it from one side is the palace, where the relative bareness of the lower parts contrasts with the bristly peaks of the
dormers, belvederes, spires, pillars, chimneys, and domes; on the other
side, the church, covered by gleaming hemispheres perched on columns of porphyry and green serpentine. Around the church, luxurious
buildings, with the Baptistery, where mosaics of Byzantine inspiration

shine. It is not the majesty of this building that dazzles one most—unlike others, it doesn't tell me its name—but the harmony. The design of the Hippodrome, ridges of roofs visible on the horizon, the houses that climb up hillocks to reach the walls, the orchards and green spaces between buildings—everything seems to obey a clairvoyant spirit, one capable of happy variations. (We leave the dance. The music, the dancing, the heat, the afternoon light, the ingenuous and unworried presence of the people among the trees and on the shore of the lake. The lamb accompanies us.) In many houses there is a courtyard with a fountain and various sheltering terraces with flowers. Sculptures of heroes give a solemn air to the squares.

Marble plaques of various colors cover the walls of the church on its lower part; mosaics in blue and gray on them. (We have no glasses and drink our wine from the bottle. "Do you know *Daphnis and Chloë?*" The lamb has lain down beside us, its bells tinkle.) The other large figures on the mosaic, representing dolphins, tritons, peacocks, and doves, shine in the apse and on the walls. Two thrones, one inlaid with amethysts, the other with topazes, flank the altar, carved in wood and covered with gold.

Not far from there, on the road to the Palace, the Senate building, low and with a dignified look, two Solomonic columns in front topped by an equestrian statue. In the vestibule, a stone bull fighting seven stone leopards. Severe but delicately carved furniture, almost always inlaid with mother-of-pearl. (Is a cicada singing? Am I imagining it? If it's singing, why doesn't it fly, as in the Greek romance, out from the branches where a bird might find it and come hide between Roos's breasts? Why doesn't it start singing in those summers? I'd catch it under the black blouse.) On the ground, marble slabs laid in geometrical designs and rugs woven by whim. The windows, without glass, are protected by brocade curtains or thin alabaster sheets.

A strong wall surrounds the palace, the King's Keep, a city within the city, with pavilions and salons, living quarters, baths, library, and church, barracks and workshop, a jail, a weaving room, amidst vegetable and flower gardens, ponds and terraces laid out scientifically: on them one can receive the sun and contemplate the exterior. In addition to this, long arcades allow me to continue on protected from the sun as I go from one hall to another. In the silence the delicate hooves of the lamb resound like those of a colt. (We go into an amusement park. Roos, her hair loose, her temples exuding sweat, the sleeves of her blouse rolled up to her elbows, soft pink splotches on her face and even on her arms.) In the main hall of the Palace I see the throne, empty, surrounded by golden lions and silver trees, with birds of precious stones singing eternally in their branches. The lamb trembles and goes off bleating: there is a real serpent in one of those trees.

We go on holding hands, Roos singing a Rhine ballad in a soft voice, the ribbon and brim of her hat fluttering with her long strides. Normally, her gait is different, moderate. We spin on the roller coaster, and, just as one day in Chambord, amidst the sound of innumerable motors in two tempos, I shout her name, I shout her name in a circle and the sound of the vowels undulates with the undulation of the seats on the rails. We go up in the Ferris wheel, we see the rooftops, horizons, the world, she holds up the scarf with both hands, the fantastic griffin and the flowers fly over our heads, I fill my lungs with air and I say "Roos," slowly, "Roos," the name now forms a perpendicular circle, the wheel is decorated with the streamers, the ribbons, and the garlands of the "R", the "O," the "O," the "S," and suddenly, at the top, Roos's hat falls off, spins among the spokes of the Ferris wheel, is lifted by the wind and carried far off with the long green ribbon.

Now we are in a quiet *brasserie* between the Quai aux Fleurs and the Rue du Cloître de Notre-Dame, we're the only customers at this hour and the waiter is wearing rubber-soled shoes. The floor, paved with light-colored lozenges, smells of fresh floor wax. Roos's left hand is resting on the red tablecloth. I take it between mine. The smell of violets has vanished—and the other Roos, the one from Vincennes, seems to have fled, lost in who knows what invisible shipwreck, with the sounds, and the light, and the intoxication of the afternoon also finished. How can I bring her back?

"Roos ... We've never seen each other's room or country. We met each other as people adrift in the world. I don't know what scent your dresses have in their closet; how you arrange your nail polish, your lotions, your creams, what color your bathrobe is, what position your slippers fall into when you take them off to go to sleep. I know even less what your father's like and what he works at. Whether the sun in Eltville comes in the window of your room in the morning or in the afternoon; if there's some bird or dog in the neighborhood that you might hear; if you hate the dog, if you love the bird."

The waiter comes over, silent, with the tray of meatballs and wine. In her literary French she describes the room she has at the Alliance, she lists her records and her books, talks about the Rhenish landscape and the clothes she wore when she was fifteen. Through the glass door I catch a glimpse of the cupola of the Panthéon under the violet light of dusk, the garden behind Notre-Dame, and a large tree across the street beside the Seine. Polished copper vessels on the walls reflect that clearness and the same purplish reflections seem to streak Roos's voice.

"You said you didn't know anything about my room. You don't know what kind of a man my husband is either, and what he did for a living. He's a kind of archaeologist. His field of activity is ancient ship-wrecks. When he got sick, he was investigating a sunken ship off the coast of Sicily. Do you know how many years old? Thirteen hundred. It's incredible what can be studied in a ship buried for a thousand, two thousand years. The art of naval architecture, maritime routes, the kind of trade that existed between two countries. That ship was carrying a cargo of capitals and friezes in Proconnesian marble. It was on its way to some city being built, possibly in North Africa. It was coming from Constantinople. The captain's chest was intact. We would have known nothing about him or about his ship if it hadn't been for that storm. He was a Syrian and he had two daughters."

Our happy afternoon is going away. How long did it really last? The ship under the sea, off the coast of Sicily. The young daughters of the Syrian captain.

"Roos, these last hours! . . . Do you think we can be happy facing things whose end we know to be near?"

Her face, thoughtful, is turned away, toward the sky that's growing dark. The cities transubstantiated in her come and go like waves, all seeming nocturnal and autumnal.

"Yes, maybe. Who knows? . . ."

She and I embracing by the Quai aux Fleurs. We go along quickly, and this rekindles her exaltation. "I'd forgotten about your trip. What a pity you're leaving! How many minutes do we have till train time?" Boats, lighted up now, stretch out along the Seine, excursionists on board. Some answer our waves. I shout from the quay, beside I don't know what bridge, at the boat that passes and to the equestrian statue across the river in front of the Hôtel de Ville: "*J'aime cette femme*, it is my love, her name is Rose. Rose!" With my arms I make a rose unfold as large as the night that is being born. She takes me by the hand and urges me, laughing, to walk faster. Half lost among the flower stalls, we can't find the yellow lights of the subway entrance right away.

I leave her in front of the Dupontparnasse looking for a taxi, I run to the hotel, go up the stairs three at a time, come down in leaps, drunk with wine and joy. She's waiting for me in the cab. Breathless, I sit down beside her, I tell the driver Gare du Nord. She doesn't take her hands off mine: she squeezes them. Jets of lights coming from the shopwindows, from the streetlights, and other cars are projected through the windows of the taxi, they cross over her face, over the hundred cities in her face. What if the train has left? We'll come back, she'll go up with me, see my room at the Hôtel Sainte-Marie, help put my clothes and things in place, give life to the curtains, the easy chairs, the walls, the floor, and the ceiling with her presence, and who knows what will happen? I shouldn't be going. This is the day, the moment I've waited for for so long.

We run among the passengers, the griffin on the scarf eating the flowers: he roars, barks, growls, and sings, transformed into a bird. The announcements that precede the departure are already echoing among those sounds.

"Goodbye. Send me a postcard."

"Roos . . . I was happy this afternoon! I feel as if I'd been inside a drum. A loud drum. As if I were surrounded by a rhythm. A roll. The drum."

She holds me by both arms and, for the first time, for the first time, she kisses me on the mouth. She offers her face for me to return it. I kiss her on the mouth. The train is leaving. I run. The train is leaving. She waves with the beast surrounded by butterflies.

T
Cecília Among the Lions   13

Praça do Entroncamento: stone benches under the mango trees and, through the foliage, the moonlight on Cecília's face. Everything alters that face, which is sensitive like sleeping waters and in which I discover new aspects at every instant. Am I wrong to believe that every mobile and immobile thing, disordered, is reflected in it?

I tell her about the incident of the day before, in which she took part without knowing it. I cross the Boa Vista Bridge. In front of me, among the pedestrians, a woman is going along. She has the same build, the same height, short hair like hers, and the same sandpiper walk. Then some indication that I can't define—perhaps the feet touch the ground with a little more weight—convinces me of the contrary. This doesn't stop her image from enwrapping the body of the strange woman seen only from behind and taking possession of it, replacing it.

"I know it's not you. That certainty, however, helps me conjure up only a part of the vision imposed on my senses: the other one, the one in front (I can't see the face and breasts), continues to exist as if it belonged to you."

As long as the woman doesn't turn toward the river, breaking up the face present in my spirit with the reality and violence of her own face, I follow a hybrid being at a distance.

"Half you and half a stranger."

Cecília's double and still-undeciphered being trembles in my arms as if struck in the depths of her substance. The impression is so clear that I hold her tighter, trying to keep her from losing hold of herself.

"Can that be what I lack, Cecília? A vast love like the one I have for you, which puts its stamp on everything?"

Her eyes become somewhat more oblique, somewhat duller—as if they didn't see me—and at the same time they sparkle with greater intensity. I think I see, inside the female eyes, two more. Male? What I seek is not she and it is not in her. (The hoarse voice and the bitterness of melancholy.) She, Cecília, can only be at best a part of the course that will lead me to the end of the search. In the same way, at the age of twenty, it is necessary to keep on living to arrive finally at twenty-five. It might be too that the end of my search could be nothing more than the beginning of a broader and more precise search. A glowing veil of shadows passes over her eyes again. There is something in them, yes. Not male, perhaps. She stares at me as a tamer does into the lions' core before opening the cage.

The Fat Woman and I, at the desk covered with papers left by the dead man. Policies, notes on his existence as an employee, historical notes, receipts, birth certificates, lottery tickets, samples of paper money withdrawn from circulation, newspaper pages with news from World War II, clippings from the *Official Bulletin*. I separate and classify this residue.

She puts a drawer beside me: "Throw what's of no use in here."

She looks well in that satin dress. The catamonk, sitting on the table, impassively observes the selection of papers.

"Shall I get rid of the villa, Abel? I like it. But left alone in this big house? So many rooms!"

"The Treasurer left a reasonable inheritance. With that and the pension you won't be in need, ma'am. In short, you can retire."

"Show some respect for your mother." (She runs her chubby hand through her tinted, curled hair.) "What man would take a second look at me now? I'm yesterday's newspaper. Trash."

The wind has stopped. I unbutton my collar and loosen my tie. "I think I'll take a swim."

"Coming back from the Seventh-Day Mass to have fun on the beach!" (The catamonk licks its hand. Looking alternately at me and at the Fat Woman.) "Aren't you going into mourning, Abel? A black tie at least. An armband."

"I feel too happy for any funeral show."

"I know, I know. There's no hope for you. You were seen holding hands with a chippy waiting for the bus. Don't you want to know who told me? Your wife. She was at the Mass."

"She gave me her condolences. I thought they were for the Treasurer."

"Abel, Abel!" (The catamonk jumps into her lap and she starts to laugh.) "Who's the victim? The one who came with the old women, I'll bet my ass."

"Why do you say 'victim,' milady?"

"Did you lay your cards on the table? Your marriage and everything?"

"She knows. She says it matters, but not that much. First, of course, she suggested we just be friends. I answered that spiritual love is depraved. Isn't it, really?"

"Spadework, eh? Well, look. What I want to hear is you singing that song to her family. Do they know?"

"One of her brothers already called me."

"Brothers? Doesn't she have any parents?"

"No. She lives with some relatives on Rosa e Silva. One of the brothers works for the Police and the other one is a clerk in a notary's office. If you must know, they're not rich. Why did you use the word 'victim'?"

A week and there still seems to be a nauseating smell of withered flowers and lighted candles in the house.

"When she came in, all she could see was you. She was devouring your face with her eyes. There didn't even seem to be any dead man or

other people in the parlor. Female eyes and pretty ones. Then she noticed that I was your mother and turned her eyes toward me between
her lashes. I've had experience with a few things. If I were you, I
wouldn't get too involved with that girl. I could feel it in my flesh when
she turned to me: the look sounded heavy with energy. Turned into a
voice. A male look, Abel."

The cat, tail raised, back arched, watches me closely, its purple
irises glowing. An animal with fear.

"You saw it clearly: you've got a good eye. But could you see
everything? I can see more. Opposites are reconciled in Cecília. Solitude and multitude. Delicacy and strength. Giving and receiving.
Straightforward and devious. In a word: whole. Before her I consider
myself a diminished being." (The cat, less tense, continues to observe
me, vaguely shadowed, with his eyes of a night monkey.) "Don't you
find hybrids attractive?"

On the bus I examine the reproduction of a bas-relief in the
Louvre that shows man as a fragile bark floating on the sea of the
world. The winged skeleton at the stern symbolizes the material, the
old man amidships the immortal spirit; the woman in the prow, holding up a swollen sail in her outstretched arms, is the life force: guard-
ian of blind passions and unreflected impulses, she makes the boat and
the other passengers go forward. Present in me, the image and the enchantment of Cecília. In this way: a text that is known by heart, that
can be grasped by the mind—a whole—and repeated word for word.
While I look at the figures, however (the bus window open and the dry
midday wind beating on my face), Cecília, a familiar text, is a sleeping
acquisition—present and discreet, silent. The bus picks up speed on
the Avenida Norte. The accord existing between me and everything
that forms this moment having been altered (the rhythm of the ride,
the constancy of the wind, and the revolutions of the motor), I raise my
head. The wind, with growing force, blows over me, coming from the
mangrove swamps, and inflames me, inflames me, I grow larger. Not
only the wind: I am invaded by wind and speed. My chest inflates
against the wind like the sail in the relief, the speed bellies it out—and
suddenly, caught up in the wind, in the speed, occupying it without
fitting into it, created from the wind and the acceleration, is the image
of Cecília. This presence and the name, hers, which forms in my
throat, coincide, a bond. I don't pronounce it and the knot in the bond
suffocates me. Suddenly it is loosened, the name is loosened, a cut in
my throat, the name is pronounced, it bathes my chest, all ruddy, a

fan. Brilliant and ruddy. A pulsation—and it spreads out, the fan. The bus goes back to its previous speed. The presence of Cecília comes out from the depths where things sleep, it is nothing but a known text, one not remembered: it accompanies me, so neatly.

Derby-Tacaruna, the canal, slowly excavated, restores a part of Recife to the status of an island. The bald tongues of earth on both sides of the canal, on which vehicles cannot pass and which stretch out for yards and yards, are given the arbitrary designation of Avenue. But the houses, built in a casual way roundabout, reject this uncomfortable presence, and the windows of the façades avoid it. Between the houses and the sides of the canal, up and down, which people cross (but almost always in groups, fearful of that dimly lighted barren), vegetation grows without any gleam, short in height and harsh. A few brave trees. The waters of the canal only change in volume, thanks to the tides: high tide or not, they are always muddy, dark, they stink of rotting carcasses and sleep under a layer of mud that low tide reveals. At that time the smell of rottenness gets stronger; touched by the wind, it reaches the homes far off.

I await Cecília's arrival. The brothers have threatened to attack me, and she suggests I meet her in this deserted place. Do the waters smell bad? Even so, they are other waters. Reflecting the Moon, they dull it—and, reflected on them, they receive an imprint from the Moon. The vegetation is less aggressive in the moonlight. The voices of the batrachians and the many insects in the shadows weave and interweave threads of voices tied to threads of voices. A gray horse without harness, its mane drooping, is tugging on a rope, trying to find something to eat among the sour-leaved bushes. At intervals it snorts between its lips. The pounding of the hooves on the soft ground resounds like brief enigmatic formulas exchanged between the quiet Earth and its feeling of being alive, it, a beast of burden, old and with hardened joints, in repose now, ferreting about for hidden greens. The snakes slip off for far away, hide, coil about the more distant plants, accomplices.

Cecília, I and Cecília, sitting on the ground—not far from the horse, among the twisted bushes with spiny stalks—the head of one resting on the half-raised knee of the other. We see the people who go along the canal using the cement wall, but they don't see us. She replies to the *raison d'être* of my expressions and makes me see the courage in reaching a certain kind of resignation. I must accept my status of one banished from Eden. We are not inaugurating, she and I, a world.

No world at all. None. We are not separated from or exempt from evil. Evil, fate, and inheritance are part of us. Contrary, however, to the fortunate solitary ones of Eden, we are far from being the protagonists of any fable of fall and expulsion: we are born expelled and fallen. We have, therefore, the alternative of accepting the status of degraded ones and realizing, through actions rife with generosity and rage, the nostalgia of the Garden. On the other hand, the jaguars of today only lick their own skin. But the turbulent globe we live on is populated with men.

Lying on the leaves, side by side, we are led through the stars by the Earth. We are holding hands in silence, and Cecília's presence broadens, rises up, comes over, a wave, wrapping me up, a wavering wave, as if seen from a height. The horse, closer by, swishes his tail and his loose mane. His hooves among the plants, cautious. Cecília turns and rests her head on my shoulder. Her breath warming my skin, she says that she loves me, ten, twelve times, in a soft voice, as if the people in the distance might hear her or as if the words that she repeats, spoken more strongly, might lose their intimate and secret character. Inhabitants of Cecília, liberated, pass in the distance or cross through me. One among them keeps coming, perturbed, in raw leather sandals, the brim of his straw hat drooping around his head, hiding the burning glassy glow of his eyes. His passage is just like that of a strong wind: all bend over somewhat and lower their heads. The snakes come closer. The horse seems to be made of moonlight.

The air is hot and stifling in spite of the sudden downpour. I open one of the windows. The waters must be already carrying off shacks in the swamps of Campo Grande, in the garbage landfill of Coque. I wake up when the rain becomes strong again—and then the limits of sleep are broken, fluctuating in the room are numerous streamers tables chairs planks, everything charged with an arbitrary meaning. They express priority and enwrap me, me, a half-awake swimmer. Does that idea of priority come from Cecília's presence? Does she soak up everything, even destruction?

The cloister of Santo Antônio vibrates under the explosions coming from without, from the Rua do Imperador. All Saints' morning. I'm in the center of the courtyard on the stones worn down by the sandals of the Franciscans and the shoes of visitors. I observe, for the tenth time, the tiles from Holland that in the open air decorate the guardrail of the upper gallery of the cloister. A thousand? The band, capriciously stretched out above the arcades and columns, decorates the mirror of the four parapets that mark off the courtyard. Men working, blue, children busy at their games, marine monsters swimming, ships, the blue gallop of knights, and indigo flowers unfold in blue vases. A bird, giving the impression of being lost, alights beside me. Can it have fled from the Ark of the Flood, represented in the panel of Portuguese tiles that decorates the ground-floor wall to the right of the entrance? Confused, rust spots and two white stripes on the top of its wings, eager. What bird is it? When the image of Cecília rises up whole for me, strange, I remain motionless, even knowing that it is impossible to retain such a vision without its immediately becoming deformed. That's how I behave facing that familiar bird. *May your stay be long!* Without moving. But the bird, like a dog pointing the way to the hunt, the bird, a fugitive from the Ark and the Flood, seeming to return to the wall from which it comes, deviates, flies in the direction of the panels that show the Creation of the World and the Death of Adam, whirls toward them, crosses the sunlit courtyard diagonally, and brushes, on the opposite wall, the tiles of the Tower of Babel. Its coming and its flights give me the feeling of a written phrase that I—a contemporary of the Tower and the Confusion of Tongues—am incapable of understanding. It goes off quickly into the great morning full of explosions. Where can I have seen a bird like that?

O

The Story of , Twice-Born 21

Across from the Cine Metro, on the afternoon of the last Sunday in August, I am waiting in vain for Inácio Gabriel. Evasive answers to my telephone calls to the office. Inácio Gabriel on the sheet (the despair knowing that he is agonizing and dying a few steps away from me, in the Charity Hospital), Inácio, his hands crossed on his thin chest, dressed as if he were coming to meet me, but with his feet bare. There is a lighted candle at the head of the bed, and a man weeps in silence, his back toward me. Through the open window I see some trees, tall buildings, construction and scaffolding, the sky of this beginning of September. A sparrow flies. Have we done everything, Inácio, everything we could? Have we said everything?

Illustrated books existing there in Grandfather's library among bound collections on jurisprudence and the law: *Costumes dos Insetos, The Sea Around Us, La Vie des araignées.* Inês, when I talk to her about the customs and varieties of beetles: I mustn't be afraid of anything, my room is protected against insects. Answer her? I go back to the illustrated books in silence.

Tell me, Inácio, why do the passages by which we make our investigations of the world always take the shape of a rectangle? Rectangular the shape of windows, doors, pictures, and even on a roll of papyrus the writing has been organized into a page: a rectangle.

He, from his dark rectangle:

"In many pictures (expressions, with their rectangular format, of attempts at access to the world) another window is drawn, another rectangle."

I, among the living:

"In them the contemplator sees twice—or, rather, sees three times—what's in the rectangles of the painting, what's revealed beyond the window represented there, and through all this, still, the infinity of things."

Inácio Gabriel smiles and opens a window that isn't there.

Have we done everything, Inácio? Have we said everything? No. But the bird, this one, the restless bird you make rise up in me and whose name, I know, is Avalovara, doesn't fall silent or leave or die with your death. Even when I reveal it to Inês, even when I do that and she tells me that there's no such thing as dying, there's no such thing, it remains there, enchanted, even then, when I shout, spit into Inês's face that death is death, that you're dead and no enchantment can bring us together again on any other Sunday afternoon, even when I shout out those words—not these, others similar to these, perhaps more brutal, certainly more impassioned—with such violence that my grandmother comes running and asks what's the matter and orders me to be quiet, even at that instant I know that the Avalovara is watching over me and transmitting something of your condition to me: by his gaudy feathers, his secret song.

Orff's music, cut by the sound of our kisses, of my deep sighs. A letter from Catullus to the whore Ipsitilla: "Stay home, Ipsitilla, don't talk, wait for me, use your arts and fineries so we can consummate the amorous sacrifice nine times!" The room is about twice as long as it is wide; only one of the two side windows is open, the table is on that side; where we are, lying on the rug near the other window, no one can see us. With his left hand Abel takes pleasure in testing the resistance of my right breast and that of the newer breast that grows inside the other one. I have my right leg bent, the thigh resting on his flank. In that position, the penis, which with my right hand I press back over my own buttocks, clings to my vulva. The light doesn't hit us directly. There is a shadowy and bluish clarity all through the room. At the point where we seek each other, that clarity, absorbed in the reflections of the furniture, the glass, the walls, anoints our skins with a kind of intangible and vaguely golden varnish.

Inês in her room, bending over her suitcase, facing me and trying to smile. I won't answer that tight laugh. She's finished the work she was paid for, and now she's leaving. I'm clawless; corroded by Inês's seduction is the spur I carry in my head or in some other part of my body. I'm still debating, but debating in vain and suspiciously—that's the truth—whether the doors are opening (onto what, after all?), I'm debating in order to convince myself all the more that leaving is impossible. My grandmother knows this; and she sends Inês away.

"What did I do?"

"I don't need your services anymore."

"Can't I stay a few more days? While I look for another job?"

"No. Get your things together. You certainly must have some savings. You can stay at a boardinghouse."

By the door of her room on the ground floor in the back, I see her packing her bag. Sewing equipment, cheap perfume, her photograph beside her employers and the child who, adolescent now, is watching her from the door. She smooths the clothes she is putting into the valise with her fingertips. One gets the impression that the cloth was woven from spiderwebs. Discreetly, she puts in a dark bottle wrapped in plastic sheets and I can see the label: Inês has started to disguise her first white threads. The room has a peculiar odor, a mixture of insecticide and face powder. How many days will that discordant mixture remain in the air? (The windowed wing of the second floor. The two wicker chairs and the two birdcages, always quite clean—without birds. Inês speaking to the nonexistent birds in falsetto, giving them water and birdseed. As if all that weren't enough, every so often she has one of the birds die and buries it in the garden with a trowel and is sad for the rest of the day.) She lays her work dresses to one side, one of them is dirty.

"I don't know whether or not I should wash it before I leave."

I look at her fixedly, a stone, I look at her, a worn-out instrument or one that is going obsolete, Inês, that oilcan, always lubricating the joints of things, I look at her—a servant being fired, gathering up her things. I pick up the scissors on the night table, I pick them up by the tip and offer them to Inês. I don't say a peep. The gesture. The silence. She looks at me startled and lifts her hand to her mouth: the incisors appear between her thin lips. A suffocated laugh and hesitation.

"No . . . What will she think of me?"

But she also reaches out her hand and accepts the scissors. She cuts in two the dress she intended to wash. She cuts it into two, four, eight, twenty pieces, she chops it up, the fragments fall onto the red tile floor, into her bag, onto the cot, the night table, the wicker chair, she executes the operation methodically, showing her incisors at intervals (but now they have something of the fangs of a dog threatening to bite), there's nothing left to cut, she closes her hand over the scissors, sits on the bed, hesitates, lifts her arm—it's four o'clock in the afternoon and hot—she wounds the mattress three, four times.

She leaves the scissors stuck into the place the center of her bony and solitary body had occupied for years. She combs her hair, with gentle movements now, as if it were the hair of a doll or were precariously attached to her scalp. She puts it into braids. No, into ponytails. Smiling, still startled, she picks up her bag and leaves. If she wished she wouldn't have to say goodbye to anyone: my grandfather is in Court, my grandmother is in her room.

She goes out into the garden, opens the outside door, closes it, looks around hesitantly, picks a direction at random, slightly bent from the weight of the suitcase.

Over my left arm, his head (light in spite of the impression of weight and mass); his right arm under my armpit. The persistent and skillful pressure on my tongue of his large, spaced teeth. The sole of my left foot softly resting on the top of his right foot. Ingratitude is the world's reward—the singers are saying somewhere. But I'm grateful, I'm grateful, not in my mouth but all over my flesh, for everything I've purged to attain this moment, for the intensity with which my body responds to the nearness of the body of this man, for the strength with which my hips drag him toward me, for the way in which the forest has been peopled for us, and for the light-footed fauna of the rug, for the blind anxiety with which we embrace, for the temperature of this time of day, which allows me to display my nakedness and soak myself in his as if my eyes were mouths and I were dying of thirst, and seeing him naked takes away but also intensifies my thirst. I'm also grateful for the dull, polished glow of our bodies. He looks at me in silence, he looks at me from close by (the gold-streaked blue of his eyes), and his left hand, descending over my stomach, touches the inside of my thighs. I open my nostrils, I open my eyes, I open my mouth, I open my arms, I open my hands, I open my pores, I open my throat, I open my arteries, I open a space, I open passage, I open fins, I open wings, I open a fruit, I open a skylight, I open the windows, I open a gate, I open a street, I open a clearing, I open a path, I open a road, I open a cleft, a trench, a ditch, a channel, a fissure, a breach, my legs, I open my legs, my thighs, my feet, my knees, I open my sex and he invades my flesh. I give a cry of jubilation.

My grandfather in the large double bed, inert, his legs stretched out. On the right, at the head of the bed, the lamp is on, with a piece of crochetwork thrown over the shade to soften the ocher light of the bulb even more as it outlines his figure. The people around, even the stranger whose goatlike hooves show, poorly disguised, under his trousers and who accompanies the anguish of the old man on his mortuary bed as if he were reading the name and dates inscribed on the tomb of some distant relative—all are half dissolved in that light. The furniture too—the glass-doored case full of unread books, the wardrobe with one of its doors half open, the bureau with mountings of chiseled bronze. Grandfather's face is the irresistible center of this scene. He is covered by the sheet from his feet to his sternum, and it isn't known to what mad costume his slippers, on the small gray rug to the left of the bed, belong: all of his steps in life have been reckoned up, and he—more than we—knows that. His hands on his chest, his body stretched out and already partially into dust (the death-agony worms are devouring it), the docile posture, like the one imposed on the dead, because we are ruled by repetition in that too, all represent one of the possible ways of inscribing the word "capitulation." He takes on the ceremonial form of the dead, the posture demanded of the dead. That's how Inácio Gabriel is when I see him without life. The struggle is long, unequal, and one cannot even say to the adversary: "I surrender." She has her moment, her subtleties. A ritual. Does God create us, Inácio? If he does, he sends us off, forgets about us afterward, decrepitude and death are our problems. I created them; now they can go to hell. There it is, the proof and testimony of this, this consumed animal. And all alone, given over to himself, notwithstanding those who surround him and watch him impatiently, settling accounts with no ray of hope, putting his short breath up against the

lions of death. Forty or more gasps a minute. The fish emerges from
the depths, leaps up over the surface of the sea, and returns to the
waters. My grandfather opens his eyes, but he doesn't turn his head:
he looks straight forward, he looks at the wall, everything he still sees
of the vast and varied world is that piece of wall, he looks at that piece
of wall and is serious, as if reading the brief of his own existence.

P

Julius Heckethorn's Clock 3

The clock with which we are concerned and which, as far as is
known, has no replica in the world, is of German manufacture. Its
creator, Julius Heckethorn, a mathematician, harpsichordist, and expert on Mozart, is a collateral descendant, according to trustworthy
information, of that Charles William Heckethorn who, in London at
the expiration of the nineteenth century, publishes a highly specialized
volume in octavo: *The Printers of Basel in the Fifteenth and Sixteenth Centuries: Their Biographies, Printed Books, and Devices.*

Julius's father meets the girl Erika, youngest daughter of the
Haeblers of Lübeck, on a business trip. He marries her and moves to
Germany, where he sets up a workshop for the manufacture of jewelry. He is supposed to have given up his British citizenship; in any
case, everything leads one to believe that he never crossed the Channel
again. Julius, born in 1908, the premature and only child of that union
with Erika Haebler, is still a child when his father realizes the secret
desire of his life: the acquisition in the Black Forest—a region that is
known since the sixteenth century for its fame as a center of clockmaking and that the industrialist A. Junghans revolutionizes after the
Franco-Prussian War with the installation of his factory, where the
contribution of craftsmanship is practically reduced to zero—of a
workshop specializing in sound mechanisms for clocks of all kinds.
Thus, Julius Heckethorn's first years are spent among carillons that
ring night and day.

One can imagine how his dreams are crossed with a continuous
striking of hours.

With the War of 1914, two unforeseen events pull down this fragile, tranquil child: a trip to England and the silence of the days. He falls ill, but not owing to the absence of his parents: he is anxious for the presence of the carillons. His grandfather, trying to compensate for that desire, hires a music teacher. It isn't known who suggested the harpsichord, an instrument on which Julius, without ever becoming a master, does succeed in being far more than a mere amateur.

O

The Story of Ꝋ, Twice-Born   **22**

Without his dentures, which had been tossed into some cabinet drawer amidst unread instructions, eyedroppers, and bottles of medicine, it is impossible to recognize a dignitary of Justice in my grandfather. Rather, it is old age, devastating and rapid—like a mechanism that is out of rhythm and begins to work in an accelerated way. Day by day I witness his fall. Fall? A demolition. Every night he sits down at his desk and speaks with the voice of Wisdom, an old man much older than the one of the night before. Until only this remains of everything: his blood (a very small amount, as much as a bird has), almost motionless in his veins, his transparent hands, his eyes, which no longer reflect light and images, a faded face—neuter—and those lips sunken into his mouth. One of the young men, who ignores my mother as he leaves the church (now a mature man and not in mourning), puts a lighted candle in the old man's fingers. All bend a little farther over the bed. The end of the cycle, of the passage fulfilled in blindness. My grandfather, happier at that instant than so many others whom he judges in life—his judgment, if there is such, not dependent on hands as coherent and cautious as his. No files. That's already an advantage. An intense and caustic perfume overwhelms me. My mother, breaking the barriers of the banishment imposed upon her, treads the family bricks once more under the protection of death. Simultaneously I hear the death rattle of the dying man and my grandmother's impassive voice: "Even today you're not really wanted here. You may leave." The perfume evaporates.

Seventy steps lie between the deathbed and my grandfather's study. The lights out and the vague reflections on the glass of the bookcases. I sit down in the ownerless chair, I turn the metal lamp on. I can see almost nothing except my hands and the few objects that are left on the desk: folders, glass paperweights, stamps, the useless visor. Something is complete now. I don't witness the death agony of Inácio Gabriel. I see him in the hospital, dead already, wearing the same thin clothes that he has on at our last meeting, his feet bare, a trace of affliction on his eyelids; the hours preceding his death, however, I do not see. I see the death agony of my grandfather and with that the empty space is filled. Yes, I know well, the two deaths aren't identical. Is that important? Inácio spares me, he doesn't let me know that he's dying, but I add up the fee that is coming to me. In his intentions I can see a man dying.

I'm on the *qui vive:* there's a strange presence throbbing (but silently) in the study. A rhythm. No, not a presence: a hollow, an orifice through which the world is emptying out. My grandfather's absence? Muffled voices rise up in some part of the house. A dragging of furniture, rapid steps on the stairs, a chair falls. A rhythm. With uncertain fingers I put the visor on my forehead. My field of vision is enlarged with that, I can see the gilt letters on the bindings shining on the shelves and Olavo Hayano in the leather chair, arms crossed, his elbows on his thick knees, his feet firm on the floor. He stares at me with his distant and disquieting look. I should ask in a tone of suspicion and with a shadow of anger what he is doing in the study. I don't speak.

Hayano, however, as if the question had been asked (and likewise the whole scene flows as it has been written to be fulfilled), explains:

"I came in here for the quiet. I've got a sound that bothers me night and day. I'm trying to identify it. A constant buzzing, not exactly like the song of cicadas or the chirping of crickets, not even the noise of a saw. A mixture of all those sounds and others is what I hear at each and every hour. When I wake up, I hear it. Penetrating, continuous. I hear it even when I doze off and in my sleep. Maybe that's why there are so many dead people in my dreams. Angry dead people."

Angry dead people? . . . He repeats most of the phrases, putting them together in a different way; he's almost motionless while he speaks, either his arms or his head or maybe his fatness retards or hinders his gestures. He gets up. His droning voice, slightly nasal and somewhat stupid, rises. He's near the desk, the light brings out the earthy color of his face. Angry dead people?

"In spite of the buzzing, I can distinguish other sounds quite well, real sounds, and I can appreciate them. For example: I enjoy listening to your voice very much."

His look is fixed and mistrustful. All the things he has on—not just the jacket, somewhat worn, a little tight—look as if they'd been borrowed.

"Actually, there's still some kind of dissonance in your voice. A childish ring. That's it, your voice has something infantile about it. At the same time, it's the voice of a woman, with its own timbre. No harshness. I can perceive that very clearly through the buzzing."

Coming together with Olavo Hayano is like crossing a ford with mud up to my mouth to reach—perhaps—the other side. He tells my story: I must have set out on the road to meet him. His function is to encircle me, break me down, demolish what has been built up in me, try to impose his world, his way, on me. A prolonged struggle. Nevertheless, it hasn't been foreseen that somebody, whoever it might be, is obliging or inducing me to make the crossing. I have to go on my own account, on my own account, with the air of one who doesn't know that catastrophe is certain and as if moved by hopes. I, a decorated coffer with certainty at the bottom—the vial, the poison. I, loved and lover, in the eyes of others and in my own eyes: enameled coffer with floral motifs, radiant. But I, being the coffer, know, I know without clarity, yes, without clarity, but I know, what I contain under lock and key—the vial, the poison. Go on, blind girl, deck yourself out and enter the game that's not too different from the one that destroys your mother. Love this man and his emptiness, cleave your hands and feet to his. Then let there be the struggle to cast off the yoke, only in that way will you be able to attain being. Because if there isn't any way out for the milliner, there is for you. Moreover, every valid way out of your labyrinth must pass through this sieve. Olavo Hayano is something to fulfill. A rite. Then, without eyes, I begin to free in myself the love or the signs of it for a man I don't love. I take the eyeshade off my forehead, I toss it back onto the desk. No use wasting time.

Getting ahead of Hayano and tightening the rhythm of the scene, I say: "I'm still very young. I'm in school."

"You already know more than most people. It's enough to look at you. Besides, it isn't necessary to get to know more than you know. Knowledge is painful. What then?"

Emptiness, emptiness. A swallowing. I turn out the lamp and at the same time, with a quickness that contradicts all his movements, he turns it on. I can see that he's pale, greenish. The emptiness. When he comes in with his mother and sits down in the living room, I a child, on that rainy morning, the emptiness that surrounds him repels me, drives me away. When he confesses to me the beginning of deafness, the buzzing, it's just the opposite: he attracts me, and I'm on my way.

He helps me with his impersonal voice: "I'd like to make you happy."

Laughter comes to my mouth, vomit. I swallow it. The conversation takes on the free and at the same time mechanical fatal appearance of a game of checkers.

The repetition of other openings that are old and therefore no less decisive: "I haven't got anything, you know. My parents . . ."

"I'm not interested in them. I'm only interested in you." He leans over the desk, he stares at me from close by and, for an instant, his look plumbs my eyes, hesitating. I lower them. "I want you to be my wife."

Eyelids still lowered, I remain silent. I don't answer. I mustn't answer. My left hand rests loosely under the lamp, so that Olavo Hayano can take courage and touch it. He takes it between his, kisses it. My expression is that of a person who has been compromised into reflecting on what there was and also of one who perplexedly weighs one's own uncertainties.

My black camisole beside the silver teapot, absorbing a little of its soft glow, the silver absorbing its blackness. The silk stockings, almost invisible, on top of my shoes. Abel on top of me. Inside of me his knob, his fist, his arm, inside of me the throats of the singers, their distant voices (*eis aiona!*), Abel in me, inside me, block and tackle, splitting me and binding me. I open my legs even more, I move my pelvis (he comes, he breaches the hold), and I feel him, firm and severe, I feel him up to where I can feel him. The butterflies beat their wings on the broad sides of his staff. They're red, they're green. My vulvas lick his grapes.

Long and futile hours of the wake. On the streets, in the city, maybe the night is a living creature, mobile and growing, generating other nights. Here it is decomposing. The shepherds on the pottery are growing old, their instruments are turning to dust. I breathe in a dead air, heavy with smoke. I look at the old man. His forehead speckled with sweat, his dentures badly placed, his jaws tied up with a handkerchief. I untie the knot of the handkerchief, I watch the mouth unclose. Someone opens the fringed curtains in the parlor, opens a

window, and exclaims: "What a beautiful night." At intervals, in the
Charity Hospital, the lament of a sick person rises up. Voices behind
me. "A great man." I clench my fists. Will he serve Justice dead more
or less than when alive? Footsteps to my left, the soft sound of feet on
the carpet where the young girl is having fun on the swing with flowered ropes: the stranger, without anyone's paying attention to him,
passes among us with the somber look of an old dog.

Dressed, without taking off my shoes, I turn out the bedroom
light and throw myself onto the bed. Have you seen death already,
Inês? In what part of the world today are you pouring your indulgent
words onto things? I contemplate death face to face and this test makes
me glad. You don't protect me. You're absent when old age destroys
my grandfather with its swift rhythm. Without your protection the vision of death devastates me, death reveals itself clearly before my eyes,
Grandfather is dead, dead and quite dead, his jaw opening and his
false teeth shoved between his dry gums. You're not present to stretch
out a veil between me and the destruction of the flesh so clearly dem-
onstrated here. Goodbye, Inês. Steps in the room, steps of the goat-
man, the stranger. The Hernidom? We look at each other, he standing,
I lying down—and his look means nothing. Why is he here? Can I be,
like him, a creature of the abyss? Both silent. Our look: two hollows,
one facing the other. A mirror opposite another mirror. I leave him, I
walk through the house again. The empty vase-holders on either side
of the clock. My grandmother shut up in her room. Several windows
open and the people motionless, not speaking, their faces more and
more pale and cadaverous. My steps echo, echo. The piano with its
brocade shawl. The tenderne, the first noises of this one more day,
some men sleeping in the chairs. The rooms remind one of the coaches
on a night train. I go back to my room. I don't see the stranger
anymore.

The singers fall silent. The pendulum comes and goes, the slow
pendulum. We rest. My left leg, extended, between Abel's knees; the
other one bent. Delaying the end to the maximum, keeping it near, not
letting it take us—as long as possible. He strokes my half-raised hip;
with clenched fists I pound slowly on his back. In the silence our sighs
echo, my moans and the muffled words he blows at me. The room
darker and now a tremulous light. A long and decreasing succession of
thunderclaps born above us among clouds I can't see descends in the
direction of all the points on the horizon. A cupola. Animals cross in
us, restless, stags with lions, sheep with dogs. Pulling away a little,

Abel slips a palm between my stomach and his, fondles my pubis. I pull him to me with force, I close my rings, doubly, around his axis— he is two in me. His tongue penetrates my left ear, it seems to spread out in my bodies, I feel the swelling of my bodies agitated by hot, harsh tongues, by the burning breath of seventy mouths. I don't know what to do with my own mouths and I start crying out. Tongues out, I lick the air. I don't know if my moans keep time to the rhythm with which he knocks at the entrance to my uterus or if he is using my cries as his rhythm. It's four-fifty-three.

T

Cecília Among the Lions   **14**

An old man, shirtless, exposed to the lukewarm November rain, is fishing with a net, taking advantage of the rising of the waters in the canal. Cecília's open umbrella is the same one with which she gets off the bus on the day I glimpse with surprise the peopled thickness of her body in front of the State Museum. Red, the fabric looks blue or gray at this hour of night and far from streetlights. Pellets of rain beat against the taut material. Her eyes glow in the shadows and, intimately, the heat of her flesh warms me through the clothes we wear—a breath in opposition to the damp exhalation that the canal gives off. A memory without remembrances now, Cecília's face. Hidden, silent, the creatures that are remembered or imagined in it. Rarer and rarer with the rain are the people who cross the vacant lots. The fisherman, standing on the wall, throws his net into the water. Is he after dead fish?

Cecília asks me if the Treasurer's death is truly accidental. I tell her about the conversation on top of the Bank and I put forth the idea that there are arbitrary suicides. Others, however, don't go beyond being a reinforcement: the dead man collaborates with death. He has an understanding with it or participates, in a certain way, in his own end. In the Treasurer's case, since life is really a thread, almost nothing is left when it's cut. Consider this: the thread unraveling itself. So clear!

Someone waving a flashlight traces a twisting path in the darkness from the other side of the canal. Cecília, her eyes fixed in that direction and seeming to believe that the one carrying the light is bringing another object with him, nameless, destined for her, a terrible object, a sentence written down or a weapon, starts to talk.

Maybe, she tells me, I have a tendency to see in the world a stage setting where destinies—individual or collective—flow. Is she mistaken? Does it occur to me at times that the world isn't an inert element? That it's a compulsion, Abel, maybe a character?

She admits perhaps it was possible to catch a glimpse of the Treasurer's life at the end. You can mark on your watch the moment in which a fighting cock, battling with another, begins to give in. There is a reason for that: the spurs, the beak, and the fury of its adversary. The Treasurer is massacred and yet his liking for parties certainly comes from the world. It already was or could have been—or not?—the disfigurement of a force. When you see or say you see—as in his case, and in others—capitulation as a simple auxiliary act, whom are you serving? It leaves the cruel side of the world sheltered from accusation. That side. Cecília can't succeed in naming it and has trouble identifying it clearly. Can we, in spite of all, deny that it exists? Isn't that what leads Marilyn Monroe to suicide?

She goes on talking. She's going to lend me some studies that she's read on the reality of the Northeast. The phrases roll together, separate, and suddenly, obeying a sinuous tie-in, she affirms: "In the work I do, seeing so much suffering close at hand, it hurts my teeth to say 'I'm happy.' But the fact is, I am." She adds that beyond a certain measure one can't possess and at the same time know: "I have, yes, and a lot." It's not known. Untenable. (The one with the flashlight, on the bridge, indecisive, some hundred paces from us and the silent fisherman.) If we knew? We'd explode. She can, however, with a clue, she can measure or evaluate how much these meetings increase it. You can die for so many reasons! "I'm afraid of death, Abel. So afraid! I don't want to die." She didn't want to. Now death doesn't mean anything anymore for her: and that's the clue, the measure of her happiness. In the papers she read the news about a double suicide. A couple, students, each at home, separately. Nothing was preventing them from coming together and no one knows the reason for the suicide. She, however, knows. She knows and I, too, am not unaware why they died. Was it a surrender? No. The two died because they were driven to a degree of joy that incinerated vileness, fragilities, fears like that of death—and they answer the instigations of that experience in their own way, they kill themselves, burning with jubilation in the rarely attained nucleus of fervor. Of fire. An exalting love like ours instigates us to die. One dies crushed and one dies exalted.

The man with the light, accompanied by someone now, having crossed the bridge, explores the side of the canal where we are. Both in raincoats, cautiously leaping over puddles. The fisherman casts his net again. He gathers it in. If death, in the depths, were to grab the net, would that patient old man fall into the snare, sinking down and becoming entangled in its cords? Cecília, tight, clutches me and tips the umbrella a little in an attempt to hide us. Close by, the two men. They're not talking. The flashlight, as if by chance, wavers and catches us. One second. They draw off.

"Where shall we meet tomorrow, Abel?"

"Not here."

"Where, then?"

Her breath burns my face. She throws her head back, bites my mouth. The impulsiveness of her gesture.

I'm standing and beside me there is someone lying on a bed. The house where we exist—I and the anonymous shape in the dream—doesn't separate us from the outside world. So I can see innumerable bonfires on the fields bathed in moonlight. A blinding brightness suddenly illuminates the night and the walls of the house. The person on the bed doesn't know the nature of the flashes: when the thunder sounds, dull and muffled, he bends over and tries to find the origin of the noise under the bed. The thunder, he supposes, is in his chamber pot. But thunder and lightning are only announcing the windstorm. For reptiles, the wind is a crawling phenomenon; it stirs the dust, moves the trees, turns over the trash, it doesn't fly much higher than locusts and bats. In my dream the wind that the thunder and lightning announce begins where clouds usually end, and it doesn't blow in a horizontal direction, it rises up vertically in the direction of some point even farther away than the great heights where it is born. All the air of the Earth is now moving in its direction, with insects and birds drawn by the vortex, and perhaps the waters follow it. Can it be for this reason that the sea roars so strongly? It is the fish who are clamoring, fearful. The bonfires in the fields become livelier. Sucked by the wind, the flames become longer, rise up, fly in the direction of that invisible magnet. The sky is peopled with ascending lights and glows with the rain of fire upside down. The flames, reaching a certain velocity and height, go from red to white, become darker and fly more rapidly, more and more rapidly. The action of the wind, prolonged, becomes stronger and weighs upon me. There is no more shape lying down, or bed, or walls. Everything, roots and foundations, is being pulled up from the ground like the bonfires. Then I hear my name, pronounced by a singing and slightly hoarse voice. I turn around: Cecília is standing, naked, under the fires, with her short hair and her body of an adolescent boy endowed with breasts, followed by a cohort of lions whose tawny fur reflects the moon and the flying flames at the same time. I sense that the air—and life with it—is being sucked out from within my trunk. I unclench my teeth, the air comes out of my mouth, a vomiting, I vomit the air I hold in my mouth and where I read, with tracings in blood, the word "fire" and the name of Cecília. Field and heavens are extinguished and the wind dies down. Cecília is still standing in front of me, the weight of her body resting on her left leg, dominating the lions under the moonlight. A sound similar to the ebb tide on Milagres Beach roams among the powerful and fearsome animals.

Over the quiet sea an incandescent star passes. No human form on the whole extent of the beach. Cecília lying down, her flank turned slightly in my direction and her purse serving as pillow. Her eyes, lighted by the distant stars (a knight, step by step, passes through her body, whistling) and the lights of the ships anchored in the distance, stare at me. The beacon cuts the night. The ram, lying down, chews his cud in peace. Cecília stretches out her two hands and takes my head, pressing it against her breasts. Children run and hide at the approach of the knight. I open my mouth, breathing in the calm wind and Cecília's voice. My eyelids: I close them. Her words all around: she's talking about struggles, but I don't know what she's saying. I hear her as if reading, the text being disturbed and certain mystery being added to the reading by the passage printed out of place. Those words that are not understood touch me. My hand advances along her thighs and she grabs it with a quick movement. Her heart is beating strongly under the pressure of my face; her legs are crossed; her legs stretched out; her whole body tense. I begin to kiss her. On the breast, on the shoulders, on the hands. In a little while, the stiffness is relaxed. Her heels, erratic, sketch in the sand.

The ram gets up with a leap and takes a few steps, moving his head. I sharpen my ear. A thin and meaningful whistle, coming from I don't know where, cuts through us. The waves break some distance away from us. Another whistle, this one sharper, answers the first. From the other side? Yes. Two new whistles indicate that there are movements on the sand, near us—or demarcate the encirclement. The encirclement. I get to my knees, looking around. She rises up. Her head against the halo—distant, peaceful—of the lights of Olinda. Maybe we can still escape. Cecília, rejecting the suggestion, grasps my arm, makes me turn around, and kisses me. I see the shape of a man over her shoulder, an imprecise shape. He is approaching slowly, with cunning and caution.

"Let's go, Cecília."

"No."

"Your brothers?"

"It might be. They won't hurt us."

"That's what they're here for."

She raises her bust and head even higher. I take a quick look at her delicate figure, incapable of frightening a bird, taking on a posture of challenge—and I clearly perceive our helplessness. I lack the necessary instruments of defense—neither muscles nor weapons (quick, rigid muscles). A feeling of nakedness and dependence. My love, alone, doesn't constitute protection. Cecília, unarmed, stiffens her body and doesn't seem to measure the difference in forces, undisputed now: four figures are spying on us, the thickness of the threat blackening us. She shakes her bust, silent, draws in the sand with her fingers. Does she find what she's looking for? A stone? Her hand closed. Three of the strangers keep their distance, all bareheaded; the fourth, wearing a helmet, holds a club. Police? He heads to where we are. He can take his time: his three chums bar our eventual flight. The one with the helmet: "What are you doing there?" One of the three lets out a thin and avid laugh. Without answering, I get up; I help Cecília up. The ram has disappeared. "Are you deaf? Deaf?" Cecília puts her purse over her shoulder and has her shoes in her hand. The three civilians close in the square while the other man orders us to show our papers. Papers? An intimation expressed in a dead tongue or one still larval. The presence of the intruders seems clear to me. It takes on a drastic feeling of expulsion, nothing casual. I clutch Cecília's hand and make the decision to leave as if the four individuals didn't exist. But the one with the helmet sticks the tip of his boot between my ankles and trips me. I fall, with my face in the sand, and before I can make a move they roll me over with kicks at kidney level. The tail of the beacon, curved, passes among the stars. My attacker, helmet in hand, kicks me with every attempt at rising, and Cecília is defending herself from the others. I'm startled by the quickness with which she avoids the blows of the aggressors and the obstinacy with which she protects herself in silence, not giving a single shout for help. On the ground I manage to grab the policeman's leg and make him fall. I throw myself, my arms open, at the ones mistreating Cecília. One of them grabs me and squeezes the breath out of me. A hard, broad hand. I bite it and I hear a muffled roar. A quick blow on the back of my neck knocks me down. I try to get up. All I can manage is to roll over on my shoulder and catch a glimpse of Cecília's body, losing its balance, slowly ceding and falling, slowly, slapped again. I hear a moan, a cry, a call, each one thrown out by a different voice—and the stars grow larger, blinding lakes. The footsteps of the offenders go off quickly. The herd. The beach trembling under the weight of those steps on the sand as if covered by a band of rhinoceroses. I close my hands, trying to keep myself on the surface of my consciousness in that way. If only there were a rope in my hands, a cord capable of pulling me up out of that deep cave where I'm floating! The lakes of the stars grow and diminish. A softening comes over me, a simulated peace, the sweetness of dying or cutting ties. A honey. A nothingness. Abel! My name knocks on the doors of the darkness (how many times?) and stops me from giving in. In a little while I move. Cecília is sitting with her hands over her sex and her legs extended out together in the exact position in which beggarwomen without the strength to walk ask for alms on the sidewalk. Her wounds are bleeding and she is shaking. From pain? Her teeth chatter over my name. Maybe from cold, her body uncovered, exposed to the wind of the beach. I can't manage to take off my shredded shirt. I wet Cecília's torn slip, try to wash her body, the cuts, trying to make my swollen hands light. I hurt her and at the same time I see how round and firm her breasts are, how soft her aching stomach is, and how delicate the line of her back in the starlight, slightly raised up at the soft curve of her shoulders. I make her get up. Why doesn't she go into the sea? Just for a minute. It ought to be good for her. She tries to keep her back to me and finishes undressing. Her thin body, her thin ribs, her tiny behind, almost like a child's. Hesitantly, she goes toward the sea. I call her. She stops. The beacon, the firmament, the wind, the waves. Cecília keeping herself from being seen in the front.

"Come back to me. I won't touch you if you don't want."

She obeys. I see her then, I see her as I see her in dreams, but without lions surrounding her and without fires. She comes close, slowly, resolute in her slowness. The clear line of her teeth and eyes (I can almost hear the buzzing of fever in them) fastened on me. With my left hand, I heft the form of her breast, I accompany her waist in the direction of her flank, in my palm I feel the wool, the desired pubis. Among the hairs: the quivering penis. I draw back my hand quickly, the hand bitten by the invisible weak viper. Cecília takes it and lays her head on my shoulder. Led by her fingers (they tremble uncertainly), I feel along the soft damp walls, between which there emerges—alive—the penis. Real and unlikely. Simultaneously our knees weaken. We fall, embracing, our foreheads joined. Coming from Cecília's body, fifteen or twenty children surround us, ragged, dirty, barefoot. With their hollow eyes they stare at us. A motionless circle.

We are in a taxi with noisy springs, and the leather of the seats is rough, making indecisive turns along the streets, Progresso, Soledade, Ninfas, Conde da Boa Vista, and Padre Inglês. The driver, apprehensive, looks at us in the rearview mirror. He finally asks if we don't want him to take us to the police. Cecília, hugging me, trembles: she moves her head resting on my shoulder, saying no. I lower the glass. "No, no police." The gentle night wind, full of voices that wander along the street, softens the pain of the wounds.

"I think it would be better if I took you home, Cecília."

With the tips of her fingers (so cold!), Cecília rubs my face and asks that we delay going back a little. The driver, impatient and bewildered perhaps, suggests dropping us off at the First Aid Station. I thank him and tell him: Casa Forte, Estrada das Ubaias.

R

Ꝋ and Abel: Meetings, Routes, and Revelations   15

With the window closed and a candle lighted on the dresser, Ꝋ's tale evolved, mutilated and not always comprehensible in the early dawn, mingled with the sound of the waves, the sparse crowing of the cocks, the interminable flight of the night birds, and the smell of the sheets that give off an aroma of cinnamon sticks. The flame moves to Ꝋ's quicker movements, and the shadow of her body, agitated, makes the boards creak. The flowers on her kimono, still open, give strength to the lushness, and between Ꝋ's skin and the space that enwraps it there is something like a light untouchable transparent down, a name-less material, light and fleshy, a mysterious gradation.

Somebody, able to do everything and not able to describe himself, puts on a disguise, that of emissary from himself, visiting us and living among us. An im-perfect and difficult way of speaking, like all of them; a discourse in which it is explained. The emissary, made up of the same substance as the one who molds and manages him, is as if joined in his hybrid nature to the Lamp, the Polished Surface, and the Reflection. What are the names of this visible emissary and this hidden sender?

♂ sitting on the bed and I stretched out, resting on the pillows: her profile outlined against the flame, her lips half open and silent. The color and the vivid glow of the candlestick, attenuated, are echoed in her loose hair. At first I think that the paleness of her face announces some debasing confession. But what stands out in that half-leaning profile is the opaqueness (against the light, one couldn't see it if she were pale), it passes through her skin and bones, fugitive, a transpar-ency just like that of clear grapes, in the pith of which we glimpse the shadow of the seeds, another face, a twin, looks at me through her temples and doesn't talk to me, we're all silent, but from the silence in which it is locked up it seems to be saying: "Hear me." The vision shuts off at the precise instant in which the face not hidden also turns to me, and agile signals—clear signals and shadowy signals—rise up to neck level, sinuous and swift, they disappear in the forehead or be-tween her breasts, an exasperated swarm of insects, black and white, tiny. She takes my wrist (the temperature of the rings) and with her right hand strokes my face. She bends over, leans her head on mine, and one breast, coming out from among the flowers of the kimono, is crushed, tepid and fragrant weight, against my flesh, having become sensitive, as if I were made of tongues.

"I open my hands before my eyes in the heart of the night and I don't see them. I create a cocoon of shadows. I question my trade as a writer in the face of oppression. I remain listening to the reply that is forming in the most protected and inviolate point of my body. The machine of oppression reaches me through the walls and the flesh. All of its guards and artifices are asleep, all—surrounded by scaffolding, casements, and weapons—and it, the machine, is operating. Machine or dog? There's no way to escape its breath."

"Few medical treatises deal with the Yolyp. This, I believe, favors the lack of awareness on the part of the parents. Almost always, they perceive only that they have brought something unique into the world when the child has reached the age of twelve or thirteen. An absolutely inexplicable detail: there are no Yolyps of the female sex. They are all male."

Her forehead on mine, she in the center of the room and the shadow on the wall, her mouth half open on my mouth, her profile against the flame and the secret eyes staring at me from deep inside. Eclipse, transparency, shadows. In a while, there they rise up out of absence, one and the other, both tense with drastic contrasts that are not always discernible, both duplicates, and, more than duplicates, above measures and limits, the two women I love rise at points far removed from years and the world, they pass through me, I entrust myself to them, at a given moment they concentrate and take on my obsessions, I grind their names on my teeth and the two names seem to meld, the first name: constant clarity, resplendent tide, Roos, swarm of fires; the second: Cecília, armed with virility, those I love and before whom, humble and startled, I subview the face—full of voices and signs—of the world, there they rise up. I introduce the first allusions, difficult and hidden, between 'O''s pauses, and my tongue contorts when I speak. Does she hear me? The extinguished lights on the motionless carousel and the sheds, the waves break up, and our voices mingle, solemn and inflamed, mouth to mouth, the truth creaking in our teeth without tricks and also without captious emphasis.

"From the age of twelve or thirteen, the face of the Yolyp begins to be visible in the dark. Anyone can see it under those conditions. Even he."

"The word consecrates kings, exorcises the possessed, effects enchantments. Capable of many uses, it is also the bullet of the unarmed and the animal that turns over rotting carcasses."

"Not everyone can glimpse the Yolyp in the dark with the same clarity. Some only perceive a very light halo; others distinguish it with xylographic relief."

We live together every day with written narratives and this hides their mystery. A voyage is in the text, whole: departure, course, arrival. In it there is the going and the staying; that is, flux and permanence coincide.

"The face that can be seen in the dark, completely different from the one that is seen in the light, is the true face of the Yolyp."

"I know quite well: there are, there have been, other evils on Earth, always and numberless. Oppression, a phenomenon that tends to legitimize many other evils and, in general, the most prosperous, reduces the word to a spoil of war, part of the invaded territory. The writer battles under oppression with a confiscated set of goods."

A great butterfly with black wings rises up on the ceiling, two more by the door. The candle goes out. I don't move and I remain undressed, even if I grow cold with dawn and the rapid gusts of wind make the window latch groan. Can I be speaking in vain? Both, Roos and Cecília, aren't they listening to me in ☺, estuary and confluence?

The foreign woman, going back and forth between the frontiers of going and coming, surprising in the constructions of her tangible and fantastic spaces, full of towers, birds, fishes, tracking animals, and raised banners, the foreign woman, slippery and luminous (plants turn toward her face), the fragile and populated androgyne whom I love, who gets undressed, multiple, before the window opened onto the dazzling summer afternoons of the Northeast, heavy with scents, with blue, and the buzzing of flies—those women so fundamentally loved who incorporate themselves into the world forever are a cloud of dust and a sound in the world, there I see them under an unexpected perspective, one that doesn't even frighten me. Could you be, Roos, in your fluctuation between coming and going, a more subtle and anticipatory version of Cecília's oppositions? Isn't there in correspondence to the clarity that is one of your gifts—as night corresponds to day and death to birth—a certain constant of blackness, associated since the eclipse to the presence of ☺? Besides which, I do not know how and to what point, you reverberate, hidden, I don't know to what point, in the symmetries, in the rhythms. I tend to believe, Cecília, that the doubleness of your being covered with figures rises up again in ☺, in this case a triple, dual, and single being, and also I wonder now if I don't hear your voice in her mouth at times. I would never say, however, that you are fragments or simple inconclusive attempts of this one who, I still don't know how, revives you two. Each one being absolute and, in a manner of speaking, unlimited, none of you is everything. Integral, in spite of this, they do not constitute solitary realities: in their integrity they come together in an all—sum and summula of totalities—not superior or more perfect than the unities included.

"The true face of the Yolyp is not necessarily horrible. Some, in the dark, present a face with purer lines than those on the one made of flesh, the daylight one, the one everyone knows. What is frightening is not the monstrous look of the face; it is the fact that it is a matter of a different face, one hidden to our eyes when lighted up and revealed precisely when there is no light that isn't its own."

T

Cecília Among the Lions   15

In the peacefulness of the night, they both appear before us. They. Cecília and Abel, all covered with scratches, little more than naked, dressed only in their arms, their hands, and torn bits of cloth. The birds trill, startled by the strange voices that invade the silence where we live. They ask: "Visitors? Visitors? Tiu? Pio?" Bruises on their faces and dry bloodstains on what was left of their clothing. They seemed to be poisoning themselves, the two of them (two?), sucking in the air corrupted by their own fleeting and predatory love. They bow out: they save themselves. Broken and battered. They glow, even like that, within their bodies. No. A different body, a body of desire, burns intact inside the body of flesh covered with welts. Abel looks at me, looks at me through Cecília's body, looks at me with triumph (he, the loser), and we see him winged, plunging into Cecília's inviolate center. Cecília looks at me, face to face. Her look a block—black, broad, brilliant, a sheet of stone, impersonal and thick. She snaps my heartstrings with that look. As if saying: "Be damned. Help me and be damned. These wounds are Abel's vespers." Visible, tangible, the sign of fire that enwraps them and encircles them. Encircles them? It isn't an arc. Almost. An interrupted arc: the almost invisible ends don't meet and can continue on. Continue on? Cecília, Abel, Cecília, enclosed and held within it—the loop. Snare. The needle, magnetized, doesn't point anywhere. Abel refuses the help I offer him ("Take care of Cecília!") and sits on the bench, the album on his knees. The porch light is out. Why the album, then?

We, Hermenilda and Hermelinda, take Cecília to our room. She shudders where we touch her on the skin. Has her poor flesh been so scourged? From aggression or desire? We outdo ourselves with solicitude. Suspicious, Cecília watches us, her fists clenched. Seeing the candles lighted in front of the small shrine, she tells my sister: "Turn out the light." I obey. In the closet, I look for one of our dresses, old, light, and clean, that she can wear. I hear the cry. A sob? Sob or cry: without wishing to, in the discreet light of the candles, I see Cecília's double and doubtful sex. Obverse and reverse. Sheath and knife. I bend over by the foot of the bed, by the head of the bed—and I receive a kick, my sister's look. I stroke Cecília's injured feet, I stroke Cecília's face, I kiss her hair and with the almost extinguished heat of my body I try to warm her winged, firm feet.

I leave the room and Cecília follows me, older in my mallow-colored dress, silk, with wild roses on the bosom. From behind Cecília, from the door of the bedroom, I see Abel standing in the dining room. The arc of flames unites them. He turns toward me and toward me, the album still in his hand. Doesn't he see us, perhaps? The way in which he looks at Cecília from between his swollen eyelids reveals a strange joy. His expression is that of a man freed of choices. He has embraced contraries in one of those rare earthly incarnations.

According to her habit, left over from olden days, of leaving the entrance unlocked, the Fat Woman lies down whenever she feels like it and leaves the house open for anyone to come in. "Is that my son Abel? I'm here on the bed. Come here, man." Directed by her voice, I open the door to the room.

"What if it hadn't been me?"

"I only asked for the sake of asking. I know your footsteps."

The black hulk seems even vaster in the darkness on the canvas bed without a sheet. I sit in a broken-down wicker chair with a pillow on the back.

"You never come around! Have you abandoned your old lady?"

She laughs. The whiteness of her feet, intensified by the black dress, stands out in the shadows. She crosses them.

"Why are you shut up in here? This morbid room!"

"Resting my eyes. Now that December's here! All this brightness in the world can even give you a headache. Between noon and two o'clock, you know: I come in here."

Lucíola came to visit her and ask for some money. She said she'd seen Dagoberto lying drunk on the street. Lucíola's husband, always involved in bad business deals, is going around without any means of support again. Result: Lucíola is pregnant, while the oldest of the six stepchildren is going on sixteen. Cesarino swears by everything that the Treasurer jumped in front of that truck. "Could it have been like that, Abel?" In the corner and at bed level, two small dots fixed on me: the eyes of the catamonk.

"I don't know. Maybe. We'll never know."

The sound of the waves dully reaches the room. The sea, under the two-o'clock sun, continues to gnaw at the walls and floors of Milagres.

"What about you and Cecília? Are you still together?"

"We're still together."

The meetings in distant and poorly lighted places. The canvas bed groans under the weight of the Fat Woman.

"Your wife was here again. She's all upset, Abel. Be careful."

The cat with the monkey's head slips away into her left ear, slides along her throat, disappears and reappears under her skirt, between her knees. It curls up beside her very white feet. With a sudden movement she shoos it away and sits up on the bed.

"You smell like medicine. Why? Come over here beside me." (My head between her hands, she takes a deep breath.) "Where did you get that drugstore smell?"

Before I can answer, and with an agility inconceivable in such a heavy body, she leaps from the bed, opens the door of the room, and clutches my face, turning it toward the light. "What the devil is all this? All bruised!" The catamonk climbs up her legs and curls up in her stomach, trembling. "I was attacked." "By whom? Why?" "I don't know. Cecília and me." "Take off your shirt." "It's not necessary." She starts to unbutton it. The catamonk leaps out of her belly and hides under the bed. On occasion it sticks its short neck out, examines me, and goes back to its hiding place. "Was it those brothers?" "How should I know!" "What do you mean you don't know? They might have been sent by them. Remember? One of them is a clerk with the Police." "Bastards." "And you, why don't you get rid of that little lady? So many females in the world! It can't go on like this. What ever can they be thinking about?"

Without putting her slippers on, she goes to her room, climbs up on a chair, takes down a shoebox from the top of the closet, blows the dust off the cover, and tosses it into my hands. "It's yours." In the box there is a revolver and a handful of bullets. I give it all back to the Fat Woman, without any explanations. "What? Are you going to keep on getting knocked around? Do you want to die like another Eurílio?" The cat comes running, leaps onto the living-room table, and is inlaid on her shoulder. "Maybe you're right. It's too much already having put Janira into this world. Killing her own children!" She puts the revolver into the box and the catamonk opens its arms on her breast, its back toward me. "How long has that gun been here? I didn't know about it." "Five or six months." "Who brought it, the Treasurer?" "He's the one."

The palm trees, beyond the porch, are motionless in the hard light. The window curtains have halted, the birds and hunters are still.

"You're sucking a dog's ass over that girl, aren't you? You're going to keep on seeing her. So, the time of fucking in the underbrush is over. You two come here to the villa. Naturally, I won't hang around spying on you. I'll take off. I'll go walking on the beach and you two can get together. I'd like to see if those sons of bitches—brothers or brothers' thugs—will have the nerve to invade my house." (The cat with the monkey's head runs among the living-room chairs, climbs up onto the piano, and slips among the brightly colored vases. It returns to the Fat Woman.) "Motherfuckers! Doing that to you. Your face is still half swollen."

I head toward the cistern. The zinc roof, even protected by the foliage of three or four trees, explodes in the violent sun. In that same spot—where the City would later rise up inciting me to the search—an archaic rite has been fulfilled several times in me. I scrape my thighs (am I twelve or thirteen years old?) and between them I hide my still infantile penis. The Map is clearly outlined. I imagine my being male and female at the same time. Recife, my country, the whole Earth, a deformed and arbitrary map. I run my left hand, of a boy, across the scratched flesh and the chestnut-colored pubic hair; with the right one, feminine, I open the invisible immature sex, bent back, hidden between my thighs. This is how the world rises up—in the world, me—and with this the imponderable old order returns, which, mistakenly, I believe appeased: "Go, man, seek the City." The body that exalts me then and knows the pleasure (acid still) of the flesh is mine and is not. Seek the City? Where and how? Isn't the hunt over? A pair. Seek, Abel, the City that has risen up and dissolved here. The dampness of the ground penetrates my body and the zinc roof is distended under the heat. The sound of a mandolin and juvenile voices crosses the silence.

Sounds rise up from the pantry the tin of the basin under the strong jet of the faucet tinkling of cutlery water chinaware set down on granite splash of spigot and the voices. The wind softly moves the lamp. The shadow of the paper shade, in motion, dislocates the connection between the few pieces of furniture and the walls. I open the drawer (its smell of gunpowder) and I examine the already extensive piece about the four old women. In the villa, concisely described, they still probe each other and talk. Each one wants to instill the memory of her own life in the spirit of the other septuagenarians; the others will have to forget what they have lived and remember only what they have heard. All, however, hear three narratives, the narratives of their sisters. Even though they are different narratives and chaos may arise at the same time in all of them. That's not what happens. Sisters, they have always lived together and their memories are similar. In that very way, the narratives are all identical, flowing, crisscrossed, and monotonous, among the four characters. One and then all of them perceive this. *"Am I hearing the story of my life or have I really forgotten everything I have lived and am telling, thinking that the twin chronicles of my sisters are talking about me?"* Wouldn't it be safer to invent a biography? Rather than this, which has been diluted by the mutual recounting of events that they doubt even when they have lived them. A general and almost simultaneous decision, with which everything becomes disjointed. Memory assimilates invention, and each old woman, who has such a desire to impose the telling of what she has lived on the sisters, no longer speaks of herself: she tells about an invented being. The four old women and their narratives pass each other in the numerous rooms of the villa. Four? They discover that they are five. The tales, as in an alchemist's jar, may have created still another being. Which among the five old women (and all invent and narrate) can the clandestine one be? No one knows, and an impatient hatred takes possession of them all. Each wants to see the others dead. Survival would be the testament and proof of their own identity. This is the reason behind the evil and lurking desires—which, when I began the story, didn't seem clear to me. The old women will then go on to confuse the number of rooms, doors, plates. Will they have lost the notion of quantity? They do not know and will continue not to know whether they are four or five. Hatred and the necessity of outliving the others continues, exacerbated. The first old woman dies. The second and third die. The story closes with the image of the last two octogenarians, looking at each other in the parlor, seated, their fists clenched. Are they looking at their own image? They themselves don't know. They don't know and they have forgotten everything except the hatred and the obstinacy of enduring.

I go through the empty villa. Listening for the desired sound of Cecília's shoes (open the gate and come, cross the porch, come!), I don't hear my steps on the mosaic tile. Five months exactly since I met her at the house of Hermenilda and Hermelinda. My mother, sitting somewhere on the beach under the umbrella with faded sectors, the vigilant monkey in her body, is watching the maneuvers of the jangada rafts. I pass by the mirror in the living room and I see myself. Dull marks of attack on my colorless face, vaguely frightened. I sit down in the rocking chair. The blue wooden frame, the young spinners on the wall, the portrait of the couple: the Treasurer's jutting jaw and the caustic—albeit somewhat perplexed—look of the Fat Woman at the age of twenty.

The iron gate creaks. I see marks of attack on my face, I sit down in the rocking chair, Cecília's light strides make the porch lighter and the afternoon more placid, her shape looms up in the doorway, laughter follows her and other shapes enter, working people, the women with baskets on their heads, the men with wax-palm hats, their faces dried out by the sun (wrinkles of the scratches of a dagger?), hands as hard as firewood and bare feet like hooves, their clothes in tatters. Cecília, laughing, a yellow blouse, a full skirt, with designs of birds and flowers, runs in my direction, with such drive that the curtains vibrate. The smell of farmhands—baked sweat and mud. The hoes, the sickles, and the machetes clang against the walls. Cecília's skin burns like this hour of the afternoon.

My head on the firm lavender pillows, on the lace coverlet put on by the Fat Woman—over which, crosswise, she laid out in addition a rust-colored linen spread, with which I partially cover myself—I watch Cecília undress. The multiple odors with which the room is impregnated—coming from those sweating glasses filled with soft drinks and coconut milk, from the trays with pineapple slices, mixed in with the dry smell of the cinnamon leaves scattered on the floor—envelop her: her body seems fruity and shadowy to me. Her new light-colored shoes lie upside down on the mat that serves as a rug. We are protected a little from being seen from the outside by the one-piece net lace curtain with the rampant lion biting the Moon. It is difficult, even without the curtain, for us to be seen by anyone who might pass by the side of the building. The room, chosen and arranged with great care, is located in the wing opposite the porch, on the lower part of the property. We are, in this way, exposed to the brightening daylight and hidden: the height of the window hides us. We hear the leaves of a

flamboyant scratching the panes (their blood-red flowers open in January), we see the branch that reaches out to touch the curtain and invade the room, we see the indigo sky, immense white clouds—and we
are not seen. The roar of the sea, not too violent, dies at Cecília's feet.

This love, soaked in the never-conquered anxiety of atoning for
my unhappy acts and choices, is magnified by the circumstance that in
Cecília's body (Cecília: body and bodies, men and women, her fables),
I can love in a single way, undisturbed by purifying interference—
putting a distance, however, between the spirit and the numerous and
concrete beings I love. Outside her body a love like this is impossible
or can be realized only as a mental operation. Can it be love, then? Her
androgyny still adds new and provocative meanings to our relationship. I don't see them clearly and I must guard against deciphering,
which would mean deciphering Cecília. I contemplate them with as-
tonishment, as if for the first time I were contemplating a geometric
figure, a sign, an echoing of occult memories, symbolic suggestions,
and still undiscernible connections.

Not everything here is a secret or a barely intuited truth. I can see
quite well that in Cecília contraries are reconciled; and I cannot isolate
the Woman and the Man in her flesh. Male and female, she doesn't
distinguish the irreconcilable parts merged in her body. Does she love
doubly, then—woman, man—or does the diffuse male implanted in
her appraise me hostilely? Is there, in this case, a tone of repulsion in
her surrender? It might be that the male and the female crossed in
Cecília (perhaps she looks at me with four eyes, two of a woman and
two of a man) love each other in an absolute, albeit incestuous way, a
love impossible for ordinary beings. All of my gestures, words, acts—
segregated and alone as I am—would be a simulacrum of that love,
crossed through with mysterious inferences. In the codices of the alchemists, a hermaphrodite, the image of the wedding between Sun and
Moon, dies and rots away to be reborn: from it the White Stone is obtained, the ferment for the New Beginning. In all this a resemblance
between the androgyne and Janus, the two-faced god, is imposed. On
finding it, my relationship with Cecília, as I judge it, takes on a strange
and even frightening expression. Indispensable, nonetheless, for my
dealings with the world, arriving at the understanding, albeit imperfect, of the function of chaos and its nature. The two faces of Janus,
engraved on so many monetary effigies, represent, I have read, perhaps
in Ovid, a vestige of his primitive state: in the darkness where the
world still doesn't exist, when everything is light and heavy at the

same time, Janus, god of thresholds—and therefore of sallies and returns—is called Chaos. He is joined simultaneously to order and disorder. Are my investigations, in this case, written in Cecília?

O

The Story of Ó, Twice-Born   23

Do I hear, before the open window, the sea on the nearby rocks?
Has a child, weeping, crossed the dimly lighted corridor of the hotel
with light shoes on? Am I breathing in the motionless air? Is someone
talking in some nearby room, a man's voice mingled with the waves? Is
there an answer? My bridal wreath hangs from a tall coatrack. The
name of the city is Itanhaém, and everything surges up—everything:
walls, furniture, clothes, movements, sounds—in the words without
number of my narration, hour after hour, until, losing my voice, I keep
on telling within myself the story of my own wedding and so many
other events, not always perceiving the links of my discourse. In a
convulsive way, with leaps and bounds, I describe the daily and irrational progress of my loveless love. Are my feelings and acts those of a
person in love? Nevertheless, this love is tricky, a spell. I describe it
and I describe the darkening days when I make myself alien to the
mechanism that had been destined for me for a long time, I describe
the apartment on the Avenida Angélica where Hayano lives with his
parents, the grimy rugs, the damask armchairs worn by use, Julius
Heckethorn's clock, a whole series of scenic elements that reveal an
abundant life in its declining phase, I describe the ceremonial teas,
Hayano's father, tall, mule-jawed, sitting at an angle because of the
constant pain in his spine, and closing his eyes to savor the brew, Bilia,
short and compact, is still not so fat when I see her cross the garden in
the rain beside her son in his Military Academy uniform, Bilia, hair
trimmed at the back of her red neck, ceaselessly eating chocolates and
sweets, not very comfortable—it's obvious—in the chair (she has always lived reclining on beds and sofas), looks at her son from time to
time through tight eyes, with an adverse expression, yet praising him,
exalting him, he will get the highest grades, everyone will see, I describe her voice, rolling in her throat between thick walls of fat, her

laugh coming from her esophagus without a trace of change in her face dulled by fat, I describe Hayano's look of realization, the calmness with which he listens to Bilia's tormented words, his confidence in the promotions announced with such insistence and firmness is evident, all that bothers him is the buzzing in his ears and the dreams he always complains about, the only ones he remembers, where only the dead appear, angry, in a thousand situations, this and nothing else makes him apprehensive, I describe the buzzing and the angry dead who argue in those nightmares, I describe Natividade, hardening the remainder of her life in an old people's home paid for by Olavo Hayano and for no reason repeating "I raised that boy," I describe the black face, the lost look, the hands without strength, the laugh that seems to flow in beads around her neck, I describe our mechanical visits to the home on certain Saturday afternoons, in Jaçanã, I briefly describe the nurses, the servants, Natividade's roommate, more advanced in years than Natividade, eyes of a child, thin ankles, a bow in her hair, dressed in a floral pattern, blue flowers, always singing and dancing the tarantella (a way of evoking gay and distant Neapolitan mornings), I describe the painted statue in the garden of the home, lifesize, showing a man with an open umbrella, water comes out of the tip and flows down the sectors, the zinc umbrella produces its own rain, it rains over that mannikin while the inmates stroll in the garden, in the sunlight, I describe our trip to the home before our wedding so Natividade can see my gown and see Hayano in his dress uniform, there is a silence among the old people when I arrive, in white, the long train, the flowers, the water falls from the gray umbrella, Natividade hugs me, her friend dances the tarantella, the old people follow me through the garden, we cross that dusty part of the city by car, its lumber mills, its heavy traffic, its lime deposits, and its houses with dirty walls, a boy disturbs the silence of the chapel on the hot and oppressive afternoon, I describe the sudden rain, shifting winds shake the two cypresses on either side of the entrance on Marquez de Ytu, there I am taking off the wedding dress and tossing it over this chair in one of the rooms one never enters (the European magazines from 1912 and the vials of perfume that only smell of past), I describe the automobile trip, and Hayano's upset and anger when he discovers the run-down conditions of the hotel where he finds himself obliged to spend the night, the foundation of the hotel doesn't exist when I describe it, but everything matches my description, the mattress with its weak springs, the bulb hanging from a wire over the tall-backed bed, the harsh spread, the pink walls, the bed lamp with little flowers on its yellow shade, the vanity with three oval mirrors, the gray curtains with orange and black designs, the faded rugs on the shiny wood of the floor, the tall coatrack with the wreath on one hook, a child weeping through the poorly lighted corridor, and I myself standing by the open window, listening to the sea beating on the nearby rocks and breathing in this air, this air as motionless as stone.

Sitting in front of the mirrors on the vanity, I put the wreath on and examine myself. Twenty-three and fourteen years old, I and I, blended in the reflection, serene and terrified, combing the silvery and tawny hair, the abundant hair, loose under the wreath, I, in the face of the mirrors, hair, flesh, and clothing almost not fitting into the ovals of the glass, my eyes, the color of dry leaves and with the look of a snare, stare with double strength at the ancient image (it might be thought that moving under the light of the bulb is the model on a postcard from before World War I, with her fleshy arms, narrow brow, and pale somber face), my protruding lips could be just like those of a black woman if marked off with less precision, and my full breasts under the loose clothing, decorated with ermine, ribbons, lace, flowers, sashes, trim, and bows, exhale a cool smell of jasmines—the odor given off by Wrath in repose—and I don't know whether of moth-eaten postcards, too.

Hayano comes into the room, comes over to me, and takes off the wreath. I desire him, it's an acid desire, with the taste of vinegar, I burn with desire and I burn with terror: I would like to flee, but I want to stay, I stay (the pact signed on the night when I struggle and I struggle on the floor, I struggle, until dawn comes up, it's established: we'll be one and one, united, in the face of everything that comes, we are one, I am one), he lays me down on top of the sheets, the lamp beside the bed is lighted, the bulb hanging from a cord is lighted and is reflected in the center oval mirror, with something meticulous in his movements, Hayano takes off my lace camisole, he falls on top of me, phrases spoken by a man echo in some nearby room. Hayano breaks my hymen, my hymens, the chandelier above us, crystals and silver objects slowly oxidizing in the shadows, the man's words echo without response, held between Hayano's arms, I struggle, I struggle from pleasure and from horror, he knows me, he rapes me, I shout drunkenly, I weep with fear. Hayano's sex wounds me, it tears me twice, icy, and then I feel the Avalovara, the bird, left in me by Inácio's passage, double over, pierced, as if Hayano's cold glans was the coming of a harsh and sudden winter: the bird loses its beak and voice, is reduced to a skeleton, engraved in me like the skeleton of a fossil in stone—without voice, without plumage.

A group of drunks pass by on some street near the hotel. With slurry voices they sing scattered verses from old carnival songs. What time can it be? Three o'clock? Hayano lights the oil lamp inside the red glass. The night lamp and the bulb on the cord are still lighted, he looks at my nakedness. With a closed fist over my eyes, I let him do it and don't try to cover myself. Did I feel pleasure? Yes, but I don't know if it's really what one should feel. He drops down and kisses me on the face. I open all my eyes, carnivorous flowers, I stare at him, eyes open. Why is the end of his sex icy? Stealthily, he reaches out his left hand for the lampshade. With one of his unexpected and quick movements, he makes the light fall on my face. I hit the lamp, the lamp flies and falls to the rug. Hayano grabs me by the hair and tries to see into the depths of my eyes. We struggle on the bed. What for? I stop trying to get away, to get my face away, my eyes, and I face him, my eyelids open, all of them, so that he can see—and he sees, and shouts that I have four eyes in my sockets, one pair inside the other, Julius Heckethorn's clock ticks on, a thunderclap on the right, another on the left, distant and spaced explosions, his monotonous voice shows accusation and disdain. What eyes are those? How is it that he never saw them?

With studied slowness, I close the newer lids over their eyes. Does he only want to see the look that everyone perceives, the look that sees him without the relief and color with which he should be seen? Let him see it. He still stares at me for an instant, he lets me go, he picks up the extinguished lamp from the floor, he turns out the ceiling light, and asks my pardon, he lies down. Only the light of the oil lamp is left in the room.

He falls asleep, but sleep doesn't come for me. That's how it is, I say to myself. Exactly. By the light of the lamp: stucco, walls, curtain, his face, the mirror. Can all men have a cold glans? He snores, restlessly. It's hot.

I get up and open the curtain more; I need air. Hayano stirs. I cross the room, naked, I open the closet, I look for a camisole without so much decoration. I catch sight of a holster. Empty? I bend over, I heft it: it contains a pistol and smells of horses. My lower abdomen aches, I feel raped, I take the weapon out of the case and aim it at the figure lying face down on the bed. Is there a pistol? Then nothing is lacking—I state. I add that the time is approaching. I put the weapon back into the holster and put it in the place, the same place, I took it from. In the end I don't change my camisole: with measured movements I put on the one I was going to replace. I lie down, I close my eyes, I hear him murmur. That's when the wind blows, a wind so cool that I shiver and cover myself. I fall asleep.

Suddenly I open my eyes: the wind must have blown the oil lamp out. With my back to the man, I can see nothing and I want—it's a demanding desire—to know what time it is. The night seems long to me, I have the impression of having slept for days on end. I try in vain to turn on the night lamp. Is the power off in the Hotel? In the whole city? Apart from the sea and the waves breaking on the rocks, I hear nothing. There is a remote halo in the room—perhaps the light of the stars—and the temperature has gone down. I get up to close the blinds and the curtain. At that moment the beam of a searchlight sweeps the walls. I take advantage of it to look at the clock: it's two minutes after four. The light is coming from a ship anchored offshore as if lost in time, and it's impossible to imagine why its searchlights are speaking to the city at this hour of the night. I fold my arms because of the cold, I turn toward the sleeping man. He snores and I see him face on. The beams from the searchlights turn on and off rapidly. A message? For whom? Message or not, that blinking bothers me. Something is missing in all this, in this room where I'm breathing with my mouth open, in this minute I am living, a discordant element here, of this I am sure. I say to myself, in spite of everything: "It's now." But *what* is now? I don't know.

In the end, I do know. It's hard for me to make out, that's certain, the reason for everything in the tangled web of this hour, even though I know that it means a result, the answer to a calculation: other innumerable hours are here and are echoing. The foreseeable ceremonies that are in the sequence and the rhythm resemble a domination over the future (or what bears that name of future). My gestures and the circumstances that surround them are like a ceremony. Like a robot, I go back to the closet, I open the door and bend over. A dog barks and is answered. The light from the ship beats on the wall, quicker than before. I take the pistol out of its holster, I close the door again, I draw back a few steps, I stand in the center of the room. What are the searchlights saying? . . . Entering and leaving the shadows is Olavo Hayano's profile. I turn the doorknob, I go through the door that opens into the hallway. Uncertain, I go off. Something in the scene reflects a determined moment of my life and I have a clear feeling of that. A door slams, far off. The waves explode on the rocks. I go back to the room and leave the door open. The other one, on a different floor, continues slamming. I sit down before the oval mirrors of the vanity. The dog is still barking. The searchlights from the ship keep on pulsating. My face and my dress—the raised bust, the lace, right arm, eyes, the hair falling over my shoulders—rise up and disappear, in triplicate. I open my collar, I feel the flesh of my breast and I turn the barrel of the pistol toward me. The explosion resounds as in the bottom of a cistern.

P

Julius Heckethorn's Clock 4

In the bosom of his paternal family Julius Heckethorn receives an upbringing that matches his nature and is not very prudent in light of the years engendered deep in the heart of other people. He reads a great deal, principally musty and little-known works. In one of the books printed by typographers of Basel and recorded by Charles W. Heckethorn, he finds indications, incomplete and vague, it is true, of a domestic clock provided with three systems of chimes and inspired in part by the planisphere clock built in 1344 by Santiago de Dondis, a physician-astronomer of Padua: the triple-sounding apparatus, single and synchronic in its origin, had to be divided into sections, remaining thus so exposed to chance that it well might never be heard again in its entirety. It is not stated, the incunabulum says, whether or not it had at least been begun, and there is very little information about the project outside of its being unworkable according to some experts. Julius is still a child, but he is enthralled by this wild dream and the notes taken on that occasion stay with him for years.

With the armistice, the carillons of his father fall silent. The latter, before perceiving that his bankruptcy is irremediable, discovers that the wife for whom he has left and forgotten the land where he was born is having intimate relations with an agitator. Deceived by his wife, by life, by History, by youthful resolutions, and by the fantasies that nourish him at other times, he commits suicide with a bullet in the head. The bullet and the revolver that he uses in his last gesture are English, a kind of funereal reconciliation with the United Kingdom.

The erstwhile maiden Erika Haebler disappears in the smoke, the dust, and the detritus of 1918.

While he makes progress in his musical apprenticeship—revealing, with some precocity, a predilection for Mozart—and strengthens his liking for books of scant circulation, Julius opens up a new field of interest, the art of clockmaking. It isn't hard for him to apprentice himself to a factory in Southampton, where, thanks to his theoretical knowledge of the subject, he is promoted to fitter. His desire to return to Germany becomes evident at this time, so that he can rehabilitate, if possible, the carillon workship that survives in his memory, Mozart and the harpsichord notwithstanding, as an Eden peopled by sounds from which he feels himself expelled.

At the age of twenty-one he finds himself in Cologne at last. He pays his expenses by playing the music in vogue at teatime on the piano in a hotel near the Cathedral. The heiress of a well-to-do broker from Münster, pale and fragile, in the city to undergo prolonged and, furthermore, hopeless tests at a clinic (she is suffering from progressive blindness), is attracted to that young man with refined manners who speaks the German language with a British accent.

O

The Story of , Twice-Born   **24**

Four-fifty-six. I suck in Abel's mouth, I speak in his mouth, inside his mouth, I say that I love him, with his tongue entangled in mine he says that he loves me, the word "love" rolls between our teeth. Made of thick clouds, swift and premature, the November night enwraps us. Echoing, a dull and mobile thunderclap unfolds: circular. I close my eyes. Another night, interior and porous, encircles me: I'm in the country, somewhere on Earth, a flat place. I hear the trees, their huge dripping crowns suspended in the shadows, I hear them as if they were waterspouts, my whole body hears them. They're full of fruit. There's a beating of wings above us and that beating of wings creates the celestial space in the darkness—the way a call in the silence creates a presence. The sky above me, with the weight of its stars. My body sees the stars. The sky is black, the luminaries are black, and the birds light, and the trees fruitful, and I, and the flat place where I am lying. The Avalovara is reborn in the asphalt, free of the muteness and immobility to which it has been condemned ever since the hour when Olavo Hayano rapes me with his cold glans; the skeleton of the fossil ingrained in my flesh (like a name in my memory) takes on feathers, unties itself, light, with its bones of air, fireworks breaking the compact shadows. I open my eyes: Avalovara, the bird of my contentment.

A rainy, hot March. Lying on the sofa among pillows, before the open curtains of the apartment, I hear the vehicles passing on Consolação, and I stroke the scar. When I'm not reclining on the sofa, I walk listlessly among the gaudy easy chairs and the gilt frames of the paintings of the kind Olavo Hayano collects, I change the place of the bric-a-brac I detest—hookah pipes, glass animals, Japanese dolls— which are joined every week by other similar ones, I lie down crosswise on the double bed or I stay in front of the mirror, combing my hair. Idly, I try on my light flowered dresses. One of the three rooms in the apartment adjoins the cement area onto which the upstairs tenants throw fruit rinds, used bags, scraps of paper, and newspapers. There, at the end of the afternoon, a fast wind blows, caught between the walls; it spins for an hour, two, with such velocity that the newspapers are lashed into shreds. I stay in front of the window glass looking at the spirals of trash and thick dust. Under that same window, when it rains, the pluvial waters gurgle, sucked in by I don't know what drain hidden among the tiles. That sound and the wild wind in the courtyard are the two things in the house not bought and imposed by the owner, the only things. I take possession of both and they take me.

For the hundredth time Hayano breaks the silence and asks me: "Why?" For him, everything, by compulsion, has a cause. For the hundredth time I don't answer and silence is installed between us once more. He insists, after the pause, his voice neutral and a little anxious: "What was the reason? I have the right to know." Are those April days as luminous as I see them? Do I see them so clearly because of the energy that's being reborn in me? As my strength returns, I stroke the mark of the bullet less and the insistence with which he interrogates me grows: "Why did you try to kill yourself? With my own weapon! What if you'd died?" He rejects, without explanation, my attempts at exchanging a decoration or arranging the furniture as I like it. He doesn't even allow me to choose my clothing: he accompanies me to the shop and picks it for me. A snipper, he cuts off my steps. Father and protector. Dozing in me is the serpent from Inês's breath, my whole rebellion consists of hiding, to avoid examination, the books I'm reading and of firing maids, whose uniforms pass from Antônias to Franciscas, to Ritas, to Edwiges. Also, facing the courtyard, paved and dirty, I have the benefit of what is not Hayano's. A lot of newspaper pages there, there, the wind blows in August, but in September there are few that fall into the courtyard trap and it doesn't rain that month, nor does it rain in October. At night I listen closely to myself and seek out the remains of the spur. Under its red glass, the oil lamp trembles. I breathe in Hayano's absence as one breathes in an odor of bones.

Decked with all the colors of a peacock, the Avalovara reminds one of an illuminated manuscript. It is almost possible to read in it. The tail is long and curved, with copper reflections. The wings, six, of a sky-blue green shade when at rest, display on the inner side, when open, circles of many colors laid out with symmetry on a scarlet background. I see them flapping and I hear nothing. It flies, the bird does, from the table to the floor and from the floor to the top of the clock, as if it were hollow, a bird of air. Traced across its breast, purple bands and stripes. From the delicate head, seeming to be decorated with a diadem of small flowers and topped by a kind of tongue, descend long, light-colored feathers, similar to pennants. The rest of the body a brilliant pink. A reddish short beak, slanted eyes. When it flutters, breathless, the motion of the six wings gives off an odor of kapok, and flying doesn't appear to weigh it down: its whole body is wings. The rain falls, it falls onto the tops of the buildings, cast down with force by the wind, it crosses through the scaffolding, becomes entwined in the trees, washes the walls that face the Southwest.

In the Triassic period, the great saurians strolled across the face of the earth as if they were eternal. The little mammals, discreet and light-footed, arise. The saurians don't even notice them. They continue at their ease, moving bones that creak like the timbers of a ship, but they are already condemned; the subtle intruders, who cannot face up to them, drill their eggs and suck out the contents. Any weapon is good for survival against the stronger, and for reducing them to nothing. I'm not hunting for love, or jubilation, or other exaltations in the strangers with whom I lie down in strange beds: I am hunting Olavo Hayano, I get him—that's my shell, my cannon—by opening my legs to others. Nor are these others always clumsy in their caresses, and sometimes they show themselves to be skillful between the sheets. My joy, when it comes, is mute, hidden, I grind my teeth and cry out: "Hell!" I cut myself into pieces, like Inês, prodded by me, cutting up her dirty uniform. I let myself be offended and in that way I offend, tear. But the spur starts to grow again, in the thighs, in the face, in the eyes, I don't know where—it grows. I still receive Hayano's cold glans in me and I continue sterile. He makes no comments.

Heavy, low thunderclaps—great iron wheels advance across salon floors, doorless and as broad as the Earth. The Avalovara, frightened, comes down from the clock, flies over Abel's back for a second, and alights on the carpet. Two or three feathers fall off, take flight, return to its body. I make a discovery: it's a composite being, made up of birds as tiny as bees. A bird and a cloud of birds.

Hayano brings a dog to the apartment, a small police dog with stinking breath and perverse eyes. Under the hair of its chest, hidden in the sparkling pelt, is a small cartilage, a hard point, like the head of a pin. Abel's hands stroking my hair, the violets that are born in my hair. *Morde me.* He bites my lips and the pressure of his teeth makes bells in my stomach tinkle. Hayano: "Why the shot?" I turn my head, reticent. The dog sniffs me, follows me, showing its teeth. Affection? Suspicion? The bird takes flight and looks at itself in a mirror. Bells in my stomach. I, happy? Behold me happy. The dog grows as it lies down, or gets up, or eats, or growls. Now, on its chest, piercing the hide, there's a beak. A curved beak, as if a bird of prey, stuck in the dog, were trying to slash it and get out. None of my movements escapes its canine look, as if it were furnished with ready-made teeth. The serpent comes out of its lethargy, coils around my ribs once more, sticks out its forked tongue. It's testing the weather. I wrap Hayano's razor blades in raw meat and throw them into the air, in the direction of the dog. It grows and swallows them greedily: it keeps on looking at me, growing and observing me. Want some more? I throw it the last piece. Wrath, the serpent, moves its tail and head. A blinding explosion, it must be a nearby lightning bolt. The bird, by the open window, flaps its three pairs of wings. Hayano strokes the hairy corpse. From the beak in the dog's belly a thread of blood flows. I hear Hayano's question, his dull and distant voice: "Who killed it?" "I did." "What about the bullet in your breast?" Twice I feel Abel's sex in me, duplicated, a fork. I: two. Double penetration and joy. A slamming of doors, Hayano turns the lights on and off nervously. He flings shouts and complaints at me. I go into the elevator, I go to the roof of the building. Through the mist, a lighted sign, red and white, appears and disappears. The rain falls more heavily and beats against the window beside which I and Abel love each other, dense, torn by the wind, it comes in

through the other windows and wets the floor. Nanny goats and lionesses fly in our bodies, looking behind. From the top of the building I
see the lights of night. The cables of the elevator groan and creak. At
some point a word resounds with insistence, a name, someone calling:
the silence of my body finally ends. Abel's copper-colored hairs brush
my body. His bipartite branch comes together inside me, clefts similar
to the clefts of a pomegranate, the green and red butterflies escape
through the slits, they flutter on my body, flower on Abel's shoulders,
and then rise up, plaited, made of wool and silk, in the designs of the
rug, motionless. This large lighted sign, which appears and dies, with
its stars, its shield, its letters, in what branch of time does it wander
and drift across my path? An explanation is insinuated in an enigmatic
way in that lighting up, that going out. Scattered pieces come together
and I think I can glimpse the reason why I shoot myself in the breast
on my wedding night. Revealed is the structure that up to now has
been incomplete and inaccessible to the thicker part of my understanding. Four-fifty-eight? Light-colored objects and the walls retain
the glow of the lightning. I go back to the apartment—its glass animals,
its bric-a-brac—I turn out all the lights. The Avalovara (its wings wide
open, its little wavy leaps) moves around me and Abel. Hayano is
snoring now. I can distinguish clearly among the murmurs that over-
flow from his struggle with the furious dead the question, as always:
"Why?" The lamp inside the red glass. I put my hand over the glass,
the flame goes out. A shriek seems to come from the street, come up
through the building, and take me: instigating voices are talking in my
body, coming and going. I go back to bed, nothing changes the darkness of the room, as wide as I can open the eight eyelids, an unexpected (or expected?) face rises out of the shadows, endowed with a
dim and foggy light, an untouchable face, as if shaped in phospho-
rus—and I see the answer demanded without cease all these many
years, yes, I see how I leaped on my wedding night, while the searchlights whirled in the room, over an unusual element lost in time, a ship
(ghost?), a ghost absence, I see myself start again, turning the barrel of
the revolver against me, the sequence described on the days when I am
narrating my life, I see what I know and in spite of everything I need to
see with my eyes so that such knowledge will be complete; I see,
Hayano is a yolyp. I raise my hand to the scar. The butterflies proliferate, my cutoff voice is mixed with the two animals that roar in our
conjoined bodies, bark, bellow, bleat, and low, I bend my knees, I
stretch out on the floor, slowly, my face against the floor, the bird cir-

cles us, lightly, it whirls about the room, it rises a little, for the first time I follow Hayano's dog, the hawk beats his wings on his dog's trunk and this leads me, tongue out, through a twisting underground place, the descent is arduous, but we descend, Inácio Gabriel's bird flees through the window, returns (it passes through beams and tiles), I and the dog finally come out of the gallery, I discover a brown valley, recumbent beings people it, lightning bolts tear the dark afternoon and illuminate the bird, I am still trying to go down but the last stage of the descent is steep, I halt, the Avalovara shines in the air as if it were hollow and the lightning were flashing inside of it, I sit down on the top of the cliff, my feet hanging, the pendulum goes back and forth, Abel and his aura, coming from times forgotten by him, reach the inflamed center of my being, let long pauses be attributed, with a period, to these commas, from the side of the valley two strangers pluck tortoises and, dragging themselves along the ground, imitate their march, the Avalovara gains altitude in the agitated air, penetrates a spiral that broadens the course of the thunderclaps, over slopes covered with muddy water, factories, huts knocked down by the rain, children drowned in the torrent, four-fifty-nine (*Morde me!*), lizards and other small slippery reptiles leap out of the valley and stick to the soles of my feet, vast is the circle drawn in the clouds by the Avalovara, and we are the center of its flight, I rub my feet to free myself of the reptiles, when some fall others jump and cling to my skin with force, I have them always on my feet during the time the vision lasts (*Basia me!*), the Avalovara climbs even higher amidst the lightning flashes, and suddenly I perceive that a bird just like it—or the same one?—almost legible and also made up of small birds, is flying in our united bodies, light, among the branches, the butterflies, the crocodile, the rabbit, and the animals with noisy throats. It flies in us and sings. Strange: it sings in duet, with a human voice, and one impregnated with compassion.

T

Cecília Among the Lions   **16**

Naked and only keeping her bracelet with gold stars and coins on her arm, Cecília comes over to the bed. She kneels, the couched penis resting between her thighs and her large round breasts as if suspended. In the light that passes through it, on the curtain the Moon and the lion, new figures are revealed from her changing and peopled being. Could this be memory—hers and mine joined? No. It probably is, at most, an imperfect and vivid metaphor from Memory.

If the inhabitants of that body had the character of images, of representations, they would be limited to repeating words and actions from another time, given over to another reality, exterior to them and already gone beyond. The autonomy of such surprising creatures, on the other hand, is broad. They resemble the beings of memory in not being always visible in Cecília's body, present always, like individuals shut up in a salon. They rise up, succeed each other, are extinguished, harass; and the space they occupy, if occupied, is immaterial, not physical space.

To suppose that Cecília, in spirit and in flesh, is changed when other bodies abandon the soft curvature of her shoulders, her breasts, or her hips—and that they act outside those limits—would be erroneous. Such bodies, as opposed to the abstract personages of memories, coincide with men born of women in two basic points: they act as a function of their own impulses and resolutions; they occupy, in varying degrees (it being understood that their existence is true and in no way imaginary), a physical space, not an immaterial one. When, finally, they leave or invade the sensible limits of Cecília's body, they don't really diminish it or increase it.

Cecília, on the lace coverlet, knees half apart, hands above her head holding on to the brass bars, waits. The pale and tense face, closed eyes, unrhythmical breathing. Men and women, idle or engaged in rustic tasks, including the farm laborers who invade the villa with her (they plant and weed in Cecília's flesh, without the sound of those chores reaching me), move in her body.

They are, her body and those bodies, on top of the lace coverlet and the red spread, at the same time bodies and surrounding space, are bodies and also atmosphere—a pleasant, shady atmosphere filled with fruity odors. I kiss her concave parts: between breasts, throat, navel, waist, armpit. With my tongue (children play in her thighs, farther and farther apart), I blow on her erect and even then not-virile penis, embedded in the femininity that envelops it. Are two simultaneous voices calling me in her mouth? Two voices, one grave and the other sharp, moan: "Come!" With extreme care I pierce her, she trembles from head to foot, I tremble and for three times I feel Cecília's impatient nails upon my back and I am admitted to the world of her body—

where three times with varying degrees of intensity I find her. What does a man know of the fall at the instant he loses his balance and tumbles? He suffers the accident and his experience is a dizzying kind of knowledge. Such are my passages through Cecília's core. I perforate the world from which so many living things erupt and which doesn't open up at all, not at all, at the introduction of my body. Now I break it, I cross it, and so limited are these admissions, so swift in their neatness, that entry and expulsion seem simultaneous.

I see myself, first, during the brief moment in which Cecília, sinking her teeth into my shoulder, orders in a hoarse voice: "More!" I see myself facing her, both standing and naked. She, holding an orchid against her flat breast, she shows her silky and desirable member; I feel, I, with the weight of her breasts, the weight of being female, and I wait for Cecília to penetrate me. My father, merry, protects us with a scarlet canopy and carries a heron on his shoulder. I see him with the canopy and the bird, I see him through my eyes and I also see with his. Little animals, light as words, fly around me and Cecília or walk through our bodies: spiders, crickets, ants, Mayflies, wasps, fireflies, Spanish flies, scorpions, locusts, all with gender changes. The crickets chirp, nocturnal; the locusts buzz. Cecília grinds her teeth and throws her head back.

This movement corresponds to the second raid into her substance. She, thin, light dress, runs in front of me, happy, her left hand held out toward me. We are accompanied by (and we are penetrated by their presence) men and women of the people: stevedores, cashiers, shoeshine boys, fishermen, sluts, washerwomen, circus performers, maids, seamstresses, wall painters, washerwomen, street peddlers, nurses, vendors of hairpins, of birds, of pins, kindergarten teachers, stonemasons, sextons. Gliding over us as if winged are beasts of land and water: frogs, otters, cowfish, rheas, conch shells, turtles, shrimp, rays, sea snails, lizards, cougars, also with a switch in their gender. Deep under our feet, the sound of many voices, angry or festive. Hearing them, I understand: the men and women who cross us are alive, but mute—their clamor and laughter buried.

Are arches and columns incorporated, in my last vision, into the organic world? Do I really see them while a child's voice behind us imperiously describes the wedding? The figure of the Bishop, imposing, raising his hands as if he were declaring us joined (woman's face), suggesting a solemn and broad space. Let there be those groups of children given over to their childish games and those vases with flowers. The Bishop's open arms emphasize the sumptuous vestments. Cecília and I, kneeling, are one. Hers, in the body we form, the left leg and arm; mine the right arm, the right leg; our heads two; one breast, the left, exists on our chest. The right hand holds the left hand. Our heads turn, forehead to forehead. Our body, broken honeycombs, exhales the carnal pleasure. Splendor? The flesh: a throbbing flame. We shout and we fall. A gulp, two throats, a single shout. I hear the noise of the sea and I see the bars of the bed, the fronds of the coconut palm, the lion rampant. Bloody and long clouds, with reflections of gold, illuminate Cecília's glowing body; arms held high, the penis still pulsating. Lying on the mat, the ram ruminates on cinnamon leaves. Cecília turns and embraces me again. The coins and stars on her wrist tinkle.

A brief season of love without questions and indifferent to all kinds of plans. We go through the rooms and parlors of the villa, always naked or decked out in old collars and hats that we find in the bureaus. Cecília, Leonor's mandolin on her breast, under the rays that cross the colored banners on the window, her head and body stained red, blue, green, plucks single notes from the instrument. Does the opposite of the world exist within the world or not? The universe: is it, too, an androgyne? Questions soon forgotten.

The months of this intoxicating summer, with its torrid days and sudden sunsets, echo like the keys of an organ pressed successively and with a blending of the sounds. In Cecília's flesh—comparable to memory and imagination, space opened up to my impassioned testimony, where the operation of those twin faculties could be sensed—a new phenomenon occurs. Rising up in her multipliable flesh, where at the time we make love for the first time, and only then, I invade the nucleus (invasions or admissions that last the time of a rifle shot), rising up and disappearing with the same rapidity in the midst of the other men and women are beings of another kind, full of strength and as if illuminated from within. I can't see them well, they vanish so quickly. Undressed, they wear only their rings with precious stones and their hats in the form of horns, but one feels that they're armed and their look has the weight of steel. They bear black or white numerals on their foreheads. With weeks of interval, in the heart of the night, the impulse of search awakens in me. Search? But where? What? I pronounce Cecília's name as if conjuring and I fall back to sleep. The grace of seeing her and my baseless desire absorb and extinguish everything. Things buzz—doors, furniture, tiled floor, air—pounded by her presence. When, at the end of the afternoon, she kisses me on the porch and leaves (and how many times, on turning at the gate, does she still run, come up the steps, kiss me?), the walls of the house creak. The vacuum and the silence reach every bone. I light two skyrockets, which explode and throw into the almost nocturnal sky the glow of strontium and magnesium. My mother translates, on the beach: "You can come back." But what I write or pronounce, with those explosions and luminous scratches, given off so high up, is the name of Cecília. I lie down on the disordered bed, impregnated with all of her presence and her loving words. The Fat Woman: "Hey, I got so much sun and wind I'm going loony. You'll wear yourselves out. Is she really that good in bed, Abel? You can tell me. And my thinking she was half man!" It's more and more necessary to hear Cecília's clothes falling onto the mat in the room, while the wind moves the branches of the flamboyant; and to repeat, always under new forms, guarded by the lion rampant, our triple pleasure. One afternoon she suggests to me, my face on her shoulder and one leg on top of mine: "Why don't we kill ourselves, Abel?" The sound of the sea is dissipated in the room. "It would be perfect, don't you think? Ascension and explosion. A luminous end." Observing me from the door, under the droopy hat, with his burning look, is the restless man, the one who inoculates others with his fever. I get up and look for the revolver on top of the closet. The shoebox is empty: not a trace of the weapon or the bullets. In Cecília's body, stretched out beside me, a couple (I don't see them) are chatting idly about the table on which I presume they are. Lying down too and holding hands? Torrid summer hour. Maybe they're naked like Cecília and me, they're all alone, he's explaining to the woman how much he loves the table that serves them as a bed. He's loved it since childhood for being the way it is, long, heavy, solid, beveled at the corners, with its legs turned on a lathe. Two things, mainly, have always attracted him to that piece of furniture: the length, the solidity, and the color. The woman corrects him, laughing: weren't there three items? There were three, yes. The color more than anything. Look at that golden color, honey and red wine. A cool place, even on days like this. Time and again he's lain on it, face down, feeling the coolness of the wood and breathing in the never-extinct perfume of the varnish. The perfume that no word can transmit. Don't you think so? The woman also finds the table's perfume pleasing. So delicate! Delicate and constant—the man becomes precise. Delicate like the smell of rice, and faithful, lasting, indifferent to seasons and the time of day, a perfume he knows he'll find waiting for him again no matter where he might have been. The woman confesses that she doesn't have too high a regard for furniture made of soft wood. Still, she does appreciate fragile doors. In the summer, at noontime, she was in the habit of lying down someplace in the house on the warm brick floor. Doors, moved by the breeze, would softly beat on their jambs. No one in the lassitude of that time of day had the energy to get up and close the doors or open them once and for all. They would pound: a brief and fragile scale verging toward silence. Those sounds, like the cicadas, were the voices of summer. The man: "Did the hinges creak?" Yes, some of them, a little. The Fat Woman warns me: "Be careful, man. How far is this going to go? It's been going on a long time!" I reply that I don't know and, really, I don't want to know. But do I or don't I know? This blindness that we accept and intensify, Cecília and I, is it really a question of someone who doesn't know anything? Is this great ardor with which we consecrate ourselves one to the other a question of someone who doesn't know anything, receiving and giving all the goods our prodigal lovers' indigence has at its disposal, locked up in the light and heat of the fugitive summer as on some precarious island that will soon be covered by the sea?

Sitting naked on my knees, in the rocking chair, with a large white plumed hat on her head, Cecília tells me the fable conceived by one of the inmates in hunger and madness: "There is, somewhere in the world, an egg whose dimensions are impossible to calculate and where God keeps a grain of light. This is in case all the fires of the universe go out. Then, with a shout, God will break the egg and out of it will fly a bird made of sparks, who will grow swiftly with the speed of light. But it could happen that the world would still fall into darkness. Foreseeing this, the bird bears an egg, where God hides light." I take her in my arms and carry her through the rooms, stating that she is that bird. She pulls in her feet, afraid of bumping them on the furniture and doorways. The white plumed hat falls to the ground. Then I see the children without names and with an unbearable look, their numbers on their foreheads.

The last Monday in March, dusk, blood-red clouds in the inland sky. Cecília and I sitting on the rocks on Milagres Beach. Ebb tide. The flesh of her waist presses against the band of her green skirt and her nipples stand out under the black blouse. Rustics, spread out through her breasts and stomach, hats in hand, in shirt sleeves, are pulling a cart. In the reddish coffin goes the body of a woman pepper-picker. The widower, fingering a red rosary, follows the cortege. In the distance a dog chases the waves when they flee and flees when the waves return. The sea, for him, a toy or a child. Without speaking, I hold out my hand; Cecília takes it, serious.

"My wife wrote me. She promises to do everything so I'll get what I deserve."

"Does she say what you deserve?"

The reflection of the sunset, purple and ruddy, lights the edges of other clouds, very high and dark: chestnut-colored. Rain clouds? They continue on rapidly in the direction opposite to the sunset clouds, almost motionless. In the distance the broad and imprecise profile of Recife.

"No, she doesn't say."

Cecília's light-colored sandals, with slight marks of use on the insoles. Our fingers intertwine. The heat of her flesh and the blood pounding in her delicate pulse, making the little silver rings and little gold fish vibrate.

"Abel, I'm pregnant."

She looks at me, fixedly, a bit pale, her knees bony and harmonious at the same time—and her bust turned toward me, thrown at me, surrounded by the space of the afternoon, as the day dies, the farm workers accompany the death cart and the agile dog plays with the waves, farther away each time.

"I have a child of yours inside me."

Two strangers, jackets on their arms, come slowly toward us. The purple and red of the horizon grows stronger. Fluctuating on the waters, translucid, is the corner of Recife. An active smell of oil mixes in with that of the sea, with its aroma of iodine or green chestnuts, but the perfume that dominates all the others is Cecília's. Cologne, soap, and powder mingled with the fragrance exhaled by her womb and thighs: of a sex bathed in many waters and agitated, humid, awake. Impregnated, of course, by that multiple odor, the green skirt. The two strangers pass by us, go on. I lean over and rest my face on Cecília's still soft stomach. All the smells invade me, intense.

Threats from the brothers. Shouting over the telephone, they demand that I induce or oblige Cecília to tear out the bastard as soon as possible "and assume everything." They mean: pay everything. I hang up every time without answering. But my blood clouds up, darker and darker, with the frequent instillation of those voices. A stirring up identical to the one that occurs in the arguments and fights in which I am involved during the murky months of my marriage.

Cecília disappears: a week without seeing her. Is she avoiding me? Why? Is she afraid to hear from me what her brothers demand and determine that I say? Is she making decisions without discussing them with me? I order Callus Face to find her, no matter what it takes. He comes back without any word about the message, with confused allegations about the belt of the Zodiac, the direct movement of Uranus, and the strength of his Legislator, who is against his function as messenger. The lines, almost always busy, make my attempts to get a connection to Rosa e Silva difficult, the same as to Social Services. When I get to speak, others answer. I leave messages or hang up the phone with a silent curse.

Sitting at the unvarnished desk with the drawer smelling of gunpowder, I examine the almost completed short story. Within the wood and walls dry wings crackle. Tiny insects in contortions. It's nine o'clock in the morning. The door opens and Cecília's two brothers invade the room. The taller one, grabbing me by the arm, talks with his mouth next to my face; the other, farther away, aims the barrel of the automatic at me. They smell of leather and ground garlic.

"We're giving you twenty-four hours to make Cecília decide." (The disaster, existing in the vastness of time, is nothing happening. An empty form, it sucks us in. Cecília and I: the pith of that empty shell and irradiating force.) "You don't want somebody just to solve this problem with a kick in the belly, do you? We give you twenty-four hours."

Cecília's face, made brutish, swims on the surface of theirs. They leave me, with their garlic-and-tannery smell, both throwing me an inclement look in which I think I glimpse—can I be mistaken?—a touch of pity. I put on my wristwatch. As I put away the manuscript, I hear a sound in the air, as if a bird made all of teeth were spreading its wings—and I remember the automatic pointed at me. Who could have stolen the villa's revolver? The sound of wings in the room. A thousand cockroaches imprisoned under the boards are making vain efforts to fly and are gnawing at each other.

A

Roos and the Cities **21**

A letter from Roos, faithful to that pendular movement so like that of two trapeze artists who never oscillate symmetrically, is waiting for me on my return from London. She's gone to Le Havre for her company and will be back this week, on the twenty-first or twenty-second. She asks me, if I don't have anything on, to reserve Sunday afternoon. It's been more than six years, April 1951, since she first came to Paris and her mother took her to a park. There were so many flowers! She's never forgotten it: "It's not Buttes-Chaumont. Maybe Parc Monceau, yes, maybe. Would you like to see it with me?"

We pass by the haughty fence, gilded on top, through which we can see the regulars, the yellow chairs, doves, the round lights on green posts. The clock, in the elegant pavilion at the entrance, shows five minutes to four. The doubtful sky, however, predicts rain and the Sun may not return. I describe, unable to express what I want to say, the brief scene near the Azores on board a ship of the Chargeurs Réunis. I'm on the quarterdeck and I turn my face: a gull follows on the larboard side, almost within hand's reach. It moves its head a little and doesn't even seem to be flying. For a few minutes, it accompanies the freighter at the same speed, as if suspended, Roos, in the cold February air—and it makes me joyous to see its right eye turned toward me, sharp, a beak. Then there was a movement of wings. It dipped and disappeared.

Roos, desolate and not very attentive to my spotty tale, looks at the sad-looking columns, a few black swans, the trellis with climbing vines. "No, this isn't the park. We've lost our outing." "We can make up for it. It's too late today. But why don't we go to Chartres this week? By now I should really be on the other side of the World. I'm still waiting, did you know? Something has still got to happen between you and me. An ending. A beginning." "I'd like to go too." "So? Friday? Saturday? We can spend the night there. While it's still dark, we'll go to the cathedral and watch the stained-glass windows rise up with the sun. Bring your camera. I'll bring some film. We can have a picnic. On the banks of the Eure. We'll come back at nightfall. A celebration. Our goodbye. In Chartres . . . I'll see your body." She takes a few steps, slowly. The purples, yellows, and rusts of the green rows of trees, perhaps her memory has multiplied them over the six years since 1951. "Our bodies . . . should they be seen?" "You know they should. It's as if they've been blind up till now."

She stops and looks at me straight on, at these words of mine. Birds sing discreetly hidden in the branches. The wind rustles her hair slightly.

"When shall we go, Roos? Saturday?"

"Yes. Saturday."

The hours that follow: a golden waiting. The rub of drawers being opened or closed is refracted in the perfume of the woods; my shoes in the dawn, the leather of my old shoes smells of milk and sedge; unfolding, detaching themselves from the whiteness of the sheets of paper are linen sheets, summer clouds; I see our meeting not located in time, but at some pleasant place, and I get the impression of going through the hours toward where, by the river or on the plain, Roos awaits me in a certain way.

On Friday she calls me on the phone. Did I get the film? Bring it. She'll bring the camera. At five? Ten minutes before (I check my watch by the small round clock on the Palace in the Luxembourg), I'm waiting for her, between the white statues of Bathilde and Mathilde, queens of France. I hear the fountain in the center of the garden and the sound of the vehicles on the streets that surround it. Roos, in a red dress, comes to meet me. Thick drops of rain, silvered by the sun, fall around her with a soft sound.

"I've come to say goodbye. I'm leaving tomorrow."

I ask where. I don't hear the answer. What difference does it make, if, as she says, she's going away and not coming back? She can't even postpone it for two days. Problems have come up, she's going to take charge of the branch office.

"So, Roos, all of a sudden . . . Everything's over."

In order to comfort me, she remembers her ill companion once more: he thinks that ends are a tricky notion. Couldn't we, Roos, leave tonight? No. She still has to go back to the office and get a whole set of instructions. Credentials, documents. What time is she leaving? In the morning. I put the film in the camera and I take her picture in silence. In the background, the tree trunks, the pensive statues on their pedestals, Berthe or Bertrade, Sainte-Bathilde, Sainte-Geneviève, other distant statues, amphorae, the people in the park, doves flying, space.

"I can't believe it, Roos."

In the Colosseum, in Roos, in the center of the Colosseum, on the point of jumping, falling into the lower part of the structure, in the Colosseum, as in the center of a fantastic bone heap, a great jaw, the symmetrical arcades and the buttresses, many of which are in ruins, between one arcade and another, and the arches behind the arcades and the windows and doors above the arches, the vaulted corridors, the incomprehensible empty spaces. Could there be a connection between all those passages? The ghosts of the lions transformed into insatiable rodents with humps, roaring in Roos, from the pits up to the higher parts and from the seats to the pits, gnawing the stones with old worn teeth.

"In the waters around Halicarnassus there is a cemetery of ships. Abel: imagine that all that's happened is there."

The dialogue is vague and mindless, I don't even know why we talk again, I and Roos, in truth, are talking to ourselves, or this isn't talking, we're talking to no one, to a corpse, from inside our deaths, because we'll never see each other again and the sum of her existence no longer has substance, I know.

"Yes, Roos, I can imagine. A whole past, waiting."

I see her in the finder, tiny, inverted, diffuse, with her red dress, smiling, looking at me, a flower in her hand (was I the one who brought the flower?), in profile, the camera explodes between my fingers, the click of the shutter, the turning of the film, Roos, fleeting and mobile, caught in motionless snaps, in which tomorrow, afterward, afterward, I will try to regain—what? Will she rise up in some one of the photographs just as I see her from the castle where Da Vinci's ashes rest? Roos, a vision, something impossible, the fleeting one, close by, darkening, clear, the almost one, the one I glimpse, the one who passes through, lightning, glow, the one barely visited, the intangible, the inconclusive coming, the perpetual going.

With the film still in my pocket, I go to the Weigels' in search of refuge and also to make my farewells. On the very next day, as soon as Roos has gone, I'll be leaving. The old man, sustained by three fragile women, is struggling in the bed. Tense and curved, an arch. All of him—tongue, head, eyes—is turned to his right. From his mouth a liquid streaked with blood hangs. I help the women in the last phase of the attack and I scarcely know how long it lasts. One minute, two. With the spasm over, the sick man closes his eyes, his body softens, he falls apart, pale, sweating. Suzanne asks me if I'm going away. "Tomorrow. I'm sorry I came by at a time like this. When he wakes up, tell him that Lev Nikolayevich was here." "What about . . . her?" "She's leaving tomorrow too." I embrace her, I kiss Julie on the forehead. I clutch Mme. Weigel's hands: once, well cared .for, they plucked the mandolin. The girls see me to the door. Leaning on the cold railing, I go down the stairs. A heavy sob rolls down the dark steps. A pebble. The door is closed violently.

I quickly pack my bags. Tourist folders on the dresser, in the drawers, on top of the table. Some cities seen, others that will never be. What's the name of the city that Roos is heading for? Can't it be this one, the one I have to find? I'll never see the City, and Roos I'll never see again. Black birds and dead dogs fight on the bed.

I go out into the night, I walk through the city and I see it emptying out. Lying down, I, with a whore; I embrace her as if I were embracing a being made of wire and hair of the dead. I ejaculate my hate, my testicles sob, I weep through my penis, I hear it moan. I still haven't dressed and already the woman of whom I only saw the purse or shoes is leaving. She goes downstairs. I remain in the room, a room with naked walls, with nothing that can be stolen. White ants cover my hands, my sex, my face. I wash at the faucet, they rise up again. I wash again, trembling, I dry myself quickly, I fling myself down the stairs.

A beggar follows me silently. Now and again, like a bear trainer, I give him a coin. Sugar for the trained ponies. Rats as big as pigs cross the alleys and run along the bridges. Roos. R - O - O - S. Ravenna, Oviedo, Orléans, Salzburg. Deserted avenues, full of parked cars. The windows closed. A desert almost the equal of Roos's cities. Rhine, Riga, Rome, Rhodes, Rotterdam, Rhône, Rouen, let them go to rape and ruin. The only human being: the one who follows me, slinking, somber. Sagres, Salonika, Seine, Salamanca, Samothrace, Sodom, Saragossa, Sèvres, Sidon, and Syracuse summed up. An angry wind blows down those names, mingles them, splits them up, throws them against other names and other winds. Two cats cross paths noisily among the yellow street lights on Nôtre-Dame Bridge. The mendicant is masturbating. Seine, Florence, Nuremberg, Bern, Murcia, Vienna, Cartagena, Linz. The sky grows pale, my follower disappears. Salerno, Budapest, Sparta, Genoa, Sorrento, Reims. Let walls open up, whole arsenals fly through the air, fires spread, the waters rot in reservoirs, gutters crumble, tile roofs fly off, telephone wires flail the air. Sitting on the curb, across from the Alliance building, next to the kiosk with theater posters and Dubonnet ads, I await the appearance of Roos. Between me and the iron gate, beside the trees that are still wrapped in mist and that separate the direction pointers, small carts with garbage. Roos, the Venetian scarf around her neck, opens the main door. She is preceded by pairs of birds, like flamingos, restless. Naples Ancona Coblenz Nantes Burgos. We go along beside the Luxembourg in the direction of the Gare d'Austerlitz, we cross the Seine (a dog, in the Tuileries, bites its black tail with phosphorescent teeth) in the direction of Saint-Lazare. Bilbao Pamplona Liverpool Lyons Dublin Antwerp Groningen Monte Carlo brindisi ulm lübeck. The bars closed—Boulevard Saint-Michel—the cafés closed—Boulevard Malesherbes—Jardin des Plantes—shops closed, post offices—constance brunswick—but the city awake—pavianancymilan—it moves a little in the morning mist. At such an early morning hour, what can the Bois de Vincennes look like? Cre monacor int hali cante granadapalosopor tobor deaux, a suburban train on the elevated tracks to the left of the Gare d'Austerlitz, the yellow numbers and the red hands of the clock at the entrance on Saint-Lazare (why so many clocks in the station?), pushcarts with mail sacks, messna brussls cogne oxd plym gena ogunc ul onia omnia let them fly away and fall to dust.

We go down, down, we go along under the high ceiling of the Gare d'Austerlitz, we go through, heading for the mortifying, narrow platforms, the long vestibule of Saint-Lazare, I embrace her for a long time, I embrace her, for a long time, she tries to smile, her eyes are damp, her eyes are damp, but the air is cold, she tries to smile, but the air is cold, in the waters, in the waters around, around Halicarnassus, there is a, Halicarnassus, a cemetery of, a cemetery, ships, of ships, on the platform the announcement of departure sounds, on the platform, of departure, the announcement, sounds, I help her on, there is a smell of violets in the air, the train starts to leave, I help her on, smell of violets, the train starts to leave, she waves to me. She waves to me, I take a few more steps, I take a few steps more, and I see myself without anything, once more without anything, without anything, once more, and blind, and blind, facing my dimming solitude, facing my dimming solitude.

R

Ơ and Abel: Meetings, Routes, and Revelations 16

We fall silent. Ơ, her body stretched out beside mine, has one arm over my shoulder. I hear clearly, pronounced by unequal voices, four or five disconnected words: "crosier," "sacellum," "matins," "faburden." As if someone were speaking from inside the mattresses or from outside, close by the window. I sharpen my ear. The magnificent black birds have quieted down.

The river journey passes on and it is forever mobile in its fixedness. It must be tempting and I make the attempt. There is a herd and the enigmatic ground shows the passage of a cow, whether black or white I don't know. I look and search for expression.

The glass jewels on Ơ's sandals take on a black tone, and her skin—so imponderable and somewhat unreal—absorbs the receding light. A sudden wind crosses the peaceful streets, twirls her hair, her dress flutters, the flowers in the fabric, she laughs and gives me her arm (this weight, this indefinable lightness!), her face next to mine, thin wrinkles woven in the eyelids. Closets, drawers, trunks, cellars, the bottom of barrels, chapels are shadowy. The November cicadas are silent, fooled by the night that filters in through the branches of the trees; moths begin to stir in their daytime hiding places and indecisively venture out into the murky half-day. *Cancellations and suspensions of political rights: new list expected by today.* The band of the total eclipse, however, is a few miles away from Rio Grande. Led by inaccurate reports, we take extensive and expensive trips in order to observe, in its fullness, a phenomenon that is foreseen as incomplete in the city. Will this deception, however, read in a different way, still be a deception?

"Extirpation, Abel, will be death, yes, it will be death, we know. Pulling out the heart and staying alive? Even so, if you do reach the extreme point (you have to free yourself of the dead animal in your body), do you hesitate? Rarely."

Water and land in an oval that inclines from Northwest to Southeast feel the action of the eclipse. The egg of that rare and brief night, whose upper edge, born in the Pacific, joins California to Georgia in an arc, cuts the Atlantic and, descending, reaches the extreme southern part of Africa, takes in the Caribbean and Mexico, the whole of the South American continent, an extensive deserted area of Antarctica, growing dark as the center is approached: a tangent over the thirty-second parallel, at the level of the almost always flat grazing lands along the border.

The rockets on the platforms, three already empty, stand out along Casino Beach, potent and precise, aimed at the stars with their water-bird beaks. They are surrounded, an agitated, compact arc with a radius of almost a mile, by a crowd that grows slowly silent, kept at a distance by well-armed troops from the 9th Infantry Regiment and the 3rd Guards Battalion. All entry is blocked by soldiers, so that the vehicles—strung out along the sidewalks, in the bushes, off the roads, or on the edge of embankments—form a barricade of cars behind the crowd, solid and without any order, their windshields reflecting the truncated sun.

"What is frightening about the phosphorescent face of the Yolyp is that it is always invisible. Also the way it reveals itself; in the dark. It hides like a goblin inside the everyday face. Like a goblin? No, like a stranger. Some are handsome—they look like angel faces—and, even so, they're frightening. What happens, then, when—in addition to its being mute and strange—the face is deformed? That's the way it is with Olavo Hayano. In him, the hidden face, out of my reach, is that of a monster."

Invisible bodies, with pale vestiges of conversations, of other sounds, metallic or glassy, drift in lightly through the plain tile roof or through the half-open door of the pavilion where Natividade's large body lies, larger after death, two big candles on either side of her head and two beside her feet, three of which are out so as to avoid waste, covered by a cheap sheet, with her heels extending beyond the short bier, meant for old people, beings who shrink—the bodies and sounds pulsate among the cobweb-filled beams, slide along over the backless benches, agitate the single flame and the edge of the frayed sheet. They're old Sundays that visit the black woman, still smelling of olives, bay leaves, onions, cheese, wine.

In the shadows of the garden, three shapes advance and an impersonal nun's voice alludes to the relations between the old people and death: "They get violent when they find out that one of the inmates has given up his or her soul to God. Only after it's grown dark do we bring out the body for the wake."

Her white habit and the face of the man (he walks bent over, his head bowed)—touched slightly by the light that marks the corners of the windows, closed today with excessive precaution—flutter among the hidden sunflowers. The steps of the woman who follows alongside the nun falter at times or become lighter, as if she were softening the weight of the body, intent on the creaking of joints, coughing, the dragging of bedpans, and the broken phrases that fill the dormitories. The nun has gone ahead, and she opens the door and the couple appear in the candlelight: he corpulent and indecisive, she with her face half hidden in her loose hair, a thin brown raincoat over her shoulders. The sister, hurriedly and looking away, lights the other candles—the four, now, mark out a rectangle—and kneels on the floor. The man, holding back his tears, uncovers the black woman's face. The woman, on the other side of the dead woman, her narrow forehead leaning forward and her whole face illuminated by the four flames, stares at the man through half-closed eyes, and inside of those eyes two other eyes stare at him, dark, without contemplation, open and dark, with specks of gold. She says to herself: "The grief he feels doesn't redeem him in any way." She opens the always unclosed mouth even more, as if the air were heavy.

"Before the age of twelve only two things distinguish the Yolyp from other children: in all of his dreams, in all, images of dead people with attacks of rage rise up; and around it or inside it (impossible to know) there is an emptiness. The substance of things passes through the Yolyp and passes on to Nothingness. But not all perceive that emptiness or suction. At first, the Yolyp doesn't recognize the characters that rise up in his dreams: until the age of twelve, normally, we see few dead people. Some time passes before the parents identify those furious shades that slam doors and attack each other with shouts, whips, and sharp objects, and learn in this way of the nature of the being that has been engendered by them."

"Under this oppression, the simplest acts—buying a postage stamp or being happy—are touched and become the nuclei of questions. Every alternative becomes a dilemma and no choice can escape that. Furthermore: even though the oppression is a brutal phenomenon, the weight and meaning of the acts, their force, grow in proportion as they come to dominate the spirit. It follows that creative acts are particularly exposed to such an emergency."

Side by side, lying on the bed under the sheet, we resemble those funereal monuments of happy couples, or of those who try to make of their own marriage, perhaps deplorable under the conjugal canopy, an edifying example, a model for newlyweds and a canon for the family. The recumbent statues of husband and wife, always carved in clothing of great ceremony, eyes closed and hands on chests, lying side by side with modesty, suggest a perfect and indestructible union, but they don't touch each other: they are, after all, parallel. We, with eyes open and turned toward the still invisible ceiling, are naked and holding hands. Of the sculptures, we have only the immobility and the muteness. Simulating eternity, we avoid moving, the hard sobbing having ceased (we weep, then, for ourselves and for some dead), and we no longer wish to talk, fearful that new words, as in a text that has reached a certain degree of precision, would be superfluous or harmful. On the other hand, we refuse to sleep, tolerating a caustic presence: the discovery of this solemn love that extends its urticant leaves out in us. The union in the flesh, we know, is now extemporaneous between us. In our bodies, desired and still strange, where bitter memories echo— sterility, death, and other damage—we discover a certain sacred character, as if we are cleansing ourselves in abstinence, holding hands, mute and surrounded by darkness, for the mutual and inevitable knowing. A sabiá thrush sings, in the distance or caged. In the foliage of his multiple body? In his body or in the world, other birds and cocks hear him and respond.

Her profile is born from the shadow, and the glimmer of dawn delineates the wrinkles of the sheet.

T

Cecília Among the Lions   **17**

"You've got a mad-dog look. Did you go and do it? Did you get the girl pregnant?"

My mother speaks in a low voice and that precaution transforms her. She tosses her purse onto the table, sits down in the only chair, pulls her dress up to her knees. I sit on the bed.

"Who told you that story?"

"Do you really want to know? Your wife. She was at the villa just this morning. Full of sweet talk. I denied it, you know. But I want you to tell me if it's true."

"Was that any reason to leave Olinda and come here to the boardinghouse? What's so urgent?"

"It's urgent, all right." (Her mouth even smaller and her thin eyebrows more arched.) "You ought to know that she didn't let go of her purse for a minute. The purse looked heavy."

The catamonk stares at me with its yellow eyes. It slips through her legs, sits on the floor, and kneads its claws on the sheet, its muscles tense.

"Is it true, Abel? Then be a man and settle the thing. You two move into the villa right now. I'm sick of talking to the walls."

"Later, maybe. Not now. You just missed running into the brothers here. One of them is armed."

She puts her hand into the neck of her dress and shows the scar on her shoulder.

"You see that, don't you? It's a souvenir from my *student* days. You know what school I studied in. I know the world and the world's boarders, man. Two guys like that, who only go around when they're yoked together, do you think they'd have the guts to shoot anybody? They won't shoot anything. I'm more afraid of your wife. I want to know, are you coming or not?"

Nighttime corridors in the Pedro II Hospital. Leaning on a cane, a nun prays aloud by the doors of the rooms. This is the place where Cecília, eager and innocent, lives part of her days, arousing the virtue of making demands in those who accept not having rights in the world as a norm. Somebody on the ground floor is repairing a metal object, and all I can perceive is sound, from the flour sacks covering the screens of the infirmary to the windows that end in a curve, opening up to the April morning. Cecília comes in (the nun's voice invades the infirmary for an instant), enters and embraces me silently. Green lions move slowly on the polished granite.

"Cecília, what about the child?"

"Growing."

A woman with gray hair, lying down, watches us. Cecília's face and hair at the age of fifty. Do I love her? Yes. My love for Cecília goes beyond her carnal glow. It includes, enduring—and transformed—her decadence, reaching the limits of the time she doesn't know.

"A revolver's missing from the villa. Was it you?"

"We're together, Abel. For better or for worse. I wouldn't do that."

I breathe in the air through my mouth—the air smells of lions—and I look at her straight in the face. Her eyes of fire scratch me.

"Cecília, I came to get you."

The walls of the villa tremble with a joy different from that which the Treasurer, still confident, animates and presides over. The pastoras, shaking their tambourines decorated with colored ribbons, sing in the living room. Their feet and the great red-and-blue bow in Diana's hair mark the rhythm of the song. Modesto Canabarro, his white beard, waddles in front of the orchestra that comes along the porch. The Fat Woman goes over to Cecília, kisses her on the cheek, weeping with joy, and she makes a great point of taking her bag. The catamonk runs through her breasts, leaps onto my shoulder, passes on to Cecília's shoulders, accompanies us, climbs up the Fat Woman's haunches again. The poor and grimy men of the LET SPEAK orchestra, barefoot, enter with us. The smell of sweat mixes with the perfume of the ripe oranges and the lilies. Deafening, in the parlors and rooms of the house, the instruments and the fourteen sharp voices of the girls echo. The ram bursts forth from among their long dresses. The catamonk leaps from the Fat Woman's hair and runs to Modesto Francisco das Chagas Canabarro. Behold us: the Old Man with his knees bent, the tail of his frock coat to one side, and the catamonk inside his top hat, the musicians holding the trombone, the bass drum, the clarinet, the cornet, the bombardon, the dancers ecstatic, hands on the point of hitting the tambourines, the Fat Woman lugging Cecília's minimal baggage, Cecília among the musicians, her back to me, but with her head turned toward me, laughing over her shoulder, and I, half bent over, like someone who was going to pick up the ram in his arms.

I'm dragged out of bed before dawn with the news: my wife and the shot in the ear. Dead? Yes. The light of morning filters in through the drapes; hunters and the hunt are outlined on the curtains. To reveal and to revolve, always, what a man has of rottenness: a disquieting aptitude. Whom did the shot really hit? Basically, Abel, you want me to die. All right, so be it. A shot in the ear. The Fat Woman's voice explodes: "She killed herself because she wanted to." Of course. Dead, however, she manages to provoke this dirty happiness in me. It injects forever a predatory element, pus, into the blood of my days with Cecília. Cecília rises up, bends over, and leans her head on my knees.

I'm sitting down. Where? The brothers will certainly rest easy now. The Fat Woman's voice and her agitated steps. I wanted that death. Yes, that's it. No matter what, everything has become clear. I'll marry Cecília. But I'm aware, while I decide this way, of everything precarious and doubtful in this solution, so absurdly desired and so suddenly possible. Possible. It isn't what I wanted anymore, however. It assumes the form of a battle now, wrathful and useless, against an intangible being located beyond the circle of the living and therefore immune.

Hammocks hung near the cistern, in the shade of the mango trees. My father, still silent, remains by our side. He moves lightly and steps cautiously, blind-eyed. He is bound by the conviction that he has no right to anything and that the fraud of existence is legitimate. In the tops of the mango trees, touched by the shore winds, the new foliage surges, wine-colored. I read the finished story to Cecília, a representation perhaps of the world I know and where old voices—even in me— seek to impose truths whose substance has dribbled away forever. My mother sweeps the ground around the hammocks. Voices of geese and roosters rise up in other restful country homes. We fall asleep listening to that and to the sound of the sea—strong or distant, according to the tides. Walks at night, the Easter Moon and the May Moon shine and die over the sloping streets of Olinda, with boys and girls sitting on the sidewalks, Alto da Sé, the view of Recife lighted up, Cecília squeezes my hand and laughs. (The lions climb up onto the roofs, twitching their tails.) Vases with flowers, arranged by the Fat Woman, appear in the bedroom. Beings from Cecília's body slip into mine when we embrace. People she might have known, memories, of which she might have spoken and which, thus, in a short time, people me, in the darkness, stealthily.

Forming with the embryo in Cecília's womb, there is another embryo of shorter gestation, an embryo that enwraps us, that makes us luminous, lighter, fiercer, more disdainful, larger, and its fullness is to coincide with the precise minute of the event. What's its name? Hallelujah? Gloria? Exultation? Does it have a name? It lifts the weight of the world from our shoulders and we almost don't notice when the newspapers circulate again after three weeks on strike. Sleep, deep, is like a festive wakefulness. The blood circulates in veins with a sound of tinkle bells. Do we breathe? Our lungs fill with honeysuckle, trinkets, and peacock feathers. The ground we walk on is familiar to us.

Contemplate, Abel, the twin whom love favors, as it does you. Enjoy, while you can, her movements, the rounded curve of her shoulders, her voice, her firm and severe sweetness. The embryo has still not reached its full development. The light of the Sun exists, the stones, the horse, the cart exist, we exist. Missing, however, is the meeting, the junction. Everything, in the empty spaces of time, driven by the currents of time, the threads I could have tangled, cut, on the night I am beside the cistern ready to dive and die, everything weaves and meets. The nameless embryo reaches fullness. Without suspecting anything, we reach the apex.

The sand of the beach, the calm sea, and the motionless palms reflect the red sky. For the first time in the year, Sun and Moon, the Sun still hidden and the Moon new, stroll together, on their separate courses, across the double field of Gemini. No one, as far as the eye can see, except me, Cecília, and the lamb. We go along the beach embracing, she in a somewhat faded cotton dress, where the pale green leaves remain: use, a kind of autumn, has parched the yellow flowers. I can already perceive an alteration in Cecília between her stomach and high breasts, and her footprints—the first of the day with those of the lamb and mine—on the bloody sand that smells of sargasso go a little deeper. The rush of the foam. The back of an animal, broad, also reddened and reflecting the light of dawn, advances slowly, cuts the waters. Birds come from far away and alight on it. The strongest waves, Cecília and I run, laughing, pretending to be afraid they'll catch us and wet our ankles. The lamb leaps, bleating, and the Mary-flour crabs, translucent, flee among our feet, hide. Cecília's smiling face, with the stripes from the pillow and still smelling of camomile. We've eaten nothing; nor have we washed our mouths. Her tongue, on waking, tastes of fasting, unleavened bread—and the salt air lightly slips in between our teeth. I tell Cecília now what she confided to me one rainy night beside the canal. To die at this moment wouldn't be difficult and would have no import. Cecília, generous, permits me to enjoy during a few weeks, without measure and without pause, the fullness that man only receives in bits and, even when there is little punishment, is diluted all through existence. She dispenses with partiality the goods within her reach, making me sole beneficiary of the fortunate and favorable part of the years (how many?), and puts me out of reach of the other, negative part. She saves me from the rotten, dark, bitter, harsh, dry ones.

Yes, the embryo that enwraps us both is mature, and I stay by Cecília's side in the certainty that we are stronger than everything, protected—by love, by jubilation—against all manner of deceit, surprise, ambush, snare, fall. (How mistakenly we read, instructed as we are with tricky letters.) In the distance, a net cast into the cistern of the world, coming along the beach, a horse pulling an uncovered gig rises up. Behind me I hear an unknown voice calling me. I turn around: my father is speaking to me for the only time. I smile at him as he keeps his distance, timid. I continue the walk. In the midst of the sound of the waves I hear the muffled and still distant, but not too distant, pounding of the horse's hooves. The horse approaches slowly and the driver seems to be in no hurry. The wheels go along slowly, marking two parallel tracks in the sand. Inhabitants of Cecília surround us now, happy and a little frightened. I am puzzled by the absence of the ram, the gig is near, the horse's steps slow down. Cecília sees it first: "Look, Abel, the horse is coming alone, pulling the gig." At this moment, at fifteen or twenty yards from us, the animal stops. When the net gets caught at the bottom of the cistern, I can guess whose hands are the ones working underwater in the darkness. Here, beside Cecília, in the light of the day that is beginning, inebriated, loaded down with bene-fits, convinced of our immunity, and disdainful of Death, of its wrath-ful annihilating power, is there a sense somehow in this driverless vehicle of the presence of the Woman with one side of her face miss-ing? I take Cecília by the hand, help her in, and I take the reins myself. The horse lifts its head and leads us toward the end.

Cecília, in her cotton dress, smiles under the straw hat, her feet spotted with sand. Cecília goes along beside me, and her body, that memory, vibrates. The horse goes on docilely, there are specks of sun on Cecília's face, she grasps my arm and looks at everything, at the blue sky, at the copper sea, at the fish that pass through the transpar-ency of the waves, at the horse's haunches, at our shadow on the sand, she laughs and kisses me, her face glowing and her whole body flooded with a joy that she never showed in such a full and evident way. She is dressed in a glow that blinds me, and even the leaves of the print, the yellow flowers, seem to recover their clarity and original colors. Cecília is brighter than this May dawn. We go along Milagres Beach, and at every turn the wheels of the gig uncover pieces of walls half buried in the sand, remains of doors or beams, broken tiles, iron-ware. The large rocks piled up along the coast to deter the constant and ever more biting pound of the waves are being conquered by the waters. But the waters are green under the morning, and the blue sky no longer enters through the windows of those demolished dwellings: with its light it floods the cubes formed once by walls that now are dust. We get out of the gig. We walk along the rocks, fingers inter-twined, among the remains of parlors and bedrooms (where many couples must have made love, and similar to the one where the Fat Woman puts us up, with its smells of fruits and a lion at the window), vaguely touched by that warning of things. Suddenly, in a single movement, assaulted by the exciting notion of our existence and the gifts we bear, we turn to each other and embrace. Cecília's face is burning and also her slightly slanted eyes. We get back into the gig. The hand that will take the reins of the animal and make it back up in the direction of the sloping rocks placed at the edge of the sea to hold back the waters is the same one—perfidious and more active this time—that holds the net in the bottom of the cistern. The horse backs up. I try to get him to go forward, he keeps on backing up, slowly. Cecília is frightened, the horse, still walking backwards, is pushing the buggy in the direction of the trap, the precipice, and he suddenly can't do anything against the weight. The right wheel loses its support, drags us, sucks us in, it's completely violent, quick, tumultuous, I shout for Cecília, my body leaps and is inserted into the rocks. I hear the cart and the horse rolling over me, a hard cold thunderclap sur-rounded by teeth and claws of steel, a round windy creature, made up of a hundred lions and so luminous that it lights me up inside, beating on the ground, on the wet stones, for a long time, cresting them, bruising my back, where is Cecília? The horse, caught in the shafts of the buggy, is struggling to get up. Cecília, motionless, one of her legs caught under the twisted neck of the animal. The waves reach her and also wet the horse. I shout Cecília's name in vain and go down the rocks. No one to ask for help. Cecília, pale, wounded, blood from her nose and mouth, eyes open, her dress in shreds. Impossible to pull her from under the horse, who continues to struggle, the veins of his neck like ropes. I loosen the harness, he lifts up his body, and I carry Cecília, inert, up above, under the light of the highest Sun, I lay her on the sand. Her eyes so luminous, open, dull, not reflecting anything. Some movement. Is she breathing? The leap of a fish. Necessary to save her, save her for me and for other mornings just like this one. I look around. Still no one. The wind wafts the hat far off. I take her face in my hands, her eyes still open, indifferent to the light. You and the net, Abel. Why don't you dive? Muffled roars of lions. I call her one more time, but this call is already poor in conviction, even though I don't want it to be, I can't admit that Cecília, male-female, strength and compassion, donor and beneficiary, Cecília, is dead.

Suddenly, I cross through a gate, a limit (I hear the voices of brothers and sisters, the sounds of their instruments)—and I accept, split from head to ankles by the vision of my absolute weakness, I accept the truth, resigned, as those deprived of the vague and concrete gifts of the Earth, I mold myself to the truth and I begin to live in the world without Cecília. Whorish. Nothing. On the curtain in the bedroom, the Lion bites and splits the Moon. The horse, still harnessed, is struggling on the rocks. Whoreborn world. Cecília's body frees its beings: sick and famished, people with no chance, whom by her compassion—also dead—she tries to rescue. The Earth is surrounded by a stinking breath of farts, from bursting, filthy assholes. I'm kneeling by Cecília's lifeless body (farewell, happy afternoons and child that I don't have!), and I probe her secrets, her prodigious substance. A circle of popes, all naked, their miters tipped over a pit, their rear ends turned toward the Sun, vomiting into the abyss. Life: shit and pitch. The great wheel, with its innumerable ball-bells, rusty, and with crêpe ribbons flying among the spokes, comes out of the sea and comes spinning in my direction. Future and dream, certainty and assurance, projects engendered in ignorance, can go fuck themselves. Ragged, sick, tottery people (coming from where?) leave Cecília's body as one leaves a plague-ridden city. A cloud of dark birds, coming from the sea and multiplying in the air, covers the Sun for a moment and a brief, illusory night darkens beach and sea. Age-old nuns, in trussed-up habits, thread garbage and dung on bloody twats. An old man, squatting, comes in his hand. I am before Cecília and in her core. The wheel passes through me, retracing the track of that joyous afternoon when Cecília and I, with the *pastoril* group, go along the beach holding hands. I bite the eggs of deception and spit them out, all chewed. Shit! Old saints with horns on their breasts, their white cunt hairs black with crabs, screw with donkeys, with goats, howling black prayers. The *pastoras*, wrinkled, dirty, beat tambourines made from the skin of balls, their mouths corked with pricks. Whorish and bitter fate. They all go away. Along a path, at a measured step, his back to me, the solitary knight goes whistling. He enters a shady area. Where are the children with numbers on their foreheads? I don't see them, and the mad beings are no longer nearby. Suck, world, suck the immense cunt that bore you again. Cecília's insides are empty and the waves are dragging the harnessed horse toward the sea. The sea devours the place where Cecília dies. In the distance, two shapes approach on the run. My father, standing beside me, waits for me. He finally perceives that I'm not

going, makes a gesture, and goes away. Where, I don't know. I get up, I
look around, I see myself alone. Then I stay on all fours, I put my forehead to the ground, I sink my fingers into the edges of my behind, and
I roar, I shit, I roar, I shout at the world, whore, weeping, whorish life,
I talk through my tail, I blaspheme through my tail, between the teeth
of my asshole that eats earth, I shit on the ground with my mouth,
all of me is transformed in the sewer of words, shitting dead words,
the shell of words, inside the dead girl, I can't even recognize them
myself, strange, talking is nothing and no one hears me anymore, I
don't hear myself, no one anymore, no one. The sea beats on the
rocks.

E

Ơ and Abel: Before Paradise   1

End and beginning. Ơ and I, face to face, side by side, back to
back. Sun, Moon, Interference, Darkness, Convergence, Route, Cadence, Balance. Back to back, side by side, face to face, arms in a "T."
Where? Out of the times of Charlemagne the trochoid maps emerge
and with them navigators take to the sea. The waters on those maps
are designed like a "T" on an "O": a "T" on "Terra." Can we be, us,
with our arms open, "T" before "T," surrounded by the world, a map?
What waters could be evoked in us, then, with their fishes?

P

Julius Heckethorn's Clock   5

The construction of the clock that Julius Heckethorn has in mind
is facilitated, in an indirect way, by the governess who accompanies
Heidi Lampl during her stay in Cologne. The month of May passes.
The nights and the mornings, darker and darker for the girl, follow
upon one another, luminous and warm. The governess, a bit intoxicated by the air and by her role as confidante, sets up the meetings of

the young patient with Julius and, on her return, extols to the family as best she can that gentle and somewhat timid artist who speaks with equal enthusiasm about Mozart and Sylvester II, pope, clockmaker, and one who understands celestial mechanics. In August, Julius goes to Münster and the Lampls accept him. The marriage takes place in January 1930, without pomp and a little hastily, so that the bride, twenty years old then, can still catch some glimpse of the ceremony: total blindness is rapidly enveloping her. With the help of his father-in-law, Julius Heckethorn sets himself up in the region where he spent the first years of his childhood and restores the carillon factory. Then he dedicates himself to the planning and building of the clock that he still vaguely conceives.

Julius's first intention is to use an oil or a water clock as his basis. Current clocks, which run by leaps and are what we are used to, seem to him to corrupt a notion that the first instruments for measuring time, like the hourglass or the sundial, restore and transmit in a less unfaithful way: that time is a flow, a continuous and indivisible phenomenon. He reflects a great deal upon this and upon the almost impossible balance between modern processes and archaic elements that the future invention demands.

Even though he doesn't arrive in his conclusions at any kind of mysticism, like the one he ascertains, owing to the influence of the cabala, in the grammarian Vergilius Maro's thoughts on the alphabet— nor are his conclusions always comparable, in his associations, to the capricious similes of Isidore, author of the *Etymologies,* where we find the affirmation that the pen, the quill, with the cut at its tip, represents a unity that becomes duality, constituting, therefore, a symbol of the Logos, the divine Verbum, expressed equally in another duality, that of the two testaments, the Old and the New, a view certainly emanating from Cassiodorus, for whom the fact that when we write we hold the pen with three fingers is related to the idea of the Most Holy Trinity—Julius Heckethorn thinks that a technical conquest equally important in scope to that of writing, that of the measurement of time, will never be gratuitous. It is impossible, when working with clocks, to stand apart and not obey the silent voices. For little as ears hear them, hands and imagination can never ignore them. Even less so can he admit that Gerbert of Aquitaine, whom he admires more than Mozart, the inventor of the leaping clock, a man of knowledge so varied and so uncommon that he was on the point of emerging as the protagonist of legends making him out to be a wizard, and this in spite of his having ruled over Christendom during the years that mark the passage, hoped for and lived through in fear, from the first to the second millennium—or, rather, precisely from 999 to 1003—under the name of Sylvester II, is presented in a period of such profound religiosity as the one responsible for an artifact devoid of any importance. And what can one think of Gerbert's having knowledge of Arab science?

E

℧ and Abel: Before Paradise   2

Man is guided on his voyage by incorrect maps and other false aids. Is he always lost? No. Maps exist that are visible in the dark: we enter things, sometimes, behind what they are. Could one say that next to ℧—on those sparse and perhaps mad days—even when she is silent and I have my eyes closed, I read and hear nothing? Her body fills me with words and images. Such words and images that I can't grasp them and I almost never know what they represent. We wouldn't act with so much precision, however, if we really didn't know what is fit and proper for us. Archaeologists, impatient and not lacking the joy of a light glowing in their intimate being, interrogate the hermetic text written in a spiral on Phaistos' disk. They know that the probability of deciphering the writing is nil, in a manner of speaking, but they do not desist and they always go back to it. On the disk, with the undeciphered signs following each other in a spiral, separated by vertical lines, there is an incomprehensible vociferation that certain ears can hear. The text, coming from without, enters the disk at the edges.

R

℧ and Abel: Meetings, Routes, and Revelations   17

The end of the trip is drawing near, the train passes through suburban stations whose names I don't read and where shapes wander along damp platforms. The panorama tends to enlarge in a vertical di-

rection: under the wheels of the coach I see gloomy streets, blackened
roofs, country homes with banana trees and trellises—and then metal
viaducts lift the tracks up over the clutter of buses, trucks, cement
mixers. Taciturn men and women, on the misty morning, in all directions pierce a landscape that seems to be built on scaffolding, and even
though I see them from a distance and passing by, I can identify the
origins of many. Ceará, Bahia, Pernambuco: the North. How many
among those factory or construction workers can have voted yesterday
in the elections for the Legislature? Many wearing thin clothing and all
with bags in their hands cross the streets in a hurry, climb up path-
ways opened in the hairy underbrush divided by fences, climb up or
down the steps of the viaduct. Several, gathered in front of a lowered
gate, wait for the passage of the last car of the train. I leave the station
and I see them from close by, piled up in the back of a Scania-Vabis
truck, while I venture forth aimlessly into the still strange city that
smells of petroleum. *Gemini 12 mission successfully concluded.* The golden
light of dawn reaches the upper stories of the buildings. Women with
children in their arms and open umbrellas cut through the tight and
sluggish traffic on their way to health clinics. Near a low and extensive
building decorated with many grimy flags (Bus Station?), two men
empty large trash barrels onto the sidewalk. *Sodré: a new democracy
emerging.* Buses come and go, making sharp turns, porters bump into
passengers, and beggars, wrapped in newspapers, their horny feet
protected by the remains of shoes, snore beside the walls.

Without Ѻ's trying to hold me by her side with a gesture or
words, I get up and remain standing in the darkness of the room. I feel
a strange body under my tongue, a sewing needle. I spit it out. Another
in my closed hand. I throw it away. The words or the silence of the
hour and the darkness that surrounds me tear off my skin, I am un-
fleshed and vulnerable.

"One might imagine that a literary project not involved very
much with the surface of the real—and therefore historical time—
would not contradict, in principle, the grammar of the oppressors. On
the level on which it quests and is organized, it would follow its course
naturally and without dilemmas."

The roosters, motionless in the dawn, stare at me, their beaks
aimed at me. I would like the support of objects—and if possible
something that belonged to me, a watch, a key case, my shoes. I feel
around in the shadows and my hands go away, become detached from
my arms, my arms from my trunk, and my legs become dismembered.

The darkness: an acid? Thin blades? I wait for what might come, what should come, what must come, what cannot but come. Is it coming? My fingers let go of my hands. There is a creaking of wood and steel springs, a breeze, the waving of a blanket, the cinnamon smell of the sheets (oh summer afternoons, intoxicating, the red flowers of the flamboyant exploding in the window of the room and the sound of the sea—or the foam of the sound?—dying on the warm bricks), and her voice, almost unintelligible, is droning between closed teeth, next to my nails, my jugular, my spleen.

"Abel, Abel, I love you."

My name and the confession reach me. They remain in me, voice and words, projectiles, embedded: solid, cutting. Knives. I dismember myself so that this can happen, and now the loose parts are coming back together, joining up, and as in a trap they enclose the short phrase thrown out in the shadows. The flowers of her kimono, black, move, she comes to me, slow and certain, as if she saw me, she comes to me and embraces me: her eyes seek my face. Can a man act as if everything were as it was before, when in his heart he denies the stable life and has already gone? Here I am, reducing our relationship to a fortuitous meeting, isolated, with no connections to other circumstances and events, here I am or am certain of being, I, intoxicated and wounded, divided between a stubborn creative project and rage at a world armed with claws, on its feet, on its tail, in its eyes, on its tongue (how, in the face of this world, can one love a single being?), have I the strength to love, yes, the strength to love, only like the beasts?—no, I, inflamed and visionary animal, do not possess the strength to love, no, but the innocence and perhaps the deafness that love demands (not hearing the clamor of those massacred, not hearing the protest of those robbed, not hearing the moans of those deceived, the gnashing of teeth of the mute, but I hear), other wounds still ache and I don't want from love its sweetnesses, surprises, losses.

She takes my face, presses it against hers, burning, and her body, feverish, adheres to mine. The moving of her lips on the skin of my shoulder and her fiery breath.

"This, Abel, isn't a bedroom. It's an aspect, look and know, of the Place and the Hour when we finally meet. Take me for what I am and I'm desperate. Abel! Don't you recognize me?"

Do I recognize her? She speaks to me, where have I read about that, about the musical instrument familiar to the Hebrews, is it called "macul"?—yes, macul, its shape is unknown, it had strings—and only the name is left, only the name. Can love be, in our time, an instrument on its way to disappearance? Does only the word "love" still survive? Let it be restored, then, and, Abel, through us endure. What will become of everything if they also tear the strength to love away from us? The joy of loving? The rage of loving? The wax that plugs my ears is dissolved and I hear not Õ's words, not her voice, but I do hear the connection, the sense, the law, the order, the coherence, the relation, the totality, the symmetry, the plan, the design, the plot. Roos. Cecília. Do I love them? Yes. I love them and the extension of my love, in each case, exhausts me. I love them and I succumb to the gravity of love and of everything that this love awakens, raises up, gives action to. But the love that I know at precise instants of my life and that lifts me up for two brief periods to a feverish and even exasperated way of living, turning white hot—as if through some kind of friction—then and always a few days and nights (exalting, on those nights, those days, even misfortune, perplexity, solitude), can this not be the nucleus of what is announced with its trees growing in the direction of its roots, its singing fish, its submerged bulls?

Roos and you, Cecília. I loved you and I love, and this love is integral, no longer poorer or more limited than any other love, yes. I see, even so, that I love you in a partial way, even though absolute. Ponder and weigh, Abel: what you are beginning to accept now is as if you heard, triplicated, at three points in a large silent courtyard, the same voice pronouncing your name.

Now you unite yourself, you come and you come, you were three, and now, being one, you are triple—and the same name, the same, is, at one time, heard three times. That's it.

The understanding that I arduously reach is blinding, and in the darkness of the room another body of darkness is born. I try to stay on my feet and my knees buckle and everything on Earth, everything, seems great and pitiful at the same time. Naked, my knees on the boards of the floor, I have my face on Õ's sex, the smell of sea and sedge in the rain, a cicada sings in some far-off summer, I see what I am, what we are, two hidden beings, destined to solve the insoluble, you two are in the dawn and in the world, lost, beaten, inhabited by visions, and I cry out "What will become of us?"—the voice, smothered, vibrates as if I had shouted intensely "What will become of us?" because I see no way out and there must be one, and she bends her knees and embraces me strongly, and I cry out again what will become of us, and she answers me "We will die, Abel!"—which means "Here we are, we are to die but we're still alive and, after all, life, long or brief, only lasts a day, no one lives two days, no one, it matters that there be an hour, a minute, an instant in this day that lights up the rest and penetrates caves, cellars, I love you, with claws and teeth, love me. Will there be penury? The desolation of the times. Will the apocalypse come? The flagellating beasts? Let them come. We are bound together. Alive we are. We love. Claws and teeth."

Profuse voices come and go in her flank, voices in her body, not in the walls or beyond the walls, coming and going, distant, the voices of a mutiny. She sinks her nails into my back, musicians pass on the beach, I embrace her strongly, a flute, a guitar, a trombone, a rebec, the bare feet of the musicians on the sand, our bodies rocking, starry sky and great birds on the beach watch the bohemians pass, an arabesque blinds me in the darkness, a woman follows the four men at a distance and sways to the sound of the music (the tiny steps and the swaying of the head, the hands lifting the skirt), the sky grows pale at the line of the sea, harsh, cutting cilices lacerate my tongue, the rebec player's hat is snatched away by the wind, he runs with the bow and the rebec in the air, the others intensify the music merrily, we rock embracing, face against face, the boards creak with the movement of our bodies, so tight the embrace that my clenched hands tingle, we embrace with ever greater vehemence, we don't know how to interrupt the embrace, and we will certainly burst into sobs now. Faburden.

E

Ʊ and Abel: Before Paradise   3

Ʊ's body and mine, all we have for this meeting. Our bodies and what both carry. Standing, her hands vibrating between mine the way the city vibrates in the still tumultuous hour of the afternoon, I contemplate her. I should like her to know and it is possible that she knows: I don't see a preying animal opposite me. She responds, with the fury and the solitude that resound in her flesh, to the obscure emptinesses that gnaw at me. Does a sound run through her? Her hands in mine, vibrating (the way a bell vibrates when struck, the ground under the gallop of horses coming, coming, vibrates that way).

The wide and strong palms. The sun beats down on my head and on the cane field, a green and bristling waviness descending through the valley, mounting the flanks of the mountains, almost white in the light of the sun that falls flat on the cane field and on me. I have wandered away from the diminished group, and there is an extended silence that takes in the locusts, the birds, and the cane fields. Between hills I see a chimney and from far away, far, far away, from the edge of distances, comes the creaking of an oxcart. The invisible and severe angels who precede the coming of the City, who precede it, seem to have expelled all living creatures and all winds from the countryside. Does Ѻ's face legibly express symbols as clear and as exact as the letters that float among the tall buildings? Numerous secrets in it spy on me; and the confrontation of my body with hers waits on an effort at perforation or breaking, that face and body drag me along—stomach haunches hocks, vulva breasts shoulders, tongue, arms thighs—with all the magnets and lures and honeys, but dragging me with even greater power is the hiding place, what moves in her flesh unrevealed, or still dark and not here. Her beauty explodes in my eyes and passes through me, crosses me, runs through me, plunges itself deep into me.

P

Julius Heckethorn's Clock   6

Yes, Julius Heckethorn, among other reasons, does not disdain the fact that the Benedictine Gerbert of Aquitaine—a resident of Córdoba at a time when the splendid daughter of the Guadalquivir was only the city of the thousand mosques, fountains of mercury, and ceilings with precious stones—passed into posterity as one well versed in Arab Arithmetic and Cosmography. It is said, however, based on various precedents, that he abandons the archaic idea of water or oil as the motor principle of his clock and makes a definite choice of a leaping mechanism. Time, fluid or not, repudiates interruptions, sectionings. Is there an answer, however, for the tendency of man to impose a rhythm upon it? This rhythm rises up—is conquered—with the leaping clock.

The blood in the body moves by leaps, the lungs work by leaps, we move by leaps, even birds of most tranquil flight take off by leaps, fish swim by moving their fins by leaps, day and night are leaps, coming and going, passing and resurging, yes and yes, no and no, and the very feeling we have of existing is not continuous, it takes us and flees, now and again it attacks us, by leaps. It is a mistake to aim for the representation of time through continuous engines, never interrupted, without pauses, denying our nature, which pulsates as our pulses pulsate—and which cuts everything, as it cuts thought into words, into syllables, into letters. This makes his decision all the stronger: the presence in the mechanism of the leaping clock of hair and springs, metallic hearts of the gears, pieces found in a spiral, and, in their way, palpable figurations of time as clear as if they were the ideographic representation of the word "time."

As Julius was not a name in the world of clockmaking or the bearer of a long tradition, but rather an amateur with ideas, he recognizes his lack of credentials even to aspire to the building of an astronomical clock like the one in the cathedral of Lyons. It would be equally mad to draw up plans for a musical clock of great proportions like the one in the Prefecture of Jena; or Lunden's in Sweden; the Jacquemart of Westminster. Where is there a Charles V of France to entrust him with a commission like the famous clock in the Palace? No potentate or administrator will place an order with an obscure harpsichordist and manufacturer of carillons in the Black Forest for a tower clock (Julius has the sketch of a model inspired by the one in the cathedral of Troyes) or even any public clock, of the kind displayed on squares or public buildings, although he can imagine some that are more interesting than, for example, the one in Waterloo Station, with four faces and no visible mechanism.

On the other hand, he knows customs change. Cities no longer need clocks for their inhabitants, and the kind of sacred sense the hours had (breath of time?) has been lost for men. Information related to the rhythmic sense of time has also fallen into disuse, and now the radio has assumed the function of bell towers, informing the passage of the hours at random, in stabs—and not in obedience to any rhythm.

The original idea, then, is to build a more or less portable object, a chiming wall clock. The first sketches convince him that there will be greater possibilities of finishing the project if it has more space at its disposal. A grandfather clock, that's the ideal size. The lineage to which his creation is linked, as soon as we see it, is not that of monumental clocks; nor is it that of gracious clocks. Can one say, at least, that Julius Heckethorn, with his clock, is inscribed in an indisputable way in the annals of clockmakers? With greater justice, he could be included among the interpreters or contemplators of the universe. As evidence, during the months when he is designing the mechanism, the book that he always keeps with him is not the *Art of Clocks* or the *Notes on the Center of Pendular Oscillation,* by Jean Bernoulli of Basel, but, in a Dutch edition, the *Manual of Arab Astronomy,* by Alfraganus.

E

Ө and Abel: Before Paradise 4

The text in a spiral on Phaistos' disk, when written down, probably had a first meaning, ephemeral and already lost. Today it resounds from far away, from the impenetrable world and touches us without meaning anything, evoking the presence and vision of mystery. Isn't this language in its densest expression? That's what Ө's body is like. The caprice of those who struggle, for any reason, with writing chooses solids of unexpected form—symbolic or magical—on which to exercise the trade. Warlike deeds are perpetuated on cylinders; the restoration of the temple of Marduk is evoked in a cone; Assyrian kings had their wars of conquest recorded in a prism. Petrified on a sheep's liver, the favorable or unfavorable points are set out; and inscribed there are secret formulas destined for exorcism and divination. None of these bodies, showing deciphered texts, is equal in significance to the disk of Phaistos, with its impenetrable text. Here the text, in totally unknown characters that resist deciphering, enters along the edges, coming from the exterior world, coming from the beginning—and coiling in a spiral, spinning toward the center. From such a way of writing, it is known—with that type of certainty that goes beyond and dispenses with proofs—it is known that it has obeyed that direction. It was written and it was read, something unique in History, by making the disk spin in one's hands: the way the Earth and the stars spin. A writing that reflects, more than any other, the world and our contemplation of the world. Since it is forbidden for us, by a fortunate lack of knowledge, to know what the text expresses for certain—nocturnal to us—on Phaistos' disk, in it we hear and we read an omnivocal, prismatic truth, tied together by the spiral; it comes out of an invisible disk, of which the clay disk is the center and the final nexus of which is in the center of the object molded by the potter and the scribe. ♂'s body evokes that irradiant artifact. In it, without my really being able to know how, I capture a diffuse group of voices; and the meaning of the voices goes beyond a discourse, being a kind of approaching linkage with chaos. I am dominated by the conviction that, in the center of her body, the image of a forgotten writing (this, in turn, an image of the world and its contemplation), one can glimpse, only glimpse, a possible nexus, without laws and still remote.

R

♂ and Abel: Meetings, Routes, and Revelations   **18**

The gate of the Home opens and the tires of the hearse carrying Natividade's body crush the gravel of the garden; the Chrysler sluggishly follows it, under the gaze of a few old people sitting on the porches; the Army vehicle, parked on the street, starts up. The cortege is complete. Two nuns, in their white habits, cross themselves and close the gate—there is a quick clink of chains. The chaplain of the Home, his faded gray cassock and his moth-eaten umbrella, comes over with his senile walk and stops in the center of the garden, in the sun, beside the painted statue that also holds an umbrella: the tip pointing upward gives off a thread of water. The priest moves his lips, praying or sucking his gums. In the silence, altered only by the distant sound of traffic and the steps of the nuns in the center walk, the somber artificial rain around the statue can be heard.

"The sterility of yolyps seems to prove their accidental or experimental nature. As if a negative current, still in formation, were groping, by means of them, for the possibility of emerging in a series and shutting off the human cycle. The glans of a yolyp is ice cold."

Someone in some window or other, still holding up in the air the smoked glass with which to follow the eclipse, watches us pass, holding hands, lazy specters in the warm midday. The sun, lunar, bathes the façades of the houses and the panes give off pallid reflections. Our steps emphasize the silence on the little-traveled streets. We hear the rustle of wings as the disoriented birds take flight and women's voices pass through city blocks and reach us, as clear as if they were coming from behind the blinds. Shops closed and classes dismissed. Fifty thousand people, kept at a distance from the rockets by cordons of security forces and their automatic weapons, press together on the Casino Beach, many since the evening before having spent the Summer night on the sand, in cars, or in tents. Gaudy and countless banners, brought so that schoolchildren, if lost, can find their way, flutter over the encampment. Cornets, bells, bagpipes, whistles, broken bottles, shouts, discarded fruit rinds, drums, voices, a martial hymn. A silence runs through the fifty thousand people, a wave of silence—like a rumor—and the staffs with the merry banners grow quiet: the Nike Apache shot is being prepared, the last rocket to be fired before the eclipse reaches its height.

"I do things the wrong way from indifference—which I don't trust—and, making of my incompatibility with the times that pass a kind of justification for the continued (and, I might say, desperate) exercise of this suspect and not very official act of writing, I go on putting my literary artifacts in order. I try to glimpse and name a fragment of what lies buried under appearances. Peeping out, however, in my conflicting and hybrid texts, is History—dissonant, with no possible integration—in one of its most somber manifestations. A cyst: caustic and arbitrary."

In the limpid sky—not a nocturnal sky, but a topsy-turvy sky where night and day coincide—on the rim of the horizon, unknown constellations shine, over the roofs of the houses as well as on the seaside. In the calmness, the sound of the waters spreads out, a flock of birds passes without casting a shadow, a pitch-colored wave goes up and down more forcefully in the distance, glittering, the ebb tide is over and the high tide of the afternoon promises to be strong. A few banners still quiver, their colors altered and mingled at the top of the staff in a kind of mist, a tense and suffocated reflection.

The Nike Apache leaves with its tail of flames, climbs, invisible, through the thick curtains of smoke and sand, one hundred locomotives of wind and firebox thunder loose in the air, all the banners, awaken of a sudden, snap to attention, blown by the shot as if they were going to break away from their staffs, plastic cups, pieces of paper, dry leaves fly, the awnings on fruit stands fly, the wooden frames of roofs crack, and birds flee in confusion from the trees lashed by that wind. The wind smells of melted sealing wax. Flying over us, low, is a cloud of birds, their beaks mute: they seem to be flying with rage. On the square, muffled, the roar of the fifty thousand mouths on the Casino Beach echoes, and I show ʘ, in the ever more deep and starry sky, the Nike Apache—a trace, diamond and fire.

Pursued by the smell of carrion that comes from inner areas and by the impatient jabs of those calling the deaf elevators in parts of the building, in the corridors with burned-out bulbs, I go up the steps of the Martinelli Building. The luxurious palace is rotting, with its two thousand windows: some of the inhabitants live in the toilets. Farther and farther away, on the gloomy stairs, the sound of a hurdy-gurdy, and the same melody reaches me, tirelessly repeated, filtering through the curtains of the parlor with the evening light.

ʘ's mother, in black, which makes the glow and color of her legs stand out, contemplates us—me and the man sitting on one of the green plush armchairs—from the depths of a hatred that is incurable and can conceal nothing else. Lines like those on hands cut across her waxen face, surrounded by hair tinted madder red that touches her shoulders in waves. Her gestures sprinkle an intense and vulgar perfume. The man, with thin gloves, holding the newspaper and a horn trumpet, has something of a corpse about him—still quite young—dressed for the funeral. *President Castelo Branco, surrounded by children, giving autographs at the Fifth Auto Show.* The globe of light explodes over us as if a trapped June bug were trying to escape. The doors, the stucco, the fabric with lead-colored roses under the glass on the table between the chairs, the smell of the newspaper, the gray walls, painted in oil, with dirty green garlands, the hurdy-gurdy, the mosaics on the floor—everything draws closer: like rats that come out of their holes when houses fall silent. The man gets up, rigid, the horn at face level: "I'm very well. Look." Voice clear and devoid of everything, in contrast to ours, full of rage or anxiety, but alive.

"There are texts with preoccupations identical to mine turned toward the deciphering and even toward the invention of enigmas (which is also a way of configuring what cannot be said). Texts brought forth with serenity, and, seen from a certain angle, not contaminated by oppression. Yet no individual, once the oppression has been instituted, can escape its contagion. No individual and no behavior of any kind."

The black Chrysler and the Army vehicle follow the hearse through the short blocks of Jaçanã, with children coming down the hilly streets sitting on primitive carts, the stridency of the metal wheels on the asphalt covered with a thin sheet of sand, other children playing on piles of dirt in vacant lots, old clothes drying in the October or November sun, walls topped with barbed wire, small greasy auto-repair shops, dark little lunchrooms, the blackboard at the door announcing popular dishes in white lead letters, run-down trucks doing moving work (unconnected junk, bundles of clothing, electric appliances, and birdcages), spiritualist centers, a canary sings in the silence, and certain streets permit a fleeting sight: distant mountains between low roofs and cement posts. The three vehicles continue in the direction of the Center, through the numerous and well-marked belts that gradate the design as they do the life of the city, abandoned, poor, and similar in all ways in this section—behind which, still extending in contrasts, is the ring of slums and factories, alongside mounds of scrap iron and garbage—to a frontier town, with donkeys hauling carts over clay heights among humble houses and desolate gardens where pumpkin vines flourish. They advance, belt after belt, the streets become less twisted, dark hanging doors of corrugated steel replace wooden doors on shops, there is a multiplication—a tangled black net—of electric wires, with a few frightened birds and the rare framework of kites brought there by the winds of August, trucks and buses go up the half-pitted alleys, roll across the grimy mosaics of the bedrooms, and even the coffee cups, the pictures in the albums, and the dreams, those that still endure, are impregnated with soot. Fewer smoky façades, better-ventilated butcher shops, a few street posters ("Happy Holidays!"), more light vehicles, traffic lights, and a certain ostentation in the windows of fabric shops indicate a new circle, a more opulent one, of the many that gradually succeed each other, alongside other circles and separated from them. Until the structures of the palaces, sometimes in decay and even then proud, which govern the city, glimpsed at certain points on the route among autumnal trees and without any splendor, rise up suddenly, riddled with windows, crowned with antennas and huge neon signs, with their safes, their computers, their rumbling gratings, their crowded elevators, and the network that links and unites them, the tireless voices of telephone operators. Natividade's black carcass, heavier and heavier, slowly passes through that varied and indifferent world, alien to the design of streets and avenues, followed by the Chrysler and the few bored soldiers, on its way to the perpetual resting place of the family alongside which she has grown old in service, the sound of bobbins and chinaware, the smell of mustard and ammonia, her old body and this anachronistic cruise between the home and the resting place, dead at last, accepted at last, the silence, the inertia, and the rotting of her body enchanting the places it penetrates. Indispensable to the expert lacemaker—so that the ritual designs of lace netting may be born on the pillow from her fingers—an inventive spirit, taste, knowledge of pointwork, and a sure judgment of the values of its effects.

E

Ơ and Abel: Before Paradise   5

Her position—shoulders weighing on the pillows that make up the back of the sofa, her hands lax on both sides of her body, and both legs bent—inclines her in my direction. The pleated skirt of her dress, lightweight and black, printed with regular hoops of an intense green, contrasts, slightly raised, with the brightness of her bent knees. The measured and discreet sound of the clock beside the sofa emphasizes the rhythm of breathing. With my right arm I encircle her at the level of her neck and I can feel the weight of her head; making the other hand light—like a safecracker's—I untie the string of her blouse. The brassiere, backstitched and also black, with a thin circle of silk at the tips, just hides the nipples that immediately become distended, sensitive, on contact with my fingers. The tongues, touching, continue to be, on a more concrete level, instruments of speech. Palatal, alveolar, velar, constrictive, at times occlusive is our kiss, a language akin to that of words, neither ulterior nor anterior, able in spite of all to exist without the word and susceptible to enrichment in proportion to the broadening of the latter. Dialogue, it is true, that is intense and not too varied: a lovers' dialogue. I reveal my desire, she accepts it and responds, confesses hers to me. The shoes, green, two lanceolate leaves, lie on the branches in the rug—among which, for a moment, I think I see a shadow passing through.

The sun falls onto the cane field from its apex, and I no longer hear the voices of those participating in the outing. I lie down in the shade of a cashew tree, nauseated—I believe—by the heat and the strong light. Great and rare clouds fluctuate to the taste of the high wind. Their great slow shadows slip over the hills, darken the valley, and advance over me. They cover me—I feel the coolness of this passage—and they go away.

She contracts her legs more and squeezes my knee. Her breathing becomes even less ordered: I observe the acceleration of the blood in her neck. In this spot in the room, which the sultriness of the November afternoon begins to reach, the noise of the vehicles is less. But a mechanical saw, strident, cuts through the curtains. The word "stridor" and all of its derivatives, and the words "saw," "steel," "teeth," "shine," "blue," "wood," "worker," "hand," "sawdust" (can one single word drag along the whole existent or virtual lexicon with it?) cross through my spirit and resound in our mouths. The liquor that her warm tongue tastes of, Abel, can it not be filtered through words, then? Her breath evokes myrrh and violets in you, grapes, vines, dry leaves burning; or is what intoxicates you the smell of words through which you raise up that little universe that is somewhere between domestic and winy? The pressure of our mouths becomes less intense and Ѻ's bluish eyelids open halfway: secret irises contemplate me on the surface of her eyes, so wet and dilated that they seem to pour out of their sockets.

P
Julius Heckethorn's Clock 7

Julius Heckethorn knows quite well that in other parts of the world, and constructed with much less precise instruments, clocks more ingenious than his have come forth. He cannot compare it in inventiveness and delicacy to the water clock offered to Charlemagne by Haroun al-Rashid in which carved doors open as the water level descends; from the doors silver staffs fall onto a bronze drum with such a subtle and intense sound that it can be heard at a distance; one can, furthermore, know how many hours have passed by the number of doors already open; and, still to crown the marvel, twelve knights appear on the twelfth hour and parade before the quadrant, closing the doors, the doors of the hours, whereupon a new cycle is initiated. Similarly, Julius's mechanism will not bring forth admiration as quick and exalted as that called for by a certain sundial: the solar rays, passing through a lens, kindle a fuse; with this a cannon shot celebrates midday.

Jean de Felains, when toward the end of the fourteenth century he installs the clock commissioned by the municipality of Rouen, becomes angry with his adulators, exclaiming that the word "clock" is finer and more amazing than any object or mechanism. It is possible that Julius, like that illustrious forebear, intimately repudiates all kinds of admiration as he builds his clock. Since he demands of the observer a general knowledge of the laws governing his invention, without which it might easily appear to be fastidious, irregular, and devoid of any deep knowledge of the craft, who knows but that with it he is not aiming to enervate, displease, intrigue, perturb, disquiet, or to provoke harsh judgments?

Such pieces of work—a fact that escapes so many—do not arise easily or clearly. Most of the time, the designs and the calculations draw one away from the initial project. Barely recognizable, therefore, in Julius's final plan is his first sketch, for he abandons—without leaving any traces—numerous ideas that, once the work has been defined, seem ingenuous and recherché to him, like that of a twenty-four-hour face instead of twelve, following the renascent model at Chartres. At no moment, however, does he hesitate before the principle that his clock must be precise. This because every clockmaker must seek exactitude; and, in the second place, because it does not seem to him that a mechanism like the one he is putting together could be associated with unfaithful gears. In the realm of human possibilities and the limitations of his shop, he disposes everything so that his project will not fail. He selects the iron, the tin, the steel, the bronze, the wood for the casing. There isn't a single part—springs, toothed wheels, pinions, axles, hands, plates, anchor, or columns—that he neglects.

He dedicates extreme care to the pendulum, the design of which reminds one of a cithern or a lute. No other part of the clock is more affected by changes in temperature; and any expansion or retraction of the shaft quickens or slows the oscillation, variable, also, according to the regions of the Earth. Julius, passing over the steel-nickel pendulum of Riefler and the mercury compensator idealized by Graham, decides upon the Harrison. Harrison's ingenious pendulum is distinguished by the existence not of one rod but of several, with diverse coefficients of dilation. The disk—or lentil, as some craftsmen call it—hangs from steel rods connected at their ends by tin bars; other rods, one of steel

and two of zinc, are joined only to the upper bar. When the temperature rises, the zinc rods expand a great deal, but the same doesn't happen with the steel ones, as one can read in any manual of advanced
clockmaking written after 1728. With this the problem of changes in
temperature is practically resolved. For the adaptation of the mechanism to the various longitudes of the Earth, there is, at the lower end of
the bar, the regulating screw. The mechanism lacks defenses against
the alterations of atmospheric pressure.

The lentil, thus named owing to the shape of a biconvex lens,
whose oscillation is approximately 4 centimeters, has an uncommon
diameter: 193 millimeters; and its edges, putting a minimum of resistance to the air, are sharpened to an inconceivable limit. After rubbing
six or eight hundred millions of times back and forth like a docile bird
in the air of that glassed-in birdcage (also, in its travels by land and
sea, silks and flannels don't always protect it), the almost imponderable thinness that its edges show on leaving Julius's hands is blunted.
Even though it is new, its delicacy frightens those who know. And
what is the principal tool responsible for this result? The craftsman's
patience.

E

℧ and Abel: Before Paradise

6

The clock—the mechanical saw having been turned off—tolls beside us and we release each other: I clearly hear the discontinuous
chimes. (Half hidden in the rather tangled mass of hair, the other face,
mute and suffocated, spies on me, tense with meanings.) She asks, al-
luding to conversations that, at other places and moments during these
few days, reveal one to the other—and also to ourselves—a little of
what we are, if the chiming of the clock, in its real or apparent incongruity, tells me something. She speaks naturally, her broad hands
crossed at the level of her now naked knees, but the tone and the inflections of her voice do not correspond to the simple question that she
asks me: the words, veiled and somewhat dissonant, as if they were
escaping—and they escape—from her control, are rooted in our interrupted embrace.

"They are strange, yes."

My voice, too, doesn't obey me and I don't recognize it while I admit that the magnificent clock chimes in quite a different way from what I am used to hearing. It always, ʘ adds, tells the hour in an incongruous way and pays no heed to the fact that someone could hear the whole sequence of dispersed musical notes—one might say—in its ingenuity of sound.

She averts her face like someone trying to hide a thought, gets off the sofa, and crosses the room, barefoot. Her pink heels avoid frightening the birds woven at the foot of the trees and in the branches covered with flowers, and almost don't alight on the rug that marks off the living room. (Another rug, still larger and with designs of a different kind, suggests by its location the dining room.) Half turned and smiling, her left side illuminated by the light from the window, she looks at me over her shoulder, her left foot in the air, her solid torso, impetuous notwithstanding a certain air of lassitude—and her exuberance explodes, imposes itself. The furniture, all heavy, dark, and a little dusty, belongs to different styles; built by craftsmen of different periods and with diverse skills, it represents acquisitions over the years, all valuable. The furnishings of an old married couple with comfortable means, given to the things they possess and not, therefore, less inclined to reinforce the feeling of their own prosperity with periodic new purchases. Porcelain and silver objects, more brilliant on the side where the open window lets in the four-o'clock light, enhance some of the pieces of furniture. Photographs of other times, an old woman in a hat, children, a family group, some faded like the memory of those people that may still endure animate, in thin black or gilt frames, on the lime-colored walls—and not, certainly, because they represent well-loved and still-remembered people, but because they confer a kind of splendor to the past of the Barros Hayanos, their owners, doubtful—who knows?—of real existence. A garland painted in oils over moldings, above the photographs, linking the doors and the windows from angle to angle. All the decorations, however (the clock is still striking), seem faded before ʘ's erect figure, the obvious ostentation of the room pales and is reduced to insignificance, as are its dimensions. She detaches the physical limits of the room, makes the furniture hollow, blanches the roses in the wreaths, tarnishes the silver, wears the porcelain out, extinguishes what remains of the images in the frames. Only the rug with its foliage gains strength and color: her bare feet gather it in.

R

O and Abel: Meetings, Routes, and Revelations   19

"Rather than accept the fact that the pebble or rotting cat subsists in us, we prefer to die. Living doesn't seem impossible, bitter, or difficult to us. You don't act against life: you even want to live. But the hatred for the presence installed in your torso is stronger than everything."

The cortege slows down and waits for the light to change. On the right, coming from a tiny amusement park, a loudspeaker sounds, hoarse and invisible: it stridently invades the houses with very low walls where the leaves of the plants in the garden plots recall pieces of cassava candy. Opposite the two shooting-gallery booths, a mistreated pickup truck and in the back an old mattress. The pink peroba (*Aspidosperma gomezianum*), cut in a rectangle and therefore usable in varied designs, is the most used, among fine woods, as flooring. Hard and resistant to dry rot, it costs less than the others; this is also a reason for its preference among construction companies. The officer in the Chrysler notices a new companion and recognizes in it the Being: the head as always hatless and the nose little by little, it moves close to things with relative gestures, turned toward the center. A nun oversees the work of the servants. The servants disinfect the room and divide up Natividade's legacy—sea shells, a rosary, a few yards of lace wrapped up in tissue paper. They burn the rest. Rising up, even without wind, between the roller coaster and the carousel, are slow clouds of dust, as if the claylike earth of the Park were smoking. Crossing the intersection, agile, in the direction of the return, is the Being—the inverted strips of cloth sewn in place—he gathers up the procession and returns, his arms stiff, to the triple point. The dead woman's sex, never touched or awakened by the hand of a man and as hard as in the days when, adolescent, she picks coffee and cotton, explodes in rape, stains the white and half-unwound boll that protects it. The two booths, tarnished, full of holes that seem to be from bullets, under the intense sun have something of a collision about them. A man appears behind the truck, sees the hearse, turns off the loudspeaker. The sudden color of the Being, parallel to the deserted cross street, reveals him: the cause of the consequences.

The calendar is a net in the air, the calendar hunts the air as if air butter-flies existed. Look: the boatman follows the river, from headwaters to mouth. He follows and is present during the course of the voyage at every spot along the route. He can, at privileged moments, have the simultaneous vision—not of the whole voyage: it doesn't go that far—of certain segments of the journey. Forays.

The man's gloved hands rest on the horn trumpet. I know that many of his bones have been restored with metal plates and that his blood, obtained through transfusions, circulates in vessels with nylon repair work. "I'm quite well." Electronic stimulators regularize the arterial pressure and keep the heart active. He has grafts in the liver, the kidneys, the bladder, the lungs. To me, however, he looks healthy and well preserved, even though a little rigid, and difficult to perceive (the curtains are dark) are the double dentures, the silicone nose, a glass eye. *Armed forces to give warning.* The mother watches me with disdain, suspicion, and exultation at the same time. I try uselessly and perhaps without skill to obtain some concrete information about ʊ's true age. "Look." The carillon of the Cathedral wavers over the Sunday afternoon and the window glass trembles in its frames. Why am I here? The vibrations are dying out, a wave that comes in and goes out: the hurdy-gurdy, submerged, rises up again. "So, you're on vacation. Did you know our son-in-law?" "No." "Ah . . . You know? We never go there. We don't go out much." The rug at the woman's feet recalls a dog with the mange. The man's ears, I can see, are artificial, his hair transplanted, he has a mechanical leg. Why the gloves? With something artificial in his movements, he raises the trumpet: "I'm quite well. Look." We fall silent. I hear the jabs of the people on different floors of the Martinelli Building summoning the decrepit elevators.

"An artist can remain faithful to the questions that absorb him most intensely and still do his work, ignoring sordidness and brutality, as if circumstances were good for them—for him and for the work. Maybe he convinces himself that in this way he's preserving it and guarding it from infection. Is he deceiving himself or looking to be deceived? This I don't know. I do know that work and man, even so, are contaminated and, what is even more serious, compromised indirectly by the reality that they seem not to know. He and his work rescue an anomaly: they bear witness (deceptive witness, of course) to the fact that the expansion, purity, and sovereignty of spiritual life are not incompatible with oppression, and they even lead us to wonder whether this, in addition to admitting them, doesn't foster great routes for the spirit."

Powerful machines amplify the reach of the probings into the eclipse in all the senses. Optical instruments from several sources, installed in the densest point of the oval of shadow, are on the lookout for stars of dubious existence. ("You shoot yourself in the chest or cut your wrists so that the pebble will disappear. It would prefer to live, and if it dies it's by chance.") A fleet of large jet planes, emissaries from NASA, flying at such an altitude that they strain the imagination, study the solar rings. Over Peru, at a million feet above the Andes, in a space peopled by throatless groans, moans, and tones, the astronauts of Gemini film the eclipse and the oval of shadow where I and Ƌ lie motionless, laughing, half drunk, and with our arms open, in a deserted rectangle, and next to us the tree, a point, a grain. The Nike Apache, equipped with electronic instruments, investigates the higher winds, accelerated with the darkness and the cold, and the zoology of the upper atmosphere, revealable—as, under an adequate reagent, a normally invisible design—by the contorted and mysterious light of the eclipse.

Alone, on the square covered with stones, quadrangular, the windows closed, with stones among which weeds are growing, in the center a tree taller than all the houses without eaves, a leafy tree (solar remnants pass through it, small curved threads on the stones), between slugs of wine we chew cheese and bread, the tree looks like an ancient oak, houses without eaves, pale in the twilight glow, infested with white moths, the tree a marker in the square, the weeds growing between the stones, and we drinking wine, alone beside the tree, among the moths, alone, in the square's rectangle, the gangrenous Sun in its zenith, we look forward and backward, we, I and she, ten, beside us, as if we were awaiting the coming of the nine choirs of angels, the end of the world, the falling of the stars, or the beginning of everything.

Refrigerator trucks, semitrailers transporting wood, salt, and large steel girders edge in—wedges—between the vehicles of the cortege. Cortege? Maneuvering close by the other vehicles nearer and nearer and slower and slower, the lieutenant colonel glimpses—and then loses sight of—the hearse and the soldiers, about to cross Bandeiras Bridge. The gases given off by the thousands of exhaust pipes mingle with the thick and almost viscous smell of the waters. Natividade raises her hands and confesses to the two other old women, full of joy: "Can you believe it? I can smell a perfume of the earth. I'm going to be received! I'm going to be received by God!" The word "God" burns her mouth and she starts to weep, thrashing in the bed, trying to get up and fix her wooly hair, certain of being on the road to God, on the threshold of—and perhaps even inside—the walls of Paradise, whose smell is the same, has to be the same, as that of the earth on which she walks without any sure direction until her knees stiffen and where she only knows servitude, favors, the disguises of solitude. The virgin lye and water burns, and this operation must not be interrupted, in order to avoid—a consequence of the cooling—the deterioration of that part of the material. Eventually, the simple dampness of the air can burn the virgin lye, saving water and work in that way. Fluttering in the wind among the staffs are the white-and-red flags of the American Circus, set up on a vacant lot on the left. The man in the Chrysler looks for the hearse among the beams, planks, and girders loaded on the trucks. He only sees hurrying pedestrians, other vehicles, the dark quadrangular towers on the sides of Bandeiras Bridge, and "VARIG" signs, over which great white cumulus clouds slowly float. Ovals of dusty and dry grass divide the Avenida Tiradentes, surrounding the wild Chinese hemp palms. The cemeteries today have a festive air, with their countless visitors and the Christmas shopping keeping the stores busy. Natividade doesn't know her parents, her grandparents even less, and she knows nothing of brothers and sisters, uncles and aunts, nieces and nephews, she dies a virgin and her haunches become wrinkled without the appearance of any gentleman friend. Every year for more than thirty years, on November 2nd, at three o'clock, without saying where she is going, she buys a bouquet of daisies, goes into the first cemetery, looks for a grave—no matter whose—that is abandoned, places the flowers on it, prays for a name, imagines an affection, weeps in silence. Prick—or scratch—is what they call the reproduction on paper or cardboard of the design on which lace is woven. With variations they resemble the traditional designs, the motifs frequently occurring in Portuguese tilework. As for the tiles, they are inspired in the world and in Geometry. The whore, the fireman, and the handyman surround the Chrysler. The holster with the revolver, on the right-hand seat, has a strong horse smell. The hearse turns to the left, violating the grass in the center of the Avenue: the military car and that of the lieutenant colonel follow it bouncing, tear the canvas of the circus tent, enter. Natividade and a boy are alone in the stands. The blue canvas flaps, as do the banners among the staffs. A turboprop plane crosses space, high up, on its way to distant airports. The white-and-red banners waving. Methodically and without ever coinciding, the Being is the balance: keeping his feet between the two and, existing in him only, the opposite side, there is something occult and incomplete in his acrobatics. Coltish, he inverts and stays together, his hands from without inward, where. Applause, drums, cornets, and voices cross the hollow of the circus, the ignitions of the cars are turned off, and in the midday silence the dead woman's humiliated bones explode, broken by teeth or iron instruments. Performers appear, people from other countries, some wearing Hawaiian sandals, behind the dressing rooms a goat bleats, the poor animal tamers and foreign acrobats approach the dead woman, but the cars turn and leave, accelerating.

E

ʘ and Abel: Before Paradise 7

Tinkle bells ring in some part of the building or on the LP ʘ has put on. What is the meaning of that music, ardent from the start and jarring, with its violent chorus, its rebellious cymbals, coming from this room that was shaped to express acceptance and continuity? Am I to understand that such a harsh cantata, molded on what there is of the most elementary in man and governed, nonetheless, by a lucid and sensitive intelligence, constitutes a kind of norm—or aspiration—for the carnal rite that we initiate? All the night before, crossing between wakefulness and sleep, unknown hands hold an unfolded sheet up against the wall of my room. I know that it is a question of a brabant sheet, made flexible by use but still a little stiff, a resistant sheet, destined to go on through extensive phases of a life, perhaps more than one—and therefore without any embroidered mark or monogram—a stiff sheet washed with soap on a riverbank, blued with a mild indigo solution, dried on flagstones, sprinkled with rice water, and starched by the hand of a black woman, with an iron warmed on charcoal. All this I know, and I don't know who is holding it up in front of me, covering part of the wall. Ơ crosses the room again, her arms raised to loosen her hair, comes back to me, slowly, her hands grasping her cuffs, compressing the flesh above her wrists, her breasts stand out, and her half-open blouse shows the deep cleft between them, I go to meet her and we remain standing on the rug, face to face, she throws her head back and her hair flows, honey and steel, over her solid shoulders. Her face, in the middle of it, as if withdrawing into the shadows and growing old, the line of her nose clearer—a ridge—and wrinkles between her eyes. I read a word on her forehead, as if I had written it, and I cannot perceive what it means: the word, in a strange or nonexistent tongue, disappears before I can keep it. I sink my hands into her hair (am I searching for the word not grasped?), she embraces me, our faces together and a sound of voices: hurried, they speak in secret.

The subtle transitions. Without knowing how, a leap—and you find yourselves in another degree or zone of perception. Do I have her in my arms and is it an afternoon in November? Behold, however, it is that no more and simply the afternoon where a meeting takes place: it goes beyond, our meeting does, the condition of a pleasing episode and takes the shape of a keystone or apex of a structure that transcends it. Its success is not at stake, but the consecration of everything in our existences that we say and do. Wherever we walk, whatever our deceptions and assurances might be, now we are one opposite the other, alone—and everything depends on us. It matters little, beyond this, that we, lovers, enter some kind of future. By means of a rhythmical and happy ordering we must complete the complex framework entrusted to us. This is a confrontation without an afterward—or in which the afterward would already belong to a different orbit or cycle.

Weighing on me, clearly, as I bend my knees in a ritual or allusive gesture, is the status of officiant. She presses my forehead against the lower part of her stomach (once more the hidden voices), her body gives way, the soft knees on flowers, the hands full of rings with generous palms turned upward. I take them and look at her. Two bodies coexist in the body before me, and it can be said of neither that it is *the other one*. Nothing makes me suppose any antagonism between the two and the outlines of the faces coincide. One being and two. Only one of them tangible: one, a prisoner, looks at me, begging in the silence that isolates it: its hands, devoid of rings, are in the hands I hold. Reflections—red? purple?—throb in Ơ's neck, coming from some point in the room or born in her flesh. We embrace with a muffled shout and fall onto the rug. During the fall, I see a pair of eyes looking at us through the branches. The City draws close to the sunny vale like a cloud of migratory birds, the City and its river, lost, I search for it so much and now it rises up in the light of midday, alights on the plantation, without a name and somewhat worn in its splendor.

P

Julius Heckethorn's Clock

All the zeal that Charles William Heckethorn's descendant applies to his work would not be enough to elevate it to the category of arch-object, of a personal piece of work and one worthy of examination. We would have, if it were limited to that, a craftsman's product of high quality, lovingly constructed, but inexpressive nonetheless. The novelty of the clock that demands so much effort on the part of its inventor and builder lies in the triple—or quadruple—sound system, generated in his childhood among some ancient books.

Still faithful to the harpsichord, he chooses, to play in his project, the introduction to the Sonata in F Minor (K 462), by Scarlatti. (One would have expected him to choose a passage from Mozart, whom he never ceases to admire.) He divides the introduction into thirteen parts, numbers them in order, and, putting aside the next to the last, begins to manipulate the other twelve. To distribute those groups of notes in such a way that some are lost from others inside the clock, ring separately, and come together again only from time to time—that reunion being an event filled with intentions—is Julius's object. Hearing the whole integral phrase of Scarlatti's again will be like witnessing an eclipse. Eclipses, for him, figure among the most fascinating of phenomena that require—like everything that deserves to exist and be enjoyed—a happy conjugation of circumstances.

With this preliminary set, he designs and constructs three interrelated sound systems, designating them by the first three letters of the alphabet.

System A brings together the groups of notes 1, 5, and 11, functioning with the intervals of four, one, and six o'clock, or, if you will, fulfilling itself in eleven hours: the first time it occurs, the group of notes 1 sounds; the second time, groups 1 and 5 sound; the third, all three. This cumulative process is repeated in the other two systems.

Four other groups—the 2, the 4, the 7, and the 9—fit system B, whose cycle is thirteen hours, at the intervals of two, two, three, and six o'clock.

System C is larger, taking in five groups of notes: the 3, the 6, the 8, the 10, and the 13. Its cycle is also the longest of all, with intervals of four, three, five, six, and three o'clock successively, totaling, in that way, twenty-one.

In all these systems there are interruptions. For example: before series C sounds completely, a silence is observed; this silence waits for the sounding (but it rarely sounds) of group 1 of system A and group 2 of system B; between the sounds of group 3 and those of group 6, a new pause comes along and it is there that the melodious notes of groups 4 and 5 should vibrate, also a rare event, the same between groups 6 and 8; between the 8 and the 10; and between the 10 and the 13. The sound apparatus functions like a puzzle to be put together, of which each time we have only a certain number of pieces, always variable. These, put in place, leave many gaps to be filled; but when we have the pieces destined for those empty places, then others are missing. The set is rarely completed, and, seen by parts, it is not comprehensible.

In an intentional replica of our own existence—incapable as we are of foreseeing whether the instant to which we are turning will be decisive or not—not all of the hours are marked with fragments from Scarlatti. Many times the minute hand crosses number XII in silence, so that we never know if the next hour will make the works sing. Concluding that Julius's invention is not destined, as are so many clocks, to tell the time, seems superfluous to us. What he is trying to do is clearly seen: create a symbol of the astral order. Not, of course, in the manner of Jean-Baptiste Schwilgué, the builder of the last clock in Strasbourg, with his mechanism of solar and lunar equations, hands of Sun and Moon, celestial sphere, a shower of apparent time, and the ring of civil time. Julius wants to evoke the conjunctions of the cosmos, but poetically; not just the celestial mobile order, but the harmony of imponderables that permits a man to find the woman with whom he will join, brings on the birth of a work of art, a city, a kingdom.

We think, if we ignore its secrets, we are hearing the voice of chaos as we face the clock of this contemplator. Listening to it strike seven or ten o'clock, four notes, followed by a silence and seven more or twenty-five notes, or, then, seeing two hours pass without any sound—save that of the pendulum—coming from the works, we deduce that the mechanism, alternating silence and sound, disdains order, ignores it, and serves fury. Is this not always our conclusion in the face of phenomena that escape us? And can anyone blame us if we don't catch the sense of designs, which, diffuse, seem to refuse all efforts of comprehension? Julius is also aiming at this: to place people, as they face the sound systems of his clock, in the same attitude of perplexity that they undergo before the Universe.

Yet one intention orients him, to represent what there is of the aleatory in our existences. We know, however, that Julius Heckethorn's clock—or, rather, his implements of sound—obey a rigorous scheme. Above that rigor sits the idea of an order in the world. How, then, to introduce in the work the principle of the unforeseen and the aleatory, inherent to life?

E

Ơ and Abel: Before Paradise   8

I softly kiss the not very numerous freckles on her shoulders and I smooth her breasts, which, as she lies on her back, hang down, the nipples like the buds of a flower, to either side of her torso, voluminous. Do their hard and pointed tips announce roses without stems? Ơ's whole body, completely naked now under her dress and still decorated with the accessories she has brought for the meeting, stands out against the rug. Wavy and compact volumes. I loosen the cord of the blouse and, with the cuffs unbuttoned, the loose sleeves fall when she stretches out her arms and her bust is almost completely revealed. Pieces of our clothing, pulled off with an increasing lack of shame and a violence that seems to imitate the voices of the cantata, lie in various places, on furniture or on the floor, some in the far corners of the room. We are a little way this side of complete nudity and, I don't know why, the solitude where we are seems spherical, an embryo in its ovule. Would that we, she and I, were generating some affable and charming being, the joy of men, the age of concord, universal wisdom!

Conscious of her body, she, barefoot, doesn't let the sole of her foot touch when she walks. She moves her suspended heels as if she were walking on very cold bricks or avoiding being heard, her sleek flanks undulate thanks to that trick, and her hands, raised (a little), integrate the winged enchantment of her walk. Motionless, she supports herself on one foot and raises (a little) the other, advancing, by means of a flexing that is calculated with astuteness, the well-shaped knee, with which the trunk leans and affects a careless pose. She doesn't neglect, then, her shoulders, thrown back—and thus she keeps her breasts at the height she wants, the large nipples fuzzy like peaches and with the same golden tones. That play of shoulders, distinguished and precise, is reflected on her back, the curve above the quivering buttocks indented and emphasizing, in contrast, her contours. With all this, the line of her stomach, soft and adipose, is sketched out, tense: it recalls a bow pulled taut for the shot. Blue reflections throb in the concave of her navel, the origin of a slight descending fuzz. (The archaic choruses and the Latin verses on the LP, the rhythm of the clock, our words, spent and even so true, mute kisses, repressed shouts, the tinkling of bracelets on her arms.) With my left hand I slowly explore the gradations of resistance and the heat of her skin, hot, satiny, and damp between her thighs, harsh and like something animal in her shaved armpits, creamy in the hollows of her knees, cool and dry on her flanks, alive on her breasts, stiff on her knees. The softness and warmth of her stomach! Burning, dry, tense, limp, damp, hairless, stiff, swollen, frigid, fiery, cool, tepid, it is the same intent and inflamed material that responds to my wandering motions. Touching her, my fingers burn and wherever they alight there is a buzzing, a shudder. Can she be inhabited by swarms of bees? Beetles?

Motionless and without any desire to move, hands on my stomach, legs stretched out (distant bus engines, voices, steps on the sidewalks sound), I dream that I am lying precisely in the place I am, sleeping, I dream. The dark barrier of the wall in front of me is interrupted by a clear rectangle that has the dimensions of a sheet and is perhaps white. I wait for something to happen, and all that happens is the dissipation of the doubt in regard to the color and nature of the rectangle: there is a white sheet, unfolded, stretched out on the wall, and I can even distinguish the faint marks of the fold. Who is holding it up?

She closes her eyes and stiffly bends her head when with my tongue I follow the design between the jaw and the buttons of her breasts. I bite her breasts, a zone of indefinable texture—between solid, liquid, and smoky—I suck on the nipples, she raises a leg and throws it over mine, tinkle bells ring around the rug, a sudden luke-warm wind shakes the window, the pendants on the chandeliers vibrate, and over us a leafy branch creaks, the wind shakes it, and in my hands, in my mouth, I have the large fruits from the branch, its twin fruits, round, unique, ripe, impossible to pluck those enchanted apples, the skin of which doesn't separate them from the world, rather, it closes up the world in the pulp, and, in the world, another tree with new twin fruits, enjoyable but inseparable from the tree, in which the world once more—and always—is repeated. I hear footsteps (bare feet on leaves?), I turn apprehensively. A surprising sight: on the rug, a shape, naked woman or man, as if it spied on us and fled, it slips away among the shadowy foliage.

R

℧ and Abel: Meetings, Routes, and Revelations   **20**

A truck, with the lights on now, approaches the square, without a load, bouncing over the stones. The yellow beams of the headlights, cut by moths, light up ℧'s shape, radiant in the densest and most starry shadows, the hand full of rings holding the glass of wine, her face hidden amidst her copper hair and hundreds of wings restlessly flying over the flowers on her dress. A dog and an old man, coming from opposite points, cross the small square without seeing each other, enveloped for a second in the oscillating yellow headlights, the dog with his tail between his legs and the old man thoughtful, eyes on the ground or on nothing, a bundle in his hand, alien to the sudden cold, to the stars that shine through the November day, to the silence of the city, to the world. He goes down a street, the dog threads into another, and the sound of the truck—the weary motor, the thumping body—is lost on some side street. Our watches say five after twelve, the time of greatest darkness.

Groups of workmen, with, yellow and red, helmets red and yellow, a noisy nucleus of mobile generators, electric hammers, lanterns, are making holes in the pavement, tools and warning signs of "MEN

WORKING," making holes near the Post Office, the Post Office, the noise of the machines, floors and walls of shops tremble, the noise, the noise is muffled by the sound of engines and the angry horns of transportation that on every working day pours out 4,600,000 people, on every working day, coming from all points of the wind from all points of the wind and later and later they drag themselves back, the pavement, workmen making holes. The Vale do Anhangabaú and the two and the two viaducts over it, come off the Avenida São João, the level crossing at the meeting of those two broad arteries and all the slopes, all, streets, squares, alleys, and avenues, all, in a beam that broadens, MEN WORKING, vibrate under the weight of the vehicles. The pedestrians between cars are blocked between cars, the pedestrians, tense, their faces closed, some, pedestrians, run, hurried along by implacable whips, soil and walls tremble, din.

Embracing in the light rain—cold needles—that the wind agitates, we observe the harmonious prows of the boats tipped over on the sand. She describes the secret and true face of that individual called Olavo Hayano, the face visible only in the darkness. When she hears the man snore, she turns out the night light, scrutinizes him. He has twice the age of the daytime Olavo Hayano, and his bristly eyebrows advance under his narrow forehead in the direction of his temples: there they descend, encircling the heavy eyelids. (Almost deserted at nightfall, the lawns of Ibirapuera Park. The waters of the pond reflect the coppery clouds and ʘ's rings glitter above the direction of the car.) "Brutal and gross the nose, with broad nostrils; the upper lip prolonged; prolonged and square the jaw." Between us and the powerful battlement of buildings that close off the horizon, the compact traffic flows. I see, by her description, the mouth of the intruder half open in the shadows, the long teeth, the laugh of one who knows himself to be invulnerable. (The waters undulate in the cove, tin-colored, among the rounded crags and gentle hills of Ubatuba, drowsy, under the mist that entangles the countryside in an impalpable net.) "Tear the animal or the pebble from the trunk. You would prefer to live and if you die it's by chance. But the worst of all is when you accept the strange body and begin to think it's not so bad living with it embedded." (The impression, at times, that the gulls get entangled in the lines and then will come to fall on the two fishing boats anchored in the offing.) Hayano's ears, hairy, limp, and long, hang down to his neck, with warts. Even sleeping, he seems to be saying to himself: *"All the injustice that I do will always have the name of justice. I have more than enough strength and the indif-*

ference necessary to use that strength. Without that, strength doesn't belong to us." The most frightening part is that in that shadowy specter a part of the face is missing. "A part of the face?" "Yes, there's a gap." (Two girls are playing on the grass with a little white dog. Ö's gold-and-iron hair seems afire on the tips). We read the names of the boats half leaning on the sand. The hills and crags, of a darkness without relief, with bottle-green blotches, dissolve into blue and ash-gray.

The officer, separated from his men and the hearse, observes, between the ambitious towers inhabited by the Banco do Brasil and the Bank of Boston, the Martinelli Building with its two thousand windows and the dark sky over those buildings. The girl goes from one blackened floor to the next, with a being—fish, bird, or human embryo—growing in her trunk, goes, uses the tired elevators and loiters on the stairs with marble steps, afflicted and mute, worrying about the fall. The rain that begins, the rain, begins to fall, the rain, intensifies the disorder, the impatience, and the clamor of the horns the rain that begins, the disorder, alleys and avenues, that, the rain. The hands until then and the arms by themselves, the Being retreats at random, shallow, opens the two sides of its mouth and shouts with the voice through the half, exultant, trapped by it also and by it disconnected. The hearse enters the subsoil of São Paulo, and sounds from the surface reach the dead woman through the black galleries; drums and soldiers marching rhythmically, running, the gallop of horses, the rolling of vehicles, and the clash of tongues. The flowers of the ipê bushes explode, sulfur-colored, in private gardens and drives. Buildings should never be placed on the surface of the lot: eliminated, in that way, is the danger of lateral dislocation. Also, the organic bodies, frequent in the higher levels of the soil, do not merit confidence as a base. The bobbins, carved from resistant wood, present a head on the lower part and on the upper a tail that serves as a spool: on it the thread is wound. Its weight and dimensions should be in direct relation to the thread to be used and the type of lacework undertaken. Natividade cuts off a high note of her song, halts the manipulation of the bobbins, and decides to conquer solitude, to generate in secret a family of shadows, her own. She sings again, pregnant and happy now. Sons and daughters are born, two die a few days after birth (she weeps, locked in her unventilated room, real tears for those two imaginary corpses), the others grow and little by little tear themselves away, go off, disappear into the world: Natividade invents them and gets rid of the invention, alone once more and worn out now, with a dry uterus. Her voice echoes, strong and emotional, under the foundations of the buildings, in the obstructed corridors of the subsoil, the voice of the hours when she sews on the pillow the lacework called "full current," "flower in the square," "Cecília's laugh," or "queen's crown," they continue, voice and lacemaker, subterranean, cut by electric wires and by the voices on the telephone cables (behold, Natividade, love and breakup, transactions, trials, building, demolition), advance by curves, songstress and melody, bitten by rats and sauba ants of the abyss, muddied by the trash of the cloudburst, successively polished by the waters of pipes and contaminated by the putrefaction and feces and menstruation and urine and mucus and vomit and aborted fetuses that descend through the mouths of sewers.

"Is the indifference of the writer adequate to his presumptive elevation of spirit? In order to defend the unity, level, and purity of a creative project, even though it be a project regulated by the ambition of enlarging the area of the visible, does he have the privilege of indifference? It is necessary, yet, to know if, in truth, indifference exists: if it is not—and only this—a disguise of complicity. I seek the answers inside the night, and it is as if I were inside the intestines of a dog. The suffocation and the filth, as much as I try to defend myself, become part of me—of us. Can the spirit place itself above everything? Can I keep myself clean, uninfected, within the innards of the dog? I hear: 'Indifference reflects an accord, tacit and dubious, with excrement.' No, I will not be indifferent."

The telephone rings, someone answers at the building entrance, quick steps on the stairs. They knock on the door of the room. I wait in the badly lighted corridor. Ø instructs me for the meeting, no longer a meeting like the others, but the total, decisive meeting—we ripen for this—her voice sounding in an unexpected way, slow and placid, with a note of solitude, as one reading something written, without the irisations and dissonances that animate so much of what she says. A decisive meeting. The door of the room, open, faintly lights up the linoleum runner bearing the dim initials of the hotel. The chimes of the Cathedral ring: an hour and a half to our meeting. Still? The doorknob whines like a dog in chains trying to get loose. A pane of glass splinters as if hit. I go down the stairs (the railing has the same smell as the furniture, old and deteriorated), I go out, the hushed afternoon, I continue along among voices and steps in the direction of the Praça da Sé. Who can that be in front of the cathedral? The Anonymous Appearance? The Non-Being? The Upside-Down Hole? He: the one who is born somewhere else and only rises up where he is when he has left. He changes color, as if many transparent disks—blue, green, red—were fluctuating, crossing each other, between the Sun and the square. He and the passers-by, the vehicles, the ground, the sunlit façade of the buildings. I turn around: immense, vacillating, crystalline, and light, a pyramid of whirlwinds comes and alights, higher than the towers, in front of the cathedral without interrupting or altering the roars of vague subterranean animals and the anguished voices of the children who shout in front of the shops. Solemn. The whirlwinds spin, ribbons join their points. I open my hands. The colors of the whirlwinds in my fingers. The legs of the visage over claws that alight like shadows without grasping the oily asphalt on which they are reflected. Triangle? Angle? No, an A. Motionless claws, arisen, the A approaches, I hear the spinning, the whirlwinds. A.

How to narrate the trip and describe the river along which—another river—the trip exists, in such a way that it emphasizes, in the text, the most hidden and lasting face of the event, that where the event, without beginning and without end, challenges us, unmoving and moving? I see in the world, on the surface of the world, in its waters, a convex and a concave.

We are the only human beings beside the great tree, and in its branches some wing slips along. Over us glitters a sky constructed for other nights and meetings, the sky hidden for us and gleaming at our feet, at midnight we tread the stars that cover us now and against which a blur is projected, the black and striped foliage of the only tree. A cold halo covers and makes the terrace walls of the houses distant—and the windows are lighted purple. The line stretching between Sun and Earth crosses the center of the Moon, a black disk, surrounded by a blue clarity over which, nocturnal, the starry sky closes, a last leftover tongue, glimmering, a delayed explosion slipping on the Moon, and ☿, visible and hidden by the eclipse at the same time, her hair with the glow of fishes in the penumbra, a vague shape, waving, unreal tree, walks toward me, the moths coming and going between us as if linking us.

What fortunate and imponderable fragment, then, is undoing the astronomers' calculations? On the Casino Beach, a hundred thousand intent eyes see the Sun become totally blacked out.

E

& and Abel: Before Paradise 9

The prolonged rug is bordered at the shorter edges by two pale bands, a thin blood-colored frame surrounding two floral sequences, both with a predominance of blue but based on different models. A somewhat longer band follows, also flowered, where the flowers are joined together by a calligraphy of leaves, which stand out, gold and indigo, on a red background, obviously stylized and repeated rhythmically with almost imperceptible variations. Repeated then are the two border sequences, in inverse order now. This quintuple demarcation isolates in space the true motif of the carpeting, the festive rectangle where perhaps we advance to knowledge. In it there flourishes a vegetation born of happy meditations, alien to the idea of Evil—not the slightest sign of destruction, violence, death—and without this rejection's (how can one know, with certainty, whether it is rejection or ignorance?) overflowing into the invention of a world lacking the strength of truth. We are embracing on a fantastic square engendered in Beatitude, but the threads that join it to the perishable world remain, and without them there would only be the correspondence between this imaginative vegetation and the fauna that inhabits it. Twisted, short trunks, obviously without roots and leaning against one side of the rectangle, try to identify that side with a solid surface, a convention denied by the existence of other trees whose trunks rise up, increasing an arbitrary and vaguely celestial quality in the space of the garden. Opening out like sargassos are the branches of those trunks, not well provided with leaves, and animated, in compensation, by an explosion of red and blue flowers of varied form and neat open petals. The branches do not curve under the weight of that opulent flowering. Hares and birds, which might be cranes or ibises, birds strange to us but familiar to the rugmaker, or, also, birds that are extinct and only survive in certain imaginations, appear in various positions against the background, which is between orange and brick in color, almost always occupying—they, too, somewhat floral in their plumage and their quiet—the beautiful flowered branches. Why, no matter what their name and even with their perching on the trees, should those birds with elastic necks belong unmistakably to some aquatic species? Making present, by such an artifice, the absent fish. Thus, without any alteration in the unity of the picture, space, earth, and air (the rising of the trees, the existence of winged beings), is completed—behold, invisible—a lake.

I would be mistaken if I were to understand that the lake (and the rivers that have their origins in the lake) only belongs to this world that Ὼ and I are prowling about in through a kind of reflex. The representations are always enigmatic, allusive, fractional, and almost never contemplated in their totality. How can one introduce in an orderly fashion everything that we would like to have in a space that is necessarily limited? These trees and flowers spread through the whole area of the rug are not in any way these trees, these flowers: in themselves they sum up a vegetation of inconceivable variety. Fish, surface animals (not despised animals), and a whole ornithological population shine out through the cranes and the hares—and if, precisely, hares and shorebirds figure on the rug, it is probably among several other secret and unreached intentions owing to their peaceful exterior: they denote the reverse of violence.

But if I saw the All on the rug I would also have seen beyond the limits, and then I would see nothing more. Here I have the world, yes, but still inviolate and therefore it doesn't exist, in open flowers, in untroubled birds, in hares alien to eventual pursuers, the slightest shadows of destruction, or any kind of horror. An air of immunity hovers over everything, and even a distracted glance quite quickly guesses, not without nostalgia, that the beings woven here are immortal. The rug is Paradise, and in the sounds of the city death roars about the wall made up of the quintuple barrier of vegetable motifs.

It so happens that in this version of Paradise the trees, all loaded down with flowers, do not bear fruit: lacking is the bearer of the apple to be picked, the one that will transmit knowledge and punishment to the one who picks it. Absent, too, the human couple. In all, a half-undressed couple is making love on the rug's eternal morning and at that fleeting hour of afternoon, the man holding the breasts of his companion in his hands and sucking them in ecstasy. Is the couple located on this or that side of the flowering limits? Up to what point could they complete the representation and through what threads are they joined to it? Do they belong to the multitude of beings exposed to terrestrial vicissitudes, or do they happily inhabit the same unconquerable space where the motionless birds contemplate them? By entering the arbored precincts that are protected from evil, they can acquire the serenity that inundates it; and, also, by invading it with their perishable substance, they can render the walls useless. But, instead, they would prefer not to participate in the garden and to preserve it, for by bringing it to fruition they would introduce the death that circulates about those walls into it.

P

Julius Heckethorn's Clock   9

Elementary calculations—if we compare them to those used in the construction of the pendulum or the subtlety of the sound systems—demand a cycle of a hundred and twenty-five days and three hours for the coming together again of the stars dispersed by Heckethorn in his small cosmos. No one, unless he is perhaps a mathematician and a mathematician not unfamiliar with chamber music, has any probability of arriving at that conclusion without knowing something about the laws of the mechanism. The difficulty in establishing a starting point for the study of the cycle is accentuated by fortuitous circumstances. One could be asleep or absent at the moment the twelve fragments of the introduction sound in order. A detail still remains: even though we are close by and awake and we hear them, we will not have heard the whole musical phrase, for Julius, as has been seen, subdivided it into thirteen parts. The next to the last, not included in the three systems described, ties it to a contrivance that makes it ring every five hours. By a similar recourse, there is a jump from a hundred and twenty-five days and three hours to six hundred and twenty-five days and fifteen hours for the occasion of hearing the complete phrase of Domenico Scarlatti.

So this solution, if, indeed, it does complicate the scheme a little, also allows for exact previsions. We know, however, that Julius has reasons for introducing a precept of disorder into order. What, then, is he doing? He is constructing in an imperfect way the complementary dispositive attained—and therefore deregulated—as long as the temperature rises by the dilation of a thin zinc bar placed in an appropriate manner. Thus there are moments in which the next to the last group of notes, reaching the time for ringing, does not ring; inversely, at times it makes a leap, ringing one or two hours ahead of time. What comes of this inexactness is obvious: just as one can anticipate the insertion of the next to the last notes in the first confluence of the twelve remaining groups (to the hundred and twenty-five days and three hours), one can postpone indefinitely the perfect conjunction of the parts. With such imperfection, Julius's clock attains perfection. And just as in the project alluded to in the incunabulum printed in Basel, a whole life can now pass without the mechanism's repeating, from the first to the last note, the introduction to sonata K 462—called Heckethorn's Sonata by some adepts of the harpsichord. The symbolic value that he intends to install in his work has been attained: studying it, a person capable of translating cryptograms can read how uncertain and given to imponderables is human destiny: how Order is always exposed to being broken and how a small factor can do so much to impede or do away with harmonies.

Two or three years Julius gives to the elaboration of his plans, manipulating calculations that sap his strength and affect his life with his wife, for whom blindness has already become familiar when he finally brings them to a conclusion. The construction of the pieces, begun in 1933, a few months after Hitler's assumption of power, lasts four years and eight months. It is very close to being finished when he is compelled (as are other clockmakers, transformed into manufacturers of war materials) to readapt his workshop, with the subsequent silence of the carillons, whose sound is a kind of natural atmosphere for him.

The spectator of the world, preoccupied with balance, with happy unions, and given to fragility, will go to work for the Luftwaffe.

He gets up one night ready to burn the clock. He doesn't do it. He lies down again and for several days grinds that idea on his teeth. All food smells of glass and sand. Finally he desists. Not out of love for his work, but by understanding suddenly that something quite different from a clock, to which until then, even more than Heidi Heckethorn, he was blind, quickly takes shape in an inexorable way, sparing no one.

At the age of thirteen he reads, in a study of the Renaissance view of medieval science, the story of a man whose horns grow inside and who destroys the world as those roots pierce his marrow, go through his throat, excavate his heart, and branch out. For him, Hitler is that man. Destruction of the clock, so laboriously constructed, seems to him the announcement in a restricted way that the Führer's internal horns have burst forth in broad proportions. The clock is ready, but he isn't prepared to put it into motion. Vital questions hold him back. In his anxiety to attain the totality of things, has he not turned his back on the basic fact? Will he himself not be a mistake in the machine? What machine? The Machine of History? Should he put his invention into motion? For the hours that are accumulated through time like hordes, marked by a brutality the nature of which he still doesn't understand clearly, clocks like this are useless. A dream tells him: the faces will be made of human flesh; the pendulums, the balance scale of Death; blood, instead of oil, will lubricate the axles and the pinions; and the hands will go around backward.

He still doesn't have an answer for any single question among those which lash him when he receives a telegram from Münster: Heidi's mother is dying. He travels with his wife. As the olive-drab coaches pass through the stations, he listens to her describe a dream Germany, evoked by the names of the places and the opposite of the truth. This land of towers and myrtle, where ships sail through the countryside, generated in Heidi's shadows, moves him and aggravates his restlessness. After the funeral, the widower asks that his daughter stay in his company for those first weeks. Julius goes back alone and alone makes his decision. He stops the clock, goes back to Münster, and sounds out the broker. What he hears startles him: Lampl is intoxicated with Hitler's ideas. Without telling him anything, Julius talks a whole night with his wife, convinces her to cross the border, and, favored by his English ancestry, sets up a clock-repair workshop in The Hague, not far from the Mermanno-Westreenianum Museum. Five months later, he hears on the radio that Austria has been annexed. Then he goes to the clock and starts it up.

E

Ö and Abel: Before Paradise

My hunger and thirst, in no way satiated, suck and bite, my left hand caught between her thighs, suck in the solemn twin fruits, whose consistency, somewhere in between airy, liquid, and solid, recalls the space contained on the rug, celestial, aquatic, and terrestrial simultaneously. (The unnamed tree, which covers me and from which hang her frutal breasts over which I lean, opens up in flowers as alive as those of Paradise.) I withdraw my hand from between the closed thighs, which move slightly apart, I uncover her shoulder more, I caress the breast, and suddenly I perceive a scar under the skin. She shudders and, with a gesture that breaks her rhythm, she agilely grabs my wrist. I have probably touched a living wound. The long hand, a noose around my wrist, a rigid noose, her body rigid. The hair loose over the woolen designs. Her secret eyes come to the surface. They are still swimming on top when the being to which they belong puffs up, like a prisoner tied and gagged. The nostrils palpitate and their rhythm is that of blood in the aorta. She hesitantly directs (what gesture and night are echoed here?) my fingers to the wounded spot. The eyes return to the depths from which they have emerged.

The satin surface of the skin has suffered little at the place of the shot: a darning weave. The true scar, the trace of steel or lead, is hidden like the damage of a worm under the crust.

"What's this?"

The haste with which she answers me shows a certain challenge: "A bullet hole. A shot."

Her voice, ungoverned, rings out stridently, a shout that has a touch of insult in it. I feel the laceration and perhaps the bruising of the flesh, the broken fibers that were cured into nodules, a vacuum. I drop my face onto the mark.

"Accidental?"

At her negative reply, I want to know who shot her.

"I, myself. I, myself."

We remain side by side, only holding hands, in silence, staring at the stucco, our breathing agitated. Through the voices of the cantata and the great percussion section associated with the voices, I can hear the march of the clock, the electric saw, and fists on a door, discontinuous.

Her skin, sensitive to the heat, tends to keep its softness, the demarcations of tones of her body diluted and almost nonexistent, even in months propitious to maritime vacations, when (in the frequent absence of her husband, or, she confesses, in his company) she seeks out the shore and exposes herself to the beach sun—never, of course, during the hottest hours, preferring late afternoon or the early part of the morning. Buttocks and breasts are perhaps lighter than arms and waist, but the differences—coming in part from the way in which the bulging surfaces and not just the curves reflect the light—are the same as these on the light-painted walls of the rooms, between one point closer and another more distant from the window, opened for a cloudy day. I observe an identical gradation between thighs and legs, between arms and shoulders. The color of the underarm region, where, through the soft pillow of fat, I can only guess at vague designs of veins, is just like that of the hollows of the knees. The hair, with its glow, somewhere between silver and gold, hanging loose over her shoulders, disguises such differences in light even more and, from the feet up, the whole epidermis of that body overflowing with forms seems to be of a single tone. Standing out against the soft and uniform whiteness, which gives equal delight to hands and sight, are the nipples of the breasts, the navel, and the pubic tuft, curly, black, bushy.

Her body, refractory to the burning of the sun, is, as compensation, susceptible to the gradations of the light, a phenomenon more clearly observable in closed-in places and at certain times of day. The clouds between Sun and Earth may be light or thick, the curtains of the room may wave, a few doves may pass by the window, or, simply, her position or mine may change—and the flesh ripens, or trembles, or pulsates, or simulates a patina.

The surfeit of flesh contributes to so many and such surprising mutations. When she shifts position, the raised heels, bringing out with every step all the knowledge she has of her own body and its movements, the luxuriant fat—which is detestable in others because of the absence of light but which, in her case, evokes the female summer figures of Tintoretto or Titian, women in whom the splendor of form is also a way of expressing the opulence and fullness of Venice in its golden phase—undulates along her thighs and about the hips with a kind of liquid flow. I have before me, seeing her move, many fish tails and the surface of weirs.

Her changing hair now falls together to emphasize her whiteness. When she lifts up her hair, we see how a fuzz descends from the nape of the neck and accompanies the spinal column: it becomes more palpable at the level of the sacrum and then opens up into a trident, one prong of which is lost in the junction of the shadow of the buttocks and the others, light and curly, the upper zone of those wavy outcroppings surrounding the hollows that rise up every time the tips of the feet grip the ground. The inner sides of the arms are as smooth as the carefully depilated thighs and legs, while (strange and evocative vestige of virility) a more or less thick strip of hair that she may bleach with lotions runs between elbows and wrists. A vertical trace, half erased, descends from the navel and becomes entangled in the triangle, in its curls and rings.

R

Ѻ and Abel: Meetings, Routes, and Revelations   21

"I am in no condition to affirm—the struggle and the systems of defense too are constantly changing—that I will never give in to other methods of action. But I do know I shall always be inferior, as a man and as a craftsman, to what I would be under other circumstances. Under oppression we become worse than what we were. In the best of hypotheses we are murdered or we learn to love violence. Except that the weight of our acts doesn't entirely fit us under oppression: the position of the oppressor is not without onus. As much as he accuses, and he needs to accuse because he holds the privilege of sentence and execution, he fears—even though he rejects this—the answers of the rest. He's the one to blame, he attacks me; if I destroy myself, he's to blame; if I kill him, he's still to blame: his own murderer."

The three funeral cars twist along the avenues and streets filled with vehicles, some decorated with great superimposed cubes, in bright colors, the old body following along before the poverty of its children and the advertising signs with their images of opulence, of youth, of speed, the sultriness making the urns and roses pale, the obstructed throat, the flesh breaking up in the midst of the noise—of motors, brakes, curses, hurried steps, explosions—her songs coming and going on restful afternoons, muted, an invisible and melodious thread linking penury and prosperity (delineated in the distance are the profiles of potent financial institutions), Natividade goes along heavier and heavier through the cement and steel of São Paulo, her head peopled with voices that grow quiet and with luminous mornings that are extinguished, the paschal flowers of Lent explode in gardens and streets, surface and depth stand out in the lacework, purple cloths cover the images in the chapel of the former Archdiocesan College, the prisoners in the Women's Jail rise up all at the same time with the passage of the coffin, they stand beside the bars so that the funeral procession can cross over them, the funeral procession crosses over them, Natividade crosses over them, crosses through the mess hall, the courtyard, the latrines, the cells, dead woman and jailhouse with the same smell of bones in the rubbish heap, the Being, back to all, barks the palinode the wrong way, it's ten o'clock on the Light Station, the flower in the lacework is also called "ornate" and is formed by the crossing of threads among the weave, the black woman's young feet quickly cross the paths, run through the fields of coffee and cotton, harden with the years and the trajectories are restricted, more and more cautious and heavy the feet as if they tended toward quietude and now the bodies of the women cross through the May morning, the bodies are scratched, ankles and nails are extracted (bodies of barbed wire, those of the prisoners? of bottle shards? of butchers' hooks?), passed through by Natividade's body the bodies look like malignant gearwork, slash the scorched leather of the thick lips, pierce the blind eyes, scratch the crust of wrinkles and uncover—but without teeth, and they also cut deep—the face of the black girl who, deceived, sings in the cotton field.

My mother, in a long and disordered letter, answers the card sent from Rio Grande and is startled by my telegram. What am I doing in São Paulo when my objective is to try to get the manuscript in my baggage published in Rio? Didn't the publishers, "those swindling counterfeiters," receive me as they should have? "I opened your desk drawer and I saw some written pages. I got lonely, Abel, seeing you at your desk writing . . ." Without transition, in the style that I envy, she complains about her ovaries: "A retired brood mare like me and these stumps still feel like paining! But when you come to think of it, Abel:

isn't it better for them to pain now when what used to be the tools of my trade in that life are no good for anything?" She's waiting for me to describe, when I get back, the great eclipse. "It was partial here, about 10%. Callus Face, your great friend, was going from the porch to the rooms, his head bigger than his body, drinking water without being thirsty and talking about legislators, angles, aspects, the comatose power of Neptune, whatever the hell that is, oppositions, reigning luminaries, and other things he doesn't even understand himself. I've seen people less crazy throwing stones at saints and putting butter on communion wafers. I've got the impression that the guy has really only got the side that people can see." She concludes: "I'm no good for anything, trash, but I'm your mother, son of mine, when it gets rough, when it's tough, it's you and nobody else, and if you need anything and want anything I'll go to the ends of the earth, you can count on me for giving and taking care, no matter what it costs, to hell with everything, I'm no good for anything, but one thing I do have is love."

"Y." "T." What do they predict and where do these letters come from? (They replace, some of them, with the green of foliage like fans, the absence of trees and flowers on the Avenida São João.) "X." Isolated or united, almost always isolated, the "V" florid, the "I" a scaffolding of mobile and mirroring disks, the "H" severe and black with a thousand secret emblems. Vowels, consonants, the "S," the "U," some with such decorative strength that they're hard for me to read and others illegible for having risen up fallen, those light capitals rise up in the sultry afternoon with gruff passing winds that explode on the eardrums like pistol shots. With intrusive head and a jaw just as hard, torso with no fixed points, the Non-Being spies on me with its perpetual eyes. Follower or spy? Does it only notice me? The initials keep distances between each other that are conceivable in such a huge city, and some go beyond the lightning rods and the antennas of the important buildings that with their countless windows dominate the harsh landscape, tumultuous, punctuated with snapdragons, from where the rotten respiration of the sewers rises up and injects itself into the air saturated with carbon, black dust, and burned petroleum. *Congress upholds Castelo Branco's punitive acts. Speaker resigns.*

"My way of seeing oppression calls for a commentary. There is a time when we aspire to be an even-minded appraiser of things. We want, properly, to avoid the errors of passion. In order to judge facts we would like to have all the information. How far does one get with that? How is it that I didn't see earlier that I really wasn't a judge? I no longer wish to judge and I don't care much about having all the facts at hand. I'm a nobody, a renegade—and that's enough. I don't understand and I refuse to understand people who are my enemies. For me, they're never right: I won't justify them."

The hearse, the Chrysler, and the military vehicle, leaving behind the small marble works and the ephemeral firework stands, go alongside the cemetery: on the right, behind the extensive wall, winged figures, saints, pointed stone roofs, crosses. The dry branchwork of the trees in the middle of the drive slips along against the discolored sky; only the old trunks, entwined with parasites, are still green. The light of the Sun, filtered through the plastic sheets that cover the row of huts along the tree line, falls onto the damp ground, onto the flower women's ruddy faces, onto the flowers, and onto the Being—still alarmed and crosswise, opposite, splotches of half-grimy color. The officer's parents go ahead, and his wife remains beside the iron gate, tight and hard, forcing a kind of isolation. Six soldiers, obeying the orders of their superior, leap from the car and with effort carry the coffin, the weight of three dead people, leaden, the boards give way a little to the pressure coming from within. The weight of the iron braces delivered with the item might be less than what was stated on the invoice, or, speaking frankly, it might have been stolen. Did somebody, during the trip, take any iron off the braces? Did the person in charge of the warehouse cheat on the weight? Could the boss of the firm that sold it be himself the one responsible for the theft? Olavo Hayano puts his soldiers onto the handles of the box, tense look and tense backs.

Mortal, he doesn't belong to death; historical, he breaks the limits of a familiar appearance. Conciliated in him, host of days and nights, sheltering in his body the buzzings of the motionless and hanging bees, are the two faces of Time.

The Vale do Anhangabaú flows along the former basin of a river banished from its course by those who shaped São Paulo. Over that valley, asphalted and flooded with traffic, from morning to night, pounded by millions of feet and shaky from the passage of vehicles, the great viaducts vibrate, bridges that join the banks of a ghostly torrent. Behold a "W," vegetal and zoological (hawks on the scales of serpents, goats on the feathers of the hawks, and sunflowers on the horns of the goats), an oscillating "W," the double vertices of the base tangled among the iron of the Santa Efigênia Viaduct. The two arches on which the viaduct rests seem to open with the weight of the framework and the overloaded buses. Scratching itself on the rivets that burst like the buttons on a tight tunic, the "W" rises up, breaks away, and falls, a standard without a staff, onto the sooty trees of the square, and in the scrawny treetops a brief and unexpected Spring flourishes. I see the Anonymous Appearance through the reflections: led through and excepted, his back on the left, hands clasped, with the look of someone passing by.

The tongue of flames disappears. Could Humboldt's cosmic birds have flown, or, terrified, monsters from the upper atmosphere, in bands and closed compacts, in one single going, zap, from the oval of shadow, carrying the shadow on their down and tail feathers, behind, like the dust and wind of gallops? Does the hulking and delicate mechanism of the eclipse groan in its weights and forces? A minimal mirror still glows on the Moon, but, going against forecasts and calculations, the black disk swallows it: behold the absolute *caligo*. What name does that shout bear that rumbles suddenly through the encampment, gross and animal, given off even by those mute? A clamor of teeth? Black thunderclap? The world coming down?

The outline of the lead-colored banners waves, a glow lights them up, opens clearings and gaps in the scene, tar-colored blotches, the fifth rocket of the sequence of fifteen takes off.

A wind moves the branches of the tree on the square in the shadows, making the birds restless, rhythmic. A fan of feathers, rhythmic, Ѻ's hair throbs in the measured gust. I hear a harsh noise coming from a great height, as if all the doors of the city, torn off, were floating in the air and opening with one single blow, *roenggh*. The vast dark cloud, compact and fluttering, evokes in me and Ѻ the idea of a bird at the moment it flies over us with its shapeless song. The wings, so long that when open they extinguish many stars and the brilliant corona around the bituminous disk of the Moon, turning the brief noontime night even blacker, shake the roofs of the houses when they flap, bend the boughs of the tree, lift the dust from the stones, and throw butterflies against us, against the ground, against the houses. We bend over, our hands at the level of the eyes, doing all possible, in spite of the rubble and the wings in our eyelashes, not to lose it from view (its ebony plumage), and we laugh, choking, at its pitiful croak, a deformity: larynx of horns and old boots? Its passage is quick, a straight flight, even though difficult (the wings, far from lifting it like those of everyday birds, drag it, head and wings, alive, carrying a dead body, a bundle), in a southeast-northwest direction, seeming to evolve from a sunlit place to the center of the darkness, crosses the skies, grotesque and stupid, disappears. ☿ is in my arms, her irregular breathing, butterflies struggle on the stones and some leaves still fly. The volume, the vibration, the consistency, the weight, the heat, and the perfume, under the eclipse, of her body, desirable and yet secret. Sun and Moon extinguished over our joined heads (the plush and fevered face), the hidden daytime stars revealed. Her mouth, tepid sucking fruit, in this darkness tastes of wine and fresh bread.

E

☿ and Abel: Before Paradise   **11**

Our hands, joined, do not press against each other, and in spite of this it would not be true to say that they only touch: they are joined by a current without external signs.

"I shot myself. It had to be said. Don't despise me."

Fists pound on a door somewhere. The wrathful insistence with which they pound means someone from the outside world threatening those whom the key protects. The door is knocked down with a distant crash, we shudder and clutch each other's hands. She leans her head on my chest. I hold her even tighter against me, I stroke her hair.

"Abel . . . Don't ask questions. I don't want you to ask any. I hate questions: I've heard so many."

I hear the flapping of wings and the successive plunges of stones or frogs. Stealthy and cold, like reptiles, a smell of damp dead leaves passes between us. The birds on the branches in the rug, still unharmed, surround us, initiators of death and all manner of evil. Perhaps we bear in us the germ destined to kill them and corrupt the wood where they sing in silence. ☿, with the mark of the bullet on her body, will at the same time be the woman in the garden and the mortal tree of knowledge.

What secrets does the sheet hide and who holds it up against the wall? Drowsing and being able to wander in the unnamed state that a man enters while he sleeps and doesn't dream; being able to dream about distant or even nonexistent places and people—being able, however, half frightened and half nostalgic, to breathe in some childhood sunset or to see my dead once more—I see myself, in the dream, lying in a bed just like this one where I'm sleeping, lights out and mossy curtains closed, which doesn't stop—awake and in this dream without disguises—the light from street lamps, reinforced by the infiltration, under the tall varnished door, of the bulb left on all night in the hotel corridor, from revealing the shape of the antiquated furniture, the extinguished bulb in the shellacked wooden ceiling and, in front of me, the empty wall, light on the upper part and painted in oil up to the height of a man. The color and the designs of the painting, twirls done with a thick and half-dry brush on the still fresh chestnut paint, are not very clear: the whole bottom part of the wall in the dim light of the dream seems compact and shadowy to me. I wouldn't see it any clearer and realer awake than I see it now. From the brief and imprudent meeting in Ibirapuera Park (the long hands on the steering wheel or throwing back that hair which the sunset lights up), I carry her scarf with the lizard design. The perfume it is soaked with, which makes the absence less drastic (she is distant: not this kerchief and this perfume, vestiges of a short drive), also penetrates the dream. What is being hidden in the minimal space between the hanging sheet and the wall? Nothing?

Leaning over me, she takes on a certain celestial and rainy air: she covers me with tenderness and I give in to it, enraptured. The concentrated face is that of a person attempting to disentangle twine, as she executes slow wavy motions, touching me with breasts and hair. Her hair hangs down and her forehead gleams lightly in the midst of it, but starting with the eyebrows a nocturnal atmosphere shades off the features of her face. Placed outside it, the free dugs swing, full, roll over my torso. The beads of her necklace still touch me and the bracelets jingle on her wrists. The voices of the singers rise up with ardor, a ram smelling of jasmines goes over the rug and crosses the room, what gift do the breasts offer? I am a man full of dryness and my pity, if it exists, is sour, a caustic unguent, bone splinters flow in my blood and in me the creative act is confused with obstinacy, an affable and silent passage between people, dying with rage and gnashing the teeth secretly in order to bite, tear to shreds, and spit out what surrounds me, as one who bites, tears to shreds, and spits out the leather or rope knotted tight around our wrists. But, covering me like a canopy, her breast furrowed by a bullet—the scar, in that uncommon posture, the breasts smelling me out, shows even deeper—she makes me reborn or transforms me into another or makes me return to some festive hour. She scratches my torso and face with the nipples of her breasts, she puts them both to my mouth successively (they seem to be breathing), and something of the invulnerable harmony of the rug makes me in me, solemn, makes itself in me. I am not innocent, however, and disagreement is part of my nature: I exist inside and outside walls. The ram's tinkle bells sound at different points. He's walking in the room or entering the rug. No armistice here with the iniquities that my eye constantly accuses. Defiant and enraged, without the rage's poisoning or despoiling me. Yes, rage and defiance intact, although a state close to serenity takes shape in me. What is reduced are not the marks left in me by the good things that have been torn from me by the work of men or that I have never even managed to attain—but the ones I owe to hands like those of death. If, despoiled, I deprive myself of so many frank gestures, so many words of love, and so many ardent impulses, all of this converted inside me into unserviceable things, I see myself under her shoulders and: what is burned to ashes, the stubborn one, the silent one, the dry, the somber turns green and moves, responds, gushes, glows, without the freshness—that's true—of things new and still not offended, that lack, however, compensated for by a trace of maturation or even wisdom, so that a confession of love, ecstatic and at the same time lucid, will also be marked by my deceptions and disasters. I embrace her, her pluvial breasts flatten out against my chest, I embrace her in the afternoon light, with impetus and openness, the ram treads on the rug, the clear smell of jasmines, I exclaim with conviction that I love her, love, her I love, so there, I love you, unleashed and released shout, my beloved, I love her, I speak with three mouths, my voices are three and they are directed to the women I love. They all hear me: she hears me. Someone calls me from far away, I, perhaps, amidst the foliage of the rug.

Continuous and steady, wheel or aerial river, the tall wind plucks its strings in my direction, over the motionless cane field, the bellied clouds.

P

Julius Heckethorn's Clock   **10**

In The Hague, added to Heidi's blindness are intense pains in the eyes. Julius, apprehensive, consults specialists. His expenses grow. What comes in through the workshop is not very much. He takes on private music pupils. Heidi, however, is not the beneficiary of the florins thus obtained by her husband. His youth in London, the enchanting days when he discovers the harpsichord and Wolfgang Amadeus Mozart, Julius sees all again in his pupils. He decides to take up his musical studies again. Emma Ledeboer accepts him as a student. Applying himself in order to eliminate the vices acquired over years of solitary practicing, he scarcely notices that his debts are growing. After an attack more painful than the others, the doctors suggest that Heidi see a certain specialist in Rotterdam. Julius, who doesn't want to interrupt his studies, puts the clock up for sale. The Swedish ambassador acquires it.

On the train back, Heckethorn is afflicted by the news: Hitler attacks in the North. Inversely, a certain relief comes into his life. With the new treatment, his wife's neuralgia, which was intensifying in an intolerable way, is disappearing; Emma Ledeboer, impressed with the evolution of this uncommon student, recommends him to a chamber quintet that is set to visit America. Julius accepts the opportunity. He knows quite well that the borders of Holland will not protect him from violence. (Hitler burns Poland. England and France are now taking part in the conflict.) His plan is not to return to this continent that is becoming more and more menacing. Established in some American country, he will have Heidi come to join him. The trip is set for July. At the end of April the pains in the blind woman's eyes reappear. He accompanies her to Rotterdam once more. The doctor suggests she stay at the clinic for a few days. On May 8th, Julius returns to The Hague; on the tenth German troops simultaneously attack Luxembourg, Belgium, and Holland; on the thirteenth Wilhelmina seeks asylum in England; on the fifteenth the Dutch army lays down its arms.

J.H. does not see his wife again, one of the 35,000 killed in the

Luftwaffe's bombing of Rotterdam. On May 30th, after a trial lasting six-and-a-half minutes, in which his English origins are of no help—they contribute, rather, to his conviction—he is shot as a traitor. The invaders, aware of the uselessness of calculations and sketches for a chiming clock found among his papers, when—in this productive and destructive world—the only things that make sense are time clocks and precision chronometers, burn them along with all the other documents of the man whose life has been just the opposite of the desired harmony expressed in his clock.

Even before the air raids, in official circles the invasion of Holland is considered a certainty. Julius's clock, sold by the Swedish diplomat to the wife of the Brazilian representative, goes down into the cellar of the Embassy, carefully crated. It is obvious, with the first bombs, that it is foolhardy and useless to remain in the country. The accredited representative of Itamarati Palace, imitating other overseas diplomats in the emergency, flees to Lisbon, taking along only those objects chosen by the ambassadress, on whom he lavishes an incongruous love, in spite of their having been married more than twenty years. Nervous and turbulent, her fascination comes from a restless imagination, never applied to any defined task and always scattered into acts that are almost always ones of affectation, bordering on sheer extravagance. She brings only the crystal, the silver bowls, a sari, marbles (sometimes, all alone, she amuses herself for hours on end playing with them on the large rugs of the Embassy, some of which she uses to protect the items transported), Chinese vases from the blue period, an autographed picture of the queen, the diadem given her by an old gentleman friend from Nepal, seasick remedies, and thirty-eight pairs of shoes. Julius Heckethorn's clock, in the basement, forgotten with other articles.

It is difficult to get shipment to Brazil. The things saved from the war stay in Portugal under guard, except for the crystal, which was pulverized on the trip from The Hague to Lisbon. (For years the ambassadress refers to that loss, cursing the war that reduced her glasses to dust. She also laments for the queen (not for Holland), obliged to live in England, *so far from her gardens.*

Here she is in Peru, a new mission for her husband. The objects left in Lisbon are sent by sea. The ambassadress, who never reads newspapers, examines the news columns with care. She's afraid they'll sink the freighter. Everything, however, reaches her hands, which doesn't stop her from complaining: the sari no longer has the same colors as before, or, at least, the colors are less brilliant than those it had acquired in her imagination.

Not far distant is another trip by the couple and their belongings: the ambassador is posted to Rome. Eleven months later, the war over, a message comes from the Netherlands, with the seal of the Foreign Office, inquiring if by chance a grandfather's clock found in the ruins of the former Brazilian Embassy belongs to them. The inquiry excites them. Could they really have forgotten some clock? From the moment in which the ambassadress, shuffling the vases, dresses, decorations, ribbons, perfumes, and curtains that float in the festive cellars of her memory, rediscovers the clock, it seems urgent to her to have it back. She leaves for The Hague that very week and, on her return, uses it to adorn one of the corridors of the Embassy on the Piazza Navona, where its soft sound sometimes mingles with that of the luminous fountains.

With the ambassador's retirement, they return to Brazil. Here the nervous depressions that the ambassadress suffers in Europe and that disappear with the successive and sumptuous receptions at the Embassy become worse. She dies in 1953 under the crimson sheet hemmed with gold. She begs them to bury her with the diadem from Nepal—and under the pillow on her deathbed relatives discover several colored marbles. Widowed, the ambassador, homesick for a Europe that no longer exists and incapable of readapting himself to his own country, auctions off his belongings and travels, never to return, hoping to find friends, who have died or who don't even remember him or the ambassadress.

Now the clock is there, it's been there for twelve and a half years, facing lifeless rugs and faded easy chairs, elegant and sober, ringing from time to time with its mysterious sounds. No one believes now that the sound mechanisms, if more than one do exist, will reconstitute Scarlatti's phrase. It never even occurs (to whom would it occur?) that the gears adjusted and exposed to the calculated voluntary failure of the imperfect mechanism are calmly marching toward that miracle: the confluence of the eclipse. Will Julius, lost in the dust, hear that moment?

E
Ʊ and Abel: Before Paradise **12**

Beloved: when a man knows and passes by countless beings
without his own being broadening, advancing, and attaining, you lead
me (where, where?), and we do not go casually round the limits of this
wood passed through by apparitions. Tributaries and tributaries,
many since forever and for all of forever unsuspected, form our meeting. We undress, immersed in mutual lucid intoxication. Ah, if the
vestibule of our pleasure were also that of the unification of
knowledge!

You reign through this hour like a star. Your many kisses brush
the skin of my shoulders as if you were afraid of crushing them, you
intensify the pressure of your lips (do you want to breathe in my substance, incorporating it in you?), you continue kissing me lightly and
again strongly, but, soft or uncontained, each one of those kisses takes
on flesh and plants voices in me: I, more and more inhabited. I turn
and remain face down on the rug so that you can circle me with your
tireless kisses, you circle me, several mouths mark me—on the back,
on the small of the back, and along the ribs—and your head strokes
me and your loose hair too. The voices cry out in me, some disconnected and all exalted, cry out and do not fall silent—I lying on my
back, I with my chest on the rug, hot and agitated your tongue in my
ears, I lying flat on myself, you and I, with exuberant spirit, rolling
among the flowered walls of the Garden, your hand full of rings on my
stomach—multiple, the voices cry out, through my mouth or autonomously, in the body where you all go sowing them. They cry out. Beloved! The man you meet bends, in his maturity, with the weight of
some senile blemishes: I am hindered on certain days by an old man
and his burdens. You, certainly, impose on me some kind of violent
laws, and I recover under your inflow a fullness that goes beyond me
and that the raised sex reflects. Will I succeed in deciphering, however,
I, why I love you? You pass among the living carrying the weight of a
copious beauty whose valuation has come to be difficult. In all, how
expressive your body in its vigilant hugeness! Do not men expand,
using such a trick to oppose shrinkage and oblivion—those implacable

gnawers—what they decide to preserve as an example? You are, in a certain way, your own expansion. If my love and my desire tried to magnify you, they would invent a woman this side of you who would be, if even that, your pale reflection. Will I have to say, while you tighten my tongue voraciously between your teeth, that the beauty manifest in the flesh wounds me? The splendor of your face, of your body, by what they have of the transitory afflicts me. The ephemeral, however—it still isn't time for me to know how—is joined in you to permanence: anointed with perennialness, another presence spies on me in the space of your body. I also love you for that, and even for the feminine shapes that vividly make up your substance, adding to it a plural quality. You: estuary. Since I love convergences, what there is of convergence in your being must attract me. Is this, love, everything? No and I will not know clearly because I love you and I will be unable to reach all the numerous and even contradictory motives and meanings of this meeting. The deciphering, in the end, would be proof that everything—we and our steps and this hour—was exempt from existence.

The place I prefer to develop my incomplete juvenile meditations is the cistern, from where I hear the noisy work of the waves on the rock of Milagres and the sounds coming from the villa, singing, laughter, musical instruments. The premature July night is approaching and the retardatory land breeze, which blows strongly, throws dead leaves onto the zinc roof. Some light still remains of the day, the sand on the beach still shines, and over the maritime expanse a silvery reflection hovers. Here one cannot see the bottom of the cistern, and the slightly rippled water begins to exhale its green nocturnal odor, a blend of verdigris and iodine. The habit of tossing the net at the few fish, which helps me so much, during a certain period, to ascertain what I am looking for, is no longer necessary: lying on the cement, I let myself float uselessly to meet the revelations. This is how I am when, without turning, with strange and as if dislocated eyes loose above my head, I see a movement in the center of the cistern. Before I can identify the body that floats there in the diffuse light, a miniature and transparent city, the sea beats against the rocks two or three times.

℧ moves away from me. Sitting on her legs, her feet doubled up in such a way that the heels lose their color, she lifts her hands to the back of her neck and the long sleeves hang loosely, showing her arms. (Do the reflections that rise up and emerge there come from the rug, the jewels, or my desire?) She looks at me from inside, eyes of famine and fever, fathoms: preying animals on the point of leaping—elastic, happy, in the shadows—on their catch. She breathes deeply and rapidly, disordered, her loose breasts accentuating the agitation with which she sucks the air in through her nostrils and also through her mouth. Leaning her head over, she takes off the necklace and holds it in her teeth, her eyes almost hidden behind the uncombed hair. With the pearls still in her mouth and without taking her look off me, the flame of which doesn't weaken, she takes off the rings one by one. In spite of the cantata, the passage of the vehicles, and the mechanical saw active again, I can hear her gasping and the bracelets tinkling on the white fleshy arms. Free of the rings, she puts them with the necklace and lays them on the floor beside the rug. The shadows under her eyes, which I discover only then and which seem to grow more purple, enlarge her pupils.

"Abel, I love you."

I reach out my hand and stroke her knee. She takes my hand in her bare fingers—for the first time I see them without rings—raises it, and slowly kisses it. Then she lays it on the rug and, raising herself up a little (the black and abundant fleece grows larger between her thighs), takes off her dress, throws it into the center of the room, and flings her hair back with a movement of her head. I smell, as if the vial had been opened or broken, the penetrating perfume that she uses, and in the full light of the day I see the magnitude of her body, so scantily adorned, and the reflections that drink it in. The silver bracelets still remain on her wrists, she also gets rid of them, concentrated suddenly, throws them aside casually, the rings spin in various directions before they stop moving, I take off the clothing that still covers me, she leaps onto me—flying in that moment—and such is the drive of our embrace that my chest hits hers and we both give off a muffled shout together. Mouths and cries become mingled. A sound of water running under us and a thunderclap, dull.

R

Ơ and Abel: Meetings, Routes, and Revelations   **22**

The balance is undone: the Sun reappears—a nothingness—and all space, weakened, shudders. Slowly and in waves so neat that the sky seems to be dismantled, the light descends from on high, from the displaced lunar disk: countless concentric and autonomous rings, dazzling alternations of reflections and still nocturnal blues, heavy lightning, spiraled or circular, originating in the zenith, alight in the zenith. Before the first bird, alerted by the percussion of the light in the world, flies or sings, before the unanimous shout of the city reaches us, before even Ơ and I shout, before anyone shouts, I, violating a sealed space, I grasp and accept, in the revealing clarity of the looping lightning that lacerates—joining it immediately—the veil of things, restricting, I believe, my lack of knowledge, I grasp, weigh, and accept two truths tied to the essence of Ơ and of the world. In the moment when, the ephemeral simulacrum of the night beaten and destroyed, space resounds, the blue and the stars pale, a fugitive transparency annuls them, and I see the true sky—or one of the existent skies, usually inaccessible, who could know why, to our privacy. Less beautiful and comfortable than the sky of clouds, planets, and quasars—and simultaneously more disturbing—that swift and darkening phase of the eclipse uncovers a sky engraved by use, solid, recalling in color and penury, I would say even in texture, an old scratched wall or a privy door, with its designs and inscriptions. I translate nothing of what I disclose on high. The profusion of signs, visible from top to bottom, some blood red, a few in other colors, and almost all as if engraved with fire, attest to the origins of the investigations and convictions of men, always induced to divide the stellar vastness into zones, houses, mansions, quadrants, and circles, peopling it with gods, animals, and vehicles. How can one know, however, whether what I see are vestiges of the human surprise, or if the writing on the wall marks off our passage, or, yet, if the letters and figures—geometrical, fabulous, and domestic—superimposed on it were never drawn, having been there since forever, having been there until forever, the work consisting of men's seeing (with what eyes?) and marking off on the veiled surface that they contemplate some of the possible structures that sustain them and save them from the abandonment into which they are born?

Natividade, clutching the money in the pocket of her dress and trying to understand, stops in the middle of the stairs. How many times on these stairs and others, the office changes its address so many times, to redeem the boundless pawns of her dream, the barren and steep lot in the confines of the North Zone, almost half a mile from the bus lines and flooded in the rainy season? A hundred and sixty or more, yes, she doesn't know for certain, she has to see, less than two years would be lacking for the end of the purchase. Can she accept the fact that such sincere men had tricked her, selling the same plots of ground to different people? Twelve or thirteen years of words without basis! Sinners. The brothers of Judas flee, still on the way up. Buy a different lot? Time has passed, she's going on seventy and now resign yourself, crazy, don't begin anything, all urgent and brief, the day ends, recite the Credo and the Act of Contrition. The sooner the better. The officer's parents march arm in arm through the rows of cypresses. "A wonderful maid." "Never any trouble." "She deserves the family plot." The mother, obese, walks at a turtle's pace so as not to fall, moves her head with difficulty, and her myopic eyes are two anuses. The father's cane wounds the broken asphalt. Streaky, short flights of sparrows among the graves. The six soldiers, their shadows, and the shadow of the coffin. "Obedient." Natividade's voice, coming and coming, from numerous afternoons, comings, placid, voices, the smell of vinegar and the calm sound of the bobbins, blue daisies, and roses burned by the Sun, the sound of footsteps on the paths and the sky a flower with twelve petals, August to the left, February to the right, and November in front. The children are present at the passage of the burial procession, and only the look of the whore is one of hatred. Yellow earthmovers are working near the wall, trucks unload wood and iron, the voices and animal laughter of the men can be heard, the pile driver shakes noonday, and the mechanical saws hum. The Being, famished, bites his teeth with a tinkling of spurs and twists to turn, gone. Natividade raises her hands and observes, her voice sticky, her tongue half held by death's stitches: "I've already died and I'm smelling like the living. Water for everyone!" She had never believed, really, that she would come to own a piece of land. Cheated, she doesn't complain, and she ends up saying, shut up in her unventilated room, that when all's said and done that muddy and hilly plot is hers, not all of it, but a part, yes, she paid a lot for it and there's still justice in this world, someone has to come and give her what she bought, a few feet of Earth. Patience. Someone.

"Inside me or inside the night, I try to hear the answers. I don't pretend to be clean: I'm dirty and smothered, inside the intestines of a dog. It gives me anguish, of course, to recognize that the shadow of oppression infiltrates my frame and poisons it. On the other hand, this causes a kind of black joy in me. Let there be saved, from the guts, what can be saved—but with its smell of rottenness."

The gravediggers are closing up the wall of the resting place. Wall panels plumb-straight and lined up; layers level; mortar joints full: these are the three norms for the perfect laying of bricks. If they are not obeyed, one must increase the thickness of the paste between the layers and that of the dressing to set the walls properly. Looming up, in this case, is the cost of the work. The officer's wife, still withdrawn, still holding the bouquet of marigolds, her hand clutched and a little behind, as one carries a stone to throw at a dog, watches the operation, at the point of giving in, of joining the scene (the man and the old people are weeping without moving), but protesting—her lips half open—that someone must abstain from weeping for the old woman, black and worn out, buried with honors in the family tomb: "She never sat down at the table with them," yes, someone must reject the magnanimous, circumstantial, and vain game, be Natividade's body, assume her wrath, or rage in her place, not see quittance in that condescension, not fall into the deception of measuring a mode of being by the moments it is interrupted and replaced, as now, by another, ritual and passing. "Life is heavy from day to day, and this hour doesn't take anything away. Nothing. Nothing. Nothing." A fire burns Natividade's arms, burns shoulders and breasts, and her hands resist, loose, the flesh advancing through the fingernails. "I'm going to be received!" Nearby a tall cylindrical scaffolding rises up. The workmen move about in a world of tractors, compressors, planks, cement mixers, self-breathing centrifugal pumps, land levelers, buzzing saws, bricks, lime, derricks—and the Tower looms up, conical, hollow. So. With the bobbins placed properly, the threads rolled up on them cross in the order indicated on the sketch. The crossings are varied; and the number of bobbins corresponds in general to the complexity of the lacework. Then. Reduced, a little dry lime, Natividade's stomach. Thus. Liver and spleen fall apart into voracious black lizards. The lungs dissolve, damp, used paper, dirty. Well. Let's see. A serpent slips in among the blue daisies, penetrates the box, and bites—the way a dog bites a bone—the frightened, dusty heart of the dead woman. The workers stop work on the building of the Tower. Then. Being like that. After all.

They filter in, through the Son, He (who?) and his Time. Everything about him can and cannot be described. To attempt description would break everything, transcend everything, everything would be crushed and the duration of kingdoms would not suffer his discourse, flames exploding and biting themselves, rolling over things, we a reflection passed through and extinguished by swift red birds, a reflection on the wall, reflection and wall and curve fly the plotted shell reowereow the twisted word hic gives way to old syntax barrel broken hoops.

Under the same dazzling lightning flash that lays bare the celestial wall, in a glance so unifying that it and the space turned upside down by the concentric and undulating circles seem identical to me, faces of a single truth or reality uncovered, I catch the substance of ☿. She is made naked by the ephemeral transparency that subverts everything, and two superimposed beings stare at me, full of complacency or love, she and she, coinciding, one encrusted in the other, dug into the other, surrounded by motionless moths, the same person and nonetheless different persons, one external and one hidden, born and still embryonic in this one, silent within the woman who speaks, her lips half open like those of the woman who speaks, orbits within the orbits of the one who always conceals her, the breasts smaller, the hair mingled, and the same face, perhaps more radiant. Less unknowing and so modified in the course of that rapid instant, like the firmament and the city, before being immersed in the nocturnal atmosphere now soaked in a kind of livid dawn, I hear a bird moving among the branches of the tree: hearing it, I face the woman and the sky of always, bright, covering over again, under real even though truncated appearances, their secret identities. Canaries still imprecise new beams of light cross the air the morning ground barks the Sun multiplied a cock reflected on the houses crows under stones a brief hound many stars resurge ground and houses lose their intensity dissolve with the return of the Sun tree of night new curved beams—the Sun multiplied—are reflected on the stones under the tree, canaries cross the air, a cock crows morningly, a hound barks, and ground and houses, still imprecise, rise up again out of the brief night, many stars lose their intensity, dissolve with the return of the Sun, crescent still thin, the central nucleus of the dark stain along the boundary, on the pasture hill peopled with flocks, of rams and stunned oxen, the herons put out their wings, I hear indistinguishable voices of adults and children coming from nearby streets or from the bodies of ʘ, moths wounded by the passage of the heavy bird of the eclipse and by the return of the Sun struggle on the pavement and in the air around the bodies of ʘ, the tangible body and the body that, hidden like the sky of profuse images, numbers, letters, and marks, contemplates me from within herself.

Decorated with red lions and purple disks, a "K" alights on the Chá Viaduct, the hind legs turned down, forming an angle that takes in the whole extension—from the Othon Palace Hotel to the offices of the Light Company—the broad and brutal passage of concrete. The vertical bar of the letter, lying down, is balanced on the vertex of the angle as on a glass pyramid, with its movable disks and shaggy lions. The pedestrians who cross in all directions—terrified as if they had come out onto a field under crossfire—the urban knot formed by the junction of the Avenida São João with the Vale do Anhangabaú, avoiding those who are coming along in the opposite direction, passing those who block their run, jumping among cars that blow their horns and gun their motors aggressively, people from the North and other points of the world, all with spikes on their faces, shoulders, knees, and backs of the hands, don't seem to notice the "O" that is opening, flower or explosion, luminous, opposite the gray Post and Telegraph Building, reflected on the small glass square of the windows, a circular "O" and perhaps even spherical. Its decorations are the other letters of the alphabet, alone or grouped in names, some familiar, others not, and what dazzles in that vowel are the colors, varied and vivid. It goes away, in a short time, from the façade of the Post Office, rolls in the direction of the Vale do Anhangabaú, its colors are projected in the dusty air and light up the asphalt. Preceding the white lamb who crosses the iron viaduct, at a slow pace, visible through the curved and thin decorations of the railing, it is followed by the word "was," consequence of causes, advancing inwardly, the artful eye, neither this nor that, a sentence read in the mirror, a person sneaky and boom. The tangled sound of handbells and tinkle bells cuts the violent noise of the buses, the taxis, the shouts, the footsteps, the whistles, the blows, as if oxen, pack mares, and kids, loose, were galloping in the "O" that spins along, rolls without spokes, along the Anhangabaú and where I also read (it's finally time to go meet her) the name of ʘ, written with a firm hand.

E

'O and Abel: Before Paradise   **13**

The City, magnificent and already in ruins (prestigious texts promise the return of legendary submerged kingdoms), appears in the center of the cistern like a fish that could have grown and aged in secret at the bottom of this cube, exactly in the place where I am used to asking: "What am I looking for?" I pursue an unknown prey, years, I hunting in blindness. Can I, if I don't know the object of the search, come to its end? Compulsive, mindless, and with no hope at all is my search. Now, near, still immaterial in its transparency, the answer presents itself. I am looking for a city, this one, with its temples and its profane structures, some of a luxury offensive to me, halfway between obelisks and arches, on hills that separate a river or an arm of the sea. What city it is, however, I don't know, it has no name.

Without any objective, I leap to my feet and run toward the villa. What eyes are those that appear to me with the City and perceive it? An intelligent and acute vision? Twenty steps from the cistern and becoming aware of the first stars, a surprise in spite of having seen them for almost twenty years, I also see the grains the City is made of, movable like ants and uncountable, they go into the cistern and from the towers, and some of the cupolas no longer point at the zinc sky (voices of my brothers and sisters and the sounds of their instruments, the wind moves the foliage of the mango trees and their dead leaves), I stop my unmotivated course. The shadows growing denser in the water and on the cracked cement: and the City floating in the center of the enclosure, anachronistic, with its enameled squares, circular and no larger than finger rings. The sensuality of those building it is shown in every groin in the wall. Thus, the fortifications, an expression of military pride and brutality, seem to be born from foreign hands. Those solid walls are easily breached, they pull down the turrets, the towers, the battlements, but the private buildings and temples go too, melting like salt is the statue of the boy whose father or tutor seems to be offering him the world in a broad gesture, the whole City sinks into silence, the City dissolves into nothing, and its plunge into the cistern doesn't disturb the calm surface of the water at all, in silence the City ceases to exist and doesn't tell me its Name. The vision is dissolved, yes, it doesn't reveal its Name to me, yes, but the search of six or seven years is at last defined, I finally know what I must search for and contemplate, it being indispensable that I attempt it. Go, Abel, seek the City: that is your obligation.

The snakes flee into the midday heat in the thickness of the cane fields. The wandering shadows of the clouds break away across the countryside in my direction, cover me, and go away, the dreamed-of meeting is arranged and arranged again, the City comes to meet the man who—having tracked it like a madman through many countries—admits his lack of success and abandons the search. His route, in an east-west direction, is perpendicular to the direction of the wind, which carries the clouds toward the south.

We roll, embracing and laughing, on the long rug, the ram observes us, one of us hits a flank against the table in the middle, the table falls along with the silver teapot, aggravating the disorder that our desire is imposing, she runs her hands over my body and in a flash grabs my testicles as if she were fearful they would flee, squeezes them without precaution, sinks her teeth into my right shoulder, the perforating pains go through me and cross and her nakedness illuminates those vehement acts. The air she expels between her incisors scalds my breastbone, while (gestures of one who struggles with lute or lyre) she runs the tips of her fingers over my sex, from the base of the glans, lifting them rhythmically, above the real level of the glans. She models an imaginary stem, very long—besides tender—and the end of the stem opens into an umbrella. The scalding air of her mouth goes through my stomach, a sphere enwraps us, she kisses the knotty stem, voices run through the stem, the stem grows and the umbrella that her hand models is released, opens and opens and opens, great parasol, sudden and magical flower where voices—like birds—live. Two or three marks punctuate the uniform whiteness of her back, turning it— it is not known why—more delectable. Others arise, agitated, the flesh absorbs them: larger, they reappear in the small of the back. She explores with penetrating nails the region around my sex, seeks the obscure root of the force that raises it, kisses it, kisses it voraciously, and her hair drags over it. The balls weigh like stones and the stones burn me, eggs of fire, I open my arms in a cross, I cry out or I think I cry out her name—and the rug receives me among birds and flowers, a shot. The vision flashes in me—a shot—and deafens me, I under the umbrella on its stem, at my feet a motionless river, and ☿ from the other side, naked and severe, I, she, and the umbrella that covers me (and still the motionless river) covered by a tree of nine immense branches, tree of trees, the branches, nine, like walks and paths, uncountable signs interwoven without order, the signs, in the naked body on the other side of the river, so visible that I can well take them for shadows and braids of the flowers, of the fruit, of the foliage on the nine huge branches. That illegible net, however, constitutes her body, the same body and another, and I shouldn't believe that one is projected over the others. She: carnal and also verbal entity. Motionless, like the river whose banks, naked, we mark off, it is the clear hour, without cares, that is part of this world, seen—a flash—and then lost: a shot.

A thunderclap vibrates, distant, in the sky with few clouds and pale. Without interrupting his pace, less rapid than the muffled rhythm of drums on the racetrack, Olavo Hayano turns with difficulty the head that is constrained by its not-too-flexible neck. Unhurriedly he opens the door of the Chrysler and seems to evaluate the beating of the drums before starting the motor. In a straight line he slowly crosses the courtyard paved with irregular stones, the lowest branches of the plane trees brush the roof of the car. The sentries present arms and he continues on facing frontward, the thick hands holding the wheel firmly. Hayano, the Bearer. Sullen and fearsome.

Who is holding the sheet against the wall of the room? The answer is probably irrelevant, what does it matter, after all, if that dream sheet is suspended like a cloud or if it is being raised by the hands of dead people?—but if I know who holds it I will also know why it is here and what it means. Its multiple and snarled smell of sedge, sandalwood, cedar, glycerine, mint, fresh roses is mixed with the perfume with which the scarf and its lizards are impregnated. I want to escape the spell and, dreaming yet conscious that I am dreaming, I struggle to wake up. Can we be sleeping under the earth, perhaps? Underneath ourselves? I rise up out of sleep, out of the depths of sleep, slowly and arduously, I rise up, sleep squeezes me and I conquer it—and suddenly, hands on my stomach, in the same position and circumstances of sleep, I see that I am free. Free? The extinguished globe, a halo marking the center of the varnished casing, sounds in the street, steps on the stairs, visible in the penumbra the upper part of the walls, the perfume, smell of mint, sandalwood—and the sheet hanging over the oil paint, the sheet, not closed into the limits of the dream. I hear, awake, cloth being torn: the sluggish tearing of cloth, the singing tearing of velvet, the tense tearing of silk, canvas (a rasping, grave sound).

A V A L O V A R A

E
O and Abel: Before Paradise 14

She goes away from me, the feet almost those of a child and seeming insufficient for the body, vast, with something watery and wavy, she goes away touching the designs on the rug with the tips of her toes, her shoulders thrown back and the long hands restless beside her hips, I discover, with a sharpened look, one more secret enchantment, the dimples of the elbows, they're six or seven steps, but she does them with minute care, there's a waving of flags, something triumphal in the way she carries her body, each step is balanced on the previous step and determines the next one, and she still moves her arms back and forth in that dance. She stops beside the phonograph, her left heel slightly raised, the buttocks trembling with every movement of the body, an immense white roundness and, glistening with sweat now, absorbing the diffuse reflections more intensely. Curved over the record, her sex stands out a bit between her thighs, purple and damp on the point of foaming. A warm wind invades the room and the dahlias tremble on the table, the pendants on the chandeliers tinkle, the ram moves, the great pendulum comes and goes, the Bearer enters his home, silence, he replaces the telephone on its hook, goes through the dressers, opens his wife's closet, stockings and dresses thrown on the bed, open perfume bottles, he replaces the glass stoppers in the necks of the bottles, goes to the study and pulls out a drawer of his desk, a strong horse smell fills the air.

The process of events is long and some signs foretell them. Events come like a marine monster that ascends from the abyss and before he shows his head the waters rise, strange and foamy, the monster struggles and turns them about. Although I don't see the City, I enter into an orbit that is not very natural. Turned away by a kind of current that, separative, slips in between them and me, my few companions draw away. Do they call me or do they lie dozing? I don't hear their voices and I lie down myself. The shadow of the cashew tree, when the clouds pass, becomes deeper, takes on the look of a riverbank.

Hands held up, I hold the breasts that hang over me, and I pass my face over the pubis, kneeling; she, standing still, fondles my head and presses it at times, uncontained, against the soft hairs like a curly head of hair, where I breathe in an afternoon hotter and more echoing with perfumes than this November one, a damp hidden wood, with carnivorous flowers open in the shadows. (This desire that you discharge in your direction and whose springs rest on so many strange points of my body—resembling the impulse that leads, imperiously, males on top of females and multiplies the voices—some distinctions make it uncommon. Right? Or, on the contrary, must I locate those distinctions in you, object and target of my desire, being uncommon in the proportion that you yourself stand out from yourself?) I run my head on the fleshy parts of her stomach, I model the haunches as powerful as those of a horse—but with the resistance of cotton—I join the tips of the fingers on the column and I lower them slowly accompanying the line of the vertebrae with the fingernails as if trying to open her body, separate the two halves, I thrust my fingers into the hot junction of the buttocks, she opens her knees and her hands grab my hair violently, I bite the center of her body. (I attack in the direction of her stomach, without possible retreat: blind fascinated animal, I convert my claws into fingers of wool. Knowing you in the flesh, however, seems to make more and more unfold in consequences that intensify this adventure.) I bite and suck the center of her body, she repeats my name half reprehensive and half dazzled, the voice rises and dies in a whisper, her hands don't stop, the melodious and harsh cantata, incongruous shouting in her body, the ram runs, the metal bell, a bird cries out in the room and struggles, the explosion of wings, the gale, I love you, the Bearer hefts some bullets in his thick hand, the dull glow of the hammer and the steel, blues and coppers.

I stare at the impenetrable surface of the sheet as if facing an unknown animal armed with claws—and I try to free myself of the persistent vision in sleep. I doze and find again, unaltered, those two yards of brabant trimmed on the edges, which pass along, with everything that surrounds me and locates me, from dream to a state of wakefulness. (Joining you, whom I love and desire, I also join myself finally to the certain ambiguous unattainable vision, vacillating between coming and going; and I regain, since she subsists in your body, the fragile girlfriend—boyfriend, I could also say—who rises up, among old hats, faded gloves, and old necklaces pulled out of the bottom of drawers, the only enchanted and really happy period of my life.) I find again my hybrid dream, increased now by the multiple sounds of torn cloth and a fever that eats at me. I elude myself, trying to expel the fever from my body by an effort of will. The fever grows and I feel my heart exploding, the blood bursting into flames. I shout, the fever punishes me, my eyes fixed on the sheet that then seems to take on a meaning, even if I see nothing, on it, in the images or letters that its virginal and motionless surface seems to announce or await. I suffer, alone, without any possible help—I am under lock and key and I don't dare move— and only from my fever-battered body do I expect help. Still the rapid wrathful tearing, kerchiefs, covers, clothes.

Both standing and turned in the direction of the table, we, glued to the back of whom, passing for integral, is designated as female, the breast of whom, knowing it to be incomplete, passes for male, we, bicephalic, both right legs erect, the left ones slightly bent, in a way to leave the balls free, which the hand with polished nails and without any rings at all, turned backward, feels (do those bird's eggs belong to him?) while the other strokes its own breast, the other breast given over to the rougher hand, the right one, which imitates, on the turgid mammary, the movements executed by the left hand on the pulsating and dilated head of the member, held between the wet groins and seeming to come out from within the vagina, we, male-female, the heads side by side and turned in the same direction, one curved to the left in the manner of a dog who is going to bite his tail and in truth is giving his tongue to be bitten, my breasts, my balls, my double sex. What for me is lacking for us? (Still mixed in with the desire, manifest in what you now hold softly between your cold and impatient fingers, is the ambition to reveal or liberate that silent woman whom you resemble, whose voice seems to vibrate with a crude timbre in certain phrases of yours and whose look, even when you pale, close your eyes, remains fixed on me.)

Our feet are lighter on the floor, my pubis chewed by her buttocks, I encircle her, bite the back of her neck, her left breast in my right hand and the other breast making the other hand happy, the air heavy and the afternoon less luminous, she opens her legs and draws her feet back, twines them about my ankles, curves and I curve over her, with ten fingers she grasps the scrotum and staff that stands out in front of her, leaning along the slippery slot, anointed by the honey that the insides, afire, secrete over it and at times expel in violent jets, we float, the four feet in the air, she twists and our mouths come together, avid, her hair hangs down and flies, we go along without laws along the walls, we pass before the yellow faces of the photographs, we flutter over the dahlias, we brush against one of the chandeliers, our imprecise reflection before the glass of the clock, the winged and two-headed being, four-thirty-three, my woman's breasts and her man's member, we occupy a sphere of whims and decipherings, the machines surround us, the voices and the miasmas of the city, the Bearer, we alight on the ordered wool of the rug.

N
♂ *and Abel: Paradise*   1

On the shoulder blades, the small of the back, pleasure is formed; the last, in the pith of the eyes, is the pleasure that rises up, a clearing; the muscles of the buttocks, closed like a knot, grasp pleasure; the ears deaf to insignificant voices and noises hear only pleasure growing; between one stomach and the other pleasure insinuates itself; the mouths call pleasure and all things they scan between the closed jawbones are names of pleasure; the tips of the nails—the feet, the hands—the thickness of the blood, the marrow of the bones; the flower of pleasure descends along the column and opens in the flanks: poppy.

E
♂ *and Abel: Before Paradis*   15

We alight on the rug, I behind me and with my back to me, the double being, closed circle, mouth and mouth, double-faced, four legs, four diligent and permutable hands. The external clarity fades; the whole room, with its objects, resists the decline—premature and unlikely—each surface stands out and throbs, emitting a dull light. The dahlias flame in their yellows—dahlias or sunflowers?—the faces on the portraits on the walls and the creases in their clothing loom up, palpable, the grimy damasks and plush, the lacquer, the silver vases, the glass doorknobs, the jewels scattered on the floor tend toward a gleam of varnish, and, more than anything, the half-faded colors of the rug, its vegetation, the herons, the hares.

Is what in ʘ's flesh clamors to be freed—the tension of an imprisoned spring, controlled anxiety, latent explosion in the neuter appearance of the bomb—its beauty on another plane, more purified? She escapes from my arms and sits on my legs, half-leaning on the long agile ringless fingers, facing me, a replica, on another plane, of the intimate luminosity that vibrates in everything. The narrow forehead doesn't look higher, the arch of the eyebrows, yes, reveals a certain fright, and the eyes stare at me with an almost unsupportable glow through the thick lashes, but the nose is the same, straight and pointed, only more distended and with the nostrils puffed out, no alteration in the contours of the lips, open as if the air were never sufficient for them, it's whiter, perhaps—or more luminous?—and if I find the dazzling curls of the hair more compact, where gold and steel are merged, it must be because they're loose, undone, in disorder, damp threads flowing down the depression between the breasts. Alterations on the curves of the waist and the overflowing hips, in the volume of the breasts, in the tilt of the arms, in the thickness of the thighs? None. Yet, grandiose, her face insubmissive, half hidden in the mass of her hair, the hands lightly touching the rug, she is the same and another, she transformed and intensified, existing between the woman who enters the still dark room and this one, breathing rapidly and glowing with sweat, the distance that exists between a dull knife and the same knife honed: her beauty now has the edge of a razor.

The absolute isolation in which I see myself under the perpendicular Sun is the first announcement of the prodigy. A hawk flies quite high, flies above the clouds, the left arm keeping me at a distance, birds—some of which I identify—sing, hidden, under the damp hairs, hidden, her intent sex, a pair of canaries alights on the cashew tree and flees, discreet spasms in the straight knees, a buzzing in the axles, an uncertain and endless note, the wheels, an oxcart, the left hand gives way and the right continues hanging, protective. Bees and flies: their buzzing. She breathes the air in deeply and raises her knees, her tiny feet slip along the rug. Reflecting the wind that stirs the high clouds, a surface wind comes from the distant hills, making the stalks in the cane field wave, and reaches me, smelling of washed clothes. Among the hills, black, a plantation smokestack stands out—and this, with the sound of the cart, is all that exists of human presence. A shout still rises up, but it could just as well have come from a terrified child as from some bird unknown to me. Acute, that shout, distant— "Raah!"—single.

She extends her hand and draws it back when I try to grasp it, cat's play, the two breasts sway, the tips more and more lance-tipped, as the arm pulls, long and agile, finally I initiate the assault or she lets herself be grabbed, I pull her and go on top of her, the unknown bird calls out, suffocated laughs and moans, her tiny feet in the air, she sinks her nails into my back, her ardent cunt licks my damp palm, she holds my wrist with both hands, a low and ugly growl as if kicked in the stomach, she beats herself deep between the legs with my fist, biting her lips to the point of bleeding (words in her neck? her throat?), she softens and moves away from me, throws me aside and abandons herself, a wrinkle between closed eyelids, the red sockets, the hair spread over the exuberant and pacific representation of Eden, a species of a solemn and vaguely terrifying beauty—her steely knife edges— pale patches on her face, the motionless breast, the right hand over her sex as if it were warming itself on it (does the heart beat?), the lips the color of wax, the left arm, raised a little, keeps me at a distance. The faded images of the photographs grow in that kind of vacuum and abandon the frames in the direction of the living room.

Awakening, I tear myself away from the fever and the nightmare sheet: here I am, awake, but my heart still pounds, the invisible fabrics continue to be torn (I hear them, I hear them) as if predatory beings were dividing up the room, they tear without pause, sacks, pillowcases, veils, rend the air and the little light coming from the corridor, they tear everything but don't tear the sheet, sinister against the wall, immune to the alternation between wakefulness and sleep. The Bearer hefts the clip of the pistol in his fugitive palm, the seven lateral furrows attesting to the presence of the projectiles. I doze and I wake up and I doze, and between the two states, as if both were one, I debate, dragging real elements into the dream and bringing from it, lost, with its varied rural and domestic smells, the image of the sheet, a familiar neutral piece made indecipherable and threatening by the insistence with which—vision or dream—it imposes itself. The parlors and the bedrooms, with the presence of the Bearer, remain even more empty, there is a faucet dripping and this rhythmic sound increases. The piece of brabant, unaltered, crosses through wakefulness and dream, until someone turns out the hall light and it, in a little while, wears out (grows old?), dissipates—and also the sound of cloth being torn—disappears in a little while, so subtly that I don't know for certain when I cease seeing them. The Bearer, with a crisp and practiced shove, puts the clip into the rough butt; he puts the weapon into the leather holster. A fly, drunk perhaps on the horse smell, buzzes in the room, heavy.

The low wind blows and the stalks in the cane field also planted in me rub against each other, green, the edges like those of a razor. The solitude, at this time of day, and the open sky, or, which is also possible, the spell of the City, coming ahead of the City, little by little shades and confuses my limits. I breathe in the cicadas and the birds through my nose and mouth. Then only the cicadas: the birds fall silent or leave. My eyes descend from their sockets and come together in my throat. The cicadas' songs open up, peacock tails, five or six, perched at random, I look for the point of intersection among the sounds (that's where the balance is and, with the balance, the merged vision, a peacock of peacocks), I look for that point, and when I find or think I find the center of the polygon, the wind falls, the cicadas become silent, and in the center (or in me, since I have blended with the center) a calf lows. I rise up on my elbow. The shadow of the last cloud slowly drags along in the direction of the valley, turns the motionless stalks of the cane field blue, climbs up the slope of my feet, covers me, passes. The sky, in the sultriness of noon, pale and, in my sight, still farther away, seems on the point of breaking—a tense surface. I see then, at the point where the Sun is born, far away, a brief black spot, mobile and sparkling, gliding along with a sure destination.

A bird of great bearing, the black-winged spot glowing, having risen up on the horizon? Absurd. Not even this light made from ground lenses would approximate it. What body is this one, then, brilliant, flying in silence? No bird, even if it had the size of an ox and the framework of a roof, would be visible at such a distance. The Sun beats down flat upon the countryside: not a shadow of a hawk. New spots, several, more compact now, fly nimbly and, being many, impose themselves, even that way, like a whole: in those distant objects, which, no matter how swift, oscillate, I see a single being, still fragmentary, a fleet from other worlds, a warlike formation, pieces of a framework, letters of a name. This.

Moving in the direction of the vertical line that divides it, I contemplate the clear body and its splendor. She raises her arms lazily, lets them fall onto her head, and opens her heavy eyes, looks in no direction, vague, her raised knees move slightly and somewhat ungoverned, the milky flesh of the thighs wavering. The flanks, resting on the rug, enlarge, make that arch more willing and inviting.

E

Ọ and Abel: Before Paradise 16

I bend over and I kiss the rounded toes, the arched breast of the feet with their subtle veins, two lambs stand beside us, she docilely enlarges the space between her knees and begins to speak, her arms loose, her head restless, discordant and tumultuous voices pass each other, an impatient clamor, she opens her thighs and revealed is the access, the entrance, the way, the hiding place, the "N," the center, emerging among whitenesses and black, the ruddy beak and the multiple violet folds, a strong smell of wine saturates the air, a smell of fresh roses and burnt horn, the frothy slot is lost in the shadows, a masculine torso steals away among the trees in the rug, once more the bird calls out, my tongue is heavy, I go forward, the notions of opening, of entry, and of knowledge meld into the act of advancing, slowly descending over her, the luminous arms reach out to me, a voice among the voices implores with delight and authority "Come! Come!"—a shout—the lambs give out the bellow of an ox in the slaughterhouse, the face glows among the hairs with an inhuman and violent beauty, she digs her nails into my flank, raises the basin greedily, raises it, plunges me deep into herself.

I make myself for her body, penetrating deeper and deeper, the potent voice of the singers, the gesture of the Bearer, the belt and the holster hook, translucid sepia shapes breathe outside the frames, the bird and the cry ("Raah!"), the clock, the rhythm, the City flight noonday light, deeper and deeper the plunge, blind? No. Revelations.

The flying pieces move along over the valley, more brilliant as they move along, and suddenly I can see how different the forms are—natural or mechanical—destined for transit in the air. They fly in silence and without wings and have nothing organic or mechanical about them, they resemble a circus in pieces, uprooted along with poles and canvas, everything—reddish rugs, acrobats' brilliant costumes, parts of the bleachers, elephants—brought by a wind preceded by the calm. Let the wind that brings them bear these shapeless beings far from me! They change direction and seem to turn off toward the south. I can state, at that time, that I desire them more than I fear them. The curvature is corrected, and in the formation there is an appearance of disorder, an imbalance immediately overcome. The great irregular birds open up in a fan, grow in quantity, in swiftness, in brilliance, the Sun in its zenith and space blinding—as if crossed by particles of iron: filings—but the air is inflamed and another day, sun-laden, infiltrates the noonday light and blinds me.

She and she, you, the access, oh magical body, oh glory and privilege of the crossing, in all crossed reflected opposite surfaces into which phallus and Abel sink, space of voices and voices and voices and voices, multiple multiple mouths, our tongues a tie, the air breathed out and its acid and hot smell, open jasmines Sun noontime, another sex hidden in her sex chews the astonished glans, the rhythm of the clock, Julius the conjugated skills of sound, a child and a dog could fit in the wooden casing, Heckethorn, light winds rug wood festive song of birds, my name is uttered in some point, of the bodies?—my name a center?—the Bearer and the quick lightning flash over the buildings, she shouts my name takes my face, excited and energetic, the nose sharper and the lips inflated and sprightly ruddy flame the tongue and the four eyes open, crosses me and irrigates me, Abel, see how I receive you and my flesh regales you, oh, nevermore slander nevermore offense nevermore the solitary body nevermore, come and cross me in triumph with your flowered staff, I belong to you without norms and without requirements and I open to your entry everything I am and I possess, I-love-you-I-love-you-I-love-you-I-love-you, the lambs and their bells, the unbearable cutting edges of your face, I contemplate it and I kiss the aureoles, the peaches larger and darker, sweet, tender, ripe, my head curves between the breasts, the suction, the kisses, the skin bruised between the lips and the quick furtive signs that appear on the taut beaks, a rapid multiplication as if lanterns born in her body, magical, illuminating her (reflections? emblems? insects? glass beads?), weak lamps covered in her body, the acidulous cry of the bird, the signs flower and ferment, alive, the signs, another body in her body, fight and devour each other, nothing pleasant or placid or to be domesticated, a changing and grunting swarm, with its force of teeth and its fire of flint struck by steel, undisciplined combat, she hidden in herself, she and she, the wind and its movement, fire meteor crosses me Abel triumphal chariot a Sun high on the top of his staff, high, making happy the center of my being, the left elbow up and the hand at the small of the back strokes the silk sole of her foot, her polished heel, she raises her leg higher in the direction of the chandelier, wraps her feet around my back, and our mutual look, affectionate, is also serious and intent, each face an inscription, the fate or the opportunity of the other, the key, the verdict, the alternative, the playing card, the star, the luck.

The worst about amazing things is that they subjugate us, dragging us along by their laws and nature—and thus our fright, in the face of a new phenomenon, never goes beyond the usual limits: magic and monsters, after all, belong to our world and only he who does not enter it is really dreadful. Confused and feeling the floor wobble under my feet, I raise my hands to my face and for three times I try to see, and my sight clears up. Huge bodies, light as clouds, as swift as birds, compact, slip among each other and approach the valley, with no noise whatever and without the cashew tree and the cane moving; the world static. The shadows dance in the landscape—as broad as pastures, flood plains, herds of oxen—and the first bodies descend or sink, towers and gardens, stairways, statues, porticoes, a city, the City announced one day, sought, whose finding obsesses me, and finally is revealed, ordered, assumes, violating space and time, a particular form of existence and relieves me of the aim of the search: in the light of midday, I discern it.

The storm forming at the open window darkening the living room cars passing croaking of horns your hair wrapped around the branches in the rug seem to have grown the Bearer presses his ears with his hands opens the door goes down the stairs the emptiness around him and the two rams climb up onto the couch the march of the hands on the clock four-fifty-four the march of the sound mechanism the flash the explosion another explosion another explosion brief pause the thunder and still another explosion vibrate the panes of glass in the window casements your beauty a roar on your face the mechanical saw hydraulic blows slamming of a door exclamations kisses dizziness the sound of your sex of oranges sucked or squeezed the door of the Chrysler opens the shapes of the portraits interposed between us and the walls their naphthalene mint dust smell vague yellow spots on the 1910 hats on the veils on the lace on the boots a flash in the room their pale specters coming in a cloudburst drops blown by the wind wet the floor she raises her haunches pounds on my back imploring bites my mouth.

The discoloration of the lightning flashes movements of the walls and the shadows the frightened faces of the figure that people the living room alive the same as those in the photographs the slashing movement expands and the contracted stomach broadens a waving of the flanks and the buttocks higher in my sex the ring the other sex the sex shrewdly hidden and constrictive I dig force and power from my insignia I dig deep firm and deep as much as I can I look for a center a target a gate I am this insignia and I look for her agitated hair on my right arm and my left hand firm on the handle a passageway dragging it to me protecting it from a blow her head that of a tortured being and sounds of wings of flights near in her disheveled hair braided with knots her tongue kisses like a lizard's tail (the sibilant mobile double insatiable tongue, the blowing velvety tongue hot agile smell of varnish taste of almonds smell of mornings taste of spittle smell of kegs taste of bread smell of burnt cloth taste of milk the tongue: dances in my mouth) I dig in search of the central "Raah!" the Bearer the rain the smell of horse sidewalks invaded mud-colored water and in the room the children of the portraits ruffs sailor sepia the laced dresses silk bows at hip level your portage your portico your port behold the crossing is over and words invade me at first in a tumult a harsh and silent horde breaks out in me in me and my flesh knows it knows and suffers the presence of those mica-sheet insects quick blade of lightning the words run between us and with them chaos confusion clamor the dehorned rams ruddy ribbons bells the rams among the blooming sunflowers that hang petals gold the rain roars heavily.

E

♂ and Abel: Before Paradise   17

The City stretches out along the landscape, dominated by a white round temple and girded by a triple wall with defensive devices—turrets and battlements. When it goes away, will I not be an old man, this cane field having been cut many times by the scythes of the field workers? The elevations that flank it (on one of which I recognize a cemetery surrounded by erect cypresses), were they here or not before its coming? Does its true north correspond to mine? Torn out of the world, it has something of a simulated island about it, without water around, a territory surrounded by ruins, the limits wiped out by fantastic earth-leveling machines. Ample is the gesture of the colossus who indicates the horizon to a boy, and such obvious pride shows through on his face that I believe I can see the reflection of the sea in it and of many ships with valuable cargoes, but, in truth, I have guarantees that the City is a port—and yet I will not know if the waters that divide it and that reflect the same Sun which burns me are an arm of the sea or some motionless river, also coming through the air with its illusory bed. Another unknown quantity, full of irradiations, surrounds the event, the City comes to me and shows itself, with this the search ends but another begins, for the City appears to me to have no name (the hunter downs a nameless animal), I must, then, seek the name of the City or its equivalent, a kind of metaphor, which, concise, will express a real being and its evolution and the ways that cross in it, capable of remaining when such being and its roads don't exist. This darkness in what refers to the surroundings of the City and its name is opposed to what I know (up to what point and through the intervention of what indications?) with respect to what lies under its debatable foundations. Under the City there are others, the City exists on the bones of twelve other cities swept away by time or other scourges, I know that these cities are its pride and that the water of the cisterns, in the City, have a specific and even disquieting taste, a taste of admonition and threat. The name or metaphor of the name, like the City, must rest on the twelve buried cities.

Crossings and exchanges my tongue in my ear being the bird in the tree a breast and an arm raised her mouth shouts in my femur and the heart that beats in the throat (mine? hers?) belongs to some animal. The hands detaching our stomachs advancing in the direction of the oranges being squeezed the two hands closed over the phallus—Abel, I you—beloved—the stiffness of your—this pleasure—the pulsing of the blood—I and—oh! prodigious inflamed axis—let—yes, I thank you for—how is it possible—you don't—the breast—my love—nothing between me and the—between me and. Olavo Hayano, the Bearer, looks through the windshield the rain falls a flash of lightning looks at the wristwatch four-fifty-five hazy shapes on the sidewalks the vehicles wet the necklace the bracelets on the rug the earrings the rings wires and poles against the sky the color of raw leather black scaffolding and deserted lighted windows TV antennas and lightning rods red reflections of taillights in the downpour pavement stones torn out by the water the windows of the car closed he turns on the ignition opens a path between the buses the automobiles that advance slowly through the storm. Motionless I and she motionless sudden silence her thighs slip along my hips and her feet slowly alight on the floor.

Studded with towers and itself being the capital—or even the frieze and architrave—of a vast buried column whose pedestal and verge are made up by the twelve other cities, the City, with a topography as full of motion as the landscape of the Northeast over which, ephemeral, it descends and alights, with soft depressions between rounded hillocks, displays its eminence in everything: in the twenty-nine gates in the walls and in the splendor of the other constructions. Even the moats between the three walls, shaded strips where lemon, banana, and orange trees in bloom alternate, bear witness to plenty and pleasure in life. Certain groups—the white marble temple, the Hippodrome, with statues of chariots and horses, the Arsenal and a square palace, broader than all, in the center of a green esplanade—almost blot out the other domes and towers, the clean reservoirs, and the streets paved with stones. In them one reaches the high point of the sumptuousness shown in the material of the obelisks, the vegetable and zoomorphic motifs of the carved porticoes and façades, in the sea-green faïence roofs where the Sun is reflected.

Successive gusts of wind, quick blows, agitate the chandeliers, the dahlias, the indecisive sunflowers that open in the air, and the branches in the rug tremble under our bodies peacefully joined together. The storm, vigorous, simulates nightfall, compact shadows under the furniture, the cottony penumbra, and the spectators coming out of the portraits. Constant lightning, cerulean, nervous, and its light, as if plated, cuts the space before the thunder grows silent, threatens the joints between things, lights up the glass pendants silver pitchers accessories on the floor green hoops of the dress, it passes through the sepia faces scattered around the living room sucks in the sunflowers. Everything, when the lightning has passed, is ash and extinct fire, everything that is not her body: in it—a gift, a state, a boon—endures this precious glow, and beams of light throb in the thickness of the flesh. The hair poured out in a fan, the restless tongue in the dry mouth, and the outline of the face immersed among absolute peace, ecstasy, the solved enigma, and jubilation without fear, she keeps her fingertips on my face, gathers my face in point by point, incorporates it into I don't know what garret of her knowledge, and caresses me, erratic lack of skill, the torso, the flank, the curled hairs of the pubis mingled with hers, big-bellied. The firm trunk over the left side, with my right hand I pretend to outline (dare I touch it?) the radiant and as if forbidden face, out of my reach, sacred. Planted in her sex, I feel, without moving, each fold of the walls and its temperature, that of the innards of a still-living ox, she doesn't move and she looks at me from inside, pupils streaked with purple, neither of us moves, she or I, what moves, however, is that throat and cut, it compresses the sensitive member—and another lesser cut, a narrower throat, more feverish, tries to swallow the glans. The gears of sound get ready in the moving shadows of the clock: four minutes are left before five o'clock, the dice are in the air.

Over the splendor and harmony of the City a somber note weighs. In its dazzling richness the City has something of a rotting and perfumed corpse about it. In addition, the absence of animals—existent only in carvings, mosaics, and sculptures—and also of movement, even the branches and flowers are as if petrified, this and the erosion around the City, separating it from the roads and making it impassable to the approach of men, with their detritus and disorder, that monstrous isolation which the three lines of walls, each one three yards thick, reinforce and express, confers on the radiant agglomeration of towers, balusters, façades, and orchards a kind of muteness or insanity. The City: tortoise without a head.

Ebbing and flowing of the signs ebbing and flowing of the voices mortal combat of the signs the claws the mutilations I see her and the carnal being to whom I am joined grants me access to her mystery and somewhat difficult and precious a second reality contiguous to the one that clumsily—habit, habit—we manipulate behold then her meaning and her strength she keeps in herself what names the world the rising up the evolving the ending her flesh is also a resting place there lie words lie and are slashed wrathful brutal virulent the impetus of a stone thrown into the eye (lie? or are formed? or are sheltered?) there they are and that's why the body that I know which on more than one level and plane I know and which luxuriant copious pleasurable imitates the pleasurable copious luxuriant world of the garden with it almost mingling (fleshy curve of the shoulder with the mark of my teeth) that's why the body but which of the two? and can't there be others perhaps? the body hers is a mirror of the world channel of things arcanum of the namable that's why in it it is possible to contemplate

with insubmissive eye the consummated the effective the hoped-for
the feared pendulum clock two and a half minutes to five soft sepia
faces hats bird wings curled hair sunflowers shirtfronts canes corsets
open sunflowers I love you you I love it is you I love you whom I love
beloved I bite my jaw I bite closer and closer to the mouth teeth
against teeth muffled hoarse the moan the hidden ring and beyond the
ring in the secret of the flesh thin spider legs touch the phallus its
ankles brush the hollows of my knees its nails my buttocks it drags me
deep regular blows direction spiders (snowy cavity of armpit, shadow
of shaved hair) it sings invisible in her in me behind the sunflowers or
hidden in the eternal branches of the rug a bird and slowly she invades
me and is in me and shapes that I recognize and love show themselves
blended in our bodies presences pulsate pass voices the now runs between banks and we ourselves are there entwined we enunciated or
passive of enunciation we and what we provoke we and what we fabri-
cate we and what we ask we and what we witness we and what we
both swallow what we both hate what we both scan what we both love
dream desire what we both.

N
Ʊ and Abel: Paradise   2

We cross between each other, we go from me to me I I we I I from
me to me, loop and figure eight, mouth and mouth, we cross and are,
the sphere circumscribes us and we ourselves a sphere, mouth and
mouth (whose?) thighs arms knees ass ears (whose?) member throat
dewy vaginas pleasure taking shape burning balls hair ohs. Convulsed
arabesque lightning slow rolling of thunder thunderous thunder cart-
loads of heaped stone spilled over wooden ballast an explosion throws
them into the air the room trembles crystal chandeliers sparkle panes
casements molding clouds of rain whipped buildings lightning rods
TV antennas. Cold sepia faces identical positions those of the photographs, deer with dog teeth cover in our bodies sheep with lion heads,
youthful groups straw hats lacework children ruffs sailor, green and
red butterflies, hair eyes hands sepia color silent groups fill the room
some more visible others dim all concrete tangible, the lambs stroll,

lightning brightens round sunflowers among the sepia figures sunflowers on her breasts and shoulders and heads, in the room a bird
made of birds flies reddish beak diadems and as if decorated in silks
bows flowers the bird of jubilation of glory of meeting of pity and its
name is clear a Sun a day. The minute hand almost vertical XII the
toothed wheels execute the project of the obscure fabricant fascinated
by carillons by the confluence of factors by the precise and vulnerable
order of the universe, vehemence of the embrace hair loose glans in V
luminous teeth (names of cities and cities with fish birds insects quadrupeds no human shadow) pleasure comes with a gust that is benign
and fearful in its intensity, I under and over, two and one, I am and we
are ("Raah!"), the Bearer the rain undulates with the wind awnings
flapping damp pavement Avenida Angélica the black umbrella the
more distant buildings like muffled sounds lots of water trash in the
stream the tormented trees Olavo Hayano the Agent the Key the
Emissary, mud on the creaking boots, branches and flowers on the rug,
the rain heavier the living room less shadowy tires on the damp asphalt oh Abel dawn me come through the glass wake the birds come
dawn me oh (we the tree the square the dark Sun platbands truck the
carved sky white moths) rusty pieces squeak in the unpolished air
"Raah!" The deplorable solitude of the City, first step in the revelation—not complete, of course—of its nature, it soaks in that of melancholy and yet its orchards are full of wild beasts now. Innocent weight
of scrotums pleasurable weight soft ankles on my back the prodigal
staff opens me the prodigal staff unites me I pound on the floor with
my fists suctions and shouts nails wound me she bites my shoulder
(strong waves against the rocks of Milagres red flowers of the flam-
boyants in the square of the window and roars of lions prowling
about the roofs of the houses) your face the flowers opening your face
the days rising up the joys coming and secret lanterns revealing in
your carnal face the luminous face of words. Olavo Hayano at the entrance to the building polychrome tiles with a hunting scene the lambs
bleat terrified and spin Hayano the Conductor the sphere the Garden
still impenetrable circumspect rigid figures half devoured by moths
their mournful odor of flowers and gloves kept in traveling bags (the
indistinct colors of the hairs on the flanks loving flesh haughty breasts
graceful hips intoxicating fragrance of the pubis the outstanding
phallus the proud buttocks of daisies camellias and lilies the wise
tongue the excellent double slot) oh body verbal and resonant and
proliferating behold that supposing I invade you I am invaded by you

the bird of birds frees itself in ever greater and higher circles brushing
sheets of steel the sheets spin slowly the bird flies through heavy
clouds wounded by lightning a little before five premature complete
on the rainy oppressed November afternoon the wet umbrella on the
left arm of the Agent he ignores the elevator bounds up the marble
stairs mud on his soles. I contemplate the City, radiant and insulated,
over the cane field, I contemplate the motionless waters, the palaces
gleaming like quartz, the extremely high columns and, suddenly, as if I
were holding a bird with silky and multicolored plumage in my hands,
and, blowing on it, discover in the bird a scaly animal, covered with
lice, pustules, and worms, the City, without losing anything of its visible pomp, reveals its foulness, its sickness, its evil-doing levels, hidden
until now. I turn the vulva toward the ceiling raise it to the dark zenith
as if waiting for the trunk of the tree of the world to land on me from
on high and forever I cross my feet on Abel's active back and I raise as
much as possible the fiery vulva mouth of a howling dog my uterus
howls I howl and I open myself open myself and roar thunder love
sunflowers I extend my arms in a T the abstruse visitors and their attic
smell I keep my member implanted pounded nail blade and hilt I force
and don't retreat the lips of the perineum bite the skin of the sack I
extend my left hand along her right arm prostrate on the rug the convulsed fingers cross a kind of affliction the almost the apex the limit
the animals in us the vines in us the bird of birds the plates of rusty
metal a bird takes on plumage in our body and a great black bird a
bird not visible over the low clouds flies firmly giving out his battered
song song of raw leather cut with a handsaw Olavo Hayano on the last
steps the weapon cocked lightning teeth tongues stomachs the vulvas
throb the secret ring encircles me and underneath a tiny hot tongue
licks the head of the phallus (walking on tiptoe hands raised shoulders back the trembling of the fat) the hammers of the clock prepare the pendulum a sistrum or lute I more and more your body
more and more the voice of the great and rebellious multitude and
behold our flanks and backs break open crack split and the delight of the   lights up our   and we   us
            and the world is   and jets of flames around
the   and all our mouths cry out like   and when
we think we've finally reached the supreme limit of   the
clock sings and note after note flows the fractured melody in the
machine and we know what few or no one, live what they may
... oh beauty of your face, sharp and whetted, reigning

on a sloping bank, the magic of the City seems to me perilous perfidious infested with stings and not only that, the hammers on the clock strings precisely the strings we go from landing to landing and the City, motionless, moves, approaches slowly, Julius Heckethorn's structure goes along forming the sequence the harmony brings together what was dispersed and we rejubilant the vertigo the flight the animals that inhabit us gallop leap and cry out cold and cloudy the beauty of the City, the claws of the Solitary and Soiled (and why this silence?), I want to get loose from the City and I cannot, I shout for help, but who could come to help me, my voice is the voice of a condemned man, mouth against mouth without control we give off shouts and moans and words cut off my love what a marv I you and sheep and dogs entwine in our mouths and gazelles and lions butterflies fly about also in us helianthuses flower I ejaculate the testicles whoreborn beauty that of her face bullet on the firing pin the Bearer on the clock the next to the last group of the sequence is missing extreme delight of flesh her right arm open and our fingers locked her fondling feet on the hollows of my knees one of the legs extended more than the other and the free hand putting me pulling me entering me the next to the last group of musical notes is missing the last one sounds and the clock continues its search. Terrified facing the City and like a man who cannot count anymore on his own forces I bellow, a human expression, but the voice is a squeal, a pig shouts for me, I shout with the mouth of a swine, still thinking how wrong I am in seeking that unique City, ostentatious and threatening, and the day darkens and certain of my end I lose the notion of everything. The static figures having fled from the frames turn around with one single movement Olavo Hayano flanked by the sunflowers the umbrella in one hand and in the other the pistol the room dark the tinkling of the bells and the sound of the rain and ʊ's voice which still repeats "Abel, Abel, I love you!" the Fat Woman comes to the porch lifts her aged head and looks at the weather the Yolyp a hole in the world we wait in silence the tender fingers on my face the steel plates come together the bird of birds opens up my whole life is concentrated in the act of searching knowing or not what heavy as lead is lost in the clouds the gleaming bird of ignoble song the Bearer in the right hand death the end the conclusion the bird inside of us flaps its wings of silk and sings with a kind human voice Olavo Hayano his black and white hair his large teeth and devoured gap on one side of his face turns the barrel toward us we see his gesture well and we don't know what it means, we know nothing beyond recognition and beatitude, the ancient figures redolent of flowers and old things kept in drawers their tight coiffures shirtfronts lace hats remain motionless and turned toward the Bearer, he opens the pernicious mouth and several dogs or abonaxis birds bark at once, our pacifying bird sings louder our embrace, a new lightning flash in the room and we hear irate full of irate teeth the barking of the dogs and we cross a border and we join the rug we are woven into the rug I and I banks of a clear murmuring river peopled with fish and voices we and the butter-flies we and sunflowers we and the benevolent bird more and more distant barking of dogs a new and luminous silence comes peace comes and nothing touches us, nothing, we walk, happy, entwined, among the animals and plants of the Garden.

São Paulo, September 22, 1969–December 1, 1972

INDEX OF THEMES

SELECTED DALKEY ARCHIVE PAPERBACKS

PIERRE ALBERT-BIROT, *Grabinoulor.*
YUZ ALESHKOVSKY, *Kangaroo.*
FELIPE ALFAU, *Chromos.*
   Locos.
   Sentimental Songs.
ALAN ANSEN, *Contact Highs: Selected Poems 1957-1987.*
DAVID ANTIN, *Talking.*
DJUNA BARNES, *Ladies Almanack.*
   Ryder.
JOHN BARTH, *LETTERS.*
   Sabbatical.
ANDREI BITOV, *Pushkin House.*
ROGER BOYLAN, *Killoyle.*
CHRISTINE BROOKE-ROSE, *Amalgamemnon.*
BRIGID BROPHY, *In Transit.*
GERALD L. BRUNS,
   Modern Poetry and the Idea of Language.
GABRIELLE BURTON, *Heartbreak Hotel.*
MICHEL BUTOR,
   Portrait of the Artist as a Young Ape.
JULIETA CAMPOS, *The Fear of Losing Eurydice.*
ANNE CARSON, *Eros the Bittersweet.*
CAMILO JOSÉ CELA, *The Hive.*
LOUIS-FERDINAND CÉLINE, *Castle to Castle.*
   London Bridge.
   North.
   Rigadoon.
HUGO CHARTERIS, *The Tide Is Right.*
JEROME CHARYN, *The Tar Baby.*
MARC CHOLODENKO, *Mordechai Schamz.*
EMILY HOLMES COLEMAN, *The Shutter of Snow.*
ROBERT COOVER, *A Night at the Movies.*
STANLEY CRAWFORD, *Some Instructions to My Wife.*
ROBERT CREELEY, *Collected Prose.*
RENÉ CREVEL, *Putting My Foot in It.*
RALPH CUSACK, *Cadenza.*
SUSAN DAITCH, *L.C.*
   Storytown.
NIGEL DENNIS, *Cards of Identity.*
PETER DIMOCK,
   A Short Rhetoric for Leaving the Family.
COLEMAN DOWELL, *The Houses of Children.*
   Island People.
   Too Much Flesh and Jabez.
RIKKI DUCORNET, *The Complete Butcher's Tales.*
   The Fountains of Neptune.
   The Jade Cabinet.
   Phosphor in Dreamland.
   The Stain.
WILLIAM EASTLAKE, *The Bamboo Bed.*
   Castle Keep.
   Lyric of the Circle Heart.
STANLEY ELKIN, *Boswell: A Modern Comedy.*
   Criers and Kibitzers, Kibitzers and Criers.
   The Dick Gibson Show.
   The Franchiser.

   The MacGuffin.
   The Magic Kingdom.
   Mrs. Ted Bliss.
   The Rabbi of Lud.
ANNIE ERNAUX, *Cleaned Out.*
LAUREN FAIRBANKS, *Muzzle Thyself.*
   Sister Carrie.
LESLIE A. FIEDLER,
   Love and Death in the American Novel.
FORD MADOX FORD, *The March of Literature.*
JANICE GALLOWAY, *Foreign Parts.*
   The Trick Is to Keep Breathing.
WILLIAM H. GASS, *The Tunnel.*
   Willie Masters' Lonesome Wife.
ETIENNE GILSON, *The Arts of the Beautiful.*
   Forms and Substances in the Arts.
C. S. GISCOMBE, *Giscome Road.*
   Here.
KAREN ELIZABETH GORDON, *The Red Shoes.*
PATRICK GRAINVILLE, *The Cave of Heaven.*
HENRY GREEN, *Blindness.*
   Concluding.
   Doting.
   Nothing.
JIŘÍ GRUŠA, *The Questionnaire.*
JOHN HAWKES, *Whistlejacket.*
AIDAN HIGGINS, *Flotsam and Jetsam.*
ALDOUS HUXLEY, *Antic Hay.*
   Crome Yellow.
   Point Counter Point.
   Those Barren Leaves.
   Time Must Have a Stop.
GERT JONKE, *Geometric Regional Novel.*
DANILO KIŠ, *A Tomb for Boris Davidovich.*
TADEUSZ KONWICKI, *A Minor Apocalypse.*
   The Polish Complex.
ELAINE KRAF, *The Princess of 72nd Street.*
JIM KRUSOE, *Iceland.*
EWA KURYLUK, *Century 21.*
DEBORAH LEVY, *Billy and Girl.*
JOSÉ LEZAMA LIMA, *Paradiso.*
OSMAN LINS, *Avalovara.*
   The Queen of the Prisons of Greece.
ALF MAC LOCHLAINN, *The Corpus in the Library.*
   Out of Focus.
D. KEITH MANO, *Take Five.*
BEN MARCUS, *The Age of Wire and String.*
WALLACE MARKFIELD, *Teitlebaum's Window.*
   To an Early Grave.
DAVID MARKSON, *Reader's Block.*
   Springer's Progress.
   Wittgenstein's Mistress.
CAROLE MASO, *AVA.*
LADISLAV MATEJKA AND KRYSTYNA POMORSKA, EDS.,
   Readings in Russian Poetics: Formalist and
   Structuralist Views.

FOR A FULL LIST OF PUBLICATIONS, VISIT:
www.dalkeyarchive.com

SELECTED DALKEY ARCHIVE PAPERBACKS

FOR A FULL LIST OF PUBLICATIONS, VISIT:
www.dalkeyarchive.com